THE WATER THAT MAY COME

AMY LILWALL

First published 1st October 2025 by Fly on the Wall Press
Published in the UK by
Fly on the Wall Press
56 High Lea Rd
New Mills
Derbyshire
SK22 3DP

www.flyonthewallpress.co.uk
ISBN: 9781915789440
EBook: 9781915789457
Copyright Amy Lilwall © 2025

EU GPSR Authorised Representative
LOGOS EUROPE, 9 rue Nicolas Poussin, 17000, LA ROCHELLE, France
E-mail: Contact@logoseurope.eu

For my mum, Alison.

BLUE – PADRE – JANE –ASHLEIGH – GAVIN –TOM – GILLIAN
BIG CARLA – RYAN – GAVIN'S MUM – PINKO – MATT – PARIS
BLUE – PADRE – JANE –ASHLEIGH – GAVIN –TOM – GILLIAN
BIG CARLA – RYAN – GAVIN'S MUM – PINKO – MATT – PARIS
BLUE – PADRE – JANE –ASHLEIGH – GAVIN –TOM – GILLIAN
BIG CARLA – RYAN – GAVIN'S MUM – PINKO – MATT – PARIS
BLUE – PADRE – JANE –ASHLEIGH – GAVIN –TOM – GILLIAN
BIG CARLA – RYAN – GAVIN'S MUM – PINKO – MATT – PARIS
BLUE – PADRE – JANE –ASHLEIGH – GAVIN –TOM – GILLIAN
BIG CARLA – RYAN – GAVIN'S MUM – PINKO – MATT – PARIS
BLUE – PADRE – JANE –ASHLEIGH – GAVIN –TOM – GILLIAN
BIG CARLA – RYAN – GAVIN'S MUM – PINKO – MATT – PARIS
BLUE – PADRE – JANE –ASHLEIGH – GAVIN –TOM – GILLIAN
BIG CARLA – RYAN – GAVIN'S MUM – PINKO – MATT – PARIS
BLUE – PADRE – JANE –ASHLEIGH – GAVIN –TOM – GILLIAN
BIG CARLA – RYAN – GAVIN'S MUM – PINKO – MATT – PARIS
BLUE – PADRE – JANE –ASHLEIGH – GAVIN –TOM – GILLIAN
BIG CARLA – RYAN – GAVIN'S MUM – PINKO – MATT – PARIS
BLUE – PADRE – JANE –ASHLEIGH – GAVIN –TOM – GILLIAN
BIG CARLA – RYAN – GAVIN'S MUM – PINKO – MATT – PARIS
BLUE – PADRE – JANE –ASHLEIGH – GAVIN –TOM – GILLIAN
BIG CARLA – RYAN – GAVIN'S MUM – PINKO – MATT – PARIS
BLUE – PADRE – JANE –ASHLEIGH – GAVIN –TOM – GILLIAN
BIG CARLA – RYAN – GAVIN'S MUM – PINKO – MATT – PARIS
BLUE – PADRE – JANE –ASHLEIGH – GAVIN –TOM – GILLIAN
BIG CARLA – RYAN – GAVIN'S MUM – PINKO – MATT – PARIS
BLUE – PADRE – JANE –ASHLEIGH – GAVIN –TOM – GILLIAN
BIG CARLA – RYAN – GAVIN'S MUM – PINKO – MATT – PARIS
BLUE – PADRE – JANE –ASHLEIGH – GAVIN –TOM – GILLIAN
BIG CARLA – RYAN – GAVIN'S MUM – PINKO – MATT – PARIS
BLUE – PADRE – JANE –ASHLEIGH – GAVIN –TOM – GILLIAN
BIG CARLA – RYAN – GAVIN'S MUM – PINKO – MATT – PARIS

PROLOGUE
THE NEW NORMAL

I | January 2032
Hrafnablótsjökul Volcano

Hrafnablótsjökul cracks open one eye, but her icicle-dry eyelashes are meshed together. The moon is high and the air is swollen. Frost melts between her metatarsals, tickles its way down to the sea. She has spent millennia being hot inside and cold out; now the glacier's weight starts to lift, letting her gases expand. A bubble turns over in her belly. A puff rises to the back of her throat. She groans, swallows it, closes her eye.

Not yet. Not quite yet.

II | February 2032
Intimacy Laws

Flights are delayed. Europe isn't that keen on receiving seventy-two million evacuees, eighty million with Ireland, of course.

Still, people wait at airports, with one foot forward and one behind, as though queuing for a busy supermarket check-out; remaining vigilant for another till opening. Home is not an option, no, they've just come from there; their children have buried teddies in the garden, kissed all the walls. They have taped up the windows, rammed sandbags against the doors, blocked up the chimneys — how would they even get back inside? No, they wouldn't go home. There are planes leaving for the States, for Japan, for Australia but still people sit on their suitcases, their savings in their pockets, their budgets in their heads, waiting for Europe to lift the barrier or for Burger King and Leon and Pret to distribute their leftovers. Whichever comes first.

At midnight, the message flashes up.

ALL FLIGHTS CANCELLED INDEFINITELY.

There is a moment of hush before the crowd ripples outwards and spreads through the airport towards the Information Desk, where they are told there are buses leaving for Dover, Folkstone, Portsmouth, Weymouth, Poole, Plymouth, and waves of people roll through the airport and crash into the coach-park shaking tickets in the air and balancing their children on their shoulders and suitcases are abandoned, later to be ignored by those who stayed, those teachers and carers and waiters and pharmacists and bouncers and bus drivers who stayed, shaking their heads at the panic, recounting the time when supermarkets were empty of bread because of a piddly foot of snow. But then they stare, open-mouthed, at the big, silent TV screens, the news update that whirls on a ribbon at the bottom of the screen: *New Intimacy Law to be enforced as of Friday.*

'Intimacy law?' they repeat, confused or amused. 'Who thought of calling it that?' They laugh at first.

At first.

THE WATER THAT MAY COME

Soon enough, single people make eyes at every potential stranger. Acquaintances rush into registrars' offices and rush out as husband and wife. Husbands with husbands must now look for wives. Wives with wives must now look for husbands. 'Functional' is the term that is bandied about. Europe makes it clear that a 'return to the old ways' is long overdue. And that starts in the home.

Children are packed onto buses, clutching suitcases, rucksacks drooping; their raincoats are zipped up, their collars adjusted, their cheeks kissed. Money is sewn into linings of jeans, jackets, shoes, belts... They cry at the bus windows. Single parents wave with wobbly smiles, then return home and scour through dating apps until their thumbs ache.

That law. That irrational, senseless, stuff-of-fiction law.

Unless you come with your family, you can't come in. Europe doesn't want boats full of grimy, idle men; with their prickly tempers and derelict morals. Neither does it want hordes of licentious women, treading its streets at night. You come together, or not at all.

'Since sexual immorality is occurring, each man should have sexual relations with his own wife, and each woman with her own husband,' - 1 Corinthians 7:2 (NIV).

The sanctity of marriage, after all, indicates civilised intentions.

III | May 2032
Pinko

It's party night, tonight. Not just any party, but one of the last before the water comes.

Pinko gazes down into his hallway and thinks, for the umpteenth time that week, that all of this will soon be under water.

The staircase curls upwards, grand and gleaming. Pinko is at the top, of course, occupying that uneasy space between looking out for guests and feeling like something has been forgotten. His watch, maybe? He glances at his wrist. Nope. He is wearing a round, wooden Rolex. Bespoke. A gift from Padre *many* years ago. He smiles as he thinks of the old man, then shakes his cuff over the watch and checks his hair for wax (even though he has *only just* coiffed it into a side puff). His shoes — brown brogues, newly shined — match his belt. There is the sting of aftershave on his cheeks and his lips are slippery with Vaseline.

Is it terribly decadent, he thinks now, to worry about matching one's shoes with one's belt in the face of natural disaster? He concludes that yes, it most probably is. Although, the disaster wouldn't happen for at least a year, he reminds himself. Surely that is enough time to realise that someone has miscalculated something. Geologists can't see that far into the future. No. It is much too early to condemn the whole of the UK. For now, he must enjoy his party. His *dad*'s party. He would have been seventy today; it seems fitting that — as a non-football fan — he should have to compete with the last, ever football match to be played on British soil. Supposedly.

Pinko raises his chin and his shoulders.

Right.

Perhaps it's time to go down.

The stairs are rounded, wooden, a series of jutting lips. No square lines at all. It took his father's carpenters two weeks to replace the old, straight flight that parted two ways at the centre. Pinko camped out in the library while the new stairs were fitted. He can remember asking his father if he could use the servants' staircase instead, just to get to his bedroom. His father shook his head without looking up from his ledgers. *They're busy people, Pinko. They don't want to bump into us all day.*

Pinko inherited his father's taste for curves. And wood. All those rectangular trucks loaded with straight timber for square tables and angular chests of drawers; all those beautiful, circular ripples flattened and frozen into sheets, trapped like ants in amber. No, no... Here, at least, every circle is free.

Good old Dad.

The hall floor, once tiled, is now spirals of inlaid oak which took *ages* to make and fit. The front doorframe is curved into an elliptical arch, and at the top of the stairs, behind him (one day) will be the star: the pine tree swaying upwards, the wind visible in its needles, blurred yet sharp. With an artist like Gavin, it will be as lovely as the real thing.

Where is Gavin, anyway? It was most unlike him to arrive a) from anywhere other than Margate, and b) any less than twenty minutes early. Maybe he watched The Last Match with the rest of them...

Pinko frowns and turns back to the hall, his gaze sliding like a penny in a funnel, while he waits for the bus to turn up. The bus is wooden – as curved as it can be – and runs on biofuel, naturally. He sent it into town, rattling with champagne and goblets (carved from cherry wood), for it to return heaving with his mates. There should be about fifty of them, tipsy already, and whoever else they drag along. The front door will pop and fling itself like a champagne cork. There'll be bubbles of chat, laughter, welcomes, thank-yous. Overflowing. Any second now.

Pinko jumps as the DJ starts up. Nineties ambient dance. The round windows swell with sun as the first notes evaporate. He descends, veers to the left and looks through the archway into the formal reception space. The bar (walnut, crescent shaped) clacks with shaking ice. He winks at the barman, wanders his eyes through the window towards Blue, who is leaning on the handle of a pool net. Blue stares, buttons the neck of his green overalls, and walks away.

'They're here, Pinks,' Butler says. He is wearing a t-shirt with 'butler' graffitied across the chest.

'Okay.' Pinko claps him on the shoulder. 'Let them in, would you?'

The door opens. The guests enter. Gavin is first in line, tumbling into the hallway, laughing – drunk, perhaps? Pinko squints for just a moment, disbelieving, until Gavin stands straight, puts out his hand, 'Hello, Pinko. We've had such a laugh on the journey up.'

Pinko smiles at his blue and white scarf, shakes his hand. 'For a minute, I thought you'd had a drink.'

'Slush puppy,' says Gavin. 'A blue one. The E-numbers have made me mental.'

Pinko grins, his gaze lifting to take in the other guests, but catching on the person now standing next to Gavin.

'Right,' she says, one hand in her handbag, retrieving a tube of lip gloss. 'Where's the bar?'

He parts his lips to answer but his mates – clearly drunk – surround him, slapping his back and squeezing his shoulder, football tunes spilling out of them.

As he is swept off through the living room, he glimpses her again, striding away from Gavin and towards the bar.

The party is rather light on women, tonight.

Perhaps that's why she stands out.

PART ONE
THE STRUGGLE

CHAPTER ONE | February 2033
Jane

Today, like every day, there is no one in the street. Jane presses her cheek to the side of a satin-shiny RV Fleetwood Flair motorhome and sobs. Its smoothness smells like him, weirdly, and she feels very scruffy next to him – it – in her Primark skinny jeans and horse-smelling body warmer. In her hand, she holds her letter from Pinko Stephens which has unbottled a reserve of emotion, deep inside her belly. The words that tipped her over the edge are right near the top in long hand. Cursive. They say:

I have left you my campervan; I think it might come in handy. You can use it to drive up to the helicopter. Inverness – don't forget – on the 29th of February. Get there early, Jane. Perhaps the day before? They're expecting Paris so don't leave him behind. It's a long drive, but you should be comfortable. Ashleigh can rest in the back. I asked Blue to fill up the kitchen area with goodies (including dog food) as she'll surely be hungry – I heard that ramps up in the last trimester...

She stops reading for a moment to remember him smiling at her, his finger and thumb on each cheek, tracing down to his chin. It was something he often did, to check the shape of his smile, Jane used to think. She shakes the image away and reminds herself that he is a dickhead. Even though he has left her this RV and two weeks' supply of food for her and her pregnant daughter. Even though he has arranged helicopter tickets for them to escape disaster-struck England and flee to Finland. Even though he has built her a cabin by a lake, with bespoke in-frame kitchen cabinets (curved, of course), he is still a dickhead. She looks at the letter again, then drops her hand to her side. She should read the rest of it and be on her way, really. But another sob falls out of her because, well, why did it have to be like this? And also, even the *biggest* horseboxes she's ever driven were only half the size of this RV. But moreover, who *knows* where Ashleigh is now and Jane must find her, get to Scotland, get to the helicopter, and fly to Finland where they will live, mother, daughter, grandchild, dog, while the UK succumbs to its fate.

If that is, indeed, the right thing to do. Jane still isn't quite sure.

Paris sniffs the front tyre on the driver's side, cocks his leg and pees.

Jane smiles shakily, then thinks about all the 'goodies' for Ashleigh's 'third trimester'. Women get hungry in their third trimester or whatever it was he'd written. Dickhead. So out of touch with the mortal world. Probably, she will discover tins of caviar and pickled truffles in the glossy RV kitchen area – completely unsuitable. Jane wouldn't want Ashleigh to ingest anything he had intended for her anyway.

Oh, but that's petty, she thinks, wiping her eyes. Food is food, and so many people are going without.

But even so.

She sighs. 'Come on then, Paris.'

Jane walks around the van and decides not to read the rest of the letter. She folds it and puts it in the pocket of her body warmer. It's better to get on the road. Her heavily pregnant daughter is out there somewhere and Jane must find her.

As it happens, it is no different to driving a horse box, except that she has now driven this thing for three days straight. The food remains untouched in the cupboards, but she steadily sips the bottles of full sugar Coke that is stacked in crates behind the passenger seat. Paris has eaten his fair share of 'designer' dog food – Jane rolled her eyes when she picked up the first tin – he wolfs it down in seconds, then looks up at her, marching his front feet. She has taken one shower with the van's water supply and she relieves herself in the fields when she walks Paris. When she needs petrol, she steals it. Everybody does since the card machines went down. In this way, all her liquid needs are satisfied. But she hasn't eaten a thing.

There is a hooded figure at the side of the road, striding along as if it has somewhere to be. Jane only just notices its hand clutching a ballooned stomach before the RV is swept along in the tide of traffic. She lets out a cry and strains towards the wingmirror to see properly. The figure was the right height, had a similar gait – although it was stumbling slightly – had the same stoop as Ashleigh when she used to skulk about the house in her hooded onesie. Jane pulls off at the next junction, three-point turns the bulky RV, and hares back along the road towards the figure.

Even before she draws up beside it, she knows it's not Ashleigh. Its hood is now down and the ends of a mousy ponytail straggle about its lower back. Jane thinks back to that awful phone call months before. What's happened, Mum? Ashleigh said, hair newly cut to her chin. Jane didn't answer, simply cried on the hall floor.

Plus, Ashleigh's hair was auburn – *is* auburn – not mousy.

Jane turns off at the next junction and pulls into a field.

It is the 19th of February. Ten days to go. *Get there a day early*, said the letter. So really, she only has nine.

Nevertheless, for the first time in twenty-seven hours, she sleeps.

The outline of an empty Coke bottle blurs before her eyes. The dull evening haze presses against the steamed-up windscreen. Jane sits up, wipes her mouth. Paris is whining at her, telling her that her mobile is ringing. She swivels the driver's chair to retrieve it from beneath Pinko's bespoke magic tree (who owns a bespoke magic tree?) which must have fallen onto the dashboard . The number is unidentified – a lead maybe? She pulls her glasses from the top of her head and fumbles for the answer button. 'Hello?' but she is too late. Damn. She searches through the call history to ring back before a 'ding' from her phone indicates an answerphone message. She hesitates, then calls the answerphone.

YOU HAVE ONE NEW MESSAGE AND NO SAVED MESSAGES.

This is a message for Jane?

Jane sits up in her seat – she knows that voice.

It's Blue. I don't know if you remember me.

Blue. They met once. Grumpy. Smelled like sour apples and dirty hair.

Just to let you know that Gavin called…he's with a baby. You know,

18

Jane, I think it's your girl's baby. In fact, I'm sure it's your Ashleigh's baby.

Jane's chest tightens. So it has happened. Ashleigh has given birth. And Gavin, of *all* people, has the baby.

The thing is…well…

Jane closes her eyes, willing Blue to finish his sentence so that she can start up the engine, put this thing into drive and speed off towards the location of the baby.

I could take the bairn with me to Finland. Then he'd be there when you arrive.

Jane gapes her eyes about her. Of course Blue wants the baby. Of course he does.

But Gavin didn't seem so keen on letting him go…

Him? Jane exhales through pursed lips. A boy?

I was thinking you could talk him round, you know? Being the grandmother, and all.

His voice is rough and breathy; Jane realises her top lip is curling. 'You're right,' she says, her words steaming in the cold air. 'I'm his grandmother. He belongs with me.' Jane hangs up the phone and holds it to her chest where, in the last thirty seconds, another chamber has grown in her heart. In it sleeps a baby with pudgy eyelids and dandelion hair and she knows that, despite everything, she is thrilled to have him in the world. But Gavin. The artist. She remembers meeting him, the fidgety young man in his stripy, collarless shirt. How different the world was five months ago. She shakes the thought away and starts up the RV.

'Jesus, Paris,' she mutters. 'How on Earth did Gavin get mixed up in all of this?'

CHAPTER TWO | April 2032
Gavin

No takers at the car boot sale today. Mind you, Gavin probably looks dodgy with only a top-of-the-range camera to sell and not even a car boot to display it. Plus, by the time he's legged it up from Walmer beach, the last few stragglers are plopping their old tat into boxes, their trestle tables folded and leaning against car bonnets.

She has taken quite a fall, the owner of the camera, but she has definitely got to her feet. He waits until she pushes herself up from the pebbles, one hand clutching her forehead. Funny, when he was a kid, he'd fallen over in that exact spot. Backwards. Bruised his tailbone something nasty on those large pebbles. Apart from that, he can only remember feeling surprise, rather than pain.

Still, pinching her camera wasn't the nicest thing to do.

She might have reported it stolen by now. If Gavin can't get rid of it sharpish, he'll have to take it home.

Shame. Apart from saving for The Last Match, he had his eye on an enormous turkey, down to £9.99 at Iceland. Cooked and hugged tight by goose-fat potatoes, honey glazed parsnips and a bowl full of marrowfat peas. Not forgetting the gravy from the giblets, shredded onions curling in its depths. The gravy dish would go around the table. Firstly, to Ryan, then Big Carla, then the boys, then Little Carla, then Grandad would have refused it because onions repeated on him. He would have passed it on to Mum as she told Little Carla to wait for everyone else to be served before diving in. Then Gavin. And he would have passed it back to Grandad who would say: 'Go on, then. Ta.' But these days, of course, Gavin would put the dish back on the table and try not to look at Grandad's empty chair.

'How much do you want for it?' a teenage boy says to him. Seventeen years old, maybe? Short, neat haircut.

'Seventy-five,' says Gavin.

The boy kicks at the grass as he thinks about this. 'Would you take thirty?'

Gavin laughs. But thirty would certainly buy the turkey, no problem. And he'd have change for a Chocolate Gateau and some Aunt Bessie's Yorkshires. He could maybe pocket a couple of quid for The Last Match.

'Tell you what, come back at the end; if I haven't sold it, you can have it for thirty.'

The boy smirks. 'It is the end.'

'Not quite. Give ten minutes or so.'

'Alright,' says the boy. 'Thanks.'

Thirty is a bit of a steal but never mind. Before he hands it over, he wants to make sure it works properly. He stands leaning up against a tractor tyre as the on-button tune tinkles. An image of a woman's mustard eye appears at the screen, a string of hair against her cheek-hollow. He clicks his tongue. Not easy. Not easy to do a selfie with these bulky things. Still, it looks kind of artsy, sort of, on purpose. His hand slips into his pocket to a twin pack of pink wafers. He picks at the stiff waves of cling-film just as a brown labrador hovers into his peripheral. Gavin likes drawing dogs; he likes their em-shaped brows. Still, this dog isn't there to be drawn. 'Not for you, mate,' he says, still unwrapping the wafers. 'Pink colouring might send you doo-dah.'

The dog sits, head on one side, eyes mental.

Gavin breaks one in half and sits on the grass. 'At least it's not chocolate,' he says, and feeds it into the dog's mouth. 'That's bad for dogs. Chocolate's bad for dogs,' he says, chewing on the other half. A woman's voice makes them both look up.

'Yes. That's mine, Officer. That's my eye on the screen, see?' says the woman, the owner of the mustard eye and the camera. Close up, Gavin can see a gaping slit above her right eyebrow.

The dog backs away, still licking its back teeth.

'Gavin, you've been told.'

Wayne. Officer Wayne.

Gavin scrunchs the wrapping around the remaining wafer and stands up.

'Did you plan to sell it?' says Wayne.

Those bulbous-toed boots are always stood at ease, thinks Gavin. 'Yes,' he says. 'I waited, you know,' he says to the woman.

'I did wait to see if you got up, Miss.'

She hugs herself as if she were cold. 'Gillian,' she says.

'Gillian,' Gavin repeats. 'And you seemed alright – when you did get up – so I left,' says Gavin, inching up the tractor wheel. 'I didn't know you'd cut your head; I'd never've...'

'Alright, Gavin,' says Officer Wayne. 'We're going to have to take you in.'

Gavin looks down at the camera still hanging against his belly. He lifts the strap over his head and hands it back to the woman. 'I was going to buy a turkey for my mum.'

She reaches out and takes the camera from him.

'I did wait,' says Gavin.

'It's alright,' says Gillian. 'Don't worry.'

'Is he yours?' says Wayne, taking notes, chin jutting towards the dog.

'No,' says Gavin, patting his pocket. 'He just wanted a biscuit.'

Gillian smiles; is that a smile? Have her folded arms loosened a little? He should have helped when she'd slipped on the rocks, but in that moment, there was only Mum and the turkey on his mind. And fifty quid for his pocket. Maybe fifty-five. But his mum would have thrown it all in the sea to run over and make sure Gillian was alright.

'Come on then,' says Wayne.

'Spare any change?' says a man by the steps of the police station. He has a labrador, same colour as the one by the tractor wheel.

'Think I've got fifty pence,' says Gavin, looking at Wayne.

Wayne stalls and sighs. 'Is it in your pocket?'

'Yeah.'

'Go on, then,' he says. 'I'm not supposed to let you do this.'

Gavin digs in his pocket, produces fifty pence and slips it onto the man's palm.

'What are you like?' says Wayne.

Shrug.

'Yet you wouldn't help that lady when she fell over,' he adds.

'I was about to,' says Gavin.

'But you didn't. You nicked her camera.'

The man closes his fingers around the coin and bumps Gavin's fist with his own. Gavin thinks he sees Officer Wayne smile but maybe that is just the shape of his mouth.

'We'd better go in,' he says.

'Yeah, okay. Have you still got that fish tank on the front desk?'

Officer Wayne rolls his eyes.

A lady officer takes Gavin to a cell where he sits on the bunk and counts the bricks in the opposite wall. He did this last time too. After a few hours, eyes appear at the slot in the cell door.

'She's not pressing charges,' says Officer Wayne.

And the door clicks open.

The lady officer gives him his things back and tells him he can go. Gavin asks if he can draw the fish tank. Officer Wayne would have let him, but the lady officer says 'no'. He says he'll only be five minutes. She says, 'What do you want to draw the fish tank for?' He says he's got a craft fair coming up. She looks over at another policeman who blinks and nods at her. 'Alright.' Gavin stands at reception and sketches, tongue between his teeth. The lady officer thinks he can't see, but she keeps looking at him with her eyelids right back and the big white bits of her eyes gleaming like hardboiled eggs – how could he not see that? Afterwards, he might ask to draw her and her hard-egg eyes. Another policewoman turns up with a man in handcuffs. His t-shirt reads: ONLY ANIMALS FUCK IN FRONT OF STRANGERS. Gavin stared. The man catches him staring and says, 'Are you gonna do your missus in front of The Jury? Or die on this island?' The policewoman tells him to shut up. Gavin goes back to his drawing. He doesn't have a missus, thankfully. Egg-eyes says, 'This is ridiculous,' to him, or to her male colleague, he isn't sure. 'Do we always let him do this?'

The other policeman shrugs.

'I've finished,' says Gavin, dropping a loud dot at the edge of his drawing. 'But I could only draw two fish.' He turns his paper around. 'Doesn't matter because they're all pretty much the same.'

She says, 'Good, off you go then.'

'Aren't you gonna look at it?'

'Fuck me, it's really fucking good,' says the man in handcuffs.

'Oi, nobody asked you,' says the other policeman.

'Time to go,' says egg-eyes, 'Off you pop.'

'I'm going to sell it at the craft fair on Saturday,' says Gavin.

Egg-eyes is writing. She rolls her eyes up at him then back down to her pen.

It's alright, he thinks, Mum'll like it. She likes fish.

Then he picks up his paper and leaves.

An hour later, Gavin is taking his shoes off in his hallway. His mum appears at the kitchen door drying a small saucepan. She looks at him, then disappears beyond the frame.

'It was alright this time, the lady said that she wouldn't press charges. I got lucky.' He walks into the kitchen and sits at the table. The room smells of soapy, hot water. 'That could have been really bad.'

His mum is clattering something about in the sink.

'I got cheese,' he says, voice raised so she can hear him. 'Sliced for burgers. And bread. I'll put it in the freezer. Its best-before is today.'

She watches from the side of her head as he gets to his feet.

'Got you some doughnuts too. 10p,' he says, scraping the freezer drawers open and shut.

'Gavin, what were you thinking?'

'They were only 10p,' he says, closing the freezer door.

'You stole that young lady's camera.'

Gavin stares for a moment, then slides back into his seat at the table.

'You mustn't steal, Gavin.'

'I know.'

'So why did you do it?'

'To make some money. To bring home some money.'

She turns away and picks up a wet plate. 'Get a job, Gavin.'

'I know. I am trying.'

'How are you trying?'

Gavin purses his lips, picks at the table.

'I did some more drawings. For the craft fair.'

'I'm not sure about this craft fair...'

His eyes snap up. 'Why?'

She puts the plate away and doesn't answer.

Gavin thinks of the money he could make for a Sunday turkey, Yorkshires, a ticket to The Last Match... 'I've done so much. I've got at least four pictures that I've done this week. I've got loads in my room. And we've still got,' he says, counting on his fingers, 'four days left.'

'Gavin,' she says, stepping closer and looking right into his face. 'You mustn't steal.'

'I can do loads in four days.'

'Did you hear me?'

Whenever his mum wants to show that she is cross, she makes lines in her forehead and her lips get really thin. Gavin doesn't know how he is supposed to listen to her when she looks that cross. He takes the fish drawing from his pocket and spreads it out in front of him, but he knows she is still making that face.

'Did you do that today, love?' she says.

He glances up at her. 'Yes.'

She frowns at the drawing, turning her head as she does. Often people look at his work in this way, then their eyebrows lift and their mouths fall open, like they've found the answer to a really hard problem. Right on cue, his mum's face clears.

'Do you like it?' he says.

She laughs now, as if 'like' is not the right word. Then her face gets all serious again. 'If we do this craft fair,' she says, 'you have to *promise* me...'

'I promise.'

She holds his gaze, then reaches over to the doughnut bag and crackles it open. 'Alright,' she says. 'Alright.'

CHAPTER THREE | February 2033
Jane

Jane has one hand on the steering wheel and one on her mobile phone. She wills Gavin to answer, pick up, pick up, pick, up, but is connected to his answerphone. The RV races through the back lanes at national speed limit, even though she doesn't know the roads or where she is going. Margate, she thinks, for some reason, which is not that far away. But then her brain remembers Nuneaton. Nuneaton? Gavin was supposed to move to Nuneaton – what if he already moved? After ten miles she thinks this is stupid and pulls over to check the internet for the area code. Margate. Definitely Margate. She types Gavin's name into the search engine; he has a website now. She clicks the link and finds his gap-toothed, pale face smiling up at her, the seam of his collarless shirt tight around his neck. He wore that shirt when she met him, many moons back. She pinches her lips together and looks out across the fields that will all be underwater soon. Focus Jane, she thinks, looking back to her phone. There is no mobile number on his website, but she finds an email address. Email? Does email still work? she thinks as her phone rings.

'Yes, hello?'

It is the voice of Gavin's mum. Jane recognises it from meeting her at the exhibition last year.

'Hello,' she says. 'It's Jane.'

'Jane?'

'Yes. Ashleigh's mum.'

The woman sucks in a whoosh of breath that, for whatever reason, makes Jane well up. This is it, thinks Jane. This woman has definitely seen Ashleigh.

Gavin's mum says something that is lost in a fizz of poor network. Jane rams a finger into her free ear and says, 'Pardon?'

'Ashleigh,' says the woman. 'You mentioned Ashleigh?'

'Yes,' says Jane, frowning. 'Auburn hair. Pregnant.' Jane remembers Blue's message. 'But, she might have given birth by now...'

The woman is quiet. Maybe other people have contacted her, in want of a single, pregnant girl.

The line fizzes again. 'Hello?' Jane, says, full-on crying now. 'Hello?'

'The line's…very…bad,' says Gavin's mum.

'Ashleigh's my daughter,' says Jane, still sobbing. 'Do you have any idea…' She trails off as the line hisses and bleeps. When the bleeping stops, she hears Gavin's mum sniffling.

'Is she with you?' they say at the same time.

Jane freezes, stares at the bespoke, magic tree collapsed on the dashboard. She tries to say 'no' but is gulping for air.

'The…gone to…Liverpool.'

'What?' says Jane.

'Listen, where are you, love? Do you need someone to come and get you?'

Her voice is so kind. Jane sniffs deeply. 'No. That's fine. The line is really bad,' she says. 'I've got a car. Just give me your address.'

CHAPTER FOUR | April 2032
Gavin

Gavin has stolen another pencil from Little Carla's pencil case. He has managed to find 46p under the sofa and knows that the Yellow Label man will be doing his rounds at Tesco just after six o'clock. Sometimes they sell reduced cheese, sliced in a packet, and bread for 10p. He has £2 to put towards it, somewhere... Maybe he'll get some scones or doughnuts or crumpets or something... Cookies for 7p, perhaps. Mum'll tell him to stop buying rubbish but she'll eat one with a cup of tea in front of Eastenders. He shoehorns his trainers on, grabs his grandad's scarf, turns and calls up the stairs. 'I'm taking Grandad's bus pass to Walmer.'

'Alright love. Your wafers are on the side.'

He opens the pass and runs his thumb over Grandad's photo. Then, he removes his shoes with the toes of each opposite foot, pads to the kitchen, pockets the wafers and goes back to the hall, to the shoehorn, and wrenches his shoes on again. 'Bye!' he says, closing the door.

He waits at the bus stop with a mum and her little girl. The little girl stares at his shoes then up at him. The mum catches her staring, points out a baby seagull to distract her, then side-eyes his shoes. Gavin's mum texts him, *I've just booked the stall for the craft fair Xxx*

He smiles, stands up straight, tries to text back but realises he's got no credit.

Luke is driving today (thank God). He winks at Gavin and lets him on.

'Cheers mate.'

Luke nods.

Gavin lumbers to the back of the bus. He sprawls across two seats and looks at his shoes, lifting one foot, then the other. Mud clings to the vamp, holding one of the laces in a stiff loop. He feels down his jacket for an A5 rectangle and a pencil. His wafers are in his inside pocket as well as £2.46.

Gavin looks out the window as they roll past The King's Arms. His funds are dwindling a bit, but he's still hoping to get a tenner together for a ticket to The Last Match. It's the only pub for miles that's still—

Gavin turns his body as the bus passes The King's Arms, clutches his scarf. The wide, warm windows have been boarded up and the string of outdoor lights is loose and flailing. *Gone*, thinks Gavin. The Last Pub in town to show The Last Match.

Gavin frowns and stares into space.

A man gets on at the next stop in green overalls and a baseball cap. He is carrying a small cage. The man walks to the back and waits for Gavin to move up. Gavin moves, eyes glued to the cage as the man sits with it on his lap. A nose appears between the bars. The man leans round the cage to look at the nose, then resumes his upright position. The animal turns; disc-like ears paddle the air while its whiskers twitch.

'It's like Mickey Mouse, but grey,' says Gavin.

The owner realises that Gavin is talking to him. 'Aye. He is a bit.'

'I've never seen a guinea pig like that.'

'It's a chinchilla.'

'Oh...' says Gavin, wrinkling his eyes. 'I'm not very good with guinea pigs. We used to have sea monkeys when I was a kid.'

'It's a chinchilla, not a guinea pig.'

'Oh.'

The man stares ahead. Blinks.

'So that's like a separate thing to a guinea pig?' asks Gavin.

'Yes.'

'Oh wow,' he says, nodding. 'How much does one of them go for, then?'

The man pulls the corners of his mouth down, looks up to the side and says, 'About eighty quid.'

Gavin scoffs and says, 'Fuck off!'

The man goes back to staring ahead. Raises his eyebrows.

'Sorry about that, it's just, you know, that's a lot of money.'

'You're telling me.' The man coughs slightly, glances sidelong at Gavin's scarf.

'Coventry City,' says Gavin.

The man nods. Fixes his stare ahead.

'Did you buy him just now, then?' says Gavin.

'No.'

'No?'

'No. He's poorly. I'm taking him to the vet.'

'Oh no. Poor thing.'

'He's got toothache. It's stopping him from eating.'

'How d'you know it's his tooth?'

'Pardon?'

'He might just have tummy ache.'

The man considers this for a second, looking up to the left. 'Might do. But he keeps trying to eat on one side.'

'Oh right.'

The man looks away again.

'What's his name?' says Gavin.

'Martin.'

'Martin?'

'Yes.'

'Would you... Can I... Would you mind if I drew him?' he asks, feeling around in his breast pocket.

'Erm, well, we're getting off soon.'

'I'll be quick. I'll show you afterwards.'

The man frowns but says, 'Alright then, yeah.'

'It'll stop me talking to you, at least,' says Gavin.

The man smiles, but only with his mouth.

Gavin draws.

After about five minutes, the man says he has to get off. Gavin replies that he only needs ten seconds, he's just finishing the whiskers. The man sighs towards the front of the bus as it slows, then he starts to stand up. 'All done, look.' Gavin turns the paper around; the man glances at it, then back to the front of the bus, then back at the paper. He lifts the rim of his baseball cap, takes the paper, holds it to his nose and sits back down again. 'But...' he says, 'He's...*moving*. I can actually see him twitching.'

Gavin smiles. 'I'd let you keep it, but I'm gonna try and sell it at the craft sale.'

The bus starts up again. 'Shit,' says the man. 'That was my stop.'

Gavin stands up, whistles through his teeth. 'Oi, Luke! There's one more to get off!'

The bus slows. The man thanks Gavin, tells him he's got no cash on him, but he'll come to the craft sale on Saturday.

'In St Mary's Hall.'

'In St Mary's Hall.'

'Margate.'

'Righto.'

Gavin nods, looks back at his notepad, thinks of things that move at Walmer. The sea, the sea moves. Grasses, sheep – although most of the sheep have been pinched by now – perhaps he'll find a tree, unlikely but possible. No matter. He can draw anything, it doesn't have to move. But then again, it would be nice to have a theme for the craft sale on Saturday. He smiles, sits back in his seat, and imagines their stall with his pictures spread across it.

CHAPTER FIVE | February 2033
JANE

By the time Jane gets to Margate, it is almost ten, much too late to be turning up at people's houses. Jane hesitates for a moment on the doorstep. The front window of the small, terraced house is dark, but this is not unusual lately with all the power outages. Before she can lift the knocker, Gavin's mum opens the door in a tartan dressing gown.

'Come in love. It's chilly out,' she says, as if it is the afternoon and Jane has popped by for tea.

Jane steps inside. The hallway is dark but warm and smells like egg-mayonnaise. Feeling the carpet underfoot, she realises she can't remember the last time she was inside a home, apart from her own.

'Come through,' says Gavin's mum, closing the door behind Jane.

Jane doesn't move. Her face is shaking as she asks, 'Has Ashleigh been here?'

'She stayed here for a while, love. Lived with us, I'd say.'

Jane frowns. 'Lived with you?'

'We thought you were estranged. Didn't realise you were looking for her.'

'Estranged?' Jane's breathing quickens. She leans back against the door, closes her eyes.

Gavin's mum squeezes her by the elbows and tells her it's all alright, they'll find her again, it's alright... When Jane's breathing calms, she allows herself to be led into a candle-lit, Formica kitchen where another woman sits at a table, her back to Jane. Jane stops dead, but no, the woman is too broad, too raven. And anyway, Ashleigh isn't here. She's been told that already. The woman turns as Jane enters.

'This is Carla, my youngest,' says Gavin's mum.

Jane nods. 'It's late, I'm sorry.'

'It's fine. Sit down.' Carla smiles, scratches the back of her head with long, flat-edged fingernails. 'We'll tell you everything we know.'

Jane pulls out a chair and sits. Carla has a round face with thumbnail dimples and darkly straight eyebrows. She has one hand on her stomach, which protrudes from the open zip of her fleece, a uniform. B&M. With the other, she makes a loop with her thumb and index finger and pulls her ponytail through it. 'She's a strong girl, your Ashleigh, you know,' she says.

Jane nods, grateful that Ashleigh had another girl around. Jane asks all the questions she can think of: where did Ashleigh go? When did she give birth? How was it? Did she recover quickly? Was the baby healthy? Carla and her mum wring their hands as if under interrogation. Sometimes their answers trail off into quivering mouths and shaky voices. They loved her. Jane can see that. The doorbell rings, Carla wipes her eyes with the back of her sleeve and gets to her feet.

'Don't, love,' says Gavin's mum, 'I'll get it.' She puts another mug of tea in front of Jane, then heads out to the hallway.

'She was well looked after,' says Carla, when Gavin's mum has gone.

'I can tell,' Jane replies.

The low wobble of men's voices travels through to the kitchen. They sound tired, monosyllabic. Jane recognises Gavin and stands up at once. They are removing their shoes when she enters the hallway. They stop and stand meerkat still.

'Hello Gavin,' says Jane.

Gavin nods, clears his throat. 'Hello.'

'Jane's come to find Ashleigh,' says Gavin's mum, overpronouncing each word. She turns to Jane. 'This is my eldest, Ryan.'

Ryan has dark, gelled hair and a large zirconia in one ear. He nods at Jane, while Gavin stares at his socked feet, hair fluffed up in different directions. He looks like he's been crying. Ryan is about to say something, when his mum says, 'Let's get the kettle on, shall we? I'm just glad you boys are home.'

They go through to the kitchen. The brothers hug their sister, then settle at the table. Jane takes up her place next to Carla, grasps her hot mug of tea. 'Your mum says you went to Liverpool.'

The two men look at each other, before Ryan tips his chin and says, 'Yeah.'

Jane waits for one of them to elaborate, but they fidget with their fingers, watch their mum fill up the kettle.

Jane leans forward slightly and asks, 'Gavin, what was in her envelope? Do you know?'

'What envelope?' says Carla.

Jane ignores her. 'Do you know, Gavin?'

'She never said,' he replies.

'What about yours? Did you get an envelope?' she asks.

Gavin clears his throat and says, 'I'm pretty sure everyone did.'

Jane waits again to see if Gavin will elaborate, but he stares down at the table, mouth shut.

'Did she say anything at all before she left?' asks Jane.

'No,' says Ryan. 'Only that she needed a wee.' He shakes his head. 'Then she disappeared.'

'But…' says Carla, darting her eyes around the table.

Gavin and Ryan stare at her. Then Ryan swallows and urges her on with a nod.

'What is it?' says Jane. 'What's going on?'

Carla winces, then holds Jane's gaze as if she's about to level with her. 'The boys took the baby to Liverpool.'

Jane scowls and cocks an ear, 'Sorry?'

'The boys,' says Carla, nodding towards Ryan and Gavin, 'drove the baby up to Liverpool. Yesterday. They just got back.'

Jane squints at Carla until it dawns on her. 'Ashleigh's baby?'

Carla nods, eyes wide like she's explaining something to a small child.

'But you must have taken Ashleigh too, surely?' She looks at Gavin, then Ryan. 'Was Ashleigh with you?'

They shake their heads.

'She must have been with you,' says Jane again, eyes dancing. 'I don't understand.'

Gavin's mum places two mugs of tea on the table, then stands back with her knuckles on her hips. 'Ashleigh left without the baby, love. She left him here with us.'

The earlier conversation with Blue replays in Jane's head. He had spoken of the baby, but said nothing about Ashleigh. Blue planned to take the baby to Finland. Just the baby. How had this detail eluded her? Jane gets to her feet, snaps at the men. 'You could have told me sooner!'

Gavin's mum hushes her, tells her to sit down.

'He's in Liverpool with Padre,' mumbles Gavin.

'And from there he'll go to Ireland. Then France,' says Ryan.

Jane looks from Ryan to Gavin, her mouth widening as she takes in what they are saying. Padre. Pinko's friend from way back – they met on the Camino de Saints Jacques. *He's like Yoda,* Pinko had said, *but drinks brandy and cuts hair. You'll like him.* Jane remembers feeling warm at the assumption that she would meet Padre, that she was allowed that far into Pinko's life. Now she swallows the thought. 'Padre's taking him to Ireland?'

Ryan shakes his head. 'Gillian,' he says. 'Gillian is taking him to Ireland.'

Jane shuts her eyes and tries to make sense of all of this. Who the hell is Gillian? And why would she have Jane's grandson? Gavin's mum puts her hand on Jane's shoulder, explains to her that they had to get him out of the UK. If they were fleeing abroad, they would have taken him with them. But they were staying. They'd bought a house in Nuneaton. How could they keep the baby here and just, well, *wait* for the water to come?

'Don't talk about that,' says Carla, holding up a hand.

Gavin's mum presses her lips together, nods.

Jane stares at the alphabet magnets on the fridge and imagines her daughter's fingers on them, re-arranging them into words – nice words – animal names. Perhaps baby names. Jane would like to pick off a letter and hold it to her cheek. Yesterday, she thinks. Twenty-four stupid hours. She puts her hand to her throat to steady her voice and repeats, 'Who is Gillian?'

'Gavin's friend,' says Carla.

Gavin gazes down at his hands folded on the table.

'She needed to get out of the country,' says Ryan. 'Gavin was supposed to go with her. Someone else is going with her now.'

Jane looks right at Gavin. 'Why didn't you go?'

Gavin fixates on his folded hands and says nothing.

'Gavin?'

He says nothing. The others say nothing. Gavin's mum circles the table and puts her arms around his shoulders, leans her head against his.

Carla clears her throat and says: 'It's because of the Intimacy Law.'

'Hush, Carla,' says Gavin's mum. 'Don't.'

Jane swallows and looks away. 'Is the baby still in Liverpool?'

'Should be,' says Ryan. 'We made good time driving back.'

'Fine,' says Jane, nodding. 'Fine. No. Good. This is good. At least I know where one of them is.' She stands up from her chair, takes her phone from her pocket.

'You going already, love?' says Gavin's mum.

'Yes,' she says, unlocking her phone. 'I have my dog in the van. He'll be going crazy.'

'A dog?' says Gavin.

'Not now Gavin,' says his mum. 'It's late, Jane. Bring him in here. Spend the night.'

But she's already up and asking for Gillian's number and Padre's address, and Gavin takes his phone from his pocket and thumbs through his contacts, while his mum retrieves a plate of white-bread sandwiches from the fridge, telling Jane that she had them prepared for the returning wanderers; it would take her two minutes to pop one in a bag. Jane sighs, keys Padre's number into her phone while Gavin reads it to her, and presses the call button. The line crackles and beeps; she holds it away from her head. Ryan and Gavin look up as if they've remembered something.

'The signal outage,' says Ryan.

Jane huffs. 'I don't believe this.'

Gavin's mum turns to Jane, a sandwich bag in one hand, 'Try the landline,' she says.

'Everything's down,' says Ryan.

Jane breathes right down into her stomach and strides out of the kitchen, towards the front door.

Their mum scurries after her. 'Take this,' she says.

'It's very kind of you, but I'm not hungry.'

'No. It's our new address in Nuneaton,' she says, waving a small, business card. 'In case you need to keep in touch.'

Jane takes the card and tries to smile, but her face is wobbly again, so she stoops and hugs Gavin's mum.

'Drive carefully, love,' says Gavin's mum, into her hair.

Jane nods, turns and jogs across the road to the RV. In less than a minute, she is back on the motorway.

CHAPTER SIX | April 2032
Gavin

Bit different from a car boot sale, thinks Gavin as he stands in the doorway of St Mary's Hall and takes in the scene. Everyone's in such a rush, banking around each other with boxes and trellises with little clothes pegs and MDF cupcake stands and trestle tables and baskets of homemade jam, bottles of elderflower cordial, stained glass pictures, strings of coloured beads, cake stands, artists' easels and boxes, boxes, boxes. People have money to make and stuff to sell, it seems. Kids buzz between them, some are sliding on their knees, others – mostly the girls – are smoothing down frilly tissue-box covers or counting marzipan fruits in their little paper cases. *Perhaps you'd bring in some orange squash for the sellers?* says the vicar to a group of boys who are sliding on their knees. *Go through to the kitchen and ask one of the ladies,* and the boys do exactly that.

Gavin claps his hands together. Time to make some serious dosh.

He has a small table just near the door; great, he's the first one they'll see, and his mum has laid a tablecloth over the trestle table and has placed some large books underneath the cloth to 'create different levels,' and Gavin has a plastic wallet with all his drawings inside; he pulls them out and flicks through them. On Tuesday, he drew flowers all day, deciding that the size of the picture should match the size of the flower. His daisy one is the size of a coaster and his sunflower one is the size of a chair-back and in between he has an orchid, a rose, a dandelion and some foxgloves. Wednesday, he drew next-door's cat, Winston, while he slept in a puddle of driveway sunshine and *then* he managed to draw a pigeon while it sat blinking on a wrought-iron fencepost opposite the bus stop. And then, of course, there was the fish at the police station and Martin the chinchilla from the bus, and the picture he had drawn at Walmer Beach the day he stole that camera (although it made him feel a bit funny when he saw it – maybe he wouldn't put it out on the table) and loads and loads of trees: the horse chestnuts in the communal garden and the ash in the car park behind Tesco and the beech round by the bottle bank and that funny bush with berries by the bus stop; he'd spent Thursday and Friday drawing trees.

'How many have you got? Let's start laying them out – oof!' says his mum as she's bumped by two Tupperware boxes held against a stomach. 'No, no, that's quite alright. It's madness in here!' she says to the Tupperware carrier as Gavin puts the pictures on the table, starts to spread them out.

'The table's a bit wobbly, shall I stick something underneath it?' he says, and he scratches about in his pocket for that Tesco's receipt from the cheese and doughnuts and crouches down to the front table leg while Mum holds it steady and he's bumped again by something he can't see.

'We didn't pick the best spot, right by the door,' she says, as something trips on Gavin's feet and Grandad's scarf is damp on the back of his neck and his ears are dripping and he hauls himself up to see the drips sliding off the table and looks next to him at the boy with his hands planted over his mouth and he strains a bit higher to see his mum with her hands over *her* mouth then taking off her cardi and throwing it on the table where the pictures are, smudged and trickly. Gavin watches the pigeon's face contort and blur, then stares at the boy who starts to cry, tells him it was an accident and a lady comes, yelling at Gavin 'cause he shouldn't have his feet sticking out, no one could see him like that! Then he looks up at his mum who is pressing down her cardigan telling him he can dry them in the sun and he says, no, no, there's no point, they're all smudged, don't worry.

Then he steps out for some air.

Outside, the chinchilla man gets out of a very nice BMW, still wearing his green overalls. He strolls over, smiles at Gavin, hopes he's not too late to buy his picture of Martin? Gavin says he's sorry, but it got ruined along with all his others. The man's eyebrows arch across his forehead.

'Is his tooth better?' asks Gavin.

'Aye,' says the man. 'They took it out.'

Gavin winces. 'Looks like we've both had a bit of a rubbish time. Me and that chinchilla.'

'I'm sorry,' says the man.

Gavin shrugs.

'Listen, would you consider coming to draw him again?'

Gavin brightens, 'Really?'

'We'd pay you. For a trial.'

'For a what?'

'A trial,' says the man. 'Perhaps give me your number and I'll organise something with my boss.'

Gavin frowns at the word 'boss', but takes his notepad from his pocket and scribbles down his number.

The man takes the paper, squints at the writing. 'Gavin?'

'That's right,' says Gavin.

'I'm Blue,' says the man. He nods at Gavin, then rolls the paper into a tube and taps it against his palm. 'Prepare yourself,' he says. 'Things are about to get better for you, lad. You mark my words.'

CHAPTER SEVEN | February 2033
Jane

The traffic is bad on the way up to Liverpool; the line of abandoned cars on the hard shoulder doesn't help matters. Paris is asleep in the passenger seat, his tongue poking between his teeth. Jane is able to drive with one hand on the steering wheel, while the other gesticulates at cars in the adjacent lanes. 'Where are you all going?' she says. 'France is the other way.'

Everyone is supposed to be heading to France; it had been her plan too before Pinko came along. The ports on the South Coast of England are inundated; ferries heaving with people, making endless trips across the Channel, returning with an unlucky few who are refused entry.

She shudders as she thinks of it, the stupid Intimacy Law. There were rumours that the observation room was very cold. So much so, that couples only had to undress their bottom halves. Her gaze idles over the couple in the next car; she imagines naked legs positioned limply, like a frog ready for dissection.

The male passenger jabs at his mobile, then sighs his head back into the headrest. Must be the outage, thinks Jane. But why a network outage would cause mass traffic congestion is anybody's guess. Jane turns up the radio. It is mostly the same loop of forty songs, that she's been listening to for the past four days, punctuated by hourly news updates. The news, at least, is usually new. She honks her horn for no reason, then sinks back into her chair. If she can just get to Liverpool, then she'll pick up the baby and drive him to the heliport, where they can wait out the last few days in the RV. She will need to buy (or loot) baby supplies. Pinko didn't think of that, of course. Jane bites her lip. The next stage of the plan will rely on a great deal of hope and some divine intervention but, by a stroke of whatever miracle, Ashleigh *will* decide to join them. She has to. Jane has been turning the reasons over and over in her head since she left Kent. Her thinking goes something like this:

Ashleigh received her envelope from Pinko with a helicopter ticket to Finland inside.

But, Ashleigh being Ashleigh, didn't want any help – especially from Pinko – and was too ashamed to see her mum again. (Jane's eyes grow hot as she thinks this thought.)

However, Ashleigh had the baby, and didn't realise how much she'd miss her mum. Jane knows this feeling; there was a time when *she* was young, alone and heavily pregnant. Ashleigh probably, most *definitely*, thought that if she abandoned the baby – where she knew he would be looked after – then she and Jane could be mother and daughter again, just like before. (Her eyes heat up even more now.)

So, Jane believes that when the helicopter leaves on the 29th, Ashleigh will be there waiting for it because a) no one in their right mind would refuse evacuation to Finland b) Pinko is out of the picture and c) she and Jane can start again. New chapter. New life. Let the past be.

And with each passing day, Ashleigh will be under more pressure to get out of the UK. Jane takes a deep breath and looks at her phone. Ashleigh's a sensible girl. And the alternative doesn't bear thinking about. She'll be there.

Still no signal.

Jane creeps the motorhome forward and remembers the note left on the front door of their two-up two-down council house in Sittingbourne. There is an identical note on her bedroom door and one on the worktop in the kitchen (just in case the other two float away and are lost forever). The note has Jane's number, the promise that she will return weekly to see if Ashleigh is back, and a heartfelt *I love you*. Jane drew a heart around the whole message just to emphasise that fact. As promised, she returns every week, holding her breath as she turns the key in the door. Hoping to smell Ashleigh's body spray or hear a thumping bass upstairs or see her trainers by the door. After realising, each time, that the house is empty, she sets about checking the cupboards for missing food, the beds for crumpled bedsheets, the bath for stray human hairs. Then she sits at the kitchen table and blinks into space until her body is stiff with cold.

It is now 6:03am and the news has not yet aired.

Jane creeps the motorhome forwards.

Funny that she'd always smirked at the idea of depression. People would talk about their own experiences and she'd nod along making all the right noises, but really she wanted to suggest that *they* should give birth to a baby alone, *they* should get dumped and robbed of their life savings by someone who was supposed to love them, then *they* should bring up a child while searching for a job – that fitted school hours – to earn extra money for school uniforms, trips, shoes, mobile phones, games consoles, iTunes, avocados (when that was all Ashleigh would eat), dentists (when the NHS was full), childcare (when Jane had to work Saturdays), a Netflix subscription, a pet rabbit, a pet goldfish, a pet hamster, pet insurance, pistachio milk (when that was all Ashleigh would drink), the latest of EVERYTHING that all seemed to be the same stuff Jane wore when she was that age: Under Armour, Vans, Uggs, skinny jeans, off-the-shoulder t-shirts, owl-print onesie pyjamas, ballet flats, hair doughnuts – the number of times she swore at herself for not keeping every item of clothing she ever owned. She remembers thinking up this list while whichever friend or acquaintance wittered on about not being able to get out of bed for a month. Whatever, she thought. What-the-fuck-ever.

Then one day it struck her down. Not any old day, *that* day.

It was like being stuck in a tunnel, moving slowly through it. Jane spent four weeks carrying a haze about her, not remembering – or caring – if she'd been to the loo or had a shower or eaten. And just like that, Ashleigh slipped away.

She scrunches her eyes shut. Idiot, she thinks, as her daughter's swollen belly comes to mind. Surely Ashleigh will have needed stitches – would her wounds have healed without them? Was she wondering where on Earth all that blood had come from?

She opens her eyes, creeps the motorhome forwards another few feet.

Jane spent a fortnight in her house, waiting, phoning, researching, getting excited, following false leads, being disappointed, waiting some more. And then, of course, there was the water that might come. Evacuation sirens from her mobile had become more frequent.

THE WATER THAT MAY COME

Jane couldn't wait at home any longer.

Pinko's letter contained helicopter tickets and the code to one of three key boxes that hung next to his front door. Inside were the keys to his motorhome – curved, sleek, new – with the instruction to drive it up to Inverness. From there, his helicopter would leave for Finland on the 28th of each month, but the last one was scheduled for Leap Day. Jane had sneered at this detail. In Pinko's world, everything must be made special if the possibility is there.

The letter had also advised her to check her bank account.

She had done. It contained four million pounds.

At 9am, she parks up outside Padre's barber shop and knocks at the door. Through the glass, she sees his outline edging towards her. Her phone bleeps and she feels around for it, taking a moment to realise that the network is up and running again. The door clicks open and Jane looks up.

Padre stands small in the doorway, wheezing into some sort of respiratory mask. He wears a brown cardigan and a silk cravat. When he holds his hand up to wave, she waves back instead of introducing herself. He signals that he needs to catch his breath, then pulls the mask to his chin with unsteady fingers.

'They've already gone, Jane.'

CHAPTER EIGHT | MAY 2032
Gavin

Gavin is in the gardens on Broadstairs seafront, waiting for his 'meeting'. He's never had a 'meeting' before, except years ago with his headmaster at school. This one is with Martin the chinchilla. Well, Martin's owner. Martin's owner wants Gavin to draw him again, probably. Gavin doesn't quite know the ins and outs of the situation, but he said something about 'a trial' and told Gavin he'd get a free Nando's and his bus fare. Result.

Gavin doesn't come to Broadstairs very often – it's a bit posh – but he's noticed that there are some very nice trees in the gardens. Interesting ones. A mad palm has caught his eye; its leaves are properly spread out in all directions like a frozen fountain. He glances about to see if the man has arrived yet, but he's nowhere in sight. Gavin slides his A5 notepad from his breast pocket and takes the My Little Pony pencil from behind his ear. 'It'll make you look like an artist,' said Little Carla this morning, 'if you have it behind your ear like that.'

There is a girl doing handstands on the grass in front of the mad palm tree. She's not that much taller than Little Carla. Her three friends sit around her, watching, not fifty yards from where Gavin stands and chases lines of charcoal on his notepad. That really is a mad tree. Crazed and jagged, throwing the light about. One half of it is a bit flattened, like bedhead.

The girls have moved out of the way of the palm now. Good. But something twinkles in the grass below it. He stops drawing and strolls over to find a dropped bracelet. Pandora, it is. Little Carla has a knock-off version; this is the REAL THING. He bends, feigning an itch under the cuff of his trouser, and scoops it up. Nice. The charms are at least thirty quid each. He could sell them for a fiver. The bracelet, twenty-five, maybe? He could give it to Little Carla, but she loves the one she has. And anyway, what kind of gift would that be? Stolen from some other poor little girl. He stands up, looks about him. The girls are now treading slowly through the grass, hair held tight to the sides of their faces as they look for the bracelet.

Gavin releases a slow puff of breath and thinks again of Little Carla and the camera from the beach a few weeks back. He considers the bracelet, then the girls. The handstand girl is crying now. A man marches over to her, bends down, places his hands on her shoulders. He's got Ralph Lauren joggers, Gucci sneakers, Tag Heuer watch – designer-outlet boy. Not overly loaded. Could afford to buy the little girl a new bracelet.

'But Grandad gave me *that* one,' she cries at that moment.

Gavin pouts. Thinks of his own Grandad, of course.

'Is she looking for this?'

The man straightens. He is about thirty years old, Cartier sunglasses on his head, Fred Perry polo with the collar up.

The girl smiles with a high-pitched gasp, and bounces on her toes.

'Wow. Thank you.' The man claps him on the shoulder, eyes travelling up Gavin, then down him again. 'That's super honest of you.'

Gavin frowns.

'I mean...' The man reddens, scratches his cheek. 'What are the chances of losing jewellery in a park and getting it back like this?'

True. That was true. 'No problem.' Gavin tips his head. Winks at the little girl. Turns to leave.

'No, wait, let me give you something for your, well, I mean... It means so much to her.' He opens his Burberry Wallet, reveals a few Coutts credit cards.

Gavin raises his eyebrows.

The man sighs and closes his wallet. 'I'm being a dick, aren't I?'

Gavin laughs through his nose, then feels around in his pocket for a tissue.

'Are you going to catch The Last Match?' says the man, nodding at Gavin's scarf.

'I was,' says Gavin. 'But all the pubs 'round Margate are closed.'

The man grimaces. 'You know, there's one near me—'

'Uncle *Pink*o!' says the little girl, smacking the man's thigh. 'Don't say the "d" word.'

'Oops, sorry,' he says, covering her ears briefly. 'Sorry. Go and play. I think I should look after that, now,' he says, taking the bracelet.

'Is that your actual name?' says Gavin.

Pinko wrinkles his nose and nods.

A voice calls over from the promenade. 'You found each other then?'

Gavin looks over to see the green-overalled man, carrying Martin the Chinchilla.

'Martin!' yells the little girl, and all four children run over to the man.

'Alright, alright, don't let him out,' says the man, letting them take the cage from him.

'Is this the artist, Blue?' calls Pinko, one eye shut against the sun. Then he turns to Gavin. 'Are you the artist?'

Gavin doesn't quite understand what is going on, but he straightens and says, 'Yes.'

Blue walks over to them. 'Thanks for coming,' he says to Gavin. 'This is Pinko Stephens. My boss. He's looking for an artist.'

Pinko shakes Gavin's hand, while Gavin asks, 'Is it your chinchilla then?'

Pinko frowns.

'It's hers,' says Blue, kinking his head back towards the little girl who, despite Blue's warning, now holds the animal in her lap.

'Oh, the chinchilla!' says Pinko. 'He's great, isn't he? Lovely round ears.'

Gavin nods. 'I like his ears too.'

Pinko grins.

'Do you want me to draw him?' says Gavin.

'You can do.' Pinko pushes his wallet into his back pocket. 'But I'd actually like you to draw me a tree, do you think you can do that? Just for me to see your style.'

Gavin is a bit surprised, but nods and turns the A5 notepad so that they can see his sketch of the mad palm.

Blue and Pinko gape their eyes and step closer.

'Wow,' says Blue, turning his head to one side, then the other.

'It's moving,' says Pinko. 'I swear I can see it moving.'

'Hmm,' says Gavin, tilting it towards him so he can trace a branch with his finger. There is a glitch in it that would take one stroke of pencil to make right. He holds back while Pinko cranes to see it, not wanting to make corrections right under his nose.

Pinko presses his lips together, looks at Gavin. 'I think you're the one,' he says.

CHAPTER NINE | February 2033
Jane

'They can't have gone,' says Jane. But she knows that they absolutely could have.

Padre lowers his gaze. He is shorter than Jane, with wavy hair and a hospital crutch at one elbow. He shakes his head as if it all should have been different, and holds his mask away to speak. 'I saw you coming, you know,' he says.

Jane frowns, but doesn't ask what he means. 'When did they leave? Maybe I could catch up with them...'

Padre watches her face as she waits for him to reply. Then he shuffles aside, indicating that she should pass. 'It's high time we met properly, Jane. Come in.'

She widens her eyes. Something about the way he keeps using her name makes her uneasy. 'I'd really like to catch them. What time did they leave?'

'Come in,' he says, 'and I'll tell you.'

Jane half turns towards the RV, then sighs and ducks through the front door. He waits for her to walk to the middle of the room before closing her inside, then heads towards an archway leading to a kitchen, one foot sliding to meet the other. 'Do you want some tea?'

'No,' says Jane, and she starts to pace about. 'I don't want any tea, thank you.'

Padre looks her up and down. 'I watch a lot of people, you know. Did Pinko ever tell you that?'

Jane stops pacing. 'I don't mean to hurry you along,' she says, 'but...' She looks around the room, trying to assemble a polite sentence. 'If I leave now, maybe I could catch them.'

'It won't do you any good,' says Padre, as he proceeds through the archway.

She follows him into a narrow kitchen, 'What do you mean?'

He leans his crutch against the worktop, then reaches down a teapot. 'Rose cream?' he says, flicking his eyes towards a saucer of chocolates. 'And how is Gavin's mum, by the way?'

Jane gapes her eyes at Padre, then turns to leave. 'They might still be at the docks.'

'Jane,' says Padre.

'And I can call Gillian!' she says, feeling about for her phone. 'The network's back up. I'll call her.'

'Jane, it's never nice to have to tell someone this...'

Jane turns back to face him, her phone already at her ear.

Padre narrows his eyes, then turns back to his teamaking. 'Answerphone,' he says.

'Answerphone,' she says, almost at the same time. 'But there's signal, at last. I'll try again.'

'They're on the bottom deck of an Irish Sea ferry in a freezer van. Even if Gillian has signal, she will have turned her phone off so that she can't be detected.'

Jane cups her hand over one ear. She has redialled the number and presses her phone to the other.

Padre takes a little jug from a hook beneath a shelf full of teapots, then turns to the fridge.

'They're not answering,' says Jane. 'I'll leave a message.'

'Some people,' says Padre, 'are meant to be alone.'

His words are louder than the answerphone message, as if they have been spoken inside her head. 'Sorry?'

'I watch a lot of people,' says Padre.

'Yes, you said that.'

'And I've watched you. You are the brightest shade of gold, surrounded by an impenetrable black wall...'

'Yes, hello, it's Jane, um...I'm the baby's grandmother – that sounds strange I know but...well...I just want to come and get him. Please could you give me a call back, urgently?'

'Have you ever noticed...'

'My number is 07816...'

'That everyone leaves you?'

Jane stops reciting the number and stands with her mouth ready to say 'five'.

'Your husband. Your parents...'

Jane drops her arm to her side. 'How do you know that?'

'Your colleagues, your daughter, your animals...'

'How do you know that, Padre?'

'Pinko, too.'

'Stop it…'

'And now the baby.'

Jane stares, open-mouthed, before saying, 'You're mad.'

'No,' says Padre, 'I watch people. And I see that there is no point chasing that baby, because all you will do is drive him further away.'

'You can't really believe…'

'And you shouldn't make him run, Jane. He's only a baby.'

'This is madness. I don't have time…' She cuts off as Padre reaches forward, takes her hand and strokes it.

'I'm not being malicious,' he says. 'People have lessons to learn and yours – for whatever reason – is the cruellest. Yours is to learn what it's like to lose everyone you love.'

Jane is silent now. She listens to him as if hypnotised.

'And you don't deserve it. You have so much love in you…'

'Why are you telling me such horrible things?'

'Let him go,' says Padre. 'Catch the helicopter on Leap Day. Love the forests and the lakes and the long summer days. Love the sky. Love the Earth. But stop loving beings. They will leave you.'

Jane stands rigid, while a long tear rushes to her chin. 'This is stupid,' she says with a jolt, before dialling the number again. The line rings, then switches to answerphone.

Padre holds up his left hand and clicks his fingers. 'No network,' he says.

The answerphone cuts and is replaced by the abrasive no-network drone.

Jane draws the phone away from her ear, as goosebumps flash across her arms. 'I need to get going.' She turns and strides back to the living room and out the front door. If the baby was on his way to Ireland, then that's exactly where she was headed, but… She halts. Ireland, Jane? Alone? Even if she got past UK customs, there's no way they'd let her through on the other side. That stupid immigration law. There on the doorstep, she considers asking Padre if he will come with her; his age would exclude him from the entry test. The idea twinkles in her mind. This is crazy, she thinks, turning back to Padre's front door. Before she can step inside, he calls out from the kitchen.

'I will not leave this house until I die.'

'How did you...' Jane begins, but pushes on towards the kitchen. 'You could come straight back,' she tries.

Padre leans against the worktop, a teacup in his hand. 'Don't get me wrong, Jane,' he says, 'I'm not being wilfully unhelpful.' He puts the cup down to take a breath from his mask. 'It's simply that I *know* I won't leave this house until I die. I've seen it already, this part of my life, and now I must watch it play out.' He smiles at her, places his mask over his face.

Jane would like to close her eyes to this weirdness, but instead she balls her fists at her side and waits for him to stop talking.

'Before you leave,' he says, 'Gavin has a good heart. Remember that.'

She frowns. 'Why?'

'And...' he sighs, as if he is about to tell her something that he shouldn't.

'What?'

'Matthew will help you. If you must do this, look out for Matthew.'

Jane turns away before he can finish his sentence. She heads out of the house and hauls herself into the driving seat of the RV. 'Liverpool docks,' she tells Paris, as he scrambles onto her lap. 'We'll figure out the rest when we get there.'

CHAPTER TEN | February 2033
Jane

'I can't let you through,' says the man.

Jane stands by the passenger toilets at the ferry terminal, talking to a man whom she has identified as a member of staff. She would like to be able to use his name, but his lanyard is upside down and she can only see the plastic, rectangular back of his ID badge.

'Is there no way I can get over there?'

The man sighs, tilts his head to one side. 'Unless you have a European passport then...' He stumbles on his words for a moment. 'Are you aware of the new law?'

Paris is barking at the window of the RV. Jane can see him beyond the man's shoulder. 'Isn't everybody?'

'Then why are you asking for passage to Ireland?' he says. 'Alone?'

'Because I'm not going to France,' she says. 'I'm going to Ireland.'

'Fine,' he replies. 'Can I see your European passport, please?'

She rubs at the space between her eyes. 'So I'm condemned to this island, is that what you're saying?'

He shrugs.

She huffs and turns away. Her first thought had been to tell him that her grandson was smuggled over to Ireland on a ferry, but she stopped before the sentence reached her tongue. She has no proof that he's her grandson, and Gillian hasn't kidnapped him, she reminds herself, she is trying to save him. What good would come of dragging her back to the UK to perish? Paris's barking becomes raspy and she can hear his claws on the passenger window. She jams her eyes shut. There must be a way...

When she turns back, the guard-with-no-name is gone. She skates her gaze about and sees him by a vending machine at the end of the pedestrianised pathway.

'Excuse me!' she calls, jogging along the yellow road markings.

The guard jabs at the keypad on the vending machine and ignores her.

She draws up beside him. 'How much would a ticket cost?'

He squints at her. 'Are you having me on, now?'

'No.'

'I've just told you, you can't get into Europe without a husband or a passport.'

'Name your price,' she says, reaching her hand into her inside pocket.

'What?'

'Name your price.' She starts to count wads of fifties into her free hand. 'Go on.'

'No,' he says.

'How much are they paying you to stick around until the last boat?' she says. 'It's a fifty thousand bonus, isn't it?'

The man watches the clumps of money passing from one hand to another.

Jane stops and holds out the cash to him. 'There's a hundred here,' she says.

'I don't take bribes.'

Jane sighs, counts some more; puts out her hand again. 'One hundred and fifty, then?' she says.

The man stares at Jane's hand and licks his bottom lip. He stands very still, as if the money is a wild animal and he doesn't want to scare it.

'This is crazy,' she says. 'You're seriously going to stick around and finish your contract, when you could be on your way tomorrow, no, even tonight. Right now.'

The man flicks a glance to his left, then to his right, and ushers Jane around the side of the vending machine. 'If I do take the money, how are you going to get off at the other end?' he says.

She shrugs. 'You tell me.'

'Right,' he says. 'Right.' He thinks for a while, then: 'You know, I could have just taken the money and let you figure that out yourself.'

'I'm glad you didn't.'

'Is that your dog?' he says, tilting his head towards the barking.

'Yes.'

'You'll need to shut him up or they'll search your van.'

She nods, 'He'll be fine.'

They stand in silence for a moment, then the man says, 'Fuck it.'

'I'm sorry?'

He takes his radio from his back pocket and puts it to his mouth. 'Babe,' he says into the mouthpiece, 'there's a motorhome coming on the next crossing – a proper American style RV – can you check it out please?'

Seconds later, the response crackles through. 'Yep. Got a number plate on that?'

Jane watches as the man squints to read out Jane's number plate, while removing his high viz jacket. 'Thanks babe,' he says, when the woman at the other end has confirmed the registration number. He balls up the jacket and chucks it, together with the walkie talkie, into a nearby bin. 'Let's go,' he says, striding away.

Jane rushes after him. 'Who was that?'

'My girlfriend. She's on the other side.'

'And she's going to search my van?'

'She's going to jump on board when we get to Dublin,' he says. 'You're taking me with you on the next crossing. Then you can drive us down to Rosslare.'

'What?'

'You can drive us to Rosslare.'

'What's at Rosslare?'

'The regular ferry to Cherbourg. If you're following someone to Ireland, you can bet your balls they'll be on their way to Rosslare. It's the evacuation route for people who don't want to take their chances on the South Coast,' he says. 'Got your keys?'

'Oh.' Jane searches her pocket. They are now by the motorhome and Paris is throwing himself at the narrow, oblong door. Jane hands over the keys. 'How do you know I'm following someone?'

The man clicks the central locking. 'You're not the first,' he says, holding up a palm, 'and I don't want to know the details. Do you mind if I drive?'

'Yes, I do,' says Jane, taking the keys from him and heading to the driver's side. 'And don't let the dog out.'

CHAPTER ELEVEN | February 2033
Jane

Jane checks the time on the dashboard. 9pm. Twenty-three hours since she left Gavin's house. The port is navy blue now. Windscreens of car light dot across the waiting lanes like hovering flying saucers. She thinks of Gillian and the baby; they might even be in France by now. The man is making clicking noises in the passenger seat. She glances down at his hands and sees that he is scratching his thumbnails together. He has fat fingers. Without his yellow jacket, his hair looks sandy-blonde, rather than brown, and he has large cheeks that shudder as he clicks. Jane looks up at the cars ahead and the customs officials plodding from window to window in their high-viz yellow. In the next lane, a car nudges itself out of the queue, turns, and drives back towards the port exit. Jane sees the woman in the passenger seat shaking her hands in the air as she yells something to the driver sitting next to her.

'What happened there?' asks Jane.

'Turned around,' says the man. His voice is dry and he clears his throat. 'They got turned around,' he repeats.

'Why?'

He shrugs. 'Papers, probably.'

'Does that happen often?' she asks.

'About one in five cars.'

'Wow,' says Jane. 'Don't you ever just sneak them—'

'Hang on,' the man interrupts, eyes following something behind her.

She turns. A high-viz official is standing at the driver's window. She winds it open and says, 'Good evening,' but the official looks past her and says to the man, 'You off tomorrow, Matt?'

Jane snaps her gaze to Matt, 'Matt? As in Matthew?'

He ignores her question, nods at the official and says, 'Going to see the missus.'

The official frowns at them both before saying, 'Well, give her my regards, won't you?'

'Will do.'

The official holds up a flat-palmed wave and walks away.

'Is that it?' says Jane.

'Drive,' says Matt.

She puts the van into gear and advances, then slows and stops just before the ramp up into the ferry. 'You're nervous, aren't you?'

He fidgets. 'Yes.'

'There's some Coke in the back, do you want some?'

'No,' he says, glancing over his shoulder towards the stack of red and silver cans. 'Thank you.'

Now, he jigs his knee up and down. 'Relax,' she says. 'Matt.'

'Why are you so calm?' he asks.

'You wouldn't believe me if I told you.'

'What's that supposed to mean?'

She thinks quickly. 'I don't know why I'm calm. Not as much at stake, I guess. As soon as I've found who I'm looking for, I'll be coming back again.'

'What? Why?'

She hesitates then says, 'I've got another way out.'

He smirks. 'Is this to do with the shedload of money you're carting around?'

Jane bristles. 'If you intend to rob me...'

'I don't. But someone else might. You need to be more careful.'

Now she smirks, reaches behind her and takes a Coke from the box under the back seat. 'How long is the journey?'

'Just over two hours.'

'And she'll be at the other end?'

'Who?'

'Your girlfriend.'

His frown lines flatten out and a dimple appears high on his cheek. For a moment Jane thinks she can see what he must look like when he's at the pub or on the beach or waking up on a Sunday morning. Not a customs' official. Jane would like this face to stay for a minute. 'How long have you been together?' she tries.

'Two years,' he says, properly smiling now.

'That's not very long.'

He shrugs and says, 'Maybe.' Then: 'We haven't got any family. No parents, brothers or sisters, nobody. Not even one single cousin.'

Jane gapes her eyes. 'Well, that's certainly unusual.'

'I think that's why we've become so close. You know. We get each other.'

'Probably.'

'We *only* have each other,' he adds.

'She must have changed your life.'

'Oh definitely,' he says. 'Without a doubt.'

Now Jane creeps the motorhome into the depths of the ferry, following the waving hand of another high-viz official. 'I hate how the parking decks creak like that,' she says, coming to a halt.

Paris starts to whimper from the back. Matt turns his chair to face him. 'I'd forgotten about you,' he says. 'Come here.' He puts his hand under Paris's belly and lifts him onto his thigh. 'It's a bit much, isn't it mate?'

Jane looks about her at the other cars. From her high vantage point, she can see silver wingmirrors filled with blinking faces. 'Do we just stay in our cars or what?' she says.

'Yeah. The upper decks are too full.'

Jane almost asks if the boat is safe, but no, she doesn't want to know. Instead she says, 'Have you got a dog?'

'No,' Matt replies, scratching the top of Paris's head.

'He likes you.'

He looks up and grins. 'I want loads of dogs,' he says. 'And kids. At least two.'

Jane smiles. 'Is your girlfriend aware of that?'

'Oh yeah,' he says. 'But she's mad on cats and kittens. She says if we get a puppy and a kitten, they'll grow up as friends.'

Jane's smile widens, and for whatever reason, she starts to feel sad. 'Oh yeah?'

'Yeah. Throw a baby in the mix and the three of them will be as thick as thieves. Getting up to all kinds of mischief. My girlfriend watches hundreds of YouTube videos with cats and babies, and dogs and babies and once there was a baby and turkey. Turkeys are actually very intelligent animals, did you know that?'

'Yes,' says Jane. 'Surprising, isn't it?'

He smirks. 'I never used to be this soft. It's amazing what love can do.' Then he turns to her and says, 'Actually, I will have a Coke.'

'Good,' she replies, reaching back for a can.

He takes it from her. 'So go on then,' he says. 'What's your story?'

'I thought you didn't want the details?'

Matt hisses the Coke open and shrugs.

Jane grins despite herself. She has often wondered about the night it all began. *Pinko's party.* The sadness fills her right up to her eyeballs. She dabs at her face with the sleeve of her coat.

'I didn't want to upset you,' he says.

'No, no, it's fine,' she replies. 'I'm looking for my daughter, Ashleigh. It might do me good to talk about it with a stranger... well,' she remembers Padre's words, 'a not-quite stranger.'

Matt puts his Coke on the dashboard and rearranges Paris on his lap. 'I'm all ears,' he says.

CHAPTER TWELVE | May 2032
Pinko

The party must be over, now, if the silence is anything to go by. What a night.

The staircase is blurry this morning, but this only serves to softens its curve. He rubs at his eyes, pinching them awake. The bannisters are at once sharper. He descends, notices someone's pants on the stairs. He steps over them and is careful not to tangle his foot in the streamers or slip on the foil confetti. There is no glass, though, which is a good sign. He looks into the formal reception room – more streamers – then he winces at the sprinkling of pink confetti on his white couch; hope the ink won't stain, he thinks. Dirty glasses wait in rows on the bar. He leans over and appraises the crates of empty bottles. The bar staff must have joined in with the party and forgotten to clean up the mess. It's not the first time this has happened. He goes to order two large cappuccinos. *Two*. But no, wait, he remembers, the party's over. There is no barman now. It's morning. He turns and walks to the kitchen.

A coffee is the least he can bring her, although he can't remember the last time he made one himself.

He thinks about how they met – wasn't she with Gavin when the front door popped open? Loud and twinkly-eyed and looking for the bar. Ten minutes later, she'd found a long wizard's hat – ah yes, he'd forgotten about the hats from the bus – and was sweeping across the room as if on a broom stick. In heels. At some point, someone grabbed her waist, and someone else grabbed theirs, and a little chain of people were soon swooping about the room together. She wore cigarette trousers and a sequinned bandeau top; the night blue of both garments offset her deep, red hair. Gavin disappeared somewhere, around about the time she decided to lead Pinko's friends through a verse of *You'll Never Walk Alone*, champagne goblet swaying. She danced, jumped fully clothed into the pool, laughed, played darts and eventually ordered an Aperol-spritz at the bar at the exact moment he was standing there.

'Hi,' he said.

'Oh,' she replied, jamming her eyes shut. Trying to remember his name, perhaps?

'I'm Pinko,' he said, taking in her damp hair.

'I know,' she said, opening her eyes. 'Hi.' She hiccupped while telling him her name, then put her hand over her mouth. 'I'm sorry, I'm tipsy. And I'm not even supposed to be here. I'm crashing your party.'

'I know,' he said.

'Gavin. It's Gavin's fault.'

'Surely not Gavin. I can't believe that...'

'I was all set up for a night out, right...' she said, holding the 'night out' in front of her, between her palms. 'We were watching The Last Match in town. Me and Gavin.'

'Right.'

'After a while, he said he was a bit nervous because he didn't know anybody.'

'So you were his knight in shining armour?'

'Almost,' she said, glancing at the barman as he poured Aperol over ice cubes. 'We all got kicked out for being noisy,' she said, hiding her laughter behind her hand.

'Sounds plausible...'

'And somehow I ended up on the bus, sitting next to Gavin. Well...not somehow. I was always gonna end up next to Gavin.' She made her eyes big and bit her bottom lip. 'And now I'm next to you. You don't mind, do you?'

'Not at all,' he replied, smiling, taking the drink from the barman and passing it to her. 'Have a wonderful time,' he said, nodding, turning, leaving. She was a bit young, perhaps... Twenty-one, twenty-two?

A hand landed on his shoulder. 'Have a shot with me, my way of saying thank you,' she said.

He turned back to see the shots already on the bar. She'd ordered tequila. Yuk. Still, he said, 'Yeah, why not?'

'I know it's yours anyway,' she said, fanning her hands out to the bar, 'so I can't *buy* you a drink but I can order you one, can't I?' She handed him a shot glass.

'Alright, yes, fair play,' he replied, grinning.

'Take the salt first, on your hand, like this...'

He raised an eyebrow, 'I know, yes.' Twenty, perhaps? Nineteen? Could she be nineteen?

'Don't forget the lemon. Straight in.' She pinched up a slice slowly, as if to show him.

'Yes, straight in, alright.'

Later, outside, she asked him: 'What's it like being famous?'

He shrugged. 'I'm not that famous.'

'Not *that* famous,' she mimicked in a deep, slow voice.

'Well, I'm not.'

'But you are like, super rich, aren't you?'

He took a sip from his glass. 'Yes,' then threw it behind him. It bounced in a bush and they laughed. They'd knocked back five shots of tequila, had a moonwalking contest, ignored the other guests (fine, it's all fine; everyone's wasted *anyway*) then she found the sunken trampolines, bounced on one of them for half an hour, knee drops, forward rolls, and he asked, 'Are you on something?' She replied, 'No! And don't try to give me anything; I know what you rich boys do for fun.' And then they were sat on the leg part of a sun-lounger, side by side, with a bottle of Cordon Rouge.

'It's not sunny enough for sun-loungers,' he said, and for some reason they found this particularly funny.

She laughed for ages, then said, 'Don't worry, I'm not interested in money. Down in the town. That's how I heard of you, anyway.'

He had no idea what she was talking about, so he simply replied, 'Oh, right.'

She stood up, wobbled and sat back down again.

'Ooo... I think I'll call you a taxi,' he said.

'Shut up,' she replied, pointing a finger at him. 'You're just as drunk as I am.' As she said this, her hand landed on his inner thigh. 'So don't talk to me about taxis.'

He coughed. Swallowed. Coughed again. 'Erm... How old are you?'

The sun-lounger creaked as she sat up straight. 'Guess.'

A shrug. 'Twenty-two.'

'Nearly.'

'Twenty-one?'

A nod. 'Too young?'

'I'm thirty-two.'

'My ex-boyfriend was thirty-two.'

'Oh?' he said, eyebrows up. 'Was he?'

She creaked against the backrest, held her glass to her cheek and said, 'Before I killed him.'

What the fuck?

Killed him.

Then there was laughter. She was laughing.

Oh...

He laughed with her. She'd had him for a second, how stupid! He laughed on.

'It's the tequila, makes you happy,' she said. And kissed him.

From that point onwards, he cannot remember a thing.

Not. One. Thing.

This morning, she is sitting up in bed holding her phone. She is fully dressed but wrapped up in the duvet.

He stops in the doorframe. 'I brought you some coffee.'

Still looking at her phone, she says, 'Thank you,' then sniffs.

He squints at her as she drags the back of her hand across her eye.

'Oh dear, are you alright?'

She mumbles, 'I don't know where I am.'

He winces. Perhaps he should sit on the edge of the bed and look helpful, whatever that looked like. He'd learned to make himself the same height as someone whenever the need arose, to be on an equal footing or, in this case, to seem unthreatening, maybe? Oh dear, what an awful thought. He should sit. He should definitely sit. Plus, he really needs to put down her coffee. But then again, perhaps space is what she wants now. He leans against the doorframe – careful not to spill – and says in the nicest voice he can muster, 'You don't know where you are?' When it comes out it sounds condescending, piss-taking, but she is busy with her phone and doesn't seem to notice.

'My friend — someone — is texting me. They want to pick me up, but I don't know what to tell them...'

He tries to make her laugh. 'Your friend *someone*?'

She rolls her eyes. Watches her phone.

'That's okay...' He makes a worried face and dances his gaze; instinctively, he steps into the room.

She flinches and he freezes, walks himself backwards again.

'Um,' he says, 'just send this person my address. Here, I'll give it to you.'

She nods without looking at him, then types in the address as he says it.

'There. Won't be long now and you'll be on your way.' He smiles as if agreeing with himself, then has an idea. 'Or I can have someone drive you? If it comes to it...' he offers.

She puts her phone down. 'No. That's alright.'

He scratches around for something to say. 'It's always a bit funny the next morning, isn't it?'

She hugs her legs to her and shrugs.

He watches. 'You seem slightly...uncomfortable. Have I made you uncomfortable?'

She shakes her head.

'Have I done something wrong?'

Another headshake.

'Shall I leave you for a while? I'll let you know when, um, whoever-it-is comes to pick you up...'

'My housemate,' she says, in a stronger voice than he expected.

'Your housemate.'

'No, you can stay.' She sits back, puts her phone on the bedside table. 'Sorry... I'm just a bit...cloudy.' She scoops her hair into a ponytail and lets it fall again.

'I completely get that,' he says.

She smiles. 'Is that my coffee?'

He breaks from his lean. 'I'd almost forgotten I was holding it.'

'Thanks,' she says, reaching over as he approaches. 'Coffee should sort me out.'

'Okay. Good. Great,' he says. 'Want some breakfast?' He tries out her name. 'Ashleigh?'

PART TWO
THE ROMANCE

CHAPTER THIRTEEN | May 2032
Jane

It is midnight and Jane has been ringing Ashleigh for the past hour. It's not unusual for her to be out so late, but they have an agreement between them that if one goes out, she must contact the other every three hours. Pick up, pick up, pick up, thinks Jane. The last time Ashleigh called – no, not called, *texted* – was at 7pm. This is not *not* unlike her, but she has been quite secretive about her comings and goings of late. Jane suspects that the whole water thing has made her a bit erratic. It must be very stressful for Ashleigh. The next few months are *so* uncertain… Jane gets it, and this is why she doesn't object when Ashleigh flounces out without saying what time she'll be back.

Still, she thinks, if the shoe were on the other foot, Ashleigh would be worried sick.

Jane sighs. Puts the phone on the edge of the armchair. Catches sight of the brown edges of her fingernails and remembers that the horses will need doing again in the morning. In fact, she could even leave it until the afternoon. It seems easier to put it off than look into the eyes of those poor, doomed beings. And anyway, there are fewer now; she can usually do the whole stable block in about an hour and a half. Maybe two.

The TV plays back-to-back reruns. Jane is watching *The Wall*. Large balls jerk around a pegboard and land in the boxes at the bottom, while the contestant makes high-pitched, encouraging noises. You can't control the direction of the ball by shouting at it, you silly cow, thinks Jane. The configuration of the balls in the boxes reminds Jane – again – of the horses in their stables. Most of the thoroughbreds have been shipped off to wherever. She heard one owner mention Finland. There are now more empty stables than full ones.

Finland.

Not too close to the scramble in central Europe, and sheltered from the pending mega-tsunami, Finland seems to be very picky about who comes and goes.

Lucky old horses.

Jane looks at her phone again and thinks that the trouble with their agreement is that Jane never goes out, *ever*, and so Ashleigh doesn't really know what it's like to sit there worrying.

She clutches her shoulders with opposite hands. Hopefully Ashleigh took a coat with her.

There is a throw in the blanket box between the sofa and the TV. If Jane stretches out her leg, she can flick the box open with her foot and lift out the blanket with her toes. She does this now, face contorting as she tries to get the right angle. It takes a while, but she perseveres, her brain focussed on that task. At that moment, her phone lights up.

It's going to be a long shift I might stay the night so don't worry about driving out Ashleigh xxxx

Jane raises an eyebrow. *I didn't know you were working?* she replies.

The Last Match. Staff all gone. Easy cash.

Good, thinks Jane. Ashleigh likes making money, so this will temporarily ease her moods. *But where will you sleep?*

Don't know. They offered a room. I might taxi home later. I have to go.

Stay there, writes Jane. *Don't taxi home in the middle of the night. It's too dodgy.*

No answer.

Jane follows up with: *Okay, call me if you need a lift. Don't taxi home on your own.*

She decides to sleep fully-clothed on the sofa that night, in case they go back on their word and tell Ashleigh that she can't have a room. That's unlikely, but you never can be too sure.

Jane wakes to her phone vibrating. Daylight portions up the carpet in blocky shards and the TV has switched itself off, (or did she wake in the night and click it off?).

Ashleigh has texted: *Are you still alright to pick me up?*

Yes, she replies.

Thanks. I'll send the address in a bit.

The address blurs over itself, as Jane blinks her eyes back into focus. She has slept in her contact lenses, again. But hang on, Ashleigh was supposed to be at the Cross Keys watching The

Last Match. Then she said she was working a shift, and *now* she's suddenly in Tunbridge Wells. How did she get *there*? Jane sits up and puts the address into Google. Wow. It's one of those gated mansions right on the outskirts of the town. She has a shadowy memory of someone telling her that it belongs to Pinko Stephens.

Nah.

Can't be.

Are you sure that's the address? she writes.

Yes.

I thought you picked up a shift.

I did. Waitressing for some rich bloke. What time will you be here?

Jane blinks at the screen. *You're going to have to fill me in...*

I will. What time?

In an hour and ten xx

Why so long?

It's quite far! How on Earth did you end up there?

No answer.

Jane pays extra special attention to her mascara, making sure the lashes are properly separated. Then she laughs at herself while twisting the lid back into the pot; what the fuck was the point of that? He's just a minor celebrity, she thinks, as she teases out a few strands from her bun. She considers her only, tailored shift dress, but goes for jodhpurs, a roll neck, a body warmer and her riding boots. She prepares a thermos of tea and grabs her keys.

Jane heads out of the estate and towards the motorway. More sandbags have appeared since the night before; football fans must have hung on for The Last Match, before heading to Dover early this morning. How, thinks Jane, can one's own survival plan depend on the timing of a football match? There are signs up on some of the doors: LOOTERS WILL BE SHOT, is the preferred warning. Funny how words alone can be an effective deterrent. A few have chosen NO FOOD ON PREMISES, or, from those resigned to the fact that their homes are now fair game, PLEASE REPLACE SANDBAGS ON EXIT. Jane hits the brakes as she rounds a corner and nearly collides with a green Transit van. The New Horizon Apocalypse Trust are doing their rounds again this morning; they travel in threes, dressed in military garb and promising bed, board and a new awakening somewhere on the South Downs. They'll likely have to cover several estates today and so they park anywhere they can, like delivery drivers used to. Jane gathers herself and pulls forward, glancing at the community library. Never has it been so busy. Yesterday, they held an evacuation meeting, mainly for the elderly. Today is Speed Dating. Ordinarily, Jane would roll her eyes, but instead she strains to read the timings. Her phone vibrates on the passenger seat and she pulls over to read the text.

Be careful on the roads, pls.

Jane smiles. *I'm on my way, be ready xx*

CHAPTER FOURTEEN | May 2032
Pinko

Pinko takes a frying pan from the cupboard, but Ashleigh laughs and tells him he needs a deeper pot for porridge. He says, 'Right, pot, pot, pot...' as he looks around the cupboard, then produces another, larger frying pan. She rolls her eyes, tells him to get out the way, she'll handle it. Seconds later, she pulls a saucepan from the adjacent shelves and holds it up to inspect the size. She smiles and searches through the other cupboards, flapping them open only to push them closed again, until she says, 'Ah! Here we are.' She takes porridge oats, maple-syrup and, 'Do you like sultanas?'

'I don't know if I have any,' he replies.

She shakes a bag at him and says, 'You do. Look.'

He laughs. 'As it happens, I don't like them.'

Again, she rolls her eyes and goes back to rummaging. 'It's like you've never cooked before.'

'I've never cooked *porridge* before,' he says, sliding onto a bar stool.

Surprisingly, she doesn't seem at all hungover. Ah, the joys of youth, he thinks, as he watches her and tries to recall the events of the night before – the bedroom part at least. But for some reason, the blur of his hangover won't let the memories sharpen and the whole thing makes him feel very predatorial. He makes himself small on his barstool, pulling his elbows in, clasping his hands between his knees. Maybe they didn't do anything at all? Perhaps they simply fell asleep... For a second he wants to ask her, but the question seems too dangerous.

She looks up at him while stirring the porridge and says, 'That's right. You just relax.'

He smirks. She really is very young. He cannot remember the last time he was drawn to someone in their early twenties. They were usually a bit older, a bit more self-assured.

'Pinko, this young lady was waiting in the hall.'

Pinko and Ashleigh look up from their respective points in the kitchen, first at Butler, then at the lady.

A girl, older – early thirties, probably – with freckles and riding boots stands not two metres from Pinko with her hands on her hips. 'You could've texted me sooner,' she says to Ashleigh, but she isn't cross. She is smiling widely.

Lovely teeth, he thinks, round and straight, and those dimples are deeper than average, but – oh dear – she is addressing him now.

'I'm sorry?' he says.

'I said, thank you for looking after her.'

He stands up and bows slightly; he doesn't know why... 'No problem.'

'Quite the party, was it?' she asks, looking him up and down. She has a few curls around her face and an open, easy stance. She maintains her smile, as she scratches just above the rim of her boot. He would quite like to offer her a coffee, but instead, he rubs his neck and says, 'You could say that.'

Ashleigh pours the porridge into one bowl, then takes the pan to the sink.

'Don't worry about that, I...'

'You'll what?' she smirks. 'Wash it up?'

Pinko flicks his gaze to the older girl – the woman – who has widened her eyes at Ashleigh's remark.

'I have a dishwasher,' he replies, 'so you might as well put it in there.'

The girl – *woman* – laughs, the way people laugh when they are unsure about how to act around him; she obviously knows who he is and this deflates him slightly – *that's a shame.* Ashleigh is more natural, he thinks, as she sticks her middle finger up at him.

'Ashleigh!' says the woman, still smiling.

'Are you not having some?' says Pinko.

'Nope. We've gotta go,' says Ashleigh. 'I'm not dressed for the stables if that's where you're off to next,' she says to the woman.

The woman looks her up and down and says, 'Is that what you wore last night?'

Ashleigh spreads her arms and looks down at herself, 'What's wrong with it?'

The woman shrugs. 'I used to wear black and white when I was waitressing.' Then to him she says: 'Don't you ask them to wear uniforms?'

Pinko's eyes flick to Ashleigh and back again, 'Erm...'

Ashleigh says, 'You just met his butler. He didn't have a uniform.'

'Was that the butler?'

'Yep.'

Pinko adds, rubbing his neck again, 'We're quite casual here. And he's actually my PA...'

This time, the woman dances her eyes over him and says, 'You call your PA *Butler*?'

He laughs. She does have very beautiful teeth, and takes the piss quite easily. Perhaps the fame thing doesn't bother her... Her energy is on the outside, he thinks, visible, pulling her facial muscles in all different directions and twinkling her eyes.

'Come on. I've got to let the horses out,' she says.

Ashleigh yanks at her bandeau top, 'Right then. I'm ready.'

'Do you want to pop back and get changed, first?'

'Could do – would you mind?'

'No – got everything?'

'Thanks, Pinko,' Ashleigh says, shaking his hand. 'You'll put the money in my account, yeah?' And she winks.

'I'll have my PA do it.'

'Yes, thanks very much Pinko.' The woman waves, reveals those teeth again, her cheeks pinched upwards into doughy bumps.

'You're more than welcome.'

The hangover brings palpitations. He stands by the bar for several minutes, turning in half circles, hands flat against his cheeks, then he tries to help clear up the mess from the party.

Butler says, 'Sit down, take it easy man. Sit down, won't you? It's Sunday.'

Pinko shakes his head. 'I have to stay busy.'

Butler eyes him. 'Fine, I get that. Let's do it together.'

'Yes, good, okay,' he replies, clapping his hands with one loud pop. Keep busy. He'll work through the flashbacks, wincing as the images surface with every push of the Dyson: cold legs tangling with his in the night, a sleeping face snoring into his back. A boob.

He's sure he remembers a naked boob. He screws up his face and pushes at the Dyson.

'What's up, Pinks?' frowns Butler. 'You're pulling some weird faces.'

'No, nothing,' says Pinko, wincing. 'An intrusive memory...'

Had his brain invented that image? Brains were very good at that. Even so, the whole thing makes him feel icky. She was extremely drunk – that part he remembers – and there was no way she was thinking clearly. No way *either* of them were thinking clearly. 'Not smart, Pinko,' he says to himself, as he empties a champagne bucket.

'Are you suffering flashbacks?' says Butler, guiding a large broom across the dance area.

Pinko deflects. 'Aren't you?'

'Nope. I was dry last night.'

'That's not like you.'

Butler shakes his head, still sweeping. 'Someone's gotta stay alert. What if the water comes?'

Pinko smirks. 'That won't be for months.'

Butler makes a face that suggests he doesn't believe everything he reads. And neither should Pinko.

'Do you...' Pinko begins, wanting to ask if Butler had seen him with Ashleigh, but his mouth cannot bear to set the question free.

'Do I what?'

'No, nothing. A question for later,' says Pinko. 'My head isn't functioning properly right now.'

They clean up, while the house staff sleep off their hangovers. Pinko had always hoped that they liked him better for mucking in. Blue, of course, would be lurking in the garden in his green overalls. Impossible to stop him from doing his job. Pinko cranes his neck to glimpse him fishing something out of the pool. An item of clothing, by the looks of it. A t-shirt.

Anxiety grips him until late into the day, when he finds himself polishing the wooden spirals in the hallway floor, curve by curve, headphones on, ignoring the mini convulsions, the pangs of an unwelcome thought. He mind drifts to the older girl – freckles, riding boots – and this calms him slightly, he has no idea why... But then he's back to the unwelcome thoughts – those tears on his bed this morning. Perhaps she didn't like it. Perhaps he hurt her or ignored her while he humped away. Feedback from other sexual partners suggested that really wasn't his way; he was far more likely to be overly romantic – face stroking, little kisses, that type of thing – but he can't remember last night in that level of detail. He twitches again, then mouths along to the lyrics of *Personal Jesus* while scrubbing the skirting boards. *Older, next time, Pinko. Definitely older.*

Now, Butler appears in the large archway between the hall and the bar and says something to him.

Pinko removes an earphone. 'Sorry?'

'Lost and found items,' repeats Butler. 'Will you start up a WhatsApp group?'

'Why, what treasures have you unearthed?'

Butler approaches the far end of the hall, squats and places his findings on the parquet one by one. 'One small bag of weed,' he says.

'I'll take that to Padre,' says Pinko, reaching over and snatching the bag. 'Thank you.'

'One earring, one three-pointed hat...'

'The three-pointed hat belongs to the bus.'

'To the bus, righto,' says Butler, putting it to one side. 'One mobile phone and a wallet.'

'Oh, that's not good. Someone will be tearing their hair out looking for that.'

'Probably.'

'Have you turned the phone on?'

'Nope. It has a pin.'

'Can we charge it until someone rings it, do you think?'

Butler turns the phone upside down and studies the little hole in its bottom. 'Yes, I believe we can.'

'And the wallet?'

'Belongs to...' Butler opens it, locates a bank card and holds it to the light. 'Ashleigh Pearson.' He turns to Pinko and winks. 'Found it in your room.'

Pinko grasps his stomach. 'Shit... Really?'

'Yup.'

'Right,' says Pinko, nodding to himself for a moment. 'I'd better deal with that one...'

CHAPTER FIFTEEN | May 2032
Jane

The shovel scrapes under the straw nest and its cluster of dense brown lumps. Garland, sixteen hands and dappled grey, knocks her shoes against the ground and sways a little. Jane is bent right over next to the stable door thinking that these old jodhpurs are not as stretchy as they used to be. They seem to have moulded a gap at the top of her legs where her thighs meet and she wonders what shape it is. Keyhole, perhaps. 'Drop it in the bucket; she wants to come back in. We'll stick it on the flower bed,' she says to Ashleigh.

Garland snorts, as if hurrying them up.

'How much money did you make, by the way?' asks Jane.

'This bucket's too full,' says Ashleigh.

Jane's body stands fully upright, closing the keyhole. 'There are more over by the door. Piled up.'

Ashleigh pads over to the door, then back again with another blue bucket, picks up her spade.

'So how much?'

'Um...'

'You know,' says Jane, picking a stalk of straw from her leg, 'that you shouldn't be going to parties.'

'I wasn't... I...'

'Especially ones on the other side of the county. That you haven't even been invited to.'

'I made about seventy quid,' she said. 'Alright?'

'We had a deal, Ashleigh. You know I worry.'

Ashleigh pokes her shovel through the straw and says nothing.

Jane purses her lips. In this strange world, a mother can't allow her daughter to disappear into the night, or strop off into the sunset. The balance is complex. Jane picks her battles. 'Seventy quid's alright. Did you get any tips?'

Ashleigh scrapes up the last shovelful and heaves it into the bucket. 'A few.'

'Yeah?' says Jane, nodding for a moment for Ashleigh to elaborate. 'Nice.'

'Yeah.'

'What was he like, though. He seemed very friendly.'

'What, Pinko?' Ashleigh turns her back to Jane, checks through the straw with the tip of her shovel. 'Alright, I suppose... Posh.'

'He must have been alright to let you drink on the job.'

Ashleigh snaps her stare to Jane. 'I didn't!'

'You stink like a brewery.'

She doesn't reply, but kicks the bottoms of her wellies against the wall and scrapes up the mud that falls from each one.

'Ashleigh?'

'People kept buying me drinks. So I drank them.'

Jane draws in a long, dusty breath and observes Ashleigh. On any other Saturday morning, she'd drift about the stable yard yawning, only pausing to flop against the stall guards and chat to the horses. Today, her jaw is particularly rigid as she drives the shovel through the straw.

'Did something happen, Ashleigh?'

Ashleigh shovels through two more loads before saying, 'Like what?'

'I don't know... Girls are really vulnerable at the moment.'

'No one cared. The others were doing it too.'

'What others?'

'The other staff.'

'Did they stay the night too?'

Ashleigh yanks up the waist of her leggings with one hand. 'No.'

'You stayed there on your own?'

'I think it was nice of him to let me stay, considering I'd very obviously been drinking.'

'Oh God...' Jane dances her eyes. 'Did he know you were drunk?'

Ashleigh turns the shovel and inspects the end. 'I don't know. Probably. I don't want to talk about it.'

Jane nods again, brushes her hands on her knees. She would like to say, *you know how I feel about you drinking*. Instead she says, 'I think I'll get the fresh straw, now.'

'I'll get it.' Ashleigh leans her shovel against the wall, adjusts the shoulder-seam on her t-shirt and strides away.

Once back, she throws the bale of straw into the stable, crouches next to it and tugs at the binding.

Jane is leaning on a pitchfork, staring. 'How old is he? Do you know?'

'Come on, Mum…'

'No, seriously, I…'

She is pulling at the straw bale, not listening, and Jane thinks better of finishing her sentence. She'd only achieve some sort of derisive snort or eye-roll that would make her feel old and undatable. So Ashleigh surprises her when she says, 'Go on.'

Jane clears her throat. 'I think we shared a look,' she says, pointing between herself and an invisible face. 'I think there was a moment.'

Again, Ashleigh turns her back, kicking out the straw towards the corners of the stable. 'Are you going to help, or what?'

'Did you notice?' prompts Jane.

'Yes,' says Ashleigh, then, 'But that was all you, Mum. I think it's because he's famous. You were all jittery and making your eyes all big.'

Jane slumps a little on the fork. 'Oh really? Did I embarrass myself?'

Ashleigh shakes her head, but doesn't look up from kicking the straw. 'No, it's just that isn't really *you*.'

Jane's hands tighten over the fork handle, scaly and calloused from years of outdoor work. Further down, her eye catches on the shit caked around her boots.

Ashleigh says, 'He's thirty-two. He told me.'

'Thirty-two. Huh.'

'Yes. Thirty-two.'

Jane sways on the pitch-fork handle, eyes angled upwards.

'What?' says Ashleigh, looking over.

'Let's get Garland back in,' says Jane.

CHAPTER SIXTEEN | May 2032
Pinko

Pinko is standing at the front door of an ex-local authority, terraced two-up, two-down in Sittingbourne. He woke his driver at 3pm and asked if he wouldn't mind chauffeuring him an hour across the county. Of course, the driver didn't mind, but insisted on breathalysing himself first. There was enough time during the journey for Pinko to ask all those questions that made it very obvious he liked the woman with the freckles and the boots and the dimples. 'Have you ever had a lightning bolt moment before?' he'd asked, and, 'How much time is polite to leave between *romancing* a young lady, then pursuing her housemate?' To which the driver replied, 'We all know she ended up in your room, Pinko,' then chuckled in his smokerly way.

Pinko winced at that.

Now, the driver and the Land Rover are parked in the road opposite; Pinko glances over at it. The driver nods at him, moves his mouth as if saying, 'You can do it.' Of course he can do it, he's only here to hand over Ashleigh's wallet. The freckle-boots woman might not even be home… He turns back to the door. No knocker. No bell. A letter-box-flap yawns side-long above the Yale lock. He pokes his finger in it and lets it clatter back. A shadow grows behind the glass, presses its face up against it, eyes first peering, then surprised. The door clicks open.

'Hi.'

Those beautiful teeth. 'Hello,' he replies, putting one foot behind him, then in front, then tracing lines with it on the floor.

'Are you okay?' A giggle flutters out of her and colours her face.

'Um, yes. Well, you know the yesterday? I mean, the waitressing? Well, the party; I mean the party, anyway…your little housemate left this at the house,' he says, blinking between each word.

'Oh!' she replies, taking the wallet. 'Wow, thank you.' She grins, more teeth. 'My little housemate?'

'Yes. Ashleigh.'

'Yes, Ashleigh.'

'I imagine she was wondering where it was.'

'She's been asleep all afternoon. You must have worked her too hard.'

A wave rolls in his belly. 'Is she okay?'

'She's fine,' she says, nodding. 'She's fine.'

'Good,' he says, hands in his pockets, nodding at the floor. 'I wouldn't want...um...'

'Wouldn't want what?'

'Nah,' he says, 'nothing.' He glances back over his shoulder, then up at the guttering.

She asks, 'Was there anything else?'

As she says this, he notices she has one blue eye and one grey. Dark grey. Elephant grey. 'No,' he says, enchanted by this detail. 'It's um...a lovely day,' he says.

She leans forward and looks about the sky. 'It's not bad.'

'Enjoy it,' he says. 'The day. Enjoy the day.'

'You too,' she says, closing the door.

Later that day, when a journalist asks him about his favourite tree, he finds himself talking as if he were talking to her. He leads the journalist through the woods to his treehouse and pretends he's leading her. He shows him the giant oak in the back paddock, tells him about stretching blankets around its lower branches and sitting inside them with a flask of orange squash when he was a kid. In fact, he still makes blanket forts in this exact place with his niece. He skips the journalist over to Blue, the most loyal member of the team, been around since Dad was alive but, 'I don't want to be mentioned in whatever you're doing,' says Blue, before walking away. 'You know what I'm like,' he calls back, over his shoulder. Pinko apologises to the journalist, turns back to the giant oak, tells him about recording the birds singing up in the higher branches then playing it back into the sky to see if others would answer. He tells him that sometimes his father would come and sit with him and play noughts and crosses with the acorns and the leaves.

'That was...different,' says Butler afterwards.

'Different good?'

'I think your followers will like it.' He shrugs. 'I liked it.'

And maybe *she* would like it, thinks Pinko, if she could be counted among his followers. Although oddly, when he thinks about his childhood, she is right there in his memories. But it isn't her, couldn't be. So who is she? Who *was* she? This parallel face from his past that wears those freckles and dimples like a mask. She was the *real* one. The one with long, pinkie fingers that tapered into curved nails. She had that big, soft hair and her eyes – although a different colour – locked him in the same way. It was more of a lock than a look, yes... As a child, he wouldn't have noticed a look, would he? Unless it was a really sustained, furrowed, grumpy-adult look. Blue used to look at him like that... Still does. But the woman, with the soft hair, who was she? And why did she lock him into a look?

Later, while he cleans his teeth, his brain tries to patch together fragments of memory into a person. But he can't quite manage it. As toothpaste foam disappears into the plughole, he realises that the woman from his childhood memories is lost. He turns and goes to bed.

At one point, in the night, his mind turns her in revolutions until it is dizzy and falling and he wakes up. He opens his eye to the darkness, tries to catch her hair as it streams behind her. But she falls away from him, again.

He floats through the weekend, over Monday, into Tuesday, to another party – or rather – a birthday ceremony. He stands again at the top of the stairs and imagines the series of expressions captured on Ashleigh's housemate's face, each of them lovely. He had fumbled his words and shuffled about too much... Had he acted like an arse? The way he stood at her door, the thing he said about the weather, was that all a bit lame?

That 'other business' doesn't have to be labelled as 'other business' anymore; he can comfortably call it 'the one-night stand' or the 'sexual encounter'. That is, after all, what it was. What doesn't sit so easily is the fact that Ashleigh will surely have told her housemate all about it, the way housemates do. Funny, though, that the woman laughed when he'd said 'your little housemate'. Funny that the walls were papered, that she wore faux UGG slippers, that there were hanging baskets flanking the front window. The house was very much a home, hmmm. A lodger, perhaps, not a housemate. That would explain the slight age difference.

He twizzles a pen in his hand. It is wooden, with 'Lily' engraved along it in looping letters. It was made for Lily, his elder niece, but she is eighteen years old and it obviously doesn't interest her enough to take it home. He clicks it, tests it on the back of his hand as he thinks on. Not a housemate, so an aunt, perhaps? He was thirteen when Lily was born. Perhaps Ashleigh's housemate is an aunt.

One blue eye, one grey. He winces, squeezes the pen. Ashleigh's eyes were dark with greying edges that undulated lazily; *oyster* edges, yes, she had oyster edge eyes. Perhaps she is a sister? God, that's much too close for comfort. He clicks the pen and slides it into the breast pocket of his jacket.

The guests have arrived.

A blue jeweller's box is set precariously on the banister in front of him, followed by Butler's voice. 'I just picked it up from the engravers,' he says. 'I'm expecting similar treatment after twenty-five years' service, by the way.'

'Huh!' says Pinko, picking up the box and running his hand over the family crest. 'You'll be at the helm long before then.' He lifts the golden clasp. 'Anyway, I thought I'd get you a Maserati,' he teases, glancing up to check Butler's reaction.

The box clicks open pleasantly enough, but could they not get a circular box? Inside is a watch, wooden of course; he turns it over.

Max Hemmel
Valued Employee
Happy 60th Birthday

'Fine. You can,' says Butler. 'I'll sell it and keep the money.'
'Really?'

'It would be like giving a fish a bicycle.'

'I won't get you a car,' says Pinko. 'Unless you ask for one.'

Butler smiles and nods towards the box: 'What do you think?'

'It's great.'

'The tickets are underneath the mount,' he adds, turning to a dark-wood framed mirror and adjusting his tie. 'I'd lose the waistcoat, Pinko. It's almost thirty degrees.'

Pinko lifts the watch from its box, and the square of velveteen card that supports it. 'First class?'

'Yes.'

'Thanks, Butler,' he says, taking off his jacket. 'It's a great gift. I hope he likes it.'

'Got your speech?'

'Yup,' says Pinko, undoing the waistcoat. 'I'm bursting through the shirt, that's why I put this thing over it.' He glances at Butler. 'Walk with me a moment.'

'What is it?' says Butler, following Pinko along the landing.

'You know I met this...girl.'

'The wallet girl?'

Pinko reddens. 'Not exactly.'

Butler steps ahead to hold open Pinko's dressing room door (cherry wood, bespoke, oblong) and they both stride in. 'Who, then?' he grins.

'The woman who came to collect her,' says Pinko, discarding his shirt and selecting another from his button-cuff rail.

'Oh.'

Pinko slides an arm into the shirt. 'Why the surprise?'

'Well... It's a bit weird, isn't it? It looked like they were related and you...' he tails off, gesturing vaguely with his hands. 'Didn't you...with the other girl?'

'Do you think they're related? I'm not sure they are. Apparently, they're housemates – they could be housemates, couldn't they? I think they're housemates.'

Butler shrugs. 'She looked at least ten years older. The girl with the boots.'

Pinko sighs. 'You're right. It's ridiculous. She's completely unknown to me, like, completely and I'm, you know, *all like this*.'

Butler laughs. 'Thunderbolt, was it?'

Pinko tilts his head, buttons his collar. 'It's never happened to me before. I guess so.'

'Leave it for a few days,' says Butler. 'See how you feel. Then why don't you *ask* her what their deal is?'

CHAPTER SEVENTEEN | May 2032
Jane

Ashleigh is not taking things particularly well, Jane has noted. She has been hiding in her room for most of the week. It seems that the media is fed up with the water that might come. When it was first mentioned the whole country jumped into action. This energy kept up morale; The Blitz Spirit, they called it. The latest news is that Sydney is the hottest place for film studios, now that London is almost gone. The shift in focus – to America and Australia and other countries that are largely unaffected by the water – only serves to make the Brits feel isolated, like they have been forgotten about; the world is watching and waiting for its next drama-fix.

This is, thinks Jane, why Ashleigh has become very clingy.

As soon as she hears Jane put her shoes on, she asks her where she's going. Often, she goes with Jane – to the shop or the stables or to work – then sits in the car and waits. At least three times a day, she shuffles down the stairs, into the living room or kitchen and flops beside Jane, puts her arms around her. Who knows what has happened to her mates. They've probably gone to France already; most of them belong to married, heterosexual parents. It's different for Jane, she is alone, and she wonders if Ashleigh feels hard done by because of this. 'I'm sorry,' said Jane one day, when Ashleigh had come downstairs for a cuddle. 'I'm sorry that me and your dad aren't together anymore.'

Ashleigh pulled away, screwed up her face and said, 'Why would you be sorry? I don't even remember him.'

Jane took comfort from this, wondered what kind of person she would have become if her ex-husband had stuck around. She let the moment dissolve, before saying, 'It's okay, babe, we will figure this out. Just live your life, for the moment. The water might never happen.'

Then Ashleigh started to cry.

This was conflicting for a mother who longed to comfort her daughter the way she used to years ago. How selfish am I, she thought, to take pleasure in finding my little girl again?

She tells herself now that she should force Ashleigh back into her almost-adult self. After all, what's ahead will require resilience and faith.

Jane looks through the window and blows into a full mug of tea. The TV behind her twinkles in the reflection. She watches it without turning, not wanting to read the breaking news, but can't help catching bits of it; now she can see Becky Albright from Penzance. Jane's eyes manage to reverse the letters beneath her as she speaks. 'It's coming,' says Becky Albright. 'It's getting closer; all these months they've been talking about it with lessening urgency, the media, but the passing of time doesn't make it any less real.' Tina Singh, in Leigh-on-Sea — just over the water from Sheppey — makes a similar point. 'The government has come off the boil,' she says. 'The world is coming off the boil. Those who haven't escaped are more or less doomed.' Jane squeezes her eyes shut. Go high or get out, is the overwhelming message; every man for himself. Jane turns and reaches for the remote control. A talk show host watches on as a couple scream at each other on stage.

'We have the passports! We could leave with him now!' says the woman-half of the couple. 'But he's not my biological son!' comes the response.

Another jab at the remote control.

'The British passport application service has a backlog of over four months, according to new figures released today.'

Jab.

'People think we're mad paying two hundred grand to have it removed from its foundations and physically towed up to the Highlands, but, we spent so much time building the place... It's our forever-home.'

Jab.

'Skip the customs officials and win a one-way ticket for you and your entire family to Poprad.'

Doorbell.

Jane puts her mug on the windowsill and wanders out to the hall.

'I have a delivery...' says the delivery man, reading a clipboard. 'For Ashleigh's housemate.' He looks up at Jane and smiles.

Jane frowns, before realising that only one person refers to her in this way. 'That's me,' she says, grinning, forgetting the doom on the TV.

He bends down beside the door frame and picks up a baby tree wrapped in a hessian nappy. A green ribbon has been tied into a bow at its middle.

'It's an oak,' she says.

'Wouldn't know,' he shrugs. 'Can you sign here?'

She signs and pushes the door shut with her shoulder.

> *To Ashleigh's housemate.*
> *If you need help planting this, just let me know.*
> *Yours hopefully,*
> *Pinko*

She flops back against the door, covers her mouth with the back of her hand, uncovers it, gazes at the baby oak, reads the note again, gazes some more. She turns to call Ashleigh, who is sleeping upstairs, and tell her that there really *was* a spark! He likes her! He does! But... She shuts her mouth tight; no, perhaps not. It's too frivolous to be that happy right now. Anyway, what if Ashleigh disapproves? She probably would. Yes, she probably would. And it might make her feel weird about working there again.

Jane walks the oak to the kitchen and detaches the label.

CHAPTER EIGHTEEN | May 2032
Pinko

Pinko is sitting in the walled garden – round of course – imagining it filling with water like a large, sloshing toilet bowl. It is on the lower level of the estate, in fact, there are steps down to it from the kitchen garden. The steps are annoyingly square and perhaps it is that imperfection that often keeps him from wandering down to the walled garden, but for some reason, today he has realised that it might all be gone soon. And so he is here, thinking about that, wondering if his father is watching, shaking his head. *They're only things, Pinko. And you are one of the lucky ones.* Pinko smiles up at the sky, nods. You're right Dad, he thinks, as the phone rings.

'Hello?'

'It's Jane.'

The rain is a little heavier now and he jogs to a stone folly for cover: 'Who?'

'Jane, you know, Ashleigh's um, *little* housemate...'

'Oh!' he says, spinning to face the other direction. 'Jane,' he says. 'That must be your name. Hello, Jane.'

She laughs. 'It is my name, yes.'

He winces. 'I didn't know that was your name before, so that's why I...said it.' He clears his throat and asks, 'Did you get the oak?'

'I did!' she says, and he hears her take a deep breath. 'In fact, I was calling to say thank you.'

He registers the diphthong in her Kentish 'you', smiles into the phone. 'You're most welcome.'

'Also... I, um, planted it already.'

'Oh... In your garden?'

'Yes. Where else?'

'Not too near the house?'

'No. Not too near the house.'

'Well...' he turns in a circle and wonders if that's it. She planted it alone and so now he can't help her as he had hoped. 'Great,' he says. But perhaps there's nowhere else to go from here, perhaps it's all over before it can begin. He sits down on the bench inside the folly. 'That's really great.'

She takes another breath. 'So...'

He springs up from the bench. 'So?'

'I guess you can't help me plant it. Like you said on the note.'

He freezes, his eyes skipping through grass blades, up to the curved edge of the patio, 'Erm...' Ordinarily he would leave it at that, but his mouth will not obey him. It blurts, 'Would you like to go for coffee this week?'

Again, he listens as she draws in one, slow breath.

'I'd love to.'

CHAPTER NINETEEN | May 2032
Gavin

Gavin kneels up on the dustsheet, still and slow. He is not making movements but tiny adjustments to his position, or rather, the position of his hand that wields the smallest paintbrush in his kit. A small flick here, a mini stroke there. He kneels down, leans back, zooms out and inspects the bit he's working on, then closes his eyes and imagines an pine tree. Hmmm, not quite, it doesn't quite move like that, he thinks. He leans in and skims the other end of the smallest paintbrush through the wet paint. Good. Better. Much better. Much happier. The tree is much happier.

He puts his hands on his thighs and uses them to turn his top half to the left, then the right. The furniture on Pinko's landing is all hand-made. The speakers that hang at the top and bottom of the stairs are SONOS. He'd get maybe two-hundred quid a piece. Perhaps a bit more; try to sell them too cheap and buyers get suspicious. Ever the opportunist, he thinks to himself, shaking his head. His stare trips down the staircase, then back up and over the atrium dome, and down the inside wall to the panelled, galleried landing. Nice gaff. Not too shabby. Beats sifting through the yellow sticker counter in Tesco. The only reason Blue was on the bus that day with Martin the chinchilla, was because the chinchilla specialist just happens to live in Margate. That and the fact that his van broke down somewhere near Canterbury. And it didn't escape Gavin's notice that Blue's name was Blue. He squeezes the fringe on his scarf and sends a smile up to heaven. Then, he selects a sponge from his kit and continues with his work until he hears footsteps behind him.

'Hey Gav,' says Butler.

'Hello,' says Gavin, without looking up.

'Quick question. Pinko wants to arrange an "unveiling" of the mural.'

Gavin stops sponging and turns around. 'Really?'

'Yes. And I was wondering: when might be a good time to do that?'

'What like…' He pauses, eyes dancing, 'A ceremony?'

'Yeah, kinda.'

'Are you joking?'

Butler wrinkles his forehead. 'Nope.'

Gavin sits back, mouth open, and thinks about what that might be like.

Butler says, 'So the date? Would July be okay? Do you think you'll be done by then?'

'Oh, I'll be well finished by then,' he replies. 'In fact, I'm almost done.'

'Great. But will you be available?'

'For what?'

Butler scoffs out a laugh. 'For the unveiling.'

'Are you really inviting me?'

Butler laughs, loudly this time, bends and claps Gavin on the back. 'You crack me up,' he says. 'Bring your friends along, if you like.'

Gavin scowls. 'Like who?'

'I don't know…' says Butler, walking away. 'Or how about your family?'

Gavin lets his jaw hang for a moment, then he says, 'My mum.' His gaze climbs the tree. 'I'll bring my mum.'

CHAPTER TWENTY | May 2032
Jane

Wow. So *this* is the place he chose for coffee, she thinks as she stands outside the high, arched doorway of a rose-pink, Tudor hall. A waiter in a long, white apron is watering the bushes of lavender that smudge the angle between building and ground. Jane wonders how this type of place has been spared the doom that threatens the country, if it survives purely on the excitement of first, second and third dates; there's no fear of the future when the present is so exciting. Despite the authenticity of the weathered beams and the leaded windows, the glass door *sshhes* open when she approaches, as if she were entering Tesco. A woman with a bun stands behind a lectern-thingy and asks her if she's booked a table. Jane nods, then shakes her head.

'I haven't personally, but we have one booked,' she says, then pronounces the name she never thought she'd use in this context.

The woman smiles. 'Certainly. Follow me.'

The waiters wear gloves and carry silver domes on one hand, right up high, next to their heads. It's like a film, thinks Jane. A pianist plays jazz with his eyes closed. Great bronze globes hang from the high ceiling, their arrangements decreasing in girth as they spiral downwards. Finger-food sits synchronised, each little bundle higher than it is wide, chive stalks angled all towards the same direction, salmon shaved to the same thickness, cherry stalks bending like ballerina arms. A different waiter accompanies her to her table, where she tries to pull out a chair. He puts up one gloved palm to stop her and slides out the chair, indicating that she should sit down. She sits and thinks about her jeans, looks to see what everybody else is wearing.

The waiter says, 'Are you waiting for someone else, or would you like to order?'

'Yes. They'll be along in a moment. Thank you.'

She checks her watch, early, always early, then drums her knees with her hands. What would be a good thing to order – rosé? Perhaps they don't serve rosé here. Perhaps, coffee would be better; he'd said coffee. But what would he say if she asked for instant? With powdered cream? Or tea! There is nothing wrong with tea. She'll go for tea, she thinks, and a perfume cloud passes her, a woman following close behind with her tiny, bechained handbag. Jane looks down at her canvas tote bag on the floor beside her. What would he ask her about? About her profession, maybe. Fine, she thinks, she is quite proud of that. But what else? Hobbies? The horses, of course; that's certainly something they might have in common. And then Ashleigh, what if he asks about Ashleigh? 'Her little housemate.' Perhaps the first date was not the right time to talk about Ashleigh. That story usually sent men running for the hills. *Pregnant at sixteen? Really?* Then she'd watch their faces change as they made mental assumptions about her; her sluttiness, her lack of education, the girth of her vagina. No, she won't be a parent today. She'll save that for their next date, maybe, *hopefully*, but, then, what if this isn't even a date?

'Am I late?'

She jumps. Looks up. Pinko is standing beside her, a stem in his hand leading to the head of a blue rose. It hovers at the exact level of his smile. She notices, as other customers turn in their seats to look at him.

'Or were you early? I think you were early,' he says.

'Hi. No, yes, I'm early.'

'Okay,' he nods, struggling with the chair. Jeans, he was wearing jeans, nice ones probably, but jeans all the same. 'Oh, this is for you,' he says, handing her the rose. 'I'm not sure about dyed flowers, but the blue really is very striking, don't you think?'

'It's lovely. Thank you,' she says, taking the rose and holding it to her nose.

'I didn't really know where to suggest,' says Pinko, glancing at her mouth. 'My PA said it was nice here – you sort-of met him, actually. Butler?'

'Didn't he drive you to my house? With Ashleigh's wallet.'

'No, that was someone else. Butler can't drive,' he says, sitting down. 'The one that brought you into the kitchen that first day, do you remember?'

She does. 'Oh yes.'

'Yeah. So, I thought I'd give it a try.' He looks around, then back at her mouth. 'Quite formal, isn't it?'

Smiling, she says, 'Yes,' then, 'Have I got something in my teeth?'

'No,' he says, widening his eyes. 'No, I just... Well... You have very nice teeth, that's all.'

She runs a finger around the bread plate in front of her, looks about for a menu.

'Oh,' he says. 'I brought you something.'

'As well as the rose? You didn't have to...'

'Yes, well, only a little something.' He hands her an envelope. 'Well, not little. It's an example of the most amazing talent...'

She opens it, pulls out a postcard-sized piece of card. It is a drawing of an oak tree.

He laughs. 'And I've just realised, it's another oak tree...'

'The fully grown version,' she says.

'Yet – weirdly – smaller than the one you have at home.'

'So it is. There's something intelligent to be said about that, probably.'

'I'm sure there is,' he smiles. 'I didn't put it in a frame. I didn't want to presume that you'd display it...'

It is a drawing of a tree, but the light twinkles through its leaves – actually twinkles – and cloud shadows hang upon it like old cloaks. She would like to put it to her ear, to hear the branches fizzing. She turns it in the light to see if the movement is an illusion – it must be – and Pinko takes a breath to comment when...

'What can I get for you?' says the waiter.

'Erm,' says Jane, putting down the drawing.

'I'll have tea please,' says Pinko. 'With milk.'

'Me too,' she says, smiling. 'In a mug, if possible.'

'That sounds good. Same for me, please.'

She listens as he talks about the new artist and how they met. Then his niece Lily and how spoiled she is, but her little sister is *much* worse! Laughing, he tells her that he wouldn't change that, *couldn't* change that, says that he was exactly the same when he was younger – but how did he get to talking about that? Anyway.... He asks about her job, then listens with steepled fingers. Every so often, he nudges his ears with his shoulders, holds his chin, small, dimpled, stubbled, in the angle of his thumb and forefinger; puts his elbows on the table, takes them off, talks at length about trees. Then he talks about the café – how posh it is – while he waves at someone sitting over on another table, someone recognising him. She comments that he must get that all the time. He starts to say that he doesn't, but then admits that he does, but anyway! The café is really quite posh, and he doesn't really like posh things. He likes trees and people; he tells her as he sweeps his hair back.

'You're such a fidget,' she says.

'Am I?'

'It's constant.'

'I'm a bit...' He leans forward and searches for the end of his sentence. 'Nervous.'

'Really?'

'Aren't you?'

'Funnily enough, no,' she says. 'I thought I would be.'

'I knew I would be... I'm always nervous on——' he stops himself. 'I'm just always nervous.'

She swallows and fiddles with her spoon. 'But you're Pinko Stephens.'

'I'm...' He scratches his head. 'Not sure what that means.'

They don't talk about her family, in fact, they *do*, but Ashleigh is never mentioned. They don't talk about the water that might come, thankfully, or not – Jane knows that they have very different escape plans.

'People are still working in places like this. I wonder why?' he says, looking at the waiters, and she is relieved that he has also noticed the bubble of normality.

She says, 'Saving money. They know how much they'll need to get over, I suppose.'

For a second, he seems confused, then he looks at her, looks down, plays with his teaspoon. 'Shall we go somewhere else?'

By 9pm, they are tipsy and lolloping through his back garden, to the woods, towards his treehouse. 'Just a little further,' he says. 'I really want you to see this.'

In the car, there had been no grab for each other's clothes, no fumbling, no squeezing. No leaning in even, despite the separating shield raised by his driver (who even winked into the rearview, first). Perhaps they had wanted to, but they were busy talking about all the things they would eat once they got to his place. Did she eat cheese? He had so many cheeses! And queen olives. And apple chutney. And part-baked baguettes (from Waitrose) and chorizo, *No thanks, I'm vegetarian.* Well, we have loads of – he thought for a moment – leaves! he said. And they both thought this was the funniest thing for reasons that kept popping up in their minds, mid-laughter. Mid stiff, open-mouthed, laughter. *What about rosé?* she'd asked. Oh, yes. *So* much wine... In fact, there was a wine cellar. With barrels, he explained as he pressed a button in the door to make the division slide down, and they could have tapas on the barrels, and he asked the driver, 'Can we have tapas, on the barrels when we get back?' And the driver said, 'Certainly, Pinko.' And she said, 'Did you just ask someone to bring nibbles to your wine cellar?' And he blushed, hooked his finger over his lips. She watched him, then said to the driver, 'Can you bring some glasses too? And one for yourself.' And Pinko was suddenly rescued. So, they all stood beneath the vaulted cellar-ceiling and ate olives from toothpicks and shavings of cheese, while she found an *eye-wateringly good* bottle that turned out to be corked.

'Only a little further,' he says now.

'Into your Gruffalo den.'

'Into my Gruffalo den.'

'Make sure you behave yourself,' she says.

He makes an affronted face. 'But you just drank one of my best wines!'

She laughs, 'And I prefer rosé from Lidl.'

'So do I,' and he's about to tell her that, actually, she will be the FIRST PERSON EVER to visit his treehouse, when her phone buzzes.

She looks at the screen. 'I'll be one minute,' she says, then answers.

He walks on slowly ahead. He hears 'babe' and 'I'm out, that's all' and 'I'll be home soon,' and he turns just as she flicks her gaze to him, smiles, 'Okay, bye.'

'Everything alright?' he asks, as she jogs to catch up with him.

'That was my housemate,' she says. 'She's ill. I said I'd pick up something from the supermarket.'

She seems alert, rolling her hands and darting her eyes.

'Then I'll get someone to drive you back right away,' and he turns them both around. Back out of the woods. Back to the house.

'I'm sorry,' she says. 'I know you wanted to show me the treehouse.'

He waves her comment away. 'There'll be other times.'

She leaves and he feels hollow, as if there *won't* be other times.

Three weeks and several dates later, Pinko stands before Gavin's pine– the mural – now finished. He considers it for a moment, wonders about the gossip and the long looks and he *knows* that people have already spotted him out and about with Jane, but to invite her to an event *as his plus one* suggested something more serious. The thought excites him. He takes his phone from his pocket and texts her. *Will you come to the unveiling of Gavin's mural next month?* Then he holds the phone to his chest, waits for her reply.

CHAPTER TWENTY-ONE | June 2032
Gavin

Pinko presses his feet into the stairs, left, right, left, right, 'coz he doesn't want to scuff the wood. He's silent, although Gavin can now feel his vibrations, has learned that his paintbrush is unfaithful to him when Pinko comes pressing up the stairs.

He's not painting today, though. Neither is he sat on the floor. He's waiting for Pinko to cast his eye over the mural, one last time, and probably talk about the unveiling again. Gavin hopes that he will: just thinking about it makes him feel something like hunger inside, but not for food. As he thinks this, he unwraps the flattened waves of his twin cling-filmed wafers, like the water behind a speedboat, he thinks each time. Then he wonders what it would be like to have a speedboat. He bites into a wafer. 'Want one?' he says, mouth full, as Pinko draws up next to him and surveys the mural. He turns to Gavin, glances at his offering.

'I haven't had one of those for years.'

Gavin pushes his hand out further, reaffirming his offer.

Pinko holds up his palm. 'No thanks.'

The wafer returns, with Gavin's gaze, down to his lap.

'Well, perhaps just half,' says Pinko, slapping his belly. 'I'm off carbs.'

Nodding, Gavin snaps one in half, kneels up and reaches the wafer towards Pinko. 'I always give my mouth something to do when my brain needs to think.'

Pinko takes a bite. 'Really?' he says, glancing at Gavin, then up at the tree.

'Like busying a tearaway child – you know? Gives me a minute's peace.'

Pinko laughs as he puts out a hand to touch the mural, then withdraws it, flicking a look at Gavin. Gavin nods, 'Go ahead.'

Pinko resumes, padding his hand down the trunk of the tree, expecting to be tickled by the bark, feel the prickle of the needles. 'Gavin, it's...' he says, 'incredible.'

'Thank you,' he replies, looking at Pinko's slippers.

'You know, Gavin, I've invited some curators for the unveiling.'

Gavin wrinkles his brow. 'Oh right,' he says, popping the last chunk of wafer into his mouth.

'So maybe you could bring your sketchbook, what do you think?'

'Why?'

Pinko smiles. 'So that they can see some more examples of your work.'

'Oh,' says Gavin. 'Oh.' But the thought won't get beyond the image of his sketchbook tucked under his arm, as Pinko opens the curtains that will cover the tree. Pinko paid Gavin a more-than-tidy sum to paint the mural, and to think that there could be other people interested in his work... He starts to feel shaky, so he swallows the rest of the wafer and says,

'Jones' the Bootmakers. I didn't know they did slippers.'

Pinko smiles at Gavin, clearly expecting a different response. He lifts his heel and looks at it. 'I have so many pairs of slippers...'

'They must have been a present.'

Pinko puts his foot down. 'Why's that?'

Gavin shrugs. 'That's the type of shoe, I mean, slipper, that someone like me would wear,' he says. 'On a good day. Don't get me wrong... I usually wear socks.'

Pinko looks at the floor. 'As it happens, I'm trying to appear...' he hesitates, dancing his eyes over the floor.

'Poorer...'

'Unpretentious, is what I was going to say.'

'Having loads of slippers ain't really normal,' Gavin replies, screwing up the clingfilm.

Pinko looks back at the tree, his neck and ears red.

'Don't worry,' says Gavin, waving it away. Then: 'Are you seeing a lady?'

Pinko widens his eyes. 'How did you know?'

'And she doesn't really like...' gesturing around him, 'all of this?'

He nods. 'It's not that she doesn't like it...I just get the impression that she's...'

'Poorer.'

'More down to earth,' he says, raising eyebrows: 'Any advice?'

'What? Me? Ha! I know I'm poor but…being like me won't do you any favours.'

'I didn't mean that…but…the money thing has always been a barrier. And you're, well, always so wise.'

'No one's ever called me wise.'

'No, seriously.'

'And I've never had a girlfriend.'

'Oh?'

Gavin puts the ball of clingfilm into his pocket, clears his throat. 'I had one go – you know, with a lady – but…' Gavin tails off, turning pink.

'Gavin, you don't have to share this.'

'It makes me feel funny,' he says, his earlier happy feeling vanishing. 'I don't like to think about it.'

'Well, we've all been there, mate,' says Pinko.

Gavin smiles; the 'mate' seems weird in Pinko's posh mouth. Still, it's a nice word to hear. 'So I'm not the best person to ask,' says Gavin. 'About that.'

'Don't worry about——.'

'But, it's better that she's not into money rather than being, you know, *really* into money, isn't it?'

'Absolutely.'

'Maybe she's used to counting her pennies, you know? Going down the back of the sofa for the odd 10p. If you buy all this fancy stuff, it will make her think more about what she hasn't got.' Gavin sends his tongue up and over his front teeth. 'My mum even gets annoyed when I bring home discount doughnuts from Tesco.'

Pinko stares off somewhere around the base of the tree.

'Perhaps she likes you as you are. I mean, you're nice enough, aren't you?' Gavin checks his Nokia. 'Mum's getting a taxi here for the unveiling,' he says, smiling at the screen. 'From Margate, I'm paying for it.' Then: 'Pinko, what's a curator?'

CHAPTER TWENTY-TWO | June 2032
Jane

Jane has two things to do today. One, decide what to wear to Pinko's *unveiling* and two, help the poor Kentish animals as they careen helplessly towards certain death. She feels guilty that 'finding a dress' is number one on her to-do list, but it is key to her grand plan for getting them – she and Ashleigh – out of the UK. And it's a long-respected truth that the right dress can unlock the world.

She should be at the stables, mucking out Garland – one of three Cleveland Bays – but she isn't. This is the least of her priorities. She phones the owner and explains that she has a few 'things' to sort out, can the owner muck out Garland this time? The owner cannot. The owner is shopping in Courchevel. The owner is ten years old. The owner's mother says that it's really, very inconvenient... Jane would like to tear her off a strip but instead says she'll do what she can. She asks Ashleigh to go instead. Ashleigh refuses, goes away and thinks about the poor, unloved horse with nothing but its own shit for company (or some such thought, Jane believes) and comes back in boots, jodhpurs and a fleece zipped up to her chin.

'Are you cold?' Jane says as she heads into the kitchen. 'It's June.'

'I'm tired,' says Ashleigh. 'That makes me cold.'

Jane rolls her eyes. 'Do you want me to drive you?' she calls back into the hallway.

'No ta,' comes the reply. 'I'll bike it.'

Leylandii branches dance shadows around the kitchen table. It is windy. Ashleigh might struggle on her bike. Before Jane can say this, the front door closes and Ashleigh is gone.

Jane takes her own coat from the hall and heads off out. She walks the three streets (left, then left, then left) to her place of work. It is Saturday afternoon and the closed sign hangs aslant in the window. Jane lets herself in, calls 'Hello!' into the waiting room and then again along the back corridor.

'You ready, Jane?' comes the reply.

Jane walks in the direction of the voice. 'Have we been called upon already?' she says.

'Yep. I'm just grabbing what we need.'

Sue, the surgeon, bustles out from the back room in a scrub-top and jeans, her blond bob clipped back. She drives them to their first point of call, a cattery up by Northfleet, where a wrong turn leads them to a still, dark line of Eurostar trains. WELCOME TO DISNEYLAND KENT is graffitied on one of the carriages in a long orange squiggle. At the cattery, the manager welcomes them, face greyed and unblinking. Every morning, she says, she finds more of them, abandoned in boxes. Sometimes the mewling wakes her up.

Jane nods, looks through a low window to the back yard lined with cages. Each one contains a crowd of faces, multiple pairs of eyes.

'We won't euthanise healthy cats...' says Sue.

'I know, I know,' the woman replies. 'I wouldn't want that.'

'Have you separated males and females?

'Yes. I believe so. Some of the kittens are too small to tell.'

Jane winces. 'Poor things.'

'And would you believe that people have left their dogs here?'

Sue nods. 'You should see what they leave us.'

Sue and Jane work quickly, inspecting the cats for signs of disease, testing them for chips, checking for pregnancy, neutering, fleas... After a few hours, they report back.

'We've had to put three to sleep,' says Sue.

The manager looks relieved. 'Oh?'

Sue shakes her head. 'Too old. Too sick. And you're busting at the seams here.'

'Don't mix any new arrivals with this lot,' Jane nods towards the meowing cages. 'We'll be back next week,' she adds, looking at Sue. 'Won't we?'

'All being well,' says Sue.

In the early evening, they leave the cattery and move onto a kennel. The owner has been left with five dogs who were brought to him weeks ago 'for a holiday'.

'What am I going to do with them?'

Jane and Sue look at each other, continue the careful unpacking and checking of their equipment. 'We've just come from the cattery. They've got the same problem.'

He leans against the wood-clad wall of the main kennel. 'We work so hard to give them a good life, but when the water comes, we'll abandon them.'

'We can only do our best,' shrugs Sue. 'And believe that it might not happen.'

'I guess you'll be off to the continent soon anyway, won't you?'

'That's the plan,' says Jane.

They are late for the wild animal sanctuary. The manager is waiting for them outside, arms folded around herself, tapping the evening chill out of one foot. She thanks them for coming along at this hour. She doesn't know what to do with the lynx...

'What lynx?' says Sue.

She explains that she found it tied to her gate one morning. She had to sedate it before she could bring it in. And now she's out of tranquilizer – do they have any tranquilizer? Every morning she wonders what on earth she'll find tied to the post.

'Do you think he was a pet?' asks Jane.

'Absolutely,' says the manager. 'I've had three tortoises and a sloth, this week.'

'You need to put out a sign,' says Sue. 'Closed for business.'

'It won't do any good,' says the woman. 'And I have no idea what to do with the lynx.'

They don't know, either.

'If he's been kept as a pet, he should be tame,' says Sue. 'But it might attack the other animals.'

They help the woman to reinforce its enclosure. The lynx watches them, butts his head against the areas they are working on. Jane assesses his pupils, his ears, his tail. No sudden twitches. No fear in his eyes. No obvious anxiety. She sends her hand through the wires and he collapses against her palm. 'You're as dopey as a goldfish,' she says. When they are finished, they stand back, hands on hips.

'What now?' asks the woman.

'You'll have to let him go before the flood,' says Sue.

The lynx watches them, eyes half open, swatting his tail against the floor.

Jane arrives home just after 11pm. Ashleigh's boots lean against the shoe rack.

'It's only me!' Jane calls up the stairs.

No answer.

'Hello?' she tries again, toeing off her shoes from the heels.

'I'm asleep!' says Ashleigh.

'Good,' calls Jane. She can tick off two of today's tasks. Now for number three.

Jane is sitting at the kitchen table, scrolling through the women holding their shoulders back, sticking their pelvises out, their mouths making weird shapes. What colour would she go for, even? And would any of these sites still offer home delivery? She puffs at a strand of hair, then tugs it behind her ear. Her riding boots blur in the hallway beyond her screen. Maybe she didn't need a dress at all. She could arrive and say she'd just been riding. That would be very casual and cool, wouldn't it?

She hears the stairs creak and minimises the window. Her desktop background is a picture of Ashleigh's baby footprint in the sand at Margate; she smiles at it, then at Ashleigh. 'Hello love.'

Ashleigh stands in the doorway wearing pyjama shorts and a ribbed vest, frowning and tasting her own mouth.

'Are you okay?'

'Yeah. I think so...'

'Do you want some tea?' asks Jane, getting up.

Ashleigh shakes her head. 'No. Just water.'

'We're out. I'll have to boil you some.'

'No,' says Ashleigh. 'I'm sure that's making me sick.'

Jane lifts her eyebrows cheerily. 'We've got orange juice?'

'Can you pour me a glass?' says Ashleigh, sitting down.

'Please?'

'Please.'

Jane gets up, pours her a glass and sets it in front of her.

'Thanks,' she says, sipping, swallowing then gasping, 'You're back late.'

'I know.' Jane sits at her laptop again. 'There are just so many of them.'

'Oh yeah?'

'Yeah,' she says, reaching for her phone. 'Look, I saw a lynx today.'

'No way!' Ashleigh leans over to clasp the phone. She looks at the lynx for a long time, mouth in an open smile. 'I love its ears,' she says.

'I love *you*,' says Jane, pulling her close. 'My little tearaway who still finds fluffy animals cute.'

'Animals *are* cute,' says Ashleigh, pushing her away, then yawning. 'What you doing down here?'

'Among other things,' says Jane, 'I'm trying to get you over to the continent.'

Ashleigh puts the glass on the table with a knock. 'I'm not going without you.'

Jane looks at her screen, begins to type. 'I'm afraid you might have to.'

'No.'

'We don't really have a Plan B.'

'I can't do it, Mum. Can't we just head inland, or something?'

Jane pushes her computer aside, folds her arms, exhales loudly. 'I guess that's our Plan B.'

'It should be our main plan.'

'There's nothing in place if we head inland. No evacuation plan. What would we eat?'

Ashleigh shrugs. 'We could take a load of cereal and pot noodles.'

'Right. Yes, of course.'

'What?'

Jane rests her cheek on her hand. 'It would be like some dystopian movie. We'd end up eating our dead.'

'That's gross,' Ashleigh says, draining her glass. 'I don't want to imagine that.'

Jane flicks a glance at the glass. 'Did that go down okay?'

'I think so,' says Ashleigh, holding her stomach. 'Not sure.'

'Okay,' says Jane. 'Maybe it's the mains water. We'll keep an eye on you.'

CHAPTER TWENTY-THREE | July 2032
Pinko

Pinko sits in the hallway by the telephone table, swinging on his captain's chair. He is turning the word 'exhibition' over in his head. Jane's word. She had used it instead of 'unveiling' and he had corrected her. Like a nob.

An exhibition wasn't a bad idea. It was something he had in mind for the future, but that future was looking pretty shaky. Why not do it now? He swings some more, pushing with his knees, left to right, left to right. The more he thinks about it, the more the idea develops roots. Of course, he'd have to see if Gavin could be ready in time – he'd need a body of work – but it would be a way of bringing the spotlight to an exceptional talent. Gavin's art could end up in some top galleries in North America – no doubt about that.

And all because of Jane.

He comes back to himself, dredges up a sigh from the pit of his belly.

Here's what you do, he thinks, when you can't figure out why you like someone so much...

He laughs then, at such a teenage thought, and in his head quickly adds, *By Pinko Stevens (age 32 and a half)*.

So.

He will write a list of his ex-partners and note down all the things they had in common. Four crates of wine pass him on wheels, as he continues to swivel his chair in the large, round hallway. He finds a round, wooden, thick-lead pencil, reaches for the telephone pad (also round, unused) from its walnut mount, and starts his list.

1. Wealthy
2. Lots of make-up
3. Lived in London (still do, probably)
4. Worked/works in London
5. Brought up in the home counties/abroad

6. ~~Slim~~* Attractive
7. Independent
8. LOOKING FOR A MATCH (funny how he'd never thought about that before?)
9. ~~Never satisfied~~ High achieving
10. ~~Highly strung~~ Motivated
11. In their late twenties
12. Smiley/friendly
13. Cultured
14. Outgoing
15. Not been in the treehouse

*Conventionally attractive (although this is largely unimportant).

Pinko sits back and appraises the list, then looks about quickly to make sure no one is watching. As it turns out, he is quite a shallow bloke, he thinks, but he has started the exercise now and it seems to be helping.

Right.

Now identify which elements of this list apply to the girl you really like.

1. Attractive
2. Smiley/friendly/makes you laugh
3. Independent
4. Not been in the treehouse (but almost)

Gosh, that's really quite different, he thinks. So, what exactly does he have with Jane, that he didn't with them?

Hmmm…

That's tricky. Especially when the attraction was so immediate. Can you tell if someone is intelligent the moment you meet them? He could tell she was older. Perhaps they are both in a place where they need to be…older. He could tell that she was quite, um, natural…what does that mean? That there are *bigger things* in the world than porcelain veneers and Berluti. Like trees—yes, exactly! And trees are beautiful just as they are; does she remind him of a tree? He tries to make the thought work, but it's too abstract. He moves straight to the bottom line: the best in him surfaces whenever he is with her. And she doesn't need veneers. He likes her teeth (he touches his own teeth as he thinks this).

Now he wonders if they were related in a past life.

Now he wonders if they are related still.

Now – a pang from nowhere – he regrets sleeping with her Little Housemate, who might (also) be related to her. But he hasn't asked that question, because he doesn't want to know. And time is great at creating distance, so he will simply look at the selfie that Jane took of them both in his wine cellar and allow time to put a few more moments between him and The Night of the Party.

He winces as he remembers how she looked around the wine cellar, picking up a bottle and turning it to see the sediment. 'What will you do with them all,' she asked, 'when the water comes?'

'This is partly why I'm having a few gatherings,' he said. 'To drink them up. But some of them will be boxed and sent to Finland.'

She smirked and put the bottle back. 'Are they worth anything?'

He laughed louder than he should have, then looked at the floor and said, 'A few quid, yes.'

'You could donate them,' she said, 'to people who can't afford tickets.'

'Tickets?' he mused, screwing up his eyes. 'To what? What tickets?'

Her features spread, her smile dropped. 'To France. To the continent.'

Shame drained and refilled him, pricking at his armpits, his forehead. 'I'm donating money,' he lied. 'It never occurred to me to sell the wine,' he truthed. 'But you're right, I'll look into it,' he added.

'That's the last of them,' says the delivery driver, now stood behind him with a clipboard.

He puts the notepad back on the desk, face down, gets up from the captain's chair and signs at the bottom of the clipboard with the round, wooden pencil. He frowns at the wine as it is loaded into a lorry, then looks at the selfie again.

There she is, the soft-haired woman of his childhood, smiling the same smile. Those same teeth. He shuts her behind his eyelids and tries to conjure up her face, her hair, her eyes...

One by one, the teeth disappear.

CHAPTER TWENTY-FOUR | July 2032
Jane

The Sittingbourne Messenger is looking very empty, these days. As Jane leafs through, she wonders who is editing it, sending it to press. The adverts for local hairdressers and village-hall craft sales have been replaced by ads to evacuate the elderly – complete with emergency numbers – and offers to purchase unwanted gold. Just below, a life jacket manufacturer advertises a family deal. Jane shuts the magazine and buries it behind the sofa cushion.

On her pinkie finger, she wears her grandmother's wedding ring. She twizzles it now; wonders how much it is worth.

This is how finance works in a working-class household, when one is alone with a teenage daughter and the end of the world is nigh. Importantly, for this equation, the mother has a hot date with a rich man, in front of whom she does not want to seem poor.

Feminism leaves Jane like a stolen soul. It's not all about the money, it really isn't; a year or two earlier, she would have happily retained her dignity.

But...

She pauses, for a moment, to focus on a round-bellied stickwoman, with pitched-roof hair, framed on the wall by the TV. 'Mum' is scrawled underneath it in progressively shrinking letters.

Ashleigh was four when she drew that.

She still is four, in Jane's head. Small and soft, with chocolate around her mouth. And the thought of sending her off to Europe alone...

Jane shakes her head. Goes back to her task for today. Often, these days, her daily tasks involve staring into space, thinking, assessing... Formulating her survival plan.

So far, this is it:

Jane has four-hundred pounds in her current account. There are fourteen days until payday.

Jane has six thousand five-hundred pounds in her ISA which she has been saving from the CSA money her ex-husband sends her because he has to. This money must be used to get Ashleigh to France. From the research, a young person's ticket to France costs one thousand pounds. That's fine, she thinks, she has that. But, once Ashleigh is there, she will have to pay for accommodation and food. The shelters set up for British young people in the Pyrenees, the Massif Central and the Alps are now payable (no longer run by charities). Jane does not want Ashleigh to go to the Pyrenees, because she'll be too close to the coast when the water comes. She is not the only person to think this and so it is much more expensive to go to the other mountain ranges. If she gives Ashleigh another two-thousand pounds, that should be more than enough to get her through the first six weeks.

Ashleigh has some money saved up, apparently. Jane will not count this, as she doesn't know how much.

Total spend so far: three thousand pounds.

Jane wants to leave enough money to save herself, obviously, but knows that the game is very different for fully-fledged adults. From her research, an average ticket should also cost one thousand pounds, however, the meagre forum groups that exist have mentioned the various 'add-ons' that crop up along the way and, if she can't pay, her journey will end. Also, she needs several tools to allow her access to the continent. Tool number one: a passport. She has that so she can tick that off. Tool number two: a husband. Apparently, they are quite expensive, but if she manages to find one with the same amount of cash as her, then they'll be fine. However, the ones who are 'left over' usually don't have much money and need to be paid for. Then there are various 'documents' that might be demanded at the last minute. Jane has compiled a list of what she needs but should she overlook something, a 'replacement' could be pricey. Jane would also like to keep back one thousand pounds in case she is deported from France and needs to head up country.

Jane estimates that two thousand five hundred pounds will reunite her with Ashleigh.

If she gets there, the leftover one thousand pounds will allow them to survive for…well…for a little while. Hopefully.

In two weeks, she will be paid sixteen hundred pounds. This will be her final paycheck. Staff are leaving daily. She hopes that there will still be someone in Accounts to process her wages. Until then:

She will not pay her rent.

She will not pay her council tax.

(She stopped paying for gas and electricity when the outages began.)

She will squat for a month and use her wages to pull off her Plan A.

Her real Plan A.

And in order for Plan A to work, she needs a dress.

She closes her eyes. Has it really come to this?

One of the two clothes shops still open in town just happens to be a prom dress specialist. And those things don't come cheap.

But no. Enough dwelling. This is not a *thing* to bemoan but an opportunity to slip into without his noticing. And that means blending in, fitting in, integrating into that world.

Jane reads the text again. *It's an exhibition now, thanks to you! It's going to be fancy so get your glad rags on!*

She smiles. No one says 'glad rags' anymore. He probably thinks he's being kind, not condemning her to confront her own poverty in the most humiliating way. Jane decides that she must spend a maximum of two hundred and fifty pounds on a dress and shoes and one of those tiny handbags that trips along on a chain. She will forego any kind of over-garment. The weather is nice enough.

She laughs at herself. Two hundred and fifty pounds is one week's rent.

'Stay positive,' she says, aloud. 'Buck your ideas up.'

Jane gets up to open the kitchen door and walks to her little oak tree. She squats beside it, rubs one of the leaves between her fingers and blows at it. She recalls a conversation with Sue the surgeon that plants need as many cuddles as people. Her eyes ache and heat up, her head tilts to her shoulder as she bathes different parts of the leaf in light. If the water is a myth, if it's all conspiracy, lies or a massive fuck-up, then she'll come back to this little tree when it's bigger. She'll knock on the door and ask whoever lives here if she can come and see it and take pictures of it and if they wouldn't mind her coming back the following year to do the same thing. In her life, she thinks, she has been sent only three beautiful gifts: number one, her daughter, number two, her health, number three, this little tree.

She stands, walks back to the kitchen and hopes for number four.

CHAPTER TWENTY-FIVE | July 2032
Pinko

What does one wear to an unveiling?

He smiles at the text and immediately types out a response. *It's going to be an exhibition now, thanks to you! It's going to be fancy so get your glad rags on!*

He regrets 'glad rags' as soon as he's sent it; who the hell says that these days? Too late. It's gone. And anyway, she'll be a bit excited about getting dressed up for something. The thought cheers him, until he remembers that the world is going to end and 'getting excited' about nice clothes is probably way off her radar.

But she's always such fun, he insists to himself. It really feels as if they are on the same page, as if all that shit exists on the outside of their bubble. Maybe, he thinks, maybe that's why he feels good with her.

At least she'll be happy for Gavin, he concludes. And hopefully she'll realise that it's all down to her.

He decides to go to her place of work and surprise her with flowers, but where does she work? How little they know about each other, really. Well, it was about time he found out, and that's the thing, that *is* the thing, if he knew anything about her since their first meeting then why would he give her flowers, to stand in water while the whole of the UK...waited for the water. What an unlikely gift, he thinks. What an *insensitive* gift. So, he taps his chin, signs some documents that he hasn't read, thinks about the picture of the future and the tiny space in front of it.

And how long, how long has it been? He counts on his fingers – May, June, July – well, they are now at the beginning of July. Less than three months, much less than three months. Perhaps he would send her a letter; avoid putting her on the spot and avoid trotting out, stumbling out, tipping out a speech about 'bad timing' and 'it's now or never' and 'the inevitable' and 'having a good thing going' and not wanting that to end or to break and resume who knows when? Tricky things, horizons. Stuff generally grows on them...

Padre, for example. He smiles as he thinks of the old man.

But that situation had been exactly the same.

They met on the Camino de Saint Jaques, of all places. Padre had an oxygen tank in a shopping-buggy that scuffed behind him like an ill-treated goat, getting stuck on jagged flint and refusing to move, tipping sideways for no reason. One of Padre's shins was slit from knee to sock-top where he'd bent to set the thing right and fallen forward on a rock.

Able pilgrims would tip their hats at him, glance at the tank, the slit, and carry on.

Except Pinko.

He only meant to hang about with the old man for a couple of hours, out of pity, if he's honest, and then Padre started telling him about his life and how his partner had died of sepsis before they could do the walk together. So now he was doing it for the both of them.

Then he wanted to sit down for lunch and Pinko set him up just off the track, on a flat rock next to a bramble bush and the remains of a fire spread about like a mauled pigeon and Padre wheezed for a bit, then produced some cherry jam and mountain cheese, tore his baguette in two and gave half to Pinko and Pinko couldn't very well abandon him straight after he'd shared his lunch, so he planned to buy him dinner that evening, then part company, before bedding down in a hostel.

They ended up staying in the same hostel and drinking local beer, in wicker chairs on the veranda, and the next morning Padre didn't feel like leaving early, couldn't face another day of that thing tripping behind him – perhaps he would go back? 'Oh dear,' said Pinko. 'It's a shame, but if that's the way you feel,' he said, pulling his boots on, while Padre sighed at his oxygen tank. Then he slowly washed out one of the beer bottles, wrapped it in a t-shirt and packed it at the bottom of his rucksack.

Pinko got his head straight while he fiddled with his laces, but knew after the first boot that he'd help the old man go the whole way, carrying his oxygen tank, waiting in Burgos for three days while he got a replacement, fetching bread, coffee, tomatoes, peppers, weed, regularly tugging on Padre's spliffs in the evening, out by the bins of some hostel or up high, where the stars hung in front of them and the air plumed inky-mauve through their smoke.

Sometimes, he just had to zoom out, have a look at the map, then dive back in again. That time, he knew the ending would have been all wrong if he'd continued alone.

And what a friend he'd found in Padre.

In truth, he hadn't carried enough oxygen, broken enough bread, shared enough spliffs to warrant taking Jane to Finland. But the journey was already laid out for both of them in one straight line. And he was one of the able. He thinks some more, signs more documents, and considers the spiral parquet and how it will fair under seawater. Perhaps there'll be one more party to say goodbye and then, of course, the art exhibition for Gavin but JUST HOW SHORT-SIGHTED were all his angular, shiny, perfumed acquaintances to keep COMING to such frivolous events, when the end of the world was actually just there, just *there*?

He bends closer to the telephone table, inspects a fleck of something and sweeps it away. But this is for Gavin, he thinks, then wonders how he will say goodbye to his treehouse.

CHAPTER TWENTY-SIX | July 2032
Jane

Peering over the geranium pots that stand next to the front entrance, Jane sees that yes, there is another one. She'd seen it from the car. A hedgehog, this time, has been left in a box, curled in on itself, holding its nose with its feet. Mud clings to its spikes like a hairbrush dropped in candle wax. Must have fallen into a silty puddle, then dried out. Can it even move? She bends closer – it's probably too heavy to move itself. She picks up the box and bumps the surgery door open with her buttock.

'Got another one, Jane?' asks Vicky, the receptionist, peering into the box. 'Needs a good wash,' she says, holding the door open, while Jane takes it through to the backroom.

Jane checks its temperature, its heartbeat, its hydration.

'Fifth one this week, isn't it?' asks Vicky from the doorway.

Jane says nothing. Sniffs one nostril upwards. Blinks. The world shatters into granules, swirls and dissolves. She steadies herself on the edge of it and focuses on the things she can still control. This little life is saveable. She plugs the sink, turns on the tap and gathers up the hedgehog in gloved hands. Yes, she'll lock herself into a bubble with it and forget about everything else for a moment.

Every day, she watches people trudging past her house, plants sticking out of their unzipped backpacks, dogs on the ends of leads, some even carry birds in boxes or cages. Kids in the area have built up mud into foot-high banks, hiding earthworms inside. *You'll be safe in there*, they whisper, filling them over. One man stole an abandoned van from a field down near Dover and is now doing the rounds, collecting rabbits and guinea-pigs, mainly, driving them up to the Midlands, where he's built some sort of sanctuary. Loads of people thought he was eating them until he appeared on TV, cradling a flop-eared rabbit in his elbow. On the same day, same channel, a man nursed a slow-flying bee with water and sugar. The following evening, Jane found Ashleigh doing exactly that in their garden. Birds with broken wings are now looked after, kept in garages or sent off to school with bread and milk, children tiptoeing carefully with shoeboxes, then they are nursed until released into the sky, above tilted, peaceful faces.

Jane runs the tap warm and places the hedgehog inside the flow, rubbing the mud soft, massaging it away in wet clouds. It uncurls and flops in her hands. She tickles its belly and it tenses again; good, its reflexes are good.

Now Sue comes to wash her hands and sees Jane de-caking the hedgehog, red eyes all wet. 'Oh dear, not you too,' she says, standing at the other sink, shaking away excess water.

'It's fine,' says Jane. 'Just a bit tired, I think; could do with some food.'

Sue watches it in Jane's hands; the water glasses off it, making it stretch here, flop there and smile. *It is smiling, isn't it?* And she starts to cry too, has to turn away because, because, what now? It will be better, like some of the others – not many – and they'll take it into the back garden, release it into the grass and imagine it making bubbles on submerged land, its bloated body floating, belly up. Perhaps it will bob along next to the kitten brought in last week by a little girl, her parents with backpacks, hanging back, heads down, while the kitten clung to the girl's shoulder, dabbed at the wisp of fringe on her cheekbone. And Paris, the Pug, who snorts and paws at his cage door every time someone walks in, then retreats when he realises that it's not her, the woman who left him tied up in the waiting room last week, while he trotted on after her, only to be yanked back by his own lead. Then there was Popcorn, the gerbil, who died on the spot, two minutes after his little owner had patted him goodnight and skipped away. Good for him, Jane had thought, at least he wouldn't see it, at least he wouldn't end up floating dead on frothy water, his eyelids blasted back, his body crushed; yes, good for him. How precious are the ones who touch you because they give rise to all that you can't touch or some such shit. She sniffs again and turns the hedgehog onto its tummy. Number Five, she decides to call it – her – wanting to give her a name and at the same time not wanting to. She brings the hedgehog up to own face and watches its squidgy eyes twinkle open and look at her, right at her, its chin slack against her thumb, that smile again. 'Number Five alive,' she says to it, snorting a wet laugh.

'Wow, that takes me back,' says a voice from behind.

CHAPTER TWENTY-SEVEN | July 2032
Pinko

Pinko is at the clinic where Jane works. He has been allowed behind the desk. 'Yes, quick, come through, she's out back,' says the receptionist, taking a second to gape her eyes at him. 'Can I have your autograph?' she says, blushing.

He puts down the potted orchid that took him much too long to choose, and takes a pen from his breast pocket. 'Yes, alright.'

He glimpses the back of her, Jane, in a green tunic to the knees, a darker polythene strip ties at the back, around her waist. Her elbows are still, dimpling slightly as they apply delicate pressure, seemingly, like a fine-chinaware painter. Another woman, in scrubs, smiles at him, her wet eyes squeezing shut as she does. She notices the orchid in his hands, turns and leaves. Oh dear, he thinks, a sad event maybe?

He looks about him; there are no animals in here, no signs of life, perhaps they are kept in another room. What a job she does, what a game-changer. To think of all the owners coming here to retrieve their best friends, newly well and sparkly and full of tongues and wags and perhaps a plaster on their front leg or a lampshade around their neck. And now, seeing her colleagues – Vicky and the woman in scrubs – they seem so very smiley, as does his Jane, Jane is *always* smiling; how happy would he feel under her care? He leans against the doorway undetected, crosses his ankles, cocks an ear *number five alive* – is that what she said? Her arms are now raised, something is being held up, an animal is it? He pushes himself onto tiptoes, no, can't quite see, he'd have to give himself away.

'That takes me back...' he says.

She turns. A ball of brown swells in her hands. 'Wow, hello,' she sniffs. 'You caught me scrubbing a hedgehog.'

'And...crying.' He steps forward, puts the orchid next to the sink. 'Is he going to be okay?'

'She,' she says. 'No. Well, yes... But then no. None of them will be okay, will they?'

Pinko nods, watching the thing curl open on her palm. 'Can I hold him?' he hears himself saying.

'Her. You can, yes,' she says, tipping the hedgehog into his opened hands. 'This is a nice surprise. Sorry I'm all weird.'

'No, no... Not weird. I just wanted to see where you work,' he says, stroking the hedgehog from its forehead to its nose. 'A tiny Gruffalo,' he tries, then looks at Jane, checking for a smile.

Her lips tremble. She is trying not to cry.

'She's lovely,' he says instead.

'She's better,' says Jane. 'We'll be releasing her this afternoon, probably.'

He looks at her sidelong, while her eyes fill up and spill over. He thinks about the note on the orchid, an outstretched hand to Jane on her sinking ark. She turns, pretends to do something that isn't wiping her eyes, before noticing the orchid and asking, 'Is it for me? It's lovely,' without that funny energy crinkling the corners of her eyes and pushing up her cheeks. Her face is sour inside this room, under flash-bright lights and smells that snake through the air, around their heads and into their nostrils and inside that uniform that shimmers when she turns and this plastic floor with random ridges that he can feel through his Goodwin Smiths and, with that face, she's telling him what she thinks is important and he's about to tell her what *he* thinks is important and the two things are very, very different.

'Yes,' he replies, before snatching off the note. 'But perhaps I'll save this.'

He winces at these words as he pockets the note. The action was a little too hasty. But...not yet, he thinks.

She takes the hedgehog from him, her face hard. 'Now wash your hands,' she says, tilting her head towards the other sink.

'That must have seemed very odd,' he says. 'I'm not sure what to say.'

'Well, that's your problem,' she says with a little more sparkle, as she puts the hedgehog into a box with holes, 'isn't it?'

He smiles, slides his fingers over the backs of his hands and under the running water. 'I'm unprepared.' He looks down at his hands. 'Stupid really. I will give it to you,' he says. 'But you've reminded me that I have a few things to do first.'

CHAPTER TWENTY-EIGHT | July 2032
Gavin

Gavin's mum is in the kitchen, glasses on, Ryan's phone in her hand. She is looking at photos of Gavin's work that has been chosen for the exhibition. Her chin is tipped up so she can slide her gaze through her glasses and down her cheeks into the phone. Her mouth is grinning in the shape of a bite.

'That middle one is really impressive, Gavin,' she says, as he opens the fridge.

'Yeah?'

'I really like how it plays with the light. I think they should use this one; definitely.'

'They're using all of them, Mum.' Then, through a mouthful of rice pudding, he says, 'What middle one?'

'The one with the birch.' She adds, 'You'll have to eat it all now you've put your spoon back in it.'

'You know,' says Gavin, munching, 'birches have these little leaves that flip the light about. They look like five ps.'

She smiles down at the phone.

Gavin takes the Tupperware container and sits in Grandad's old, Windsor chair with his shoulders to the window. From this position, he can look down the whole length of the table while feeling the sun on his back. Big Carla's name is scratched into the wood, about halfway along, and whenever Gavin puts his spoon down, he reaches over and presses his finger against the grooves. It's black with age now, her name. Ryan's is somewhere on the underside, probably black too. Gavin scratched his into one of the legs with a compass; Little Carla filled it in with pink nail varnish last year. Gavin holds the pudding on his tongue and realises that he doesn't have to eat it all just because he put his spoon in twice; he could chuck it and buy a new tin. A hundred new tins, even. Soon, he could probably buy a new kitchen table! But no, not in a million years would he sell this one. Perhaps something nice for his mum, though. Although she'd never been in to jewellery, or gadgets. He'd have to have a think.

Ryan walks in and pulls out a chair opposite Gavin. 'I wanted some of that.'

Gavin finishes his mouthful, swallows. 'Sorry bro.'

'You've been fallin' on your feet these days, Gav. Last of the rice pudding. A gig with a millionaire. Tickets to The Last Match.'

Gavin nods. Funny that he was just thinking the same thing. To think that he, the former family loser, could now eat a whole can of rice pudding at the head of the table.

Their mum puts the phone in her apron pocket and says, 'There's custard, Ryan. Do you want some custard?'

Ryan holds his hands out, beckons for his phone. 'We got any peaches?'

'Do you want custard with peaches?' she says, retrieving the phone from her apron and handing it back.

He nods. 'Yes, please. Thank you.'

At that moment, the front door slams.

'All the troops have returned,' says Gavin's mum, as she opens the fridge.

Big Carla walks in, name tag shining. 'Alright?' she says, letting her bag fall from her shoulder, before sitting down at the table.

'Do you want peaches with custard, Carla?'

'Ew, no,' says Carla, pulling her mouth corners down. 'Stick the kettle on, though.'

Ryan takes the bowl of peaches and custard from his mum. 'How was work?' he says to Carla.

Big Carla yawns. 'I've been given my notice,' she says through the yawn.

'What do you mean?' says Mum.

A shrug. 'We've all been laid off.'

'Why?'

'You know why,' says Ryan.

Mum pulls a chair up to the table, stares at Carla as if she's saying something, but she isn't.

'We have to talk about the water, Mum,' says Ryan. 'Whether we like it or not.'

Gavin sits on his hands and darts his eyes down to the old, brown lino. The sun is now hot on his back and he would like to go to the living room and fall onto the cold leather couch with its lumpy cushions and net-like cracks, and stay there until this whole water drama is over and everything would just be the same except he'd have a little bit of money and Big Carla wouldn't have to work and maybe even the pub around the corner would open up again and there'd be no more sandbags in the streets and abandoned cars at the sides of the roads and Little Carla could go back to school and he could spend his days getting the bus to the beach, with all his kit, like a proper artist... But that isn't usually how this type of conversation goes. Gavin gets up, hands well inside his pockets, and pads to the living room on the balls of his feet.

'Sit down, Gav,' says Carla.

He freezes, turns and leans against the worktop.

'Look,' says their mum. 'It's that awful...I don't want to think about it.' She lets her hand whisk the air for a moment. 'You know what I mean. None of us are married.'

Carla smirks. 'I ain't doing that immigration test.'

'No, love,' says her mum. 'I'd hate to think of any of you... you know.'

Gavin covers his ears and turns again towards the living room.

'Gavin,' says Carla, 'we need to make a plan. As a family.'

Gavin would like to ignore her, but he returns to Grandad's chair at the end of the table. She's always been a bossy cow, Carla. Gavin's mum leans around him and takes his empty bowl. Her wrist bulges around her analogue Casio and there are more blotchy freckles on her arm than he remembers. To imagine those arms... in France...around God knows who...

Ryan smacks the table. 'I'm staying.'

Carla looks at him through half-closed eyes. 'We can't stay, you wally.'

'Why not?'

'Because England is about to get drowned.'

'You're sure about that, are you?'

'Don't be daft, Ryan.'

Their mum says, 'We're only ten minutes from the coast.'

'Exactly,' says Ryan. 'None of us can *leave* England. So we'll have to move inland.'

Carla puts her hands on the table, pushes herself up. 'This is daft.'

'Can we just listen to him?' says Gavin.

They look at Gavin. Carla sits down in her chair.

'If you ask Google,' says Ryan, picking up his phone, 'what's the town in the UK furthest from the coast, you get Nuneaton.'

'Nuneaton?' says Carla. 'Where's that then.'

Gavin's mum smiles. 'Warwickshire.'

'Grandad was from Warwickshire,' says Gavin.

'Exactly,' says Ryan. 'It's a sign.'

Carla smirks, rolls her eyes.

'We can't just *go* to Nuneaton,' says their mum. 'Where would we live?'

Ryan thumbs his phone for a moment, slides it across the table to her. 'Look,' he says. 'Look at that.'

'Just scroll down Mum,' says Carla.

'Five bedrooms,' she reads. 'Dining room,' she reads. 'Oh, an en-suite. How lovely. And a hot-tub?' She widens her eyes at Ryan.

'Dead cheap,' says Ryan. 'No-one's buying property in England.'

'I wonder why...' says Carla.

'We can't afford dead cheap,' says their mum.

Ryan pauses for a moment, then says, 'Gavin can.'

Again, they turn to Gavin.

Gavin frowns as he skates through the idea in his mind. A big old house in Grandad's home county, none the less. And he could definitely afford dead cheap, definitely. 'I suppose we could easily move back again, when all of this is over.'

Ryan sighs. 'Yes, Gav. Whatever.'

Three days later, Ryan goes into the garden with Little Carla, then comes back into the house looking for his phone to take pictures of this big butterfly she's found — *yes, Gavin, you can go and draw it, but I'd like to find my phone first*. He looks around the kitchen, picking up stuff that could be hiding his phone like tea towels, cushions, leaflets from that end-of-the-world cult, but he can't find it, so returns to the garden to look in the grass. Gavin goes to ask his mum, locates her in the living room, feet up on the pouffe, button marks from the upholstery in her left calf. Her glasses are on her chest, their golden chain threading about her neck. She puffs up tiny snores through parted lips and holds Ryan's phone to her stomach. He squints, even though he is standing right above her, yes, it is Ryan's phone. He is so used to seeing her with a Mills&Boon or Sudoku or the remote, that the phone seems weird in her hand with its long, dead black eye. As he eases it from her, it senses someone lifting it and shines into life. A photo appears, the house in Nuneaton. He looks at Mum, then wanders back into the kitchen. 'Ryan,' he says, voice blowy and low, 'I've found your phone.'

CHAPTER TWENTY-NINE | July 2032
Pinko

This morning, Pinko sits at the kitchen table, typing. From here he can see Blue in the boot room that leads from the kitchen. Since the little glitch at Jane's place of work, she seems to have taken over 90% of his brain. This is quite surprising. Ordinarily, a retreat like that would signal the end of an affair and he could again focus on other things like the business, or the estate or getting out of the country before the water comes. He would then let the relationship pootle along a downward gradient until it reached its end. It happened so often that it didn't even upset him anymore.

But this time is different. The words on the orchid note glow warm in his pocket. He would like to take them out and give them to her, where they rightly belong. Apart from the 'little housemate' mishap, he cannot work out what's holding him back. It's very soon – yes – but time isn't a luxury for anyone at the moment. Then there's the fact that she is so good, he thinks, with her animals; what has he done in the last six months to help the world? Thrown a couple of parties? He sighs at this thought, and continues typing, putting together his plan, inspired by her – again – just like Gavin's exhibition. Little by little, she is making him a better person. He has vans and drivers and a piece of land in the Peak District with stables, a chicken coop and a large barn. His intention is to help her, he thinks, in her quest to save the animals. Again, he pictures her teeth and wonders where he has seen her face before. This mystery, he believes, is what draws him to her. Leaning back in his chair, he stretches his arms upwards, already feeling good about his very small effort to change the world. One way or another, he'll make himself worthy of her. And then he'll take her with him to Finland.

Blue stands in the boot room in green overalls, stirring a mug of tea with the blunt end of a biro. He sucks the pen then puts it behind his ear.

'Blue?'

Blue sighs and says, 'Pinko.'

Pinko laughs at this. 'Do you remember any of Dad's girlfriends?'

Blue smirks. 'How long have you got?'

'I mean,' says Pinko, blushing, 'from when I was very little. That should narrow things down a bit...'

Blue turns to Pinko, fully framing himself in the doorway. 'Why?'

'I just have this memory. From Dad's cabin. There was a woman with biggish hair,' he says, splaying his hands around his head. 'Blonde.'

'Well, that narrows it down,' says Blue.

'God, was he really that bad?'

Blue sips his tea. Stares at nothing for a moment. Sips it again. 'Does this someone look like the booted lassie you've been wining and dining?'

Pinko picks up a coaster just to fiddle with it. 'You saw her, did you?'

'Heard her giggling from my hut.'

'Sorry about that,' he says, pressing the coaster between his hands, looking at it.

'Her name was Sandy,' he says. 'And you adored her.'

Pinko looks up. 'Who?'

'The girlfriend you're referring to. It was true love, for you at least.'

'Sandy?' Pinko smiles. 'Sandy, Sandy, Sandy... I can't remember that name.'

Blue shrugs. 'You were only about four.'

'Why did I love her?'

'Well,' says Blue, 'she used to play with you while your dad was on site. I remember, you were scared of the big slide your dad had built up there for you – you remember the one? – but you wanted so desperately to get on it. Your father said you had to learn to do it for yourself. Well, she climbed up to it, in her heels – I'll never forget – popped you on her lap and down you came. You were screaming with laughter.'

'I can't remember that at all. Funny, isn't it?'

'You used to ask for her all the time,' he says, knocking his gaze to the ceiling and back again. 'Even well after she'd left.'

'Why did she leave, do you remember?'

He shrugs. 'Why did any of them leave?' he says. 'But the others didn't look after you like she did. They were only interested in...' he pauses to rub his thumb and index together.

'But not her?'

'No, not her. I can't remember why she left.'

'Right,' says Pinko, putting the coaster down. 'Thank you, Blue.'

Blue leans around the doorframe and into the kitchen so not to step on the tiles in his wellies. He sets his mug on the side. 'I see you've got square coasters,' he says. 'Must be love.' With that, he pulls a cap from his pocket and disappears through the back door.

Pinko looks at the coaster, widens his eyes. It *is* square – where on Earth did that come from? He frowns. This conversation was enlightening, but not comforting. *Love?* He loved Sandy. But where did she go? A memory surfaces. A collection of pinecones on the floor that they'd imagined were sheep, then in a row they were a caravan of camels, then a train, and he'd never felt happier with those little objects that cost nothing at all, and the woman who sat him on her lap while he named each one. But even though he loved her, she left. Jane. *No, not Jane*, he thinks as he closes his eyes. *Sandy.* Not-interested-in-money Sandy... If *Jane's* not with him for the money, he thinks, then there is no reason for her to stay, except for him. He suddenly feels too small, too undeserving. He picks up his phone and dials her number. After three rings she answers, her voice smiley.

'Jane,' he says.

'Pinko,' she says, mimicking his tone.

'Is there anywhere you'd like to go?' he says. 'While we still have the time...' He is not sure if this is a declaration of love. At date number five (was it five?) *surely* they are not supposed to be there yet. But the sound of her voice compels him to tell her something huge, something lifechanging. Pace yourself, Pinko, he thinks. Don't scare her away.

'This sounds very final and surreal,' she says.

'All the more reason,' he says. 'Let's enjoy the last glimmers of normality.'

'There is somewhere I'd like to go,' she says, sadder now. 'London.'

The frenzy in his blood stills, as he understands completely why she would want to go there. It's such an obvious choice, yet somewhere he would never have thought of. Yes, of course; the capital city. The heart of their home country. 'London,' he says. 'That's exactly where we'll go.'

CHAPTER THIRTY| July 2032
Gavin

Gavin rubs his cheeks with the smudging ends of his fingers.

Then he draws.

He draws the bluebells in front of the house in Nuneaton. He draws the high swing-gate at the side, with the apple tree bending over it. He draws the estate agent photographer, reflected in the front room window, the camera like a diver's mask. He rubs at his cheeks again, leaving marks from the charcoal. The sky is slanted and messy in the reflection of the water (his hand keeps drawing the water even though it hasn't yet come). He sends a black line through it, scribbles it out, screws it up. Perhaps Grandad is sending secret messages to his brain. Perhaps Grandad drew the water, not Gavin. He looks around the living room for the crystal snowman, remembers his Grandad holding it up to the light when he was small and jiggling rainbows all over the walls. If the giant wave of water catches the light, will it make the most magnificent rainbow before it crashes over them? He shakes this thought out of his head, decides to sit on the floor instead of his spinny, artist stool, and looks at the leather sofa. If he squints his eyes at it, it takes the form of an ivory woman laying on her side. One chair back would be her hips, then a dip (where the arm rest is) for her waist, then the other chair back her... He screws up his eyes, he can't think the word. All those private places that women seem to have, that his mum has – yuk! – and Big Carla, and... He dissolves the next thought but it comes back at him, gyrating and shaking its chest. He gets back on the stool and just catches the bluebells swaying. Chest is a much better word than—but no...even that word is too much. Quick, do something else. Kill the thought. He knocks the charcoal against his easel and skits his eyes about for his Nokia. It is next to him.

Holding his breath in his cheeks, he calls the number.

'Mum,' he says, the following week, while drawing a smiley face on his pancake with chocolate chips. Gavin's mum is in the kitchen as usual, pulling cling-film around the left-over batter mixture. She is a bit jumpy today, he thinks. Her eyes dart after her jay cloth as she wipes down the kitchen worktop, and she breathes quickly, like she's puffed out. Ordinarily, she'd have no reason to be anxious. Gavin has already met dealers interested in his work ahead of the exhibition, throwing numbers around that Gavin wouldn't even know how to write. Then Pinko texted him earlier that day – some hotel in London wants a load of work off him to fill up the empty spaces in their bar. Only renting, mind. Still, when Pinko told him how much they were going to pay, he nearly fell off his own legs. *But they don't wanna keep them?* he asked. *They're gonna pay me that just to give them back to me?*

Turns out, that's exactly what they're gonna do.

He leans back in his chair, hands clasped behind his head; everything is tickety-boo at the moment. Except for his mum. And that's because she's worried about the water that might come. He has been sitting on a secret, waiting for the right moment. Now might be it.

'Yes, love,' she says, still a bit breathless.

He waits a beat, then says, 'I was thinking that we'll have to start packing the house up soon.'

His mum turns, stares at him for a while, then picks up the frying pan and starts to scrape the greasy, crispy bits into the bin.

He puts a chocolate chip in his mouth, sucks it, watches her.

'Because,' he goes on, 'we'll have to take it all with us.'

She lets the frying pan drop to the bottom of the sink, wipes her hands. 'I told you Gavin, I'm not leaving my home,' she says. 'You can go, by all means,' she insists, sweeping the air back with her palm. 'I'm not going to stop anyone.'

'You're coming too.'

'I am not,' she says, 'young man.'

'I've found a really good place, though.'

'No, Gavin.' She makes her eyes all wide like she really means it. 'No way.'

'I've already put in an offer.'

She is about to retort, when she stops and gasps a small, elegant gasp and puts a hand to her cheek.

She's got it, thinks Gavin, smiling his forehead down. 'You know what I've done now, don't you?

'Have you bought it?'

'I just told you, didn't I?' he says, hand splayed.

'Oh but...Gavin.'

'Wanna see it again?' He takes out his phone, skates his thumbs around the screen. 'Look, I got a new phone especially to see the photos.'

She bends to look, hands clapped to her mouth, eyes glittering.

'We're all going there. See, Ryan can have a whole shed to himself to paint his weird little men.'

'Oh, Gavin,' she says again. She bumps her hip to his shoulder and he stands from the chair to let her sit.

'And that room's already pink with unicorns and crap all over it. Little Carla will love that.'

She clasps his free hand and pushes a kiss into his cheek. 'Let's hope,' she says, 'we haven't left it too late.'

CHAPTER THIRTY-ONE| July 2032
Jane

Ashleigh has been sick on the floor of the bathroom. Ashleigh is curled up next to her own vomit; her ribs push at her skin like they are trying to break out. Jane throws glances over her in secret; is she excessively tired? No. Does she wince as she zips up her tight, riding gilet? Never. Do certain smells trigger the vomiting? Sometimes... Jane was not quite seventeen when her own, small bump started to show. The thought of her mum finding out was... well... Jane remembers the cold smell of the neighbours' wood burner, the sharp-bright stars, the gravel under her socked feet as she strode off into the night to her friend's house. Thinking back, her 'friend' was a lonely, creepy pothead who found any excuse to rub Jane's feet. But there she stayed, until she was rushed to hospital with pre-eclampsia. Jane jams her eyes shut as she thinks of how worried her mother must have been.

Easy does it, thinks Jane.

Jane books an emergency appointment with a private doctor in Tunbridge Wells.

She pays over the phone and bundles Ashleigh into the car.

She punches the address into the GPS. Arrives. Rings the bell. Knocks on the door. Curls her hands around her face and presses them up against the window.

Empty.

On the door there is a poster detailing the emergency contact information.

She calls the number.

She checks the number and calls again.

She goes back to the car. 'Arseholes,' she says to the open car window.

'What?' says Ashleigh.

'They've gone.'

'Good.'

'Why is that good?'

'I'm actually feeling alright now.'

'Ashleigh, you said that yesterday.'

'Let's go to the stables. There's that falafel van on the way.'

'You're hungry?' says Jane. 'Are you kidding me?'

'What's your problem? I'm better, aren't I?'

Jane gets back into the car and scrutinises her daughter. *You're not pregnant, are you?* she thinks, but doesn't say, of course. Instead, she chips away at this question until it is nearly unrecognisable. Then she pulls Ashleigh in for a hug.

'Are your periods okay?'

Ashleigh's head pops up. 'Why d'you ask that?'

Jane strokes a hair away from Ashleigh's face and says, 'Because you're sick.'

'My periods are horrible,' says Ashleigh, settling back against Jane. 'They always have been.'

Jane nods. 'You would tell me if—'

'Are you still going out this weekend?'

Jane winces. She has told Ashleigh that she and Sue are going to the animal sanctuaries on Saturday. She considers coming clean and revealing that she has a date in London with Pinko, instead, she says, 'I don't have to. Not if you want me to stay.'

'No,' says Ashleigh. 'I want you to go. You're making a difference.'

Lying is awful, thinks Jane, giving Ashleigh an extra squeeze, but the situation is so delicate. She wonders, again, what promise had been retracted when Pinko removed the orchid note. The next date would be crucial and she must handle it well. She decides that she has more control over the situation if it remains a secret.

But, Ashleigh has been so clingy lately...

At the stables, Jane curses the falafel van for being one of the only remaining businesses in Swale, and parts with a tenner.

Jane has spent £145.00 on an emergency private doctor's appointment that never happened.

Jane now has £95.00 for a dress.

But...

Realistically, this money sits in a metaphorical box labelled 'In Case My Sick Daughter Needs It'.

So no dress then.

By the evening, Ashleigh is horizontal on the sofa, her head on Jane's lap. She is eating Bourbon biscuits and laughing at some Amy Schumer film. Jane strokes her hair and hopes against hope it was just a bug.

CHAPTER THIRTY-TWO | July 2032
Pinko

London, she'd said; she'd wanted to say goodbye to London, see the tendrils of the apocalypse breach the tarmacked roads, see the famous grey clouds loom finally over the skyline; imagine ivy, lichen and bindweed, choking the Houses of Parliament, wrapping St Paul's Cathedral; transpose chip and rot onto famous signage, Covent Garden, Oxford Street; picture future generations climbing over upturned velociraptors in the rubble of the Natural History Museum. Real bears and wolves will make their homes in the ruins, take the tourists by surprise, or perhaps, *not* tourists but hungry people with spears fashioned from wrought-iron fencing, who return to their underground hideouts with fur wraps and fresh meat, where they will barbecue their own predators under the cracked, arched tiling of Tottenham Court Road Station.

'Will everywhere be looted already?' she asks. 'They say that Hatton Gardens is empty, windows broken and doors booted in. But the jewels have been sent to Switzerland, of course, employees too, lucky bastards. Your mates,' she adds, 'would poop themselves if they knew that the middle classes were getting into Switzerland.'

He laughs, pinches his chin, realises he's stopped laughing before she has.

'Which friends are you talking about, Jane?'

She shrugs. 'I don't know, the ones who need a tennis court in Warsaw?'

'Oh,' he says. He does indeed have friends who are concerned about not having a tennis court; although they are moving to Krakow, not Warsaw. How she knows this, he has no idea. He glances at his Converse trainer on the accelerator pedal. *Converse!* Butler raised his eyebrows at them this morning. Jane had told him she liked them, they were a nice colour. He bought another pair, same colour but leather, not canvas. He'd picked her up in the Lexus today – Blue's runaround – just to 'complete the look', as it were. Although she had wanted to take the train.

'Getting back will be a nightmare,' he told her.

She agreed, lips stiff. She knows why it would be a nightmare. He knows she knows why it would be a nightmare.

'Won't your car get pinched if you park it around here?' she asks, now.

'I've arranged secure parking,' he answers. 'If it does get stolen, it'll probably be by someone who needs it more than I do,' he adds.

She nods, smiles her head onto his shoulder.

Her hair smells like apricots. He blinks down at her, tries to say something, but then stops himself.

'What?'

'Well,' he says, then clears his throat. 'I thought we could stay in town tonight.'

'Is that so?' she replies. 'Right.'

'You know, these landmark hotels will...go.'

'Never been to one.'

'They're certainly worth seeing,' he says, frowning at the road, the parades of shops boarded up, the flickering neon of Chicken to Go and the heavy, padlocked chains securing a Turkish barbershop. Padre forms and disperses in his mind. Jane is silent. Perhaps he'd been too presumptuous.

'The thing is,' she said, 'I think Ashleigh's very sick.'

'Oh?'

She lets her gaze wander off to the passenger window, as if she is imagining Ashleigh feeling very sick at home. 'Mmm.'

'What's wrong with her?'

Jane sits up properly and sighs. 'I feel a bit bad about leaving her.'

'Why?'

'Just to go on a date...'

Now he imagines Ashleigh, ballooning between them, pushing her head from his shoulder and squishing them both into the edges of the car.

'Does her family live nearby?' he asks.

'She's been vomiting for a week or so,' she says at the same time.

'Vomiting?'

'Mm,' she replies, gazing at the piles of uncollected binbags on the pavement.

He flicks her a look. Then another. 'We can turn around,' he says. 'If you're worried.'

'I've noticed,' she says, 'she doesn't go out very often these days and, well, the last time was your party.' She looks right at him now. 'When I came to pick her up the following morning?'

Pinko shuffles in the driver's seat, his armpits prickling. 'Really?'

She inhales to say something, then seems to change her mind.

They stare at the road after that. Pinko's stomach pulses and bubbles, his throat stiffens with trapped words.

Remembering the date of the party was easy; end of May – his dad's birthday celebration, The Last Match – two whole months before. *No*, thinks Pinko. *Dismiss that thought immediately.* No matter how drunk he was, he would never, ever sleep with a woman without discussing contraception. That was the rule he would live and die by. But still, this new information hits him like a tidal wave. He'd reserved the Terrace Penthouse and requested red roses, as well as a twelve-pack of Skips (she let slip once that she loved them) and a bottle of Tesco's rosé. The concierge didn't seem the least bit surprised, simply said, 'I'll arrange that for you, Sir.' He knew she'd like that, as long as she liked the idea of staying the night, of course. And now Ashleigh crops up and he is wondering a) what kind of relationship would make Jane duty bound to look after her? And b) why her brain has led her back to the party, *his* party, as the root cause of Ashleigh's sickness.

Pinko swallows. The thought resurfaces. Ashleigh with a swollen belly, scowling at him. But no. Too unlikely and too unlucky. He'd never been bothered enough about sex to get carried away in the moment. That wasn't his style at all.

Really, it wasn't.

Raindrops spatter the windscreen and he flicks on the wipers.

He asks, 'Do you have an appointment? I mean a doctor's one?'

'Hm?' she turns to him.

'I mean, does Ashleigh have an appointment? To see a doctor?'

'In one month,' she says. 'Couldn't get one sooner. And it's only with the nurse.' Jane looks out of the passenger window. 'I made one with a private doctor in Tunbridge Wells but...it didn't happen. We think he fucked off to Vienna.'

'Bugger,' Pinko tuts and winces. 'That's frustrating.' He brakes as a woman with a pushchair hurries towards the zebra crossing up ahead. 'I mean, would she...want to see my GP? He's also a friend of mine... Won't be leaving for another few weeks.'

Jane turns her head to look right at him. 'She was drinking, wasn't she? At your house that night.'

Pinko hardens his face, looks out at Park Lane, the old shop where sultans would buy their private jets, where he bought himself a Bentley. The large windows gleam back reflections of Hyde Park and its calf-high grass; inside, the interiors are marble and dotted with made-up hostesses. He sees the golden insides of a private jet in one, in the other the stock has been replaced with enormous chesterfields and coffee tables. A couple are leafing through a catalogue, being brought leather samples. Shopping will still go on here, as long as there are customers. On the opposite side of the road, the heaps of black binbags shimmer with raindrops.

'Maybe...' Jane sucks back whatever she was going to say and replaces it with: 'Maybe she didn't spend the whole time waitressing.'

It is more of a question than a statement. Pinko licks his lips and glances in the rearview. 'Usually, the staff join the party at some point,' he says. 'I much prefer it that way.' This is, after all, not a lie.

Again, Jane's gaze wanders off to the pavement and they are quiet for a while.

Smalltalk, thinks Pinko, is all this is. About a mutual event in their history. A mutual person in their lives. He swallows and breathes deeply through his nose. Perhaps Ashleigh is all they have, in that respect.

'Has she lived with you for long?' he says, steering through a tight right-hand turn.

She snaps her eyes to him. 'Yeah. I mean...for as long as I can remember.'

He nods, waits for the barrier to lift to the Dorchester car park, elbow on the sill, fingers tracing his own cheekbone. If she wanted to tell him that Ashleigh is a cousin or a sister or a niece, the time would be now. But Jane is bashing out a text on her phone. She doesn't seem nervous or cagy, like someone avoiding the truth. Good. Okay. Still messy, but not yet unmanageable.

'Would that be alright?' she says, startling him.

'What?'

'To see your doctor-friend?'

'Yes,' he sits up straight, grips the steering wheel. 'Of course.'

'Thank you,' she says, then leans into the head rest and gazes through the window. 'Wow, The Dorchester? Wow. You're such a posh-head.'

'It's just to park the car.'

'Is this really where we're staying?'

Pinko clears his throat. 'They're offering End of the World packages.'

Jane fixes him with her stare. 'You're joking?'

'Nope,' he says, pulling into a space. 'I thought that if they were offering packages, they must be fully stocked. Otherwise, what's the point? And we wouldn't want to end up in a poorly stocked hotel, would we?'

'No,' says Jane, watching two young men rearrange tins of food in the back of their open van. An elderly lady pushes a shopping caddy towards them, with a small cat carrier balanced on top. 'We wouldn't.'

'This is like the Titanic,' she says, as they enter the lobby. She turns slowly, her gaze running about and picking things up to inspect them.

'It holds the same grandeur, perhaps.'

'*Grandeur*,' she says, nose wrinkled, teeth bucked.

He pokes her shoulder and smiles.

Two men look up from their careful appraisal of a crystal decanter. Pinko nods. They nod back. Jane nudges him. He turns. She kinks her chin towards a small wolf hound tapping across the tiles, its lead reaching without slack back to the hand of its owner. A camel frock-coat sways just above her calves, nude heels reflect nude heels in the gloss-bright tiles. Jane grins at the wide sunglasses, tells the woman that she loves that breed. The woman says thank you, continues to be pulled onwards.

They strain their heads over their shoulders to watch the dog leave through the revolving doors, but once there, the owner turns and click-clicks back towards them again, leaving the grey tarmac flickering in the revolutions of the door.

Jane notices something then and approaches the door. He follows. There are people on the other side of the road, clustered together, rucksacks bobbing; children hold hands, pick their noses, stare up at the adults with open mouths. The adults shake hands, one claps another on the back. The groups disperse, half leaving one way, half the other. 'They must be family,' says Jane. 'Or friends.'

'Hmm.' Pinko folds his arms.

'I guess they are leaving. I guess lots of people come to London to do that.' She stares on.

Pinko steps his leg out wide and plants it between her and the door. 'Want to dump the bags and go out?'

Jane turns to him, her brow low and serious. He holds his breath. 'Let's explore the hotel,' she says.

'Okay, let's do that.'

Pinko has brought a leather weekend bag that he leaves with the concierge; Jane asks if she can have her picture taken next to his portmanteau, or perhaps inside it? 'Like this?' she says, climbing inside the tall, golden cage. The concierge laughs, Pinko laughs, takes her picture, follows her through the Ballroom, the Orchid Room, the Holford Room, plucks a lily from its vase and holds it just in front of the camera lens, while she poses before a smoky mirror inside thick curls of gilded frame.

They head to the bar, where Jane stares about her, twisting her fingers, while Pinko scoots onto a velvet, upholstered stool.

'I've got studs in my jeans,' she says, teeth together, concerned.

The barman tells her not to worry about that. He shakes his head at their first requests for tequila.

'The last time I had tequila...' Pinko stops as the memory of

Ashleigh resurfaces, standing at the bar in her tiny bandeau top. The world pitches and capsizes.

'What happened?' says Jane.

'Um,' he says, 'didn't we come here for wine?'

She allows her look to linger, but doesn't push him. Instead, she turns to the barman and says, 'What about sambuca?'

He shakes his head. 'No, sorry.'

'Spiced rum?' she tries.

'Nope,' he says. 'We can't import them anymore. We've run out.'

She purses her lips, looks at Pinko, then around the room, through the shining black pillars, up to the paintings of faces under large flower headdresses and the blank spaces where the canvases-which-have-since-been-saved once gazed about the bar with following eyes.

'Wine then,' says Pinko. 'That was the original plan, wasn't it?'

Jane nods, grins then catches a tear on the side of her index finger. He dares a reassuring hand on hers and she smiles.

'Gavin's work would look perfect in here,' she says in a breathy, brave voice.

Pinko squeezes her hands and notices the brown lines snuggled into her knuckle bends.

'They're from the horses,' she says, following his gaze. 'I've been scrubbing at those little brown lines for years.'

He holds her hand to his mouth, kisses it. 'I wish I were one of those little brown lines, safe and cozy in your hands.'

Another smile ticks at the edge of her mouth; for once, he thinks, she is allowing herself to be drawn in – but no, she turns to the barman, rolls her eyes.

'Fine,' laughs Pinko, throwing her hand back at her. 'Scrub harder.'

When their wine arrives, Pinko asks to see the manager. He tells her that it's really bad form to have these large gaps on the walls, would she consider hiring some work from Pinko's personal collection?

'Gavin Smith?' says the manager. 'I've heard that name before.

He's a bit of a rising star.'

'That would be great for Gavin,' says Jane.

Yes, they all agree he's very talented, sprung from nowhere. Of course, Pinko will have to check with Gavin first... 'Of course,' says the manager. She holds out her hand to shake his, bobs her head and clicks off towards reception.

Jane narrows her eyes. 'You get things done, just like that.'

He blushes, knowing full well that it is his money – not him – that gets things done.

They glide into the brasserie, eat marble-sized potatoes and slithers of chicken, chat and laugh and twinkle their eyes at each other. Something is there, something is ready to be explored, thinks Pinko, as she smiles at him over her wine glass. Yet something isn't quite right. He holds to his mouth a spoonful of mugwort panna cotta that he suddenly cannot eat. He turns the spoon to her, guides it towards her mouth.

'This is all a bit cliché, isn't it?' he says.

She laughs and says, 'Next, you'll be ordering a bottle of champagne to the room.'

He raises an eyebrow, calls a waiter over and orders a bottle of Bollinger to be sent up to the room. As he hears himself say the words, his stomach constricts and the restaurant blurs. Ashleigh returns to him, sitting in his bed, crouched over her phone, twitching as he approaches her with a cappuccino.

Jane stares after the waiter and says, 'Right then,' standing, wobbling slightly. 'I'll go on ahead and freshen up.'

Maybe they'll compare notes? he thinks.

'Did I really just say "freshen up"?' Jane giggles, then covers her mouth. 'I haven't done this for a while.'

He tilts his head to the side and lets her laughter pour over him. The wine is making him nervous; the 'Ashleigh' flashback rolls through his mind in big, graphic stills; if only he could press pause; trap this moment for them to live inside for a while, until he figures out a way forward. Jane pulls her hair over one shoulder, picks up her bag and heads towards the staircase. He watches her, realising that he's worried she could trip, or that she might be terrified, or that if he spends too much longer away from her, cell by cell, his heart will die…

You thought you could handle this, he thinks, didn't you?

He sits back, finishes his glass of Saint Émilion, looks from a blank square of tablecloth, to a plant, then a painting, and there it is. *Mrs Fisk Warren and Her Daughter Rachel.* A print, it must be. The real thing is in the States, he believes. He blinks at it. Swallows. Slides his gaze over Mrs Fisk's pluming sleeves and pink frills, the daughter peering around the right-hand side looks more like her sister. He takes a swig of wine and holds it on his tongue, thinks again about the morning after the party, the unmade bed, the quivery voice. Mother and daughter. That thought had *never* occurred to him; surely, they can't be that far apart in age? He sits a little longer, considers this. Unless the artist was being particularly indulgent, Mrs Fisk looks very young, indeed. But then, he reasons, this was painted in the late 19th century. Or early 20th. That's just what they did then, had children young. Not now, he thinks. You don't hear so much of that now. According to Facebook, Jane is thirty-two (Facebook *never* lies) and Ashleigh told him she was twenty-one. He shakes his head, as if to dissipate the thought. Ludicrous. Impossible. But it regathers again and again, until he is laughing at himself. Your brain, Pinko, he thinks, is really toying with you today.

He takes another sip of wine and swallows, gauging the near emptiness of the glass.

The decanter men from the lobby squabble into the restaurant, hands in pockets, one shakes his Rolex from under his sleeve. 'How about some cheese?' he says to the other. They sway about for the waiter, top heavy like plates on sticks. A waitress scuttles up, hands clasped in front of her, shoulders back. She can't be more than eighteen years old. 'Do you have a table, my dear? Do you have somewhere to stand my glass?' At this, they smirk and titter. 'A menu, please. Off you pop. Good girl.' She indicates a free table, strides off to get a menu, while they hum and cough at the sight of her walking away, 'I'm not sure which side I like best,' says the Rolex one, the others nod, growl and concur. Pinko opens his mouth to say something, then inhales loudly. Looks elsewhere. Wonders where her parents are, how unsuspecting they were when their daughter went off to work this morning. Should he stay and keep an eye? he thinks, and just as the thought leaves his mind, one of them is addressing him.

'Are you...' he begins, approaching, 'Pinko Stephens.'

Pinko nods, smiles, feels a porridge-moist palm pressed into his. The man's nose rises, wrinkles; he pulls his top lip upwards then climbs the corners of his lips. Porridge, thinks Pinko. The last time he had porridge, Ashleigh had to find a pan and sultanas and make the whole bloody thing because he didn't know how. They chat to him for a moment, then wink at him when the waitress comes back, including him in their circle. He looks away, but remembers afterwards their YSL suits – like his – their Louboutins (he had a wardrobe full), their Rolexes. He considers his Converse and knows that he can't hide, that he will turn into one of them, already *is* one of them. Again, Ashleigh swells behind his eyes, before his head whirls and disperses those month-old memories. Nearly two. He sucks the droplet from the bottom of his glass, stands and traipses towards the stairs.

Two months old, he thinks.

CHAPTER THIRTY-THREE | July 2032
Jane

This is a bedroom scene, thinks Jane, in London. Up until ten minutes ago, she was simply in the decimated remains of London. Now she is in a bedroom, in the decimated remains of London. A *bedroom*. Oh god, oh god, oh god. A deep-pile, walnut, velvet, gilded, tasselled, sumptuous bedroom, while people outside rifle through the month-old piles of trash. They weren't supposed to be doing this now, she and Pinko. They were supposed to be watching *Cats* or shopping in Harvey Nicks or flicking coins into flat caps on the paving stones at Covent Garden. She goes to the window. London is shedding its skin, she thinks, as she follows a swirl of litter dancing at the feet of the lurching, backpacked wanderers on the other side of the road. A dustbin has been upturned and two foxes are eating from its innards, ears flat, no passing cars to startle them.

When did he even book the room? It was all a bit presumptuous.

Finland flashes in images through her mind; fir trees shuddering under white sunlight. Lakes like mirrors. The world, forgotten.

'Eyes on the prize, Jane,' she says aloud. Here she stands, at the end of a long history of women who've had to compromise their integrity for survival.

Maybe, she thinks, taking off her jeans, it was a bad idea to come to London. What if he wants to get her into bed before he dumps her? Perhaps she has hideously misjudged the situation. But she is quite tipsy; taking off her jeans is a struggle, let alone thinking clearly.

Her lace body shorts and matching balcony bra shine synthetic against the velvet of the bed runner. She had a feeling she might need them at some point and so rolled them up and pushed them to the bottom of her handbag before leaving the house. Now, she lays them on the bed sheets, where they look yellow against the cotton-white. She winces. They cost her £10 for the set; she bought them before she had Ashleigh.

She puts one hand to her cheek, the other on her hip. She didn't *really* think she'd need them, it was more of a case of not wanting to be in a situation where she didn't have respectable underwear. As it turns out, they are far from respectable and, if she puts them on, she'll seem bold and seductress-y. Jane reaches behind her for her jeans and starts to climb back into them.

But then what if... what if, what if...

She removes her jeans again, stuffs the yellowed underwear back into her bag and goes to take a shower.

Within minutes, she is back in the bedroom, inspecting her breasts for wiry hairs. A towel, she thinks, plucking one from the end of the bed and arranging it over herself, is very suggestive and very white. She pushes her feet into the free slippers and strides about the room, stomach sucked in, shoulders back.

He is still not here. He is giving her time to prepare herself, obviously. He said he'd finish his drink and come up, and they'd both joked about 'freshening up'.

Perhaps he wasn't really coming...

In the mini-bar, she finds a tiny bottle of gin. She opens it, downs its contents and waits for more alcohol to traverse her stomach lining.

Still no Pinko.

Now, she thinks, the towel is perhaps unnecessary. She is completely dry, after all. She throws it over the bathroom door and perches against the dressing table. After a couple of minutes, she looks down and sees the lip of her stomach pouting back into the room. She glances at the door, then goes over to the windowsill, which is higher and will not cause a stomach-lip. But the window is cold on her back.

She stretches out on the bed.

But that's too much. She may as well offer herself on a plate.

Although she *is* naked. She is clearly offering herself wherever she stands/sits/lies.

She starts to run a bath. Stops. Removes the plug. Lets the water swirl away.

It's all very uncomfortable, she thinks. All very awkward. A digital clock blinks red numbers at her. He too will see that clock, when he gets here, and the rest of the room, and her in it. Because this space will only be hers alone for what, two? three? ten? more minutes. Who knows.

She sits in the deep, angular armchair, looks over to the mirror at her stomach, holds a cushion in front of it and waits.

CHAPTER THIRTY-FOUR | July 2032
Pinko

He enters the room without a sound. She is there, buck naked, sat forward in a Bugatti armchair. She cradles the sole of her foot in her hand and prods at it – he thinks – or plucks at it. Little movements jerk along her shoulder blades so that their angles dip and rise. Her big hair has fallen over her shoulders and hangs in two equal sections beside each ear. Now a girl's face appears at her side, satin pink frills around the chin. He closes his eyes and wills himself not to think about that, whatever *that* is. He turns to the door, clicks it shut. She drops her foot, looks over her shoulder. Yes indeed, he thinks as she stands, clears her throat and smiles; the last time he did this was the event that brought them here. Ironically. 'Oh God,' he says.

She steps forwards. 'What?'

He drops his gaze to the key card in his hand. 'No. Nothing.'

She approaches him, traces a circle around her belly button.

His eyebrows rise and he catches them, pinches them together with his thumb and forefinger.

She backs away. 'What's wrong?' she says, folding her arms over her chest.

'I...um...' he starts, then strides to the bed, removes the duvet and in one matadorial sweep wraps it around her. 'I met a man downstairs,' he lies.

She clutches the duvet, blinks at him like a cold, lost girl.

'I've been thinking about Ashleigh,' he says.

'Ashleigh?' Her neck extends, the duvet is opened swiftly and re-wrapped under her arms.

'The man says there's been a lot of this sickness lately.'

'How would he know?' she asks, eyes wide.

'He's...in the medical field.'

'What did he say?'

'That we should get her to a doctor as soon as we can.'

Her face collapses, she walks the length of the room with her hand to her neck. 'What is it? Is it the water?' she says. 'I'd convinced myself that she was pregnant.'

'What?' he says, then laughs. 'No, I mean, it's...' but the lie ends there. He stares at the tufted headboard for help.

Jane doesn't notice. She grabs her phone, sits down in the armchair.

He watches her sidelong, then says carefully, 'I know you two look out for each other.'

She doesn't look up, but thumbs away at her phone.

He clears his throat. 'You must be very close...'

'So what is it?' she asks again, still typing. 'Do you think she could see your doctor friend?'

'Um,' he says, 'I can get an appointment for tomorrow, probably.'

She snaps her head up, 'Could you?'

He nods. 'Yes.' Another nod. 'Are you okay?'

'You need to tell me exactly what he said,' she says. 'I knew I should have stayed with her.'

Pinko inhales slowly as he measures her words, his eyes climbing the bed post. Just ask her, he says to himself. 'Jane.'

'Yes?' She looks up. One blue eye and one elephant grey eye. The pinecones are all lined up in his memory and she, Sandy, is watching him, waiting for his next move. No, he thinks, I cannot have this conversation now.

'I'll call my friend. My doctor friend,' he says, taking his phone from his pocket and walking to the window.

She returns to her text. 'Yes. Do that,' she says. 'Thank you.'

CHAPTER THIRTY-FIVE | July 2032
Ashleigh

Ashleigh is feeling much better today. She almost told Jane to cancel the appointment with Pinko's doctor. She would have preferred to stay on the sofa or even pick up a shift at the pub – if it was still open. The landlord texted her a couple of days prior, asking if she could come in and clean the bar. That was a bit weird. Usually, she waitressed – she never cleaned unless the KP called in sick and she had to wash up. She refused straight away, imagining the smell of chemicals in her nose; that really turned her stomach. Perhaps they needed a cleaner to help close down the pub. Perhaps they'd had one last party to drain the place of booze before heading off to France. They'd have no problem getting there, a married, heterosexual couple. Plus, they had no kids or pets to worry about. Why they hadn't left sooner was anyone's guess.

Ashleigh puts a hand on her stomach, because of habit, not nausea. She looks at the round room; remembers the last time she was here. She's pretty sure she never came into this room. It has two doorways in it that curve at the top like church doors. She came through one and the doctor came through the other, all serious, like at a proper doctor's office. He looks serious too: his thick, grey locks sit like tiles on his head, and he peers at his phone through tiny, nose glasses. Between them hangs a painting, a grey man smiling in front of a forest or woods or something, and a dog with its back legs on the man's knee, front ones on his chest. The desk in the room is round to match the round walls. She could push it right up against the round wall and there would be no gap between the two things. But she can't do that because the doctor is sat in that gap, on the other side of the desk, fiddling with his phone. She would have preferred it if he wasn't. She would have preferred this whole thing not to be a thing, especially getting Pinko involved; how the fuck did Mum pull that off? Perhaps she phoned him up pleading poverty, reminding him of that night when Ashleigh 'waitressed' for him. God, how awkward. Ashleigh pushes her fringe back and scuffs at the lines in the little wooden floor tiles; squares, she observes, rectangles – bet they get on his nerves.

The doctor has stopped texting and is now talking to her. 'What can I do for you today?'

'Oh.' Ashleigh frowns. 'Don't you know?'

The doctor glances to the left, then to the right. 'Um... No.'

'Oh,' she says, voice higher. 'I thought someone might have told you. It's nothing urgent.'

'All I was told is that you need to see a doctor and were struggling to get an appointment,' he says, clearing his throat. 'I'm here to help,' he says in a kind voice.

Ashleigh covers her mouth to stifle a giggle. It's not funny, she thinks, but she's nervous. And now he's noticed the laugh and looks pissed off like he put on his kind voice and all she does is laugh. 'Sorry,' she says.

He looks unconvinced. If he were a lynx, his ears would be backwards, flattened, eyes slitty.

'Are you going to tell me what's wrong?' he says.

She thinks for a moment then says, 'I'm sick.'

'Sick how? Have you been sick?'

She nods. 'Every day for about three weeks now.'

'Three weeks,' he repeats, noting on a pad in front of him. 'When does this happen?'

'Usually after I eat.'

'Only after you eat?'

'And if I smell something. It turns my stomach.'

'If you smell what?'

'Food. Cooked food,' she says, putting a hand to her belly. 'It turns my stomach.'

Without looking up, he says, 'Is it possible that you could be pregnant?'

She gulps, blinks at her trainers inside the wooden floor-rectangles.

'Ashleigh?'

'You can't tell my mum.'

He shakes his head. 'I won't,' he says. 'Does that mean you definitely are?'

She shrugs.

'Have you done a test?'

She shakes her head and looks into her lap.

'Right,' he says. 'Don't worry… When was your last period?'

She shrugs again.

'You don't know?'

'No.'

'More than two weeks ago?'

'Yes.'

'More than four?'

She nods. 'Yes.'

He continues to write then leans down to go through his doctor-case thingy. When he sits back up, he hands her plastic pot with a screw top. 'Let's just rule it out, shall we?'

'I can't be pregnant,' she says.

He observes her without blinking, his kind face returning. 'Have you had sex, Ashleigh?'

She feels herself blushing.

He continues, 'Because if you are sure that you haven't, then you're quite right. You can't be pregnant.'

'Only once,' she says. 'That was the only time.'

He smiles at her, a bit like Father Christmas would to a child, but that image is all wrong in this context. She winces and looks away.

'As I said, let's just rule it out, shall we?'

'Alright.'

'Bring the pot back to me.'

She looks at the pot, then at him. 'When?'

'Well,' he says, clasping his hands in front of him. 'Do you think you can go now?'

'Home?'

'To the bathroom.'

Ashleigh gapes at him. 'Do I have to pee in it?'

'Yes.'

'And bring you my pee?'

'Yes.'

She shakes her head. 'I'm not doing that.'

He sighs. 'I've seen much worse, believe me.'

She folds her arms and looks at her fingernails tucked inside her elbow creases.

'It's just to rule it out,' he says for the third time. 'Don't you want to know?'

'Yes.'

'Okay. Good. Pop through that door,' he says, pointing to the one behind him. 'There's a cloakroom just on the other side of the kitchen.'

Ashleigh nods, takes the pot and leaves.

Ten minutes later, she is back at the desk, watching the doctor as he dips something into her pot of wee. After a minute or two, he smiles.

'What?'

'Well,' says the doctor, eyes on the strip of something inside the pot. 'That confirms that.' He puts down the pot and looks at her. 'It's positive.'

Ashleigh holds her breath, feels the room swirl, hears herself say – 'What does that mean?'

'You're pregnant.'

'I can't be.'

The doctor makes his voice lighter, his mouth softer. 'Ashleigh, if this is your urine, then you are...'

But Ashleigh is still in bed, she must be, with her bobbly, fleece duvet up around her ears and her dancing solar-powered monkey clicking away on her bedside table. Soon, Jane will wake her up when she pads into her room with a cup of tea, and Ashleigh will say, 'I had the weirdest dream.' Then she will get up, pull on her chunky-knit jumper and grey joggers and they'll head off to Pinko's for her doctor's appointment. 'I can't be,' she tries, but the words are too small in her throat.

'Try to remember the date of your last period, that way we can guess at how far along you are.'

Her hands are shaking now, so she drops them in her lap and concentrates on keeping her lips steady. 'Mum can't know,' she says.

The doctor clears his throat again. 'How old are you, Ashleigh?'

She looks away.

'Is your mum with you today?'

She nods. 'She's waiting outside.'

'Do you know who the father is?'

More nodding.

'Try to think. When was your last period?'

'I'm thinking!' she says, and she is. She's thinking about that time that she couldn't go swimming, because she didn't know how to use a tampon – that was only three years ago and she'd definitely had a period since then; she remembers the party, that was in May, two months ago, and she was at the pub – she'd told Mum she had a shift – but she met Gavin and that was all a bit blurry, but they got on the bus and went to Pinko's party. And before that, before that, she'd been to class as normal, she'd been to the gym, she'd been out with the girls; she'd won tickets to Dreamland and they'd all decided to go, boys too, and Justin tried to get some Diamond White from Spar but he got I.D.ed and so they all got candyfloss, stuck it to each other, and then spent ages queuing for the dodgems. That was the night she met Gavin, yes, the memory is really clear now she's replaying it – but was there a point during that day where she'd had to change her tampon? No. No, there wasn't; she'd got home desperate for the loo, because she hadn't been all day. Apart from that, there was no event that stood out in her memory, no day that was different to all the others. The days seemed to blur and merge with no clear picture of her period.

'About three months ago. Maybe.'

'The first day of your last period?'

'Yeah.'

'Right,' he says, consulting a calendar. 'I imagine you don't have an exact date?'

'No.'

'Okay,' he says. 'That means you're about twelve weeks pregnant, then.'

'What? How can it?'

He shrugs. 'That's just how we work it out.'

Ashleigh thinks she might fall off her chair. Twelve weeks was the same as three months. In six months, she'd have a baby. She grips the edge of the desk as the room dissolves into pixels. 'What am I going to do?' she says.

'Well,' says the doctor. 'You have options.'

'You mean...' Ashleigh makes her eyes big.

'Termination, for example, yes.'

Her gaze totters along the curve of the desk. 'Is that what girls do?'

He dips his chin slightly, makes his voice a bit quieter. 'Ashleigh, how old are you?'

She flicks her eyes up to his. 'How come you don't know?'

'I don't have your medical files. This is the first time we've met. I don't know anything about you.'

Nothing, thinks Ashleigh, he knows nothing because he's not her doctor. Because there are no doctors. Because England is empty of doctors and horse-owners and proper families. England is empty of respectable people. Only the poor, broken households remain. The idiots and the criminals. The single women and their dirty, pregnant daughters. It's so unlucky, thinks Ashleigh, that it's almost as if it was meant to be. 'I'm twenty-one.' She swallows; her tongue tastes metallic and she can smell the sweat from her jumper. 'Twenty-two in August.' That was, after all, her birthday month. 'Why does that matter, anyway?'

The doctor watches her for a moment, eyes narrow. 'Okay,' he says, slowly. 'You're quite right. It doesn't matter.'

CHAPTER THIRTY-SIX | July 2032
Pinko

Jane waits in the hallway for Ashleigh. The curves are oddly relaxing, she thinks as she looks up at the ceiling. Whorls of cedar hide muted lightbulbs, like rose petals around their stamens; coving follows the curve of the wall and a pine tree shivers over the galleried landing, ah yes, the tree, Gavin's tree. She squints at it, trying to tie down the movement that darts, pixie-like, just ahead of her landing gaze. She hears footsteps swishing towards her. Pinko. She stands. Smiles.

'Hi,' she says.

'Hello, Jane.'

She winces. Her name in his mouth feels formal. 'Thank you for doing this.'

'I haven't done anything.' He stands with his hands in his pockets, swaying in a sheepish way.

She nods, leans to kiss him. He allows this, then steps back, puts his head down, pulls one shoulder up to his ear as if to itch it.

'You okay?' she says.

'Yeah, just a bit... You know.' He clears his throat. 'Are *you* okay?'

'Yes.' She scans the wrinkles around his pinched mouth, tries to imagine what could have triggered them. 'She told me she's stopped being sick, anyway. I think she was just nervous.'

'About what?'

'About...everything.' Jane looks around the room, indicating 'everything'. 'You know, leaving England, the journey. It's going to be very stressful.'

He fills his chest up, presses his lips together.

'I mean,' she says, 'the journey to France.'

'I know. I know what you mean.'

'When she books her tickets, that is. She hasn't yet booked her tickets.'

Pinko looks off somewhere behind her, then down at his slippers.

'She'll be on her own,' she adds. 'It's going to be really hard for her, so...'

'Doesn't she need to be married?'

Jane looks surprised. 'She's exempt.'

'Well, at least there's that.' He shrugs. 'I don't know what to suggest, Jane.'

She gazes at him, brands him with her stare. 'I'm not asking you to suggest...' she starts, then: 'Look,' she says. 'We have things to discuss.'

He cocks his head. 'What?'

She had the words all ready, but now they make the fat part of her tongue heavy and reluctant. 'Another time.' She bunches her mouth up to one side, goes back to the chair, sits down.

He narrows his eyes. A prompt to continue, perhaps? Or, more likely, he is bracing himself for what he knows is waiting on her tongue. He takes a breath and says, 'The orchid note.'

'No,' she laughs, then, 'Let's get today out of the way.'

'Okay.' He sighs. 'It's a strange situation, isn't it?

'Must be very difficult for you.' She presses her lips together, and looks away.

He smiles, shuffles up to her, kisses her on the cheek for a long time, weirdly, asks her if she wants...a...cup of...coffee, with holes in the sentence that are all hissy and breathy and she's sure he puts his hand to his throat as he walks away. You *know*, she thinks, that this happened on your watch. Probably some drunken mate of his who has since left the country. And so this whole thing has become very awkward.

A door clicks and Jane stands up, strains her gaze. Ashleigh slips around it, pulls it closed and pads along the corridor.

CHAPTER THIRTY-SEVEN | July 2032
Pinko

Pinko would have liked to listen to the conversation taking place in his father's round office. There was nothing to stop him from pressing an ear to the door. There is CCTV in the corridor, of course, but no one watches it – it probably isn't even on. Again, he thinks, that shouldn't matter. It's his house and if he wants to stand at a door and listen, he should.

But as he tells himself this, he realises that he doesn't really want to.

He would rather disappear into the kitchen, prepare some coffee, and return in ten minutes or so, while the doctor – his mate – is packing up his serious-looking bag and telling him, with a serious-looking face, that poor old Ashleigh has salmonella poisoning or a wheat intolerance or chronic anxiety (who could blame her?) and that he has written her a prescription and told her to rest up for a while. Pinko would look sympathetic, before getting to the nitty-gritty of the situation. He could come right out and ask him about her relationship to the person who dropped her off – Jane – as there are very few scenarios in his head where a conversation wouldn't lead to Ashleigh mentioning this.

Then again, perhaps not. Perhaps they got straight to the point. His mate was, after all, a medical professional with a diagnosis to make.

Although, surely he would want to put her at ease.

Pinko sets two coffee cups on a tray and walks back to the office.

His mate – the doctor – opens the door and stands back to let him through.

'I brought you some coffee,' says Pinko, entering and rounding the desk. 'Is she alright?'

The doctor nods, sits down at the desk and starts to pack his bag.

'What was it?' asks Pinko.

'You know I can't really discuss this with you,' he says, without looking up.

'Right.' Pinko sits down in the chair opposite. 'No. Of course not.'

'Thanks for the coffee, though.'

'Thank *you* for coming at such short notice.' He reaches over and picks up one of the cups. 'So, she's gone, then?'

The doctor snaps his bag shut and sits up in his chair. 'As you can see.'

'You don't take sugar, do you?'

'No, thank you – although, round lumps? Pinko, don't you think you've gone a bit too far with this circular business?'

'Curves,' corrects Pinko. 'Not far enough. Look at the damn parquet.'

'You can't pull up original parquet.'

'I know, I know…'

'If your dad kept it, then so should you,' he says, nodding towards the portrait between the two doors.

Pinko keeps his eyes on the coffee. 'I know.'

'And straight lines are good, you know? Trees have lines.'

'That they do,' says Pinko. 'That they do.' He nods for a moment, then tries again. 'So, she left with her housemate? I didn't see them go,' he says.

'Perhaps… I wouldn't know,' says the doctor, taking a sip of coffee.

Pinko stifles a sigh. He really isn't letting anything slip.

'Mm,' says the doctor, finishing his sip. 'She said mother, not housemate.'

This repeats in Pinko's head, echoey and slow, as if they are both underwater.

'I'm sorry,' he hears himself say. 'What?'

The doctor clatters his cup into his saucer, winces at the noise. 'I said, I assume from what she told me that her mother was waiting in your hall.'

'But,' says Pinko. 'There was only one person in the hall and now there's no one.'

The doctor blinks. 'You just said you didn't see *anyone*.'

'Well I did. But... Not her mother.'

The doctor sits back and narrows his eyes. 'You seem perturbed,' he says.

'Not at all.'

The doctor becomes his mate again, tilts his head. 'What is it, Pinks?'

Pinko sighs. 'We've been... We are in the process of...' He rolls his hands around each other. 'Me and the woman in the hall and, well...'

'Right.'

'So, I'm just trying to work out what kind of relationship they have. Those two, I mean.'

'Why don't you ask her?' says the doctor. 'The woman.'

'Jane. She told me they are housemates.'

'Oh. Well,' he says, getting up from the chair. 'Perhaps they are.'

'But,' says Pinko, '*you* said that *she* said that her mum was waiting for her.'

The doctor holds up his hands. 'Look, Pinko, I've told you everything I know.'

'Right,' says Pinko. He realises that his hands are shaking and puts down his coffee cup.

'All I would say,' he replies, putting an arm into his summer jacket, 'is that if she's a similar age to your previous dalliances, she would have only been about nine years old when she had Ashleigh. That's not really possible, is it?'

'She's a bit older. Thirty-two.'

'Well, Ashleigh is in her early twenties. Biologically, she could have been conceived when her mother was twelve, but it's highly unlikely.'

'True.' Pinko smirks at himself. 'Yes, you're right,' he says. 'I'm not thinking clearly.'

'I'm sorry, I can't finish that,' says the Doctor, flicking his eyes at the cup and saucer on the desk, as he gets to his feet. 'We've got a thing, me and Izzy, a meeting thing...'

'Yes,' says Pinko, looking up suddenly. 'No probs. Leave it there. What do I owe you?'

'No, nothing,' he replies, waving him away. 'Turns out we've got to get married.'

Pinko blinks, smiles. 'I'd forgotten that you weren't married... Congratulations.'

'It wasn't really our choice. Did you know about this stupid immigration test? We didn't want to believe it,' he says, gathering his things.

'Yes. It's awful.'

'I just can't...' he begins. 'Are you alright, Pinks?'

'Hmm?'

The doctor stares at him for a moment. 'Look, I have to go. Call me if you need anything.'

Pinko stands. 'Sorry. I'm a little distracted. I will. I will.'

'She was probably parked outside,' he adds. 'Ashleigh's mother. Not waiting in the hall.'

Pinko strides to the door and holds it open. 'Go. Good luck for today.'

'Yes. Right. Thanks.'

The door closes. Pinko draws one, long breath and puts the heels of his hands over his eyes. He imagines Jane in his house, in her ripped jeans, the maid gliding her stare over them, the chef gravitating towards them. Then she was standing in his cellar, daring him to open the dustiest bottle and drink it down there with her. And that first time, when she'd stood in this kitchen in her riding boots; that morning when a memory had been re-ignited, a bolt of lightning struck him, way before things got complicated. Before the hotel room where she stood, soft and fleshy with raised, silver lines framing her belly.

Had there been a baby?

He removes his hands from his eyes. 'Just ask her,' he tells himself, as there is a knock at the door.

He drops his hands to his hips. 'Come in!' he yells, without meaning to.

CHAPTER THIRTY-EIGHT | July 2032
Jane

Jane stands and scurries her gaze over Ashleigh. 'Well?'

Ashleigh shrugs. 'Stress.'

Jane nods. 'Right.' Then: 'Did you tell him just *how* sick you've been?'

'Yeah. Of course I did.'

'And he didn't test you for anything?'

'No.'

'Take your blood?'

'No.'

'Take your temperature.'

'No.'

'Really?'

'No. I mean... That pumpy thing. Around my arm.'

'Blood pressure?'

'Yeah.'

'And?'

'Yeah, it was okay...'

'Normal?'

'Yes. Normal.'

'Did he ask if you were pregnant?'

Ashleigh gapes her eyes. 'What? No.'

'It's okay if he did. I mean, he could have... Do you think... I mean...' Jane licks her top lip and stares at her daughter. 'You *can* tell me, Ashleigh.'

Ashleigh walks towards the telephone table where Jane is sitting. 'You shouldn't be asking me this.'

Jane holds her breath. 'If you are, I can help.'

Ashleigh turns. 'Of course I'm not,' she snaps.

'Fine,' says Jane, holding up her palms. 'He didn't tell you anything then? Like, what's wrong with you?'

'The water's not great at the moment,' says Ashleigh, leaning against the table. 'He told me not to drink the water.'

'From the tap?' says Jane, walking over.

'Yeah.'

'Really?'

'Yeah, he told me not to drink it,' she says. 'It's a thing at the moment,' she says. 'With everything that's happening.'

Jane takes a seat as she considers this. Ashleigh, it seems, has repeated Jane's own worries about the water back to her – a juvenile lie. Additionally, medical experience, even with animals, has taught her that a water-borne bug will hit the bowels as well as the stomach; that victims will sweat in their bedsheets for a few weeks, usually. They won't puke in the morning, then sit around watching reruns of *Love Island* until the whiff of tea-time fish-fingers sends them retching to their bedroom. Furthermore, Ashleigh sips on the boxed juice that Jane bulk-bought before Lidl shut down last winter. *Jane* drinks more tap water than Ashleigh.

'Did he say it could be anything else?'

Ashleigh shakes her head.

Jane scowls. 'That's frustrating.' She purses her lips, thinks for a moment. 'Oh well, I'll need to stock up on bottled water. It's super expensive, but prices will only get higher.'

Ashleigh widens her eyes, raises her voice. 'Oh, don't worry, Mum—'

'We can go to the supermarket on our way back...'

Ashleigh stares off into space, feels out her hipbones the way she often does, of late. 'We're fucked, aren't we?' she says. 'The world is going to end and we'll get split up before it does.'

'No,' says Jane. 'The world is not going to end.' She leans closer, puts her hand on Ashleigh's knee. 'And we have a plan, don't we? We'll find each other.' Jane's lip trembles as her eyes scan down to Ashleigh's belly.

'You don't know that...'

Jane scoffs, 'Oh yes I do. We will find each other. There is no other option.'

Ashleigh nods, expressionless. 'I want to talk to Pinko,' she says. 'I'm going to talk to Pinko. Maybe you could you go and get the water and pick me up afterwards?'

Jane frowns, tilts her head. 'Why do you want to see him?'

'About another shift.'

'What for?'

She shrugs. 'For some extra cash. He's got another thing coming up. The doctor just mentioned it. And he pays really well like, really well.'

Jane stares. 'But you're sick, Ash.'

'I'm better, I told you,' she replies, standing up. 'I don't even know why we're here.'

'Because you're sick.'

'I'm frightened, Mum.'

Jane folds her lips together, stares at Ashleigh.

'And I need some extra cash if I'm going to make this work.'

Jane's breathing races. 'Then I'll wait here for you.'

'No, it's okay...'

'Why wouldn't I?'

'Well...' she looks about her, rubs her mouth. 'I think I'll have to wait to see him. There's no point both of us waiting.'

Jane reaches up and clasps Ashleigh's arm. 'Does he know you're my daughter?'

Ashleigh shrugs off Jane's hand. 'Don't know. Why does that matter?'

In a parallel universe, Jane storms into Pinko's office and demands the contact details of each one of his mates so she can call them, one by one, and find out who screwed her daughter at his party. She dances her eyes over Ashleigh. Whatever is going on here, they are a heartbeat away from safe passage to Finland. Now is not the time to rock the boat.

Ashleigh asks, 'So you'll come get me in a bit?'

'No,' says Jane, picking up her bag. 'I'll wait outside, in the car.'

CHAPTER THIRTY-NINE | July 2032
Pinko

The latch rattles as if someone is struggling to unclick it. Fingers curl around the door's edge, followed by Ashleigh's head.

Her face is pale, but her cheekbone dent and nose nook and eyelid cave are shadowy. Her hair is tied into a loose bun on her head.

'Ashleigh.' It's the first time he's seen her since the party. She is washed-out and shy with her hair pulled back, very different from the mouthy redhead who made him drink tequila and dance on a trampoline. But most of all, it strikes him that she might have the same nose as Jane. He squints at it, then swallows and says, 'Everything alright?'

'Hello,' she says, turning to close the door. Then she stands and stares about her, fiddling with her fingers.

'Oh,' he sweeps his hand out towards a chair. 'Come in. Sit down, if you want,' then, 'I mean, you don't have to.'

She scuttles around him and sits down.

'So,' he says, plunging his hands into his pockets.

'You know why I saw the doctor, don't you?'

He pulls a chair up opposite her, nods as he sits in it. 'Yes.'

'Right.'

He blinks. 'How are you feeling?'

'So so. You know.'

He nods as if he does know, but he doesn't. She seems jittery, her fingers shake as she clasps them in her lap, her legs are crossed and her foot is tucked behind her ankle as if she is trying to shut herself. It is the first time he has seen her since that night and now, without her make-up, he thinks she looks remarkably young. What drew him to this girl that night? The girl that was so cocky and confident. Her energy, probably, which has now been drained by some rotten virus or parasite. He checks himself; he is being unfair. She is ill after all. Or perhaps... No. His brain will no longer go there since he has ruled that out as a possibility. Her collar bone hides a smudgy dent behind it and her hair is wiry and unwashed.

For a moment, he thinks she has come to thank him for arranging the appointment. The thought leaves him as he realises this is his chance to find out about her relationship to Jane. His eyes flick to her nose again. He drafts the question in his head, opens his mouth to deliver it, but she speaks.

'I just want to ask you,' she says, 'to keep this to yourself for now.'

He frowns. 'What's that?'

'And I won't say anything either... I haven't even worked out what I'm going to do yet.'

Pinko twitches his head to the side. 'Sorry, I'm...' He tapers out, shaking his head.

She looks confused. 'I thought you knew what the doctor told me. He's your friend, isn't he?'

It takes him a moment to catch on. Then, he seems to leave his body, float above it, and watch a young man leaning towards a young girl, who is telling him something that he doesn't want to hear. 'Oh God,' he says. 'Have I misunderstood?' he says, but she doesn't answer, she is wiping tears from her face with the sides of her thumbs.

He swallows. 'Ashleigh, does this mean...' he says, glancing down at her stomach.

'You just told me you knew already.'

'I knew why you were coming here but the – I'm sorry – the doctor couldn't, *wouldn't* tell me...' he says, squeezing his eyes shut. 'Is this really true?'

'He tested me,' she says.

'And...the party,' he says, too high, too strained. 'The party,' he says, again. 'Was it...um...the night of the party? Do you think?'

'Yes.' Her face is rigid and staring. 'I haven't done it...since.'

He responds with one slow nod, imagining his skull like a woodchipper, munching through this thought, reducing it to dust, and when it is gone, all that remains is the knowledge that he is going to be a father.

A father.

This girl is pregnant.

And he is going to be a father.

He gulps back a cry, fills his head up with breath, fists his hands in front of him and secretly remembers that many early pregnancies don't work out. This thought alone allows him to say: 'It's okay, everything's going to be okay,' and he wants to say, 'but are you *sure* it's mine?' Instead he says, 'But I never, ever...do that...without protection. Never. It's an absolute rule.'

She looks at him. Shrugs.

'Oh God,' he says.

Her face is blank. Judgemental.

'Look, I'm sorry. I will look after you. Of course I will.'

She blinks. Shakes her head.

He would like her to accept his offer and leave him to gather his thoughts. His mind is already a swirl of logistics, accommodation, paperwork and Jane – oh God – Jane.

'You don't have to,' she says. 'You've done a lot for us.'

'What?'

'The doctor's appointment and everything. Thank you for organising that. You didn't have to.'

'Are you kidding, Ashleigh?' he snorts. 'This is as much my responsibility as it is yours.'

'We can discuss that.' Ashleigh slides her arms around her stomach. 'But you don't need to get involved, for the moment,' she says. 'Just don't tell anyone.'

He would like to push the issue, to tell her that he'll be involved no matter what, but her face is now twitchy, as if she is trying to hold something in. Her eyes move to the door.

'Is Jane still out there?' he asks.

'No. She went.'

'You haven't told her?'

'I don't want her to know. I told her I'd come to ask you about some more hours.'

'Hours?'

'Yeah, you know, waitressing.' She hugs herself tighter. 'I just need some time to think.'

'Right,' he says, and he almost adds, *me too*, but instead he says, 'Of course.'

Ashleigh sits blinking at the parquet, then at him. 'Why did you call her Jane, like that?'

'Never mind,' he says, tongue quick over his bottom lip. 'You can come to Finland with me. You'll have nothing to worry about.'

'Why would you...' she stops herself, squints at him for a moment. 'Finland?' she repeats.

'Yes. Of course you'll come to Finland. Do you think I'll let you try your luck in France when you're carrying...' He takes a deep breath, calms himself.

She says, 'I won't leave my mum.'

Pinko feels itchy now, the air is too close, the chair is too hard. He stands and leans against his desk, knowing what she's about to tell him.

'I'm not leaving without my mum,' she persists.

'Who is your mum?' he tries.

'I told you, she just left.'

Pinko turns, sits back down. 'So that *is* your mum?'

'Yes.'

'The lady who was sitting in the hall, just now?' The question is useless, but feels like a lifeline.

She looks at him as if he is stupid, and for an instant he sees the sass she wore so well on that night back in May.

One, two, three seconds chip their way through time.

She opens her mouth and says, 'Yes. Jane. You met Jane the morning after your party. Remember?'

He smirks. As if he could forget.

'That's my mum. Jane is my mum.'

PART THREE
THE DECEIT

CHAPTER FORTY | July 2032
Jane

Jane is parked outside the front gates of Pinko's estate, waiting. The drystone wall, she notes, has been built entirely from rounded stones. She wonders how often sections of it fall down due to the inadequate tessellation.

Then she wonders how Pinko will react to the fact that Ashleigh is her daughter. She knows exactly how he will react. He will lift his eyebrows, look at her through half-closed eyes and say, 'I knew the whole time, you wally.' And then they'll go back to being them, dancing around five-star hotels like rich teenagers. Partying in wine-cellars. Yes, she thinks, the truth is better out. Whatever allure she was hoping to maintain by being young, carefree – not a mother – is an illusion, a complex. Hadn't they been ditched before, she and Ashleigh? But there's *no* shame in being a mother. It just makes one feel – and behave – like a frump, sometimes. And frumps don't get the hot, rich guy. Sad but true. More importantly, frumps don't get the hot, rich guy who will whisk them off to Finland before a mega-tsunami drowns the UK.

There is no time to think now, yet she is thinking. She is thinking about her daughter lying to her. It has taken her twenty minutes of hard thinking to convince herself that it must have been the party. It must have been. The more she turns it over, the more she remembers Ashleigh being weird and detached the next day at the stables. Jane blinks off into the distance. A crow limps across the road. It stops, turns, and glints one, black eye at her. In a few weeks, Ashleigh could be packed off to France and who *knows* when they would see each other again. The world is going to end, thinks Jane, and we'll get split up before it does. She replays Ashleigh's words and tries not to cry. Her hand, she realises, is gripping the steering wheel, her fingernails digging right in. There were only two of them teetering on the edge of peril, now it looks like there are three. Jane closes her eyes; all that time worrying about finding a fucking dress. When Ashleigh boards the ferry, what if she is too weak to stand? What if she miscarries in a stinking cubicle at Calais? Worst of all, what if she is kidnapped and forced into marriage?

Jane thumps these thoughts away on the steering wheel, strains to see the arched, front doorway. Still no Ashleigh. They are not having a conversation about waitressing, that's for sure.

The crow takes off, its lame leg dangling behind.

Keep your eye on the prize, she thinks. It's so much more important now.

CHAPTER FORTY-ONE| July 2032
Ashleigh

Pinko pops back up from his chair. His chest seems to drag him upright. He walks to the door, turns about, walks back again and squats in front of Ashleigh. 'I need to tell you something about Jane. Your...Mum.'

Ashleigh screws up her face. 'What do you mean?' The sentence is stretched by the drop of her chin, the clap of her hand over her mouth. 'Oh my God.'

'Ashleigh, I didn't know – you told me she was your housemate.'

'And what?'

'I thought you might be related, but I had no idea that...'

'Oh. My. God.'

'And how could she be your mother? She's not old enough to be your mother.'

But the world swells and washes around Ashleigh, blasts her thoughts from her head and roars in her ears. Lying to your mum is normal, she thinks, but the other way round... She holds her ears, shakes her head. Telling Pinko was supposed to guarantee their escape, but this new information fucks up everything. When the air settles, one thought spins on a loop in her head. 'You two hooked up.'

Pinko stands and turns around in a small circle. 'Yes,' he says. 'Well no. I'm not sure what that means.'

'Have you had sex with her?' asks Ashleigh.

'No.'

'Oh my God,' she says, leaning forward. 'You've had sex with her.'

'Honestly, Ashleigh, we haven't. I swear.'

'I think I'm going to throw up.'

'Really, what, really?' Pinko scoops up the wastepaper bin and puts it in front of her. 'Are you?'

She ignores the bin; sits looking at the wall with her hand over her mouth.

Pinko sighs and pushes his hands into his pockets. 'Look, let's get some perspective here—'

'That's so *horrible*. You and me were...' she says, interlacing her fingers. 'You know. *Flirting*...'

'No, Ashleigh, no... The whole natural disaster thing is horrible. This, ha!' he says, shaking his head. 'This is not horrible.'

'You look like you're crying,' she says. 'No, you actually are.'

'I'm just a bit...overwhelmed.' Oh God, thinks Pinko. Oh God, oh God, oh God. 'I believed she was your housemate.' Pinko goes to the window and stares out of it. It's raining – of course – and the garden is a lurid green. He glimpses the edge of Blue trimming a distant hedge and has the urge to shut the curtains.

He turns only when Ashleigh scrapes her chair back. She looks about the room, pulls her coat around her.

'You're going...'

'Yes,' she says, sniffing, 'I'd better go.'

'Fine. Okay.' He fumbles for his phone. 'Of course. I'll get you a car.'

'No. Don't worry about it.'

'I'm already on it,' he says, typing out a text, then holding up his phone. 'It's done.'

'My mum's coming to get me.' She sits again heavily. 'I think I'm actually going to be sick.'

CHAPTER FORTY-TWO | July 2032
Ashleigh

Yes, she says, this time, she's probably, really going to be sick so maybe, if he could just remind her where the toilet is... She looks about her to one door, then the other. Pinko approaches her. 'This way,' he says, pressing his hands to her shoulders. She curls out of his grasp, says she'll follow him. He goes on ahead, opens the door to the cloakroom where she pissed in a pot not half an hour before. He rushes in and puts the seat up. She stands, hand over her mouth and looks at him until he leaves, then locks the door and puts the seat down. She sits on the loo, makes retching noises and waits. An image of her mum blooms in her head, on the sofa, watching Ashleigh do her make-up at the mirror before a shift at the pub, telling her to stay safe, shrugging when Ashleigh asks her what she'll do with her evening. A rerun of *X Factor*, probably, or *Pretty Woman*. Then another image: coming home to find her with a kitten, a bird, a bat, a puppy, not leaving the house until it has eaten or walked or pooed. Next, her mum leans on her pitch-fork, gazing up at the brick vaults of the stable ceiling, wondering aloud about Pinko Stephens.

Just how were they supposed to live, mother, mother's daughter, mother's partner, mother's grandchild – who was also mother's partner's child – all together in a little, lakeside cabin?

Finland would be more complicated than she'd imagined.

She studies the toilet door and considers backing out, telling him she made the whole thing up.

And then she'd leave for France.

The thought makes her shudder. An image fills her mind. Heaving, dirty bodies scrabbling for a slice of bread, while she sits on the floor, one hand on her pregnant belly, and wonders where her mum is.

No, she thinks. That isn't an option.

She snatches a ream of toilet paper from the roll beside her and concludes that neither of these scenarios will accommodate a baby. She blows her nose. Not to mention the fact that she'll have to give birth to it.

That isn't an option, either.

After a few minutes, Ashleigh gets up from the loo, twists the door handle slowly, *slowly*, and looks around the frame. She pads heel-first to the end of the corridor, glances about the round, brown hallway, opens the arched front door and jogs along the lawn just next to the gravel driveway. Jane isn't there; she'll meet her on the road. She'll meet her on the road and Ashleigh will jump into the car and tell her to drive. Jane will raise her eyebrows – *Ashleigh's in one of her moods* – and ask her if she got a shift. Ashleigh will tell her that she didn't, that he had enough staff, that she's pissed off about that, but feeling much better now she's seen the doctor. She will watch her mum's reactions, she will tell her that someone like Pinko would make a really nice boyfriend – didn't she say that she quite fancied him, once upon a time? Perhaps Jane should try and contact him. Jane will look surprised, relieved. She'll say, *Do you really think so?* then she'll drive them home, send Ashleigh to the sofa with a carton of apple juice and some spaghetti hoops on toast and Ashleigh will spend the evening googling abortion clinics.

All of this plays out exactly as she had imagined, but Ashleigh didn't expect to notice her mum checking her phone, the way you do when you have no messages, no texts, no signs of life from someone you really, really want to hear from.

Ashleigh observes Jane from behind her laptop screen and remembers how terrified he looked. *Of course you'll come to Finland*, he'd said.

He'll be in touch Mum, she thinks. Don't worry.

CHAPTER FORTY-THREE | July 2032
Jane

Jane wakes up on Sunday to find Ashleigh doing the bleep test in the garden. Jane stands at the window and watches her run to one end, touch the fence, then run back again. The bleeps are coming from her phone (she has downloaded an app, apparently) and they are getting closer together with each round. She manages to keep up to the end. Jane frowns, but doesn't tell her to stop; she sees herself, all those years back, doing laps of the field behind her parents' house. It didn't change a thing, of course.

When Ashleigh flops onto the grass, panting, Jane opens the window and calls down, 'You okay?'

Ashleigh gives her a thumbs-up.

Pinko doesn't contact her that day, no matter how often she checks her phone.

CHAPTER FORTY-FOUR | July 2032
Jane

It's Monday afternoon and Ashleigh has started to sort out the things she wants to take to France with her. Jane hesitates before digging out an old, large rucksack for her to use, as if Ashleigh is planning a gap-year adventure. Ashleigh plays the game, returns Jane's stoicism.

Doubt swoops for Jane and together they plunge. What if her brain is deluding her? What if Ashleigh isn't even pregnant? What if Jane's own paranoia has ruined everything?

Before she goes to bed that night, Jane sits crossed-legged in front of the baby oak tree and weeps.

Pinko hasn't called today, either.

CHAPTER FORTY-FIVE | July 2032
Jane

Tuesday already. And there are only four more Tuesdays to go. At work, they have all agreed a definitive shut-down date for the end of August. By that time, there will be no Sue, and Jane can't run the place on her own. Vicky left at the weekend. Smiley Vicky with her laughing voice. She managed to find a husband on Tinder who turned out to be someone she went to school with. They hit it off and became a 'legitimate' couple. Jane remembers Vicky's screensaver – a picture of them sharing a Belgian waffle – and can't help but make the comparison to her and Pinko. What happened to us, Pinko? she thinks, but she knows what happened.

They hardly knew each other.

Pinko freaked out.

Vicky was one of the lucky ones.

Bide your time, Jane. Give it a few more days.

Jane unlocks the door and tinkles it open. She shuffles around to the desk with jangling keys; her extra-long arms trail her tote containing her rubber clogs, her lunch, some old magazines for the waiting room and a ball of knotted rope for Paris. 'Will miss you all. See you on the other side!' has been printed out and taped to the computer screen. 'Love, Vicky.' Jane flips the calendar to Sue the Surgeon's last day, just to double check there have been no changes.

Four weeks. Ages away.

Jane puts down the bag of magazines and straightens Vicky's stapler. Yes, she thinks. See you on the other side. Safe travels. She doesn't feel emotional about this. She is well inside her head today; the outside world is a blurry echo. That is, except for the little bundle of fur and legs that is probably snoozing away in the side room. The thought of him brings her to her senses like a caffeine hit. 'Paris,' she says, pushing at the swing door behind her and calling through it, 'I got you a present.' She lumps her bags onto the staff worktop and fully opens the door.

Paris's cage stands empty, blanket gone, food bowls gleaming clean in the corner. She looks in the other cages, bending to the lower ones and standing on tiptoes to see into the top row. Sue swings through the opposite door. 'Where's Paris?' Jane asks, eyes growing hot.

'Good morning,' Sue replies. 'Collected over the weekend; going on holiday to Finland, apparently.'

Jane pings upright. 'What?'

'"Pinko's Ark," which is a bit conceited if you ask me. Took all of them. He's even going to take your hedgehog, Number Five, is that what you called her?'

Jane ignores the questions. 'You're kidding,' she says.

Sue shakes her head. 'Nope.'

'But what the hell will he do with them?'

'Paris is for you, I think. And the hedgehog,' she replies, shrugging. 'He said the others can stay on his farm for now – up in the Peak District somewhere – did you know he had a farm up there? Anyway, they've gone. All twenty-six of them, and anymore that turn up in the meantime will get picked up next week.'

'But... They'll need paperwork.'

'Yep,' says Sue, nodding. 'It's going to be full-on.'

'And expensive.'

'Hugely expensive,' she confirms, setting her bag down on the counter.

Jane feels herself smiling. So, he hadn't forgotten about her. He was trying to make himself worthy, or some such shit. That's exactly how his brain works. A hugely successful, wealthy celebrity, who is constantly feeling inadequate. She pulls her uniform from its bag and reminds herself that she shouldn't tease him so much.

'Hang-on,' she says, 'what do you mean, "for me"?'

Sue puts her hand in her bag and pulls out a Mars bar. 'Sorry?'

Jane follows the chocolate with her eyes; it's not even eight in the morning. 'Paris and the hedgehog?'

'Oh,' says Sue. 'That's what the driver said.'

'Does that mean I'm going with him, then?'

Sue shrugs and unwraps her chocolate. 'Vicky spoke to him. It was all via telephone. He sent a van to collect them.'

No, Jane thinks. Perhaps he meant *for* her; he was saving them *on her behalf.* If she was going with him, then he'd ask her; he wouldn't just assume. And then there was the fact that she hadn't heard from him all week.

Panic warms her shoulders; she folds her arms to stop them from shaking.

This is his way, she thinks, of *not* inviting her to Finland.

CHAPTER FORTY-SIX | July 2032
Ashleigh

Ashleigh walks to the kitchen, looks around the door: no Jane. Again, she counts the days on her hand since that party. The doctor made a mistake. He totally made a mistake; he added on ten days for no apparent reason. She walks back up the hall calling out for Jane, stops, listens, but no answer. She taps her phone to her chest. If he was capable of making a mistake like *that*, perhaps she wasn't even pregnant. She goes to the living room, stands by the window, presses the green telephone on her screen and holds the phone to her ear. Then she says the words she never thought she'd say. 'I'd like to book an abortion, please.' A woman with a nice voice tells her that she'll have to be referred by a doctor. Ashleigh says she can't, that it's impossible to get an appointment, that the weeks are ticking by. The woman with the nice voice asks her if she is sure about her decision? Has she spoken to the father? They could fast-track her for a doctor's appointment the following week? That won't work, says Ashleigh, lifting the edge of the curtain and squinting up the path, I'll be too far gone by then. Are you sure? asks the woman. When was the first day of your last period? Ashleigh tells her (she can properly remember now) then tells her exactly which date she had sex. That was the only time. It couldn't possibly have been any other date. The lady with the nice voice tells her she is thirteen weeks and six days pregnant. Then explains, as Ashleigh lets the curtain drop from her grasp, that she is too far gone now to legally consider abortion in the UK.

Ashleigh repeats the date she had sex, counts aloud on her fingers so the woman will say – *oops! My mistake!*

But the woman tells her again that she is thirteen weeks and six days pregnant. She then tells her why it is worked out that way. Then asks Ashleigh if she is sure about the first date of her last period.

'Yes.'

Finally, the woman with the nice voice gives Ashleigh the number for a pregnancy crisis line. Ashleigh says thank you, hangs up, then sits on the floor in front of the living-room window. After a moment, she tilts sideways to lay her cheek on her hand, on the floor, her phone in front of her nose. Hours later, when the front door unclicks, she pushes herself onto all fours, tells Jane she dropped her phone under the sofa.

Over the next week, Ashleigh stops eating. Scrapes her food into the bin while her mum is in the loo. Jane notices once, starts to stand in the kitchen, watching her eat. She always notices when food goes missing from the cupboards, and so she's bound to notice when it hasn't been touched. In the middle of the week, Ashleigh decides to be a bit more subtle. She sits in the kitchen with her meals, eats them in front of Jane, makes 'yum' and 'mmm' noises before running to the bathroom to push the end of a toothbrush down her throat. She crumbles a bit of bread onto a plate and leaves it next to the sink, pours drops of milk into a bowl, leaves a cornflake to soften at the bottom. At lunchtime, she puts her sandwiches in her pocket, takes them upstairs and flushes them down the toilet. She feeds bananas to the horses, removes one square of chocolate every day and puts it in a padded envelope in her room along with dried apricots and Ritz biscuits. The food thing is getting easier to hide from Jane, but the exercise is too obvious, too noisy. She does press-ups, sit ups, lunges, squats and planks in her room with the music up loud. She starts to pad her bra, wear t-shirts under t-shirts, wince at her jutting hip-bones as she steps into scalding hot baths. When her mum goes to work, she helps herself to a full glass of vodka.

Pinko calls a couple of times, leaving messages in his posh, important voice. She would like to take his calls, but has no idea how to play this game now she's started it. This isn't normal, this just *isn't* normal, being so young and *sooo* pregnant and waiting for the world to end. It's like a film. She needs to settle everything in her mind first, get in control of the situation. This is *big,* after all. It's much easier to stay small and quiet, that way it doesn't have to be real. And anyway, what if she says something that makes him change his mind? That could ruin everything. Then again, if she ignores him too much, he might give up and ghost her – although that seems pretty unlikely. His texts are a bit much, to be fair. Every day, he promises money, tells her to see a doctor – he can arrange that, of course – or to fast track a passport application (she's already got a passport, she's not completely offline). Still, she'll have to answer him at some point. And he hasn't even *asked* her if the baby is his, which is weird as he was *obviously* too drunk to remember anything that happened that night. She almost tells him that – *how are you so sure that this is even your kid?* – until one day she hears Jane crying in the garden. Ashleigh knows what's wrong. *Everyone* knows. It's become the stupid question to ask. Yet Jane hasn't yet cried, not when she knows that Ashleigh can hear.

It's raining outside and so Ashleigh is exercising on the stairs. She makes her footsteps louder, either to cover the sound of Jane's crying or to let her know that she is there – Jane might stop if she realises she can be heard. Ashleigh's phone beeps – Pinko – brilliant timing as usual. She reads the message as she walks down the stairs, nausea spiralling in her gut and up to the back of her throat.

We leave at the end of the month. All three of us. Please think of the baby.

Her heart quickens. Mum would definitely be pleased about this; they'd get to stay together and wouldn't have to worry about the awful immigration test. It was the dream. But it was all such a mess. Ashleigh sighs as she reaches the bottom step, turns around and walks back up again. *Think of the baby.* All she did was think about this thing inside her belly, but the thought always got stuck at a crossroads. On the right was this – what she was doing – on the left was...well...a baby. Babies were cute, but hard work. Her mum always told her that having a baby when you're young means you miss out on other things. Ashleigh reaches the top of the stairs, turns and comes back down again. But there was a whole other layer to this problem. She hadn't banked on Mum and Pinko *actually* hooking up. The thought makes Ashleigh feel a little bit sick – more so than usual – but it deepens and morphs back into that same, twisted family tree. Jane with Pinko, Ashleigh and a baby, Pinko taking the role of the baby's dad... Ashleigh reaches the bottom of the stairs and turns around again. She is young, but she knows certain things never end well; keeping up a lie *never ends well*.

But the truth would ruin everything.

And if they get to Finland and it turns out she's *not* pregnant, he can hardly send them back again, can he?

Ashleigh lowers her head and ups her pace until she is jogging.

'Ashleigh?' calls Jane from below. 'How long are you going to spend banging up and down those stairs?'

Ashleigh ignores her. Continues her purposeful stamping and at each step, pretends she is squashing a banana or a cupcake or a cheese and pickle sandwich.

'Ashleigh?' repeats Jane, appearing at the foot of the stairs.

'It takes my mind off everything,' says Ashleigh, turning once again and walking back down.

Jane has wide, angry eyes. 'You can't keep doing this. You'll make yourself ill again.'

Ashleigh shrugs. 'It makes me feel in control,' she says, slightly breathless. It's true, it does, but these are not her words. She read an article on the internet about eating disorders and found a reason for her weird behaviour that Jane would buy. One that would throw her off the scent.

'Ashleigh, please.' Jane's eyes are all red and her lips are wobbly.

Ashleigh stops in the middle of the staircase and sits down. She would like to cry too but there would be no point in both of them crying. That never got them anywhere except into a spat of shouting and slamming doors.

'I just wish,' says Jane, 'that you'd talk to me.'

Jane climbs the stairs and sits on the step just below her. Ashleigh drops herself down to the same step and leans on her mum's shoulder.

'Don't worry about me,' she says, to which Jane smirks loudly.

When Jane gets up to put the kettle on, Ashleigh thumbs through her phone to Pinko's last message.

OK, she types. *I'm in.*

CHAPTER FORTY-SEVEN | July 2032
Jane

On Wednesday afternoon, Jane realises that she cannot cry anymore. Not simply that she cannot, but that she does not want to. And that awful, gut-twisting space that was filled with all that new – for want of a better word – *love*, now contains the clearest image of her mother, hands on hips, eyes hard. She bends forward and looks right to the back of Jane's eyes.

'What planet are you on?' she yells.

Jane winces. Her mother was always a shouter. Cow.

But as it happens, she's right this time. Jane dispels the image of her, flicks off the rerun of *Countdown* that drones away in the background, and gets up from the sofa.

Enough is enough.

There is a pending natural disaster. You have a daughter to look after.

You.

You, Jane.

Baby or no baby, your daughter needs to get out of the UK.

Jane walks to the kitchen, snaps open her laptop, and tries the internet.

Still working today, she thinks. Good.

Then she trawls through the ferry company websites, familiarising herself with the routes from the South Coast to France. There is no shortage of options. Dozens of agencies pop up in her searches, all promising to escort unaccompanied dependents over to Europe. For a fee, of course. The fees are high, but slightly lower than the ferry companies are charging. She scans the few forums for information on each agency; she'd like to know if they're legitimate. Would they rip her off? The overwhelming conclusion is to *beware*. Some fraudulent agencies, promising private boats to the continent, would pack the passengers into a rubber dinghy and leave them to fend for themselves in the Channel.

Jane shakes her head. Nope. No way.

Back to the ferry companies.

Jane reads through the various reviews from young people who've already made the journey, marvelling at their ability to record everything online. Her own connection is patchy, but after a couple of hours, she concludes that a French ferry service, hastily set up by the French government to aid with the evacuation, is her best option. Jane learns that they prioritise young people and provide a transfer service from the port at Dieppe to the Alps, charging one, flat fee for the whole trip. Jane pauses to look at the ceiling where, on the other side, Ashleigh is lying on her bed, probably playing with her phone. She considers calling her down, asking her what she thinks. When would be a good date to travel? Then she imagines the ensuing argument, the horrid words and Jane's inevitable return to the sofa, to *Countdown* and to the mood that has swallowed her for the last two days.

No.

Jane is in charge today.

She will not waste this productive energy on an argument.

Before she can change her mind, she adds a seat in Business Economy (who knew that existed on boats?) to her basket. The fifty-pound supplement will buy Ashleigh a reclining seat with extra legroom.

She clicks Proceed to Payment.

Jane's card details are saved to her laptop; she doesn't even have to find her purse.

She adds her security number and hovers the mouse over the Pay Now button.

This is when her face heats up, her throat swells, and one, thin tear spills down to her mouth.

No, she tells herself again. Pull yourself together. You are just clicking a button; no one is leaving today.

She grits her teeth, bracing herself to press the button, say goodbye to a large portion of her savings. But there's a knock at the door.

She looks up towards the hall, then at the clock on her screen. Six o'clock. Too late for the postman, in fact, they hadn't seen the postman for weeks.

She gets up and scurries towards the door.

As she approaches, she hears barking.

Surely it can't be...

She opens the door to Pinko's driver. On his left hip he holds a small golden pug.

'Paris!' says Jane, reaching for the dog.

'This is for you,' says the driver, as if Jane hadn't known. 'And this,' he adds, handing her a stiff envelope in his other hand.

Jane thanks him, closes the door and coos at Paris while she sets him on the floor. Then she rips open the envelope, hoping to see one of Gavin's pictures. Sure enough, there is a card inside with a magnolia tree printed on the front. She takes a moment to watch the flowers sway, the leaves twinkle – how does he *do* it? – then she opens it.

Sorry for the silence. Hope you are still coming to the exhibition? XXX

She tries to be pouty and indignant, tries to keep hold of all that strong, purposeful energy, but it slips from her in one, long squeal. This makes Paris bark and Ashleigh come to the landing.

'Oh my god, a pug!' she yells, then runs down the stairs and scoops him up. Paris stops barking, twists his head right back to see who has lifted him into the air. 'Where did he come from?'

Jane grins, pulls Ashleigh to her and kisses her fiercely on the temple.

'Get off,' says Ashleigh.

'It's all going to be okay,' says Jane.

Something in Ashleigh's face changes. She smirks lightly and looks at the dog, considering him, before saying in an unfamiliar, calmer voice, 'I know it is, Mum.'

CHAPTER FORTY-EIGHT | July 2032
Jane

There's a currant bun on the windowsill. The icing on its window-facing side has faded to cloud-matte through melting and resolidifying. A Chelsea bun, Jane corrects herself, with a dug-out crater where the cherry should be. She clasps her hands behind her neck, thinks for a moment and winces. Ashleigh must have eaten the cherry. Must have done. All those weeks ago when she was eating properly. Jane stares unblinking at the bun. Her purse is on the floor below it, upturned, inside out, a few coins constellated about the carpet, some further away from the force of the throw. Paris shuffles up and sniffs it, looks up at her and licks his nose.

Next door has left their house like they always do when they go away. Wrapped up in its shutters, trellis creepers trimmed, garden furniture covered in tarpaulin (although all stacked up on the garage roof) and the hanging baskets covered, watering globes inserted. She had watched him trim the edges of the flowerbeds with scissors, padlock the barbecue inside the shed, then climb a ladder to clean the guttering. Before they left, he pulled a huge silver cover over the car, pegging its edges to the hubcaps. As she watched them leave, she zoomed in on his wife. Fifty, about Jane's size, wearing a trouser suit under her rucksack – oh that was so her. But why, she thinks as she picks up her keys, did he put the garden *furniture* on the garage roof but not the barbecue? She takes a hanger from the coat rack, walks to the front door and pushes Paris aside with the edge of her foot. And why didn't he put the car inside the garage?

The neighbour's door is white PVC, with a knocker and a stained-glass window. The letter box is right in the centre of the door. 'Plan A,' she says, inhaling. She puts the coat hanger through the letter box, loops it over the inside handle and twists it downwards. The door clicks open. Jane steps inside, removes her shoes, looks to her left into the front room and notices the dark angles and green flares of a bonsai tree. Then she looks ahead and climbs the stairs.

Jane has seen her neighbour in clothes that are *not* trouser suits. In the summer, she wears ruffled maxi dresses, on occasions when Jane has popped over for something in the morning (once, in fact, and it was a cup of milk—*we only drink almond...*), she answered the door in a long satin robe with matching nightdress. 'Bedroom,' she says to herself now, heading across the landing and opening the door (all the doors have been closed) but, oh, she is in the box room. Literally. The room is piled high with blue plastic chests. All padlocked. Jane steps out of the room and closes the door behind her. The layout is slightly different from her own house, and not just a mirror image, but it seems that walls have been knocked down and rooms have been reconfigured. Unlike her own, their bedroom is at the far end of the landing. She enters, locates the wardrobe, holds her breath and opens it.

If you are a parent with a purse full of copper and the end of the world is nigh, she thinks...

Ah-ha.

Inside, she finds what she is looking for.

She knew she would.

Back in her own house, her own bedroom, Jane slips on the dress. Slips it off.

'I think that will do,' Jane says to Paris. Then wonders which sea they must cross to get to Finland. Baltic, would it be? No, the North. She'd never crossed the North Sea.

Jane pins up her hair.

Then wonders if helicopters can even fly that far.

Jane goes back outside, steals an artificial petunia from one of the hanging baskets next door, comes back to find trainers in the hall.

Jane puts the petunia in her hair in front of the hall mirror. 'Ashleigh?' she calls up the stairs. 'How are you feeling?'

No answer.

Jane tries to google Finland, but the internet is not working.

Jane waxes her moustache (using next door's wax). 'Ashleigh?' she yells, her upper lip stiff. 'There's bottled water.'

Jane paints her nails and flaps them next to her chin.

Jane applies eyeliner. Finds one earring, looks for the other. She only just brought them down from upstairs... 'Can you give me a sign of life?' she says, walking back up, scouring the floor. 'Ah, there it is.'

Jane slips back into the dress, looks at herself over her shoulder. It is royal blue with sequinned straps and split to the knees.

She returns to the hall and bends to put on her heels.

'Where are you going?' says Ashleigh from the doorway. 'Dressed up like that.'

'You're still alive, then?'

'Where are you going?'

'Out.'

Ashleigh sighs. 'Look, I know where you're going.'

'What?' Jane looks up.

'Don't play dumb.'

Jane smooths down the front of her dress, then touches the edge of her silly, plastic flower. She stands fully up and looks Ashleigh in the face.

'You and Pinko,' says Ashleigh. She shakes her head at her mother. 'I know.'

'Oh,' says Jane, dropping her shoulders. It must have been a journalist – although, usually they were really careful. Perhaps one of Pinko's staff – that night in the wine cellar – had snapped her with their phone and sold the picture. Jane had googled Pinko Stephens non-stop throughout his radio silence, and seen him frozen in the act of giving a Ted Talk, cutting an inauguration ribbon and standing, arms folded, in front of his massive mansion, but had never seen a picture of herself. 'How do you know?'

Ashleigh ignores the question. 'Why didn't you tell me?'

Jane remembers the time, looks around for her little chained handbag. 'I'm sorry, love, but I have to rush.'

'You know he's from a different world to us, don't you?'

'Yes, thanks very much, Ashleigh. Thank you,' Jane replies, putting eyeliner and lipstick into her bag.

'I thought we told each other stuff.'

Jane stops, gives Ashleigh a long look. 'Why do you think I didn't tell you?'

A shrug.

'You would have found it weird.'

For a nanosecond, Ashleigh seems panicked. She steels herself and adds, 'I *do* find it weird.'

'Well then,' says Jane. 'There you go.' She looks back into the mirror and adjusts the straps of her dress.

'Is that all you're going to say?' says Ashleigh.

Jane turns and stares at her, conscious of her eyes, spiky with mascara. 'How are you feeling?'

'You could've told me.'

'I didn't know it would go very far.'

'How far has it gone?'

'Ashleigh!'

'Do you love him?'

Jane pauses then says, 'No.' She picks up next door's royal blue stole. 'But honestly, at the moment, we need him.'

Ashleigh sits on the bottom stair and considers this. 'Pinko could get us out together,' she says. 'Is that what you're thinking?'

Jane stops fiddling with the stole and looks straight at Ashleigh. 'It's not a bad plan,' she says, 'is it?'

Ashleigh stands. She puts her hands behind her head and turns to face into the front room, to sigh, suck her teeth, all that moody teenager stuff, thinks Jane. Seconds later, she turns back and leans against the doorframe, smile hitched up on her cheek. It never fails to surprise Jane how Ashleigh can traverse a spectrum of emotions in just a few seconds.

'You look lovely, Mum,' she says.

Jane scoffs. 'Oh yeah?'

'Mm,' says Ashleigh. 'Is it a party, or something?'

'Gavin's exhibition.'

'Gavin?'

Fumbling in her bag, 'Yes, Gavin. He's an artist. I'm going to his opening exhibition.' She stops and frowns at Ashleigh. 'Unless you are still feeling ill, are you still feeling bad?'

Ashleigh shakes her head.

'Did you have some water?'

A nod.

'Did it help?'

A nod.

'Do you want me to stay?' Jane's gaze pings to the clock and back again.

'No.'

'Sure?'

A nod.

'Right.' Jane pulls Ashleigh's head to her lips. 'There is quiche in the fridge. Try to eat it.'

'Where did you get the dress?'

Jane is already walking down the stairs. 'Stole it,' she calls.

Jane waits at the bus stop.

Jane checks the time.

Jane pops back to the house next door, takes the bonsai tree.

Jane waits at the bus stop.

A long black car slides into the lay-by. Jane looks back at her house, up to the first-floor window, then gets in.

CHAPTER FORTY-NINE | August 2032
Pinko

Pinko is standing before the pine at the top of his stairs. Butler has done an awesome job of bringing all the bigwigs in for the unveiling. It turns out that more celebrities have stuck around than Pinko had first thought. Soon an audience of footballers, actors, TV presenters, entrepreneurs, musicians, writers, bankers – even a couple of jockeys are on the list – will be swanning about the roundhouse clutching glasses of Cristal. But before they venture across the garden to the round, hillside barn with its deep, light space and its wraparound terrace, everyone will gather in his hallway and observe the unveiling of the pine. It has been decided that Pinko will make a short speech, Gavin's mum will pull the cord.

Pinko smiles at the mural. It has surpassed his expectations. There is movement – of course – as if the tree is rotating its wrists, releasing loops of energy. The mural is in charcoal, yet somehow there is sunlight, a fierce kind of sunlight that renders the pine tree weary, the movement laboured, by dogged rotations, circles struggling like weighted bubbles. He almost doesn't notice Gavin shuffling up beside him.

'Don't forget to shut the curtain before the ceremony.'

Pinko jolts, looks at Gavin. 'How are you feeling?'

Gavin shrugs, a big grin opens up his face. 'It's all a bit grand,' he says. 'For me.'

Pinko turns back to the pine. 'You know, Gavin, I...' His words feel inadequate, so he fills his cheeks with air and blows it out slowly.

'Oh,' says Gavin. 'Thank you.'

'Wow, don't thank me; I should be thanking you. I mean, this is superb,' says Pinko, looking Gavin straight in the eye. 'It's even better than the real thing. And I love trees. That's a lot, coming from me.'

Gavin puts a hand over his heart, thanks him again. Then asks, 'How's your lady trouble?'

Pinko feels his face drop. 'Well…' he says. 'It's complicated.'

'Oh dear,' says Gavin.

Since the doctor came ten days ago, Pinko has messaged Jane once – the day before yesterday – in order to arrange her pick-up for the party. He winced as he pressed send, but she replied promptly, yes, she'd be there, and Pinko realised two things: a) Ashleigh hadn't told her and b) Jane hadn't found out. He didn't know if he was relieved, but ghosting her altogether while continuing to harass her daughter was simply not an option. Plus, Ashleigh had finally replied to his last message – about bringing them both to Finland – again, he didn't feel relieved, but as he sat in his father's office staring down the portrait of the old man, there was a sense that he was doing the right thing in a terrible situation. Especially as time most definitely wasn't on their side. Ashleigh told him to convince Jane, not her, to leave for Finland with him. That is what he plans to do later that evening. When the guests have left, he thinks, as his chest starts to feel hollow and panicky. No need to dwell on it.

'You know, Gavin, several curators have already shown interest. For overseas galleries, of course. I'll be patching them in via Zoom. We have some "ambulatory" guides; they'll be carrying screens between installations…'

Gavin squints, clearly stuck on 'ambulatory' or 'Zoom' and Pinko doesn't want to assume this and explain, so he pats him on the shoulder and says, 'It's all fine, Gavin, my…lady troubles. Thank you for asking. Let's enjoy your evening.'

Gavin looks at his feet for a moment, then straight back at Pinko. 'It's not though, is it?' he says. 'Once you get involved with someone *in that way*,' he says, and he is breathless and twitchy, licking his lips, 'the feeling afterwards is horrible. It stays with you for months. It makes you someone you don't wanna be.' Gavin's eyes are glassy now, and his breathing is quick and shallow. Pinko watches him and frowns.

'Gavin, it's okay, you're safe,' he says, stooping to look right into his eyes.

Gavin holds his stare.

'Deep breaths,' says Pinko.

Gavin does as he's told, bringing his shoulders right up as he breathes in.

'There's a lot to take in, isn't there, Bud?' says Pinko, indicating around him.

'Yeah. Yeah. I suppose there is.'

'What time's your mum getting here?'

Colour seeps back into Gavin's cheeks. He grins, checks his watch, realises he isn't wearing one, so he looks around him, then up at Pinko.

'Shall we see if she's downstairs?' says Pinko.

'Yeah,' says Gavin. 'Let's see if Mum's taxi arrived.'

CHAPTER FIFTY | August 2032
Jane

They are out on the large, curved gallery terrace with a view over the hills, down toward the turreted structure of a former windmill. Gavin has painted two enormous birches that are now propped up in the garden. The crowd is marvelling at the way the trees shiver, as if the wind is moving through them. Jane is very familiar with Gavin's work, but is still entranced by the movement of the trees. What's most striking about them is their size; they are as tall as real birches. She stands gazing at them, her heels millimetres from the rush-mat flooring, so as not to plunge between the weaves, but one heel keeps slipping – bugger – and the borrowed dress, twinkling and strappy, makes her shoulders cold. She hugs the gauzy stole around her to keep warm, but the sequins itch the soft insides of her arms. People keep asking her, 'Are you chilly?' And she shakes her head, releases her self-hug slightly. She wonders why she says no; there is, after all, no shame in being cold. No shame at all. But the other guests are producing pashminas and tiny leather jackets and Burberry ponchos and cashmere shrugs and just one of those items would cost her a month's rent; stupid weather forecast with its balmy evening. Stupid British weather. Then someone is talking to her.

'Oh, so you ride horses, interesting, I used to play polo – have you ever played?' and 'Do you breed them? Are they racers?'

She turns so that she is fully facing the owner of the voice, a tanned face with deep wrinkles and a tiny, landing-strip beard. She has been talking to him for a couple of minutes now and is glad he is making conversation – otherwise she'd be quite alone – but also wishes that he would go away.

'No, I just muck them out for people when they go on holiday.'

He lifts his eyebrows, as if genuinely interested. 'When will they leave?'

'Leave? What do you mean?'

'The UK, you know? Where's their bolt-hole? And yours, for that matter. Where will you go? The US?'

She frowns and says, 'I'm not sure I follow.'

'You know…When the water comes.'

'France. That's the only place I *can* go.'

The man looks away, takes a sip of champagne.

Perhaps she was a bit snappy… But these are not her people, thinks Jane, now standing higher on her tiptoes to catch a glimpse of Pinko, who has been largely absent, so far. He has to play the host, of course. She doesn't mind that at all, but she hasn't received so much as a quick half-wave from him since she got there. In the car, her brain had whizzed up images of her gliding about, her arm tucked under his. She looks down at her dress, her white arms puckering in the cold. Perhaps he isn't that keen, now that she is stood here side to side with all his elegant friends. Perhaps she looks overdressed and cheap.

'I like your petunia.' A woman pitches into the conversation, grinning at Jane's right ear. She is wrapped in a shawl with a gold lozenge-shaped brooch. She takes a swig of champagne and says, 'I'm off to Prague.'

'Really? Do you have dual-nationality?' asks landing-strip.

'No! But we are fond of Prague.'

'That must have cost you a pretty penny.'

'Six-figure,' she says, adjusting her pashmina. 'Almost seven.'

'I think that's quite normal,' pipes up a young man with shorts and converse, messy ringlets and a Rolex. 'Krakow was a fortune.'

'Oh, I have friends going there,' says Prague.

'Really? Have they found a house, yet? We're struggling, at the moment. Can't find anything with room for a tennis court and Milly's getting quite good, now – aren't you?' he says, putting his arm around a young girl in headphones.

'They say that Richard paid over twenty million,' says Prague.

'Richard who?' says landing-strip.

'Raymont.'

'Doesn't surprise me at all.'

'Where's he going?' asks ringlets and Rolex.

'Moscow.'

The whole group gasps and coos.

'Yes, but he's got dual nationality, hasn't he?'

'No,' says ringlets and Rolex. 'His wife has.'

'Oh yes, I knew it was something like that...'

Prague turns to Jane. 'What about Pinko?'

This heartens Jane. She has no desire to find out how these people are going to pay their way out of an unparalleled natural disaster, while the proles are forced to fuck in front of an immigration jury. The fact that this lady, Prague, assumes that Jane knows more about Pinko than the rest of them means that there is hope for her, at least.

'I'm not sure, to be honest,' she lies.

'Finland,' says ringlets and Rolex. 'What? Well go off and ask if he'll change the music,' he adds to the girl with the headphones, patting her on the bum and rolling his eyes at the group.

'Oh, Finland?' says Prague. 'I read that it's the safest place in Europe, right now.'

'Yes,' says Jane. 'Apart from the bears and wolves.' They titter, showing rows of porcelain veneers. 'I won't be sending the horses there, I can tell you...' she says to landing-strip. Again, laughter.

Pinko draws up beside her and hands her a glass of deep, golden champagne. 'What's so funny?' he asks, wrapping a thicker blanket over her shoulders. Jack Wills, nothing too flash, finally. Her bottom lip trembles, either from his kindness or the fact that she clearly doesn't fit in. This is her third glass of champagne and she is longing to tell him how annoying these people are.

He says, 'Sorry, I got caught just over there, ten feet away; it seems like someone wanted to chat to me at each stage of my journey back to you.' He smiles. 'Are you okay?'

She opens her mouth to reply. Ringlets and Rolex jumps in.

'So, you're going to Finland, Pinkster? Lucky bastard.'

'Yes, alright for some,' adds someone else.

Jane notes that Prague has pinched her lips into the shape of a dog's anus and is staring at them, Jane and Pinko, appraising their body language, figuring out how together they are.

Pinko fumbles a reply, chuckling slightly and scratching the back of his head.

Jane narrows her eyes, takes a large sip of champagne and says, 'He's not really *lucky*, is he? He's the heir to a multi-million-pound

Finnish timber enterprise.'

The others stare for a moment, then dissolve into laughter. Pinko continues to stare. Jane drains her glass, smirks at them all, then catches Pinko's eye. He twitches his gaze elsewhere and sips his drink.

While the group continues its conversation, she leans closer to him. 'I've had one text from you in two weeks,' she says, even though her reasonable, sober side is pleading with her to shut up. 'And you left instructions for me to adopt a dog and a hedgehog...'

He looks confused for a moment, before bringing a hand to his cheek. 'Oh Christ, you mean the pug. I completely forgot.'

Jane takes this in, folds her lips inwards. Then she says, 'We didn't quite make it, did we?'

His eyebrows collapse and his mouth falls open. He is about to reply, when a large man in a houndstooth suit strides over and throws his arms around him. Jane observes as Pinko's face changes from startled deer to confident fox. Houndstooth holds Pinko by the shoulders and beams at him, completely ignoring Jane. They exchange pleasantries, before Pinko is swept off into another group.

Now a different man appears next to her, with a collarless, striped shirt. He has been lingering in her peripheral for a while, also quite alone, sipping from a long, narrow glass of orange juice. He stoops to mutter in her ear, 'I'm just heading inland. Taking my family.'

'Gavin,' she says, recognising his voice from Pinko's promotional videos. 'It's an honour to meet you.' She puts out her hand and he returns his with a fist bump. 'Your work is amazing; you are so talented.'

He dips his chin, pushes his free hand into his pocket. 'Thanks.'

'And congratulations on the exhibition. It's quite something.'

'Cheers,' he says, glancing about him in a way that suggests he agrees.

Someone normal, she thinks. Thank Christ for that. She smiles at him as if he is a long-missed relative, before asking, 'So, where are you going?'

He gapes his eyes, looks about his feet. 'Nowhere.'

'I mean, you said you want to move inland?'

'Oh,' he says, 'Nuneaton. Googled it. It's the place furthest from the sea.'

Jane grins. 'With your family?'

'Yes, I've bought a house and everything. I bought it for my mum, really,' he says, patting at his own cheek and looking at his fingers. 'It's starting to rain, do you wanna go inside? My mum's in there. I'll introduce you.'

'Yes,' Jane says, tilting her head towards the terrace doors. 'Let's go and meet your mum.'

As they walk back into the gallery, she takes another flute from the champagne waiter, catches Pinko's eye as he stands listening to the houndstooth man. He blinks at Jane and looks away.

CHAPTER FIFTY-ONE | August 2032
Gillian

The gallery is a vessel for light. It holds it in and swills it about, splashes it over sleeves and high chignons, backs of legs and glasses. Many of the people here have high chignons and glasses. It's a thing that artsy people do. She has attended so many at photography exhibitions. The women, especially, twist back their hair without pinning it and dress up their faces with glasses and glowing skin. No make-up. Only jagged necklaces and matching cheekbones. Baggy, slash-neck dresses skimming quartz-smooth knees. Gillian's mum always told her she had wide, fleshy feet. A detail she forgot when she threw on her flip-flops and raced out the door, this evening. Though, she took the time to enhance the scar above her eye with light-coffee lipstick. Now, she moves towards the bench at the centre of the room and hides her feet underneath it.

The light, she thinks, should be neutralised somehow, shouldn't it? Surely the artist intended their work to be viewed under a particular light; all this whiteness was a bit rebellious. A bit *anarchic*. But then, it is a sunny evening, the seventh or eighth in a row, now.

She stands at the window for the longest time, staring at a turret that sticks through the trees like a firework poised in the grass. Very unwindmill-like, considering it's a windmill, she thinks. Way too fancy and aloof. She reaches for her camera, but lands her hand on her sternum. Shit − she left it at home − never mind. She's not really here to take photos. She turns towards the largest of the indoor canvases, spreading upwards all the way to the ceiling. A portrait of a pine. The light tangles in its needles, the branches quiver towards its core, sink and rise at the ends. She darts her eyes all about it and wonders where it will go? Where will they all go when the water comes? She turns about; a waiter offers her a flute of champagne, she refuses it, *no thank you*; he glances at her jeans, her gold flips-flops, smiles and leaves. Again, she hides her feet underneath the bench, folds her arms and peeks about. The waiter didn't seem to notice her scar. Pinko Stephens stands on the opposite side of the gallery, holding a woman's hand. To the left a group of chignons, men and women, scratch their chins while contemplating a triptych of willow branches.

'Is it...you?'

She startles. Gavin stands beside her in a collarless stripy shirt, hair held back by sunglasses.

'It *is* you!' Then laughter, he laughs. 'This is amazing! I feel, forgiven. I...' His face drops when he sees her scar.

She lets him take it in, before saying, 'It's taken a while to heal, but it's getting there.'

'But that was months ago,' he says, reaching out a hand to touch the scar, then retracting it just as quickly. His mouth hangs open for a while, before he says, 'Oh my God. I am so, so...'

A small woman wobbles up to them, glasses hanging from a chain around her neck, blonde bob set into the shape of a cycling helmet.

'Everything alright, love?' says the woman, smiling up at Gavin.

'Um,' says Gavin. 'Mum, this is...'

'Gillian,' says Gillian, putting out her hand.

'Yes, Gillian,' says Gavin. 'She's, erm, well...she's...'

'An old friend,' Gillian rescues him. 'You must be very proud.'

'Oh...' says Gavin's mum, hand to her chest, 'You can't imagine...' She puts her head on one side, shakes it softly. 'You can't imagine, Gillian.'

'Well, Gavin, I'm going to finish looking at your work,' says Gillian, gesturing around her. 'Perhaps we can catch up afterwards?'

'Yeah,' Gavin nods. 'I'll stick around. Don't you worry.'

She sits on the bench in the centre of the room, until the gallery empties out. People walk past her, at first staring at her jeans, after a while not staring or even looking. They smile and chug back the free champagne. Pinko Stephens catches her eye, nods at her, holds his glass up to her and taps at it, does she want any? She smiles, shakes her head. When there is only a handful of people left, Pinko's date comes and sits next to her. In her thirties, perhaps, night-blue cocktail dress. 'Hi,' she says, sitting down.

'Are you waiting for someone?'

'Kind of.' Gillian looks away, aware that she has no invitation, no chequebook. No dress.

The woman nudges her and says with hot, boozy breath, 'I wish I'd opted for jeans.'

Gillian runs a hand over her knees.

'It's like being in fairyland, isn't it?' says the woman.

'The trees, yes, beautiful.'

'No, I mean all these dumb...people.'

Gillian frowns. 'I don't really know anyone here...'

'They just have no idea what's going on out there,' she says, gesturing towards the balcony with her champagne flute.

A few people turn and look at the woman. She has clearly been enjoying the free champagne and is quite loud, gobby even. Gillian lets her eyes linger on a floor-length, spider-webby cocktail dress.

'Well,' she says, in a quieter voice, hoping to bring the woman down to her level. 'I admit I was wondering about the point of it all.'

'They're going to ship it all off in a few days.'

'Really, where to?'

'Finland.'

'Finland?' Gillian gives a slow nod. 'Lucky paintings.'

Gillian looks around her. Trees bend, flicker, wave, dapple the sunlight drawn around them; they hunch under the rain and lean into the wind. Her gaze stops on a silver birch; she would like to put her thumb on the bark to feel its scabby texture, but no, it will of course be smooth.

The woman drains her glass, is still swallowing but manages to ask, 'Where will you go?'

'What do you mean?' says Gillian.

'When the... You know...'

'I have to get to France,' she says, perhaps a little too forcefully.

The woman travels her gaze up to Gillian's scar, then down to her hand. 'You're not married.'

'All the men in my village have left,' says Gillian, twisting her fingers together. 'Only the elderly remain. And me.'

The woman frowns. 'Have you tried to find someone to go

with you? You know, online?'

Gillian looks Jane straight in the eye. 'I've been scammed three times in as many months,' she says. 'They claim to pay for everything – tickets, paperwork, all that – and once I've paid them my half, they ghost me.' Her cheeks are trembling; she drops her gaze. 'So now I'm skint.'

The woman says nothing for a moment. 'Is that really happening?'

'I'm an idiot, I know.' Gillian smirks. 'My sister is in France. With her husband and my nephews. I just need to be with them.'

'Can your sister send you money?'

'I'd never ask. She paid enough to get there.'

'And she had to... You know. In front of the jury...'

'With her husband, yes.'

'Was it easy?'

Gillian scoffs, 'As far as I know, it was horrible.'

'No, I mean to pass. To get accepted.'

'I think so. I think she was accepted straight away.'

The woman blinks. 'How humane is it,' she says, 'to make people go to such ridiculous lengths for asylum?'

'In my opinion,' says Gillian, 'they are testing us for passivity. For obedience.'

Gillian tails off as Pinko appears beside them. He has slipped his grasp around the woman's elbow and is indicating that she should stand up. Gillian watches the woman stand and look at him, nose to nose.

'We need to talk,' he says, close to her ear. 'If you have a minute.'

Everybody watches as he leads her out to the terrace. Some look at each other, then scurry after them to see the conversation unfold. Gillian stays on the bench, feeling more exposed in her jeans and flip-flops now the woman isn't there to shield one side of her.

'All done,' Gavin approaches, hands in his pockets. 'I sent Mum off in a Taxi. We can have a proper chat now.'

Gillian keeps her eyes on Jane. 'Okay, great,' she says, standing up.

'And thank you for, you know,' he lowers his voice, 'being *discreet.*'

'That's okay,' she says, pulling a lock of hair away from her scar and behind her ear. 'Is there somewhere we can go?'

'Yeah,' he says, his eyes fixed on her scar. 'Do you wanna go into the garden? It's not raining anymore.'

She nods.

CHAPTER FIFTY-TWO | August 2032
Gavin

Gavin smiles at Gillian; what a nice name she has. You don't hear that name so much these days, he thinks to himself. She is all dressed for summer in her jeans and her sparkly flip-flops, but her shoulders are hunched and her arms crossed around her stomach, exactly the way he remembers her in a thick duffel coat at the car-boot that day. And that scar. He can't stop looking at it. It's not like it was his fault, but... His mind flashes to the moment he handed Officer Wayne her camera. Perhaps if he hadn't nicked it, perhaps if he'd gone over to her instead, helped her get some ice on the cut, it wouldn't be as bad now. Gillian frowns at him now. Gavin realises it's because he's stopped smiling and is staring at her scar.

'Thank you for coming,' he says. 'It's really cool to see you.'

She twitches her toffee eyes about like she's a bit embarrassed. She looks nice when she does that; her eyes glitter in the light to match her flip-flops. Gavin reckons he would have considered her quite pretty. But such a weird thing happened to him since they last met. He presses his eyelids into a strong blink. No point thinking about that now, he tells himself, although his skin has gone all itchy.

'I don't want you to think I came for the exhibition,' she says, 'I mean, it's lovely and everything.' She exhales. 'You're very talented.'

'Thanks.'

'But...' She folds her lips in, stares down at her toes.

'What?'

She takes a deep breath and looks straight at him. 'I need you to help me get over to France.'

Gavin gawks at her, shoves his hands in his pockets. 'But...I... can't do that. I'm not, like, influential.'

'No. I didn't mean that.'

'Just because I'm here,' he says, gesturing around him, 'doesn't mean I'm high up or anything.'

'Yes, but...'

'And you know I would, you *know* I would. After pinching your camera.'

'Exactly.' She tents her eyebrows and says, 'You kinda owe me.'

Gavin freezes, holds her stare. 'I can give you money,' he says, his throat dry. 'I've got loads. How much do you want?'

She seems surprised for a moment, then says. 'Money doesn't guarantee anything. I'd need to be super-rich, like this lot.' She indicates around her, even though the terrace is empty. 'I need help.'

He sinks his brow and looks out across the gardens to the pair of full-sized tree portraits. They didn't sell today, but he's made a mint on some of the smaller pieces. He doesn't know how much; Butler scooted past him earlier in the evening and told him they'd sold loads. But he'd never be stupidly loaded like Pinko and his mates. They were super-rich, like, squillions getting dusty in the bank.

Then she says, 'I was thinking that you could come with me. You know, to customs.'

Gavin frowns. What was she asking for, he thinks to himself. A lift? Did she just need a lift down to Dover? He wasn't a driver anymore, but Ryan could certainly drop her off, no problem. His mum might even pack her up a lunch. Egg and cress sandwich with a bit of mustard in the mayonnaise. That was a winner every time. 'Do you need a lift to Dover?'

She looks serious. 'I mean, to see the Jury.'

He squints at her. What jury? Is she in trouble, or what?

Then, he realises.

The immigration jury over in France. It dawns on him, what it is she wants, and his stomach falls into his legs. 'You want me to do...that.'

She closes one eye to the setting sun and nods up at him.

'But...' He gulps, looks for an excuse. 'I'm moving to Nuneaton. I don't want to go to France.'

Her gaze deflates, then dims as she turns away from the light.

It comes back to him again, the weird thing that happened. With all that skin and hair and he didn't like what it made his face do – he must have looked like a chimp. Or a frog. He shuts his eyes. Puts his hands over them.

'You left me that day,' she says, but her voice is sad, not cross.

He doesn't even remember her falling. Only that she was plodding along the strip of beach where the pebbles are more like rocks, and he glanced at her camera, sitting nose-up on a fleecy blanket. When he looked up, she was prone on the pebbles, like a sleeping seal. He wanted to call out, but he'd already made up his mind that he would take her camera. For some money, he thinks now, some money for his mum. It had been a whole month since they'd had a roast. After a minute or so, she got up, clutching her head, dusting herself down with the other hand. That's when he legged it up the beach with her camera. She's right, he *does* owe her. And it should be such a simple thing to do. It seemed to be for other people, anyway.

He says, 'I wanna help, but I'm not too good with...ladies...you know, down there,' he says, splaying a hand towards her crotch, then covering his eyes up again.

She bites her lip and seems to think for a moment. 'I've run out of options.'

He nods at her predicament, paces on the spot, then says, 'What about a policeman?'

'A policeman?'

'I heard that the police are gonna be some of the last to leave. There's probably a whole bunch of them in the same boat as you.'

Gillian blinks. Lets her mouth fall open.

'And, and, they can't ask *you* can they? It wouldn't be right. It would be pervy. Especially with their being policemen.'

She shakes her head. 'I'm not going to ask a policeman.'

Gavin is now holding the side of his head, elbows out. 'Well, I don't know,' he says. 'I just don't *know.*' If only she'd accept some money, that would be so much easier.

'It's weird that you're the only person I trust, right now.' She breathes out through pursed lips, as if encouraging him to do the same. 'Calm down,' she says. 'It's okay.'

'No, it's not. I owe you all of this,' he says, turning with his arm out. 'All of this is because of you. Because you chose to let me off the hook.' And it's true. He knows it's true. 'Why can't you just accept money?'

'Look, I didn't come here to take your money. I thought you might want to help me out.' She sighs and turns away. 'Forget about it. It's a big ask.'

He is pacing about now, holding his elbows. 'I could give you two hundred grand. You could bribe your way over.'

She is quiet for a moment. 'It's okay. Seriously, don't worry.' She knits her fingers, smiles down at them.

They stand in silence. Gillian wanders to the edge of the terrace and looks out over the empty gardens. Gavin stares at her toenails. They are orange with a belt of tiny gems down by the cuticles. She has a toe ring on her middle toe and an anklet – Pandora, looks like – just below the hem of her jeans. They are very nice toes. Watching them calms him right down. He wonders, if he concentrated on her toes, he'd be able to do what she was asking him to do. Perhaps he needs to take his time, get used to all the bits and pieces that make up a body, before getting so close to it.

'I need to...' he says.

'I'll get a taxi home.' She looks around. 'I'll probably just wait out on the road.'

'I need to have a think about it. If there was some way of getting you over there, then coming *back* again, to Nuneaton...'

She blinks, her eyes twinkly again. 'Really?' she says, wringing her hands.

'Then I would do it. If I'm able to.' He winces, jumps his shoulder as his body twitches. 'But, I'd really have to go slowly.'

'Yes,' she says. 'I mean, we could practise.' She stutters a bit over the 'p' in practise, and he realises that she's scared too.

'I'd have to come back,' he says. 'I won't live with you in France.'

'Yes, yes...Absolutely. You could get back easily. There are no restrictions back into the UK.'

Gavin nods. He didn't know that. He's had no reason to find out. He screws up his face, looking from the gallery to Gillian and back again. 'I want to help you. I do. I really do.'

CHAPTER FIFTY-THREE | August 2032
Ashleigh

Jane's foot slips into the car, followed by a wisp of dress and she is gone, zoomed away into a shimmer of cool, fuzzy air.

Ashleigh spreads her hands over her stomach and looks around her room, her eyes leaping from lamp to pillow to picture frame to knee-length jumper. Oh yes, she would definitely take the jumper. It would rise with her bump, might even hide it for a while. She drums her stomach with her flat hands, wonders about punching it, wonders about falling onto something – a bed post perhaps? Or down the stairs?

But then she thinks of its little toenails. She read on the internet that it would have them already, tiny and see-through like sweetcorn skin.

She walks down the stairs, takes a bottle of water and goes back up again. Her bed is scratchy and smells like cold vomit. She arranges the duvet up around her, pulls Big Ted close to her nose and shuts her eyes.

A buzz and a ping wake her up. A text message – who would message her now? She reaches around Big Ted and takes her phone just as the front door clicks shut. It's 10:30.

'Ashleigh?'

Her name comes singing up the stairs, followed by a light thud.

Mum is tipsy, she thinks as she reads the message. Pinko. Again. *I talked to Jane. It's all sorted.*

Ashleigh wipes her mouth and breathes into Big Ted.

'Ashleigh!'

'I'm awake.'

She sits up and waits for all the waves inside her to be flat and still. Then she pads down the stairs, stopping halfway, as her vision blurs. She blinks, takes a breath and continues. Jane has put the kettle on and now has her head in the fridge. She looks up, eyes rolling a bit, and accuses her of not eating the last slice of quiche. Ashleigh drags a chair out, sits on it.

'How was your evening, Mum?'

Jane bites her lip, and lets her gaze fall to the side in a girlish way – or a drunk way – Ashleigh can't tell which. Probably drunk. She takes the milk from the door, shuts the fridge and steps backwards, treading on her dress that is too long for her now she's not wearing heels.

'Me and Pinko,' she says, 'have made some plans.' She puts the milk back in the fridge without adding it to her tea and takes the quiche. 'Big plans, in fact,' she says, removing the clingfilm and putting the plate on the table.

'Oh yeah?' says Ashleigh.

'Pinko has suggested – since we get along so well – that we try to see where this thing is going, potentially. That under normal circumstances it would develop on its own – this thing – but we're currently under a bit of pressure, aren't we?' she says. 'Do you see what I mean, Ashleigh?'

Ashleigh nods, eyes wide, fingers fiddling. So, it will happen, she thinks to herself. They will travel to Finland. Together. Her shoulders fall, just a little bit, and her breathing slows. Now it's official, she can properly work out how she feels about it. Her mum is grinning, she grins back. She hadn't expected to feel relaxed, or, somewhere near happy even.

'So, is he taking us to Finland then?' asks Ashleigh.

Jane's face falls, and for a second Ashleigh is worried that she's misunderstood. Jane leans against the edge of the table. 'You've ruined my good news,' she says, splaying her hands. 'I was so looking forward to telling you.'

Ashleigh laughs. 'Why are you so drunk?'

'Huh,' says Jane. 'Free fizz.'

'Right,' she replies, smiling. She pulls out another chair and pats the seat for Jane to come and sit down. 'Go on then Mum, tell me your news. I'll act surprised.'

Jane grins, sits on the chair, and does exactly that.

What Pinko is suggesting is that they move to Finland – all three of them – and live in one of his cabins – she and Ashleigh, just the two of them – and then at least they'll have more of a chance to get this thing off the ground. More so than if she went to France. It would certainly all end if she went to France. But, importantly, Ashleigh wouldn't have to go to France on her own, would she? And she and Jane won't have to be apart, will they?

Ashleigh is listening, but thinking about the little, sweetcorn fingernails in her belly, the tiny limbs and fluttering heartbeat. Tears pool on her waterline. All the exercise, starvation, hot baths and dark, dark thoughts, oh God...

Jane is still talking. Ashleigh nods. Sniffs. Puts a hand over her stomach. She's probably damaged it. It's so small and fragile.

'And if it all goes wrong,' says Jane, 'he said we could still stay. He said the cabin would be ours forever if we were happy there.'

Ashleigh starts to cry, rubs at both of her eyes with balled hands like a baby.

Jane stops talking, reaches over to her, 'What's wrong, darling?'

Ashleigh's body stiffens and rocks. She leans forwards and cries into her knees.

'Ashleigh, what's wrong? What's wrong, what's wrong?'

'I'm hungry,' she says, sitting up and pulling the quiche towards her. 'I'm so hungry.'

CHAPTER FIFTY-FOUR | August 2032
Jane

It worked. Thank God and all that is good.

Jane strokes the sequins, considers pinning a note of thanks to the dress, but the pin would make a hole in the chiffon. A card, perhaps? A little envelope in the bottom of the wardrobe? She folds the stole and hangs it over the rung of the hanger, between the straps of the dress. No, no card. Why leave a card for them to find in years to come, in the tumbling remains of their sodden house. And what would she write? *With love from Finland.* That would be unfair. And very smug.

Smug. Manipulative. Gold-digging, even. How does she feel about that now? Does she sit well in that saddle? Jane holds either side of her head with her hands, closes her eyes to read the memory again. She fast-forwards through her loud, drunken outbursts to the part where almost everyone had left the gallery and he approached, eyes flashing, and pulled her up from the bench. *Let's go outside, now Jane. Let's talk in private...*But no! *Why don't you just say it, Pinko?* But he led her towards the terrace, before admitting in a low voice, right to a rumble, *I know I have been very elusive but* – and cupped her other elbow and pulled her outside...

She had honestly believed she was being ejected. So she lost it, a little bit.

'Elusive? I'm living by a completely different set of rules, Pinko,' she said, 'I have the threat of that mega-tsunami just around the corner. This is life or death for me; I don't have the luxury of taking refuge in a different part of myself. And I *know*,' she said, 'I *get* that this is a weird situation and it's all so fast but,' she held up a finger, 'but what am I supposed to think? We can't pretend the water won't come. And by not talking about it...well...' Her voice had started to catch then. The back of her throat jumped and narrowed and she took a minute to gather herself. He didn't interrupt. He waited for her to continue, even though there were people listening and she really was very loud. 'Pinko, you, well, *we* are trapped in tunnels that are veering in different directions. We are...This is...' And for some reason, she brought herself down to a whisper. 'You are in control here,' she said, and she hadn't realised just how tiny she'd made her voice, until he boomed out over the gallery.

'I'd like to take you to Finland. With your daughter.'

Jane blinked, her elbows frozen inside his hands. 'My...' she said, trying to look confused. 'Who?'

'Ashleigh,' he said. 'I'd like to take you both.'

Thinking about it now, as she sits in her neighbour's empty house, safe in the knowledge that she will not suffer their fate, makes her soul soar. She twinkled blinks all over him, then the tears surfaced and spilled and poured and dripped and her face was wet against his lapel and his hand was on the back of her head and there was tapping, then clapping, then applause, and camera flashing and cheers and...

And it wasn't even a dream.

Now she hangs the little pouch of lavender over the hanger – exactly as she found it – zips the dress inside its cover and shuts it back in the wardrobe.

'Thank you,' she whispers into the room.

CHAPTER FIFTY-FIVE | August 2032
Pinko

Pinko is overseeing the last shipment of Gavin's paintings. The exhibition didn't do as well as he'd hoped. The UK based curators shrugged their shoulders at him, told him the work was undeniably good, but they'd have to wait until 'afterwards'. Those with international galleries snapped up the easily transportable canvases. A few private buyers bought the big ones. The rest – including the life-sized trees – would go with Pinko to Finland.

Of course, Gavin will have made at least four million, perhaps four and a half. He is an extraordinary talent and Pinko has the right contacts to stir up sufficient hype. So now he leans against the barrier on the roundhouse terrace, watching as his team dismantles the tree-size canvasses down in the grounds. More pressing issues return to him for the first time since last night, when he took a large sleeping pill and washed it down with single malt.

What do you do, he asks himself, when you are a young man who has made a young woman pregnant then inadvertently fallen in love with her mother – who doesn't know that the young girl is pregnant or even that she's slept with you – and you have promised said mother that you will elope with her? Oh, and the world is on the verge of disaster, so the situation is quite pressing.

Hmm…

Butler calls up to him. 'Are these for the next shipment, yeah?'

Pinko confirms this with a nod and an upward thumb, then returns to his thoughts.

She *has* been fibbing though, Jane; she never said she had a daughter, *ahem*, a twenty-two-year-old daughter. Which means she's definitely been fibbing about her age. That would make her almost forty years old. Although, she can't be older than that. No. Her skin is too plump, her neck too smooth. But, of course, he'll forgive her those fibs. She is certainly not the one at fault in this situation.

Also, if Jane *was* telling the truth about her age and *did* have Ashleigh when she was thirteen, there was almost certainly some horrific past event that she didn't want to talk about.

So that's one thing. Jane is one thing.

Then there's the other thing. The unborn baby, *his* baby. There is absolutely no way that he'll walk away from that situation. So, abandoning Jane to make her way to France is now not an option. Where Ashleigh goes, Jane will go. At some point, therefore, Jane will have to know the truth.

Pinko rests his forearms on the wooden barrier, knits his fingers, looks out over his land as the jade green gardens swell and fall away into the dark, dense wood. He sighs. The water won't cover all of this, surely?

The walk back to the main house is too fleeting, across the large lawn, past the walled garden and up towards the swimming pool. It doesn't matter, he thinks, as the urge for a dram propels him. He will be gone soon and it will have to fend for itself, all of it. He slips through the patio doors and across the living room. But one day, way in the future, he would like to bring his child back here and show them the decimated remains of their grandfather's legacy: their inheritance.

He passes the bar, crosses the hallway and heads along the corridor to his father's office.

So, this is the most favourable plan thus far, he thinks, as he retrieves a cut crystal tumbler from the glass cabinet. He takes Jane and Ashleigh to Finland, Ashleigh never divulges the true identity of the father of her baby, he tells Jane he can't continue their relationship (for some reason he hasn't thought of yet) and supports the child forever more.

This idea could work. He looks up at the portrait of his father, gives him a stiff nod and gulps back two fingers of Lagavulin.

However, he thinks, while gurning the whiskey down, the most probable outcome, if he puts this plan in motion, is this: Jane finds out that he's the father and hates him forever more.

The whiskey pushes the blood into his cheeks, tears into his eyes.

Fine, he thinks, shaking out his shoulders, pouring another two fingers. Yes, fine. So be it.

But this is the thing that has to happen, he thinks, pointing up at the portrait as if he's in conversation with it. Jane and Ashleigh must come to Finland. Once they are there, they will find it difficult to leave. At least he can ensure that the child is provided for. He raises the glass again, tips the contents into his mouth. Swallows.

He'll have done right by the baby. He can be sure of that.

(Another two fingers.)

But he'll lose Jane.

PART FOUR
THE CRISIS

CHAPTER FIFTY-SIX | August 2032
Jane

Jane is sitting on her sofa, flicking through a wallpaper catalogue. She is leaning right back into the cushions with her feet up on the coffee table, feeling a little guilty at the frivolity of it all. Pinko has earmarked several pages – from previous interior renovations, no doubt – and it makes Jane smile when she notices the 'round' designs, circles, spirals, spheres or particularly bulbous or circular flowers; gerberas, peonies, dahlias and sunflowers. She hasn't seen him since the party and, ordinarily, she would be concerned about this, were she not building up to a Serious Conversation with Ashleigh.

Jane takes a deep breath and turns the page. This week had seen a steady delivery of decor catalogues and immigration documents to her house. Then, of course, the shipment boxes (they turned up yesterday), Paris's passport, and a whole pile of sandbags to stack against the front and back door. It's safe to say that she is definitely going to Finland, she thinks, but he seems less keen on *her*. He answers whenever she rings and replies to her texts. He mentioned something about feeling quite sad, leaving everything behind, and that the reality of the situation had probably only just hit him. Fine, she thinks, as she glances over a William Morris print. She got what she needed from this, so much more than she needed, in fact. But she hadn't expected to miss him quite so much.

'Mum!'

Jane looks towards the hallway and calls, 'What?'

'There's no ice!'

Jane rolls her eyes, turns the page. 'You ate it all, Ash.' She cocks her ear for a reply, but there is none.

Whenever Jane's phone buzzes, she feels a surge of heat in her stomach. It's a feeling that reminds her of a distant time, when she had a crush on someone at school or when she first met Ashleigh's dad. The feeling intensifies with each buzz but, sadly, the texts are rarely from him. Often, it's the network provider or some sort of scam. Sometimes, his PA. She fixates on the moment he saw her naked in London, the way he jumped his gaze from her to the bed, then swept the duvet around her as if to hide her inside it. She's had a wrinkly belly lip ever since Ashleigh was born. Now, she puts her hand to the loose skin, pinches it between her fingers. But, no, stop it, she says to herself. The world is ending. He's allowed to withdraw. These feelings are overwhelming, unreasonable. The bottom line is that she and Ashleigh are among the 0.5% of the population who are escaping to Finland. Fact.

Ashleigh appears at the door. 'Is there a quick way of making ice?'

Jane looks up. 'There were two trays in the freezer; have you really eaten it all?'

Ashleigh holds her head in her hands and groans, then flings her fingers towards Jane, looks at her with laser-beam, demon eyes. 'Can you not just answer my question?' she says.

'No,' says Jane, turning another page. 'You have to let it solidify. Could take a couple of hours.'

Ashleigh turns and leaves. Jane has heard some parents refer to this behaviour as 'sass'. Jane thinks she is rude, surging with hormones and struggling with food cravings. Although the vomiting has subsided, it has left a ravenous monster behind. Jane has been pleased to catch her on more than one occasion chomping her way through a Snickers or a jar of Lotus spread. At least she's eating, but the Serious Conversation is long overdue. Jane puts the magazine down, starts to stand up. When faced with being separated from one's child, anything else becomes a minor obstacle. As she thinks this, her thoughts jump from Ashleigh's bellybutton to Ashleigh's womb, to Ashleigh's baby, to the shiny, drunk penis that put it there. Something zings through her arms to the ends of her fingertips. No, thinks Jane. I cannot manage the truth until I know we're safe.

Jane puts down the magazine, shakes out her hands. 'There's sorbet in the freezer,' she calls up the stairs. 'I managed to get it yesterday.'

'Found it,' comes the response. 'Ate it.'

A whole tub?

Last week, this detail would have made her shudder. This week, it makes her curious. Cold, tart fruit had been Jane's thing too. Raspberries from the freezer; just as well, really, as she could only ever afford frozen, not fresh.

There were plenty of other familiar tells. Ashleigh snaps when she's too hot, fanning her face with her hands and darting for an open window, telling Jane it's hot, so fucking hot that she would just rip the fucking skin from her chest and run it under the cold tap.

So that's always nice to hear.

Then there's the retching, usually when Jane is cooking something salty or spicy; in fact, sometimes Jane does it on purpose just to look over at her, see her mouth open, her tongue jump like that of a honking calf.

But the most obvious detail is the empty hygiene bin in the bathroom, month in, month out. The unopened packet of sanitary towels. The bright-clean dirty underwear.

Now Ashleigh appears at the top of the stairs, walks down the first three steps and sits. Jane looks on, surprised at this desire to be so close to her mother without shouting.

'I haven't been to the loo for four days,' she announces.

'Why do you think that is?' says Jane.

Ashleigh shrugs. 'How should I know?' she says. 'I've got tummy pains.'

Jane blinks, stares.

'Mum, you're being weird.'

'Water,' says Jane. 'Two litres. Now. And fibre. You need to eat more than just ice-cream.'

'Sorbet,' corrects Ashleigh.

Yes, sorbet. There have been nightly visits to the freezer for the sourest of sorbets – lemon and lime – and she threw a fit when she went to the corner shop on Monday, to see it had been closed indefinitely. Yet, by Tuesday, she had procured another tub.

'Where did you get *that* tub, then?' Jane had asked.

To which Ashleigh had replied, 'The freezers are still fucking on, aren't they?'

'You stole it?'

'Yes.'

'Well, wasn't the shop locked?'

'Yes. And what?'

Jane gaped at her. 'That's theft.'

'Wasn't the neighbour's house locked when you stole that fucking dress?'

Jane had pursed her lips. 'Is there a problem that you'd like to discuss?' she said, making her eyebrows high and defiant.

Ashleigh retracted her arms, folded them around her, pulled the sorbet into the belly of her hoodie and bent her shoulders around it. 'Going upstairs.' And she went.

Jane observes her now, thinks about the way she keeps spreading her hands over her belly; one or both, side by side or one over the other, standing sidelong in front of windows or mirrors, darting her gaze downwards, pretending to fiddle with her buttons when Jane sees.

'We don't have any veg,' says Ashleigh now. 'For fibre.'

'There's cereal,' says Jane.

Ashleigh scrunches up her face. She's never liked cereal.

'Fine, I'll pop out,' says Jane. 'You could do with some vitamin supplements too.' Then she tries a question, just to see her reaction. 'Have you got enough tampons?'

Ashleigh looks a bit startled, rubs her chin with her shoulder. 'Yes,' she says, then: 'Actually, no. Could you get me some?'

Jane drives to the edges of town, to B&M of all places. Not really a supermarket, but it's the only foodstuffs shop around that's a) still open b) queue free. Just as she thinks this, the purple and orange starburst sign comes into view. Below it, a line of around fifty people snakes along the pavement and into the carpark of the next unit. Jane considers queuing for cereal and unnecessary tampons, then turns the car around and heads home.

When Jane gets home, Ashleigh is in bed. She pokes her head up, arches her brows. 'You were quick,' she says through the duvet.

Jane strides in and shuts Ashleigh's wardrobe doors, bends to pick a bath towel off the floor. 'Massive queues at B&M,' she says,

'No cereal, then?'

Jane stands fully up, puts her hand on her hip. 'Nope. Or tampons.'

Ashleigh sniffs.

'We have beans,' says Jane. 'For fibre.'

'Yuk,' says Ashleigh, covering her face with the duvet.

Jane sighs. Turns to leave. Turns back again. 'Did you drink the water?'

'Frozen water,' is muffled by the duvet.

'You mean sorbet?'

'Mm.'

'You need more nutrients, love. Have you taken those vitamins?'

'They smell weird,' she replies.

Jane nods, draws air through her teeth, and is about to walk away, when Ashleigh's phone lights up on the chest of drawers. Jane double-takes, but the screen blackens just as quickly.

'Can you give me my phone?' says Ashleigh, reaching her hand out from under the covers.

Jane picks the mobile up and hands it to her, willing another message to come through just so that she can be sure. Perhaps her brain is so alert to messages from him that she imagined it. She almost asks, but instead turns to leave. Walks slowly down the stairs. Tells herself that Ashleigh didn't just receive a text from Pinko Stephens.

CHAPTER FIFTY-SEVEN | August 2032
Jane

They say that you can go off someone. Sometimes, instantly. Jane forces a metal spoon through Ashleigh's beans at speed. Later, when she washes the pan – after Ashleigh sniffed at the beans then went to throw up – Jane finds the scrape marks in the bottom. Ashleigh returned with a crusty mouth and cried for a full five minutes about the lack of food in the house. Why are you getting messages from Pinko? Jane wants to ask. Instead, she breaks into next door with her coat hanger – that she keeps on a hook by the hall mirror – and returns with a sachet of dried prunes. Ashleigh picks one out, touches it with her tongue. 'It's not shit, Ashleigh,' says Jane.

'Looks like it,' replies Ashleigh.

She chomps through five or six, making mmm and ah noises and, for a moment, the air in the house stills. Jane sits opposite Ashleigh at the table and rests her chin on her hand. You can go off someone, she thinks. And this thought ruins the calm. She pushes herself to her feet. 'Don't eat them all,' she says, and slips out of the room, knowing full well that she will.

Time to be a parent.

Upstairs she presses the call button on her phone, waits for Pinko to stutter through the usual apologies for not calling. Then the question climbs out of her throat and over her tongue like a fiendish thing let-loose on the world.

'About Ashleigh,' she says, pacing inside the gap between her bed and the radiator. 'Did you message her yesterday?'

'Yes,' he says, without hesitation.

'Oh.' She stops dead and sits on the bed. 'Oh.'

'Did she tell you?'

Jane ignores his question. 'I didn't know you had her number.'

'Well...' he says, then tails off, clearing his throat, then laughing. 'I wanted it to be a surprise...'

Jane raises one eyebrow. Then the other.

'It's silly really,' he continues, his voice bright. 'We're renovating the cabin – you'll be pleased to hear – and the builders want to know if you'd prefer dark or light wood. In your kitchen.'

Jane presses her lips together.

'You know? The cabin in Finland. So...I bet light. I said to the builder: "I think she'd prefer light." But then I wasn't sure. So I messaged Ashleigh and...well...she hasn't replied yet.'

As he says this, Jane hears his phone vibrate twice. She covers her mouth. A sentence lands on her tongue; she jams her teeth together until it retreats to the back of her mouth.

'Jane?'

She is squeezing her face now, holding her breath as tears fall around her knuckles. Then she sniffs, deep and heavy, and the game is up.

'Are you upset, Jane?'

'Mm,' she manages, then holds the phone away and takes a few deep breaths. After several seconds, she can control her mouth and her breathing.

'Jane?' he says, as she puts her ear to the phone.

'I think,' she says, 'that I want to tell you something.'

'Silly isn't it,' he says, 'the thing about the kitchen?'

'I'm pretty sure that Ashleigh's pregnant.'

There is silence at the other end of the line; she can't even hear him breathing.

'Pinko?'

'Yes, I'm here,' he says, his voice dull again.

'I just don't know what to do.' Jane flops back on the bed. 'Do you think,' she says, 'that I could speak to your doctor friend?'

'But you're not even sure she's...you know.'

'The doctor knows,' she says. 'I'm sure he knows. I'm sure she lied to me about what he told her that day.'

Pinko is silent again.

'Pinko?'

He inhales thinly, like he's sucking through a straw. 'Even if I could put you in touch, you know he has to maintain patient-doctor confidentiality. You won't get much out of him.'

'Right,' says Jane. This must be a bombshell, she thinks. Mother and daughter was the deal. Not mother, daughter, baby.

'He's a tight-lipped old bugger,' says Pinko.

'I think he has to tell me,' says Jane, 'because Ashleigh is still a minor...'

The silence hisses through several seconds, then, 'Sorry, it sounded like you said she's a minor...' He laughs a little, then says, 'She's a what?'

'I want to talk to her,' she says, 'but I've been afraid that she'll run away.' She sniffs now.

'But she's what, twenty-one? I think she's an adult at twenty-one...'

Jane frowns into the phone, wonders where on earth he got that number from. 'She's fifteen.'

He says nothing, but his breathing whistles through the phone.

'Pinko?'

'No, she's not.'

'Erm...'

'She... She's older. I'm sure she's older.'

'She's fifteen. You know this.'

'No,' he says. 'No, I didn't.'

'But I told you I'm thirty-two.'

The line is silent again.

A thought strikes Jane. 'I'm not blaming you,' she says.

'What?' he says, panicked. 'Why would you?'

'Because I'm pretty sure something happened with someone at your party. You obviously didn't realise she was so young.'

The air is so quiet... She holds the phone away from her and looks at it. But it's there, the green phone icon and the digital clock ticking through the seconds of the call. 2:31, 2:32, 2:33. He *knew* she was pregnant, she thinks, and he *knows* it happened at his party.

Now he says, 'Hello?'

She jolts, rams the phone to her ear. 'Yes.'

'Look, you need to... I need to...'

Jane holds her breath and casts her eyes about. The bedroom light glares up from the glossy, décor brochure that lays open on her bedside table. 'Is this an issue?' she says. 'For a visa or something?'

'I'm sorry I just have...a thing to do,' he says. 'I'm sorry. It's... I'm sorry,' he says.

Then he hangs up.

CHAPTER FIFTY-EIGHT | August 2032
Pinko

Pinko wheels his captain's chair towards the round patio door and stares at the willow trees that shower the windy garden. Browned grasses and dried leaves flutter from the barrowful of compost parked just in front of the doors. Blue stalks across the patio, looks up and nods at Pinko, then bumps into the wheelbarrow. The compost jolts and cascades down itself. Time pauses, flickers, superimposes over that moment and, he thinks, he could slip out through the gap in between if he allowed the swirling of the air to close his eyes and carry him behind the darkness of the present. 'Oh God,' he hears himself saying. 'Oh God, oh God...'

'Something wrong?'

Butler is at the door in cut-off dungarees and a flat cap. He's holding a tablet and a stylus. His expression suggests that Pinko doesn't look good at all.

'I don't...want...to talk about it.'

'Pinko, you look like shit.'

Pinko laughs, then feels like he's going to choke. He inhales, inhales again.

Butler approaches, bends slightly, looks into his face. 'Seriously.'

'Okay...'

'Okay what?'

More inhaling. If he can just breathe deeply for a moment, he won't have to think.

Butler says, 'Seriously, dude, you're hyperventilating. Breathe for a minute. Just breathe.'

Pinko exhales. Strangely, it seems to calm him.

'What's going on?' says Butler. 'You can tell me, come on.'

'I'm not sure.'

'Is it that bad?'

'It's so bad.'

'Why?'

'It's *so* bad.'

'Like, are we talking money or morals or *death*?'

Pinko peers up at him, sucking air through pursed lips. 'I've done something that…I'm going to have to come to terms with.'

Butler puts a hand on his shoulder and squats down beside him. 'I'm sure it's not that bad,' he says. 'Is it Jane?'

Pinko winces. Fidgets. 'I don't think I can go into it now.'

'Look.' Butler reaches over and drags the other desk-chair towards Pinko. He sits on it, bends forward and clasps his hands in front of him. 'I've not seen you like this before.'

'No, you probably haven't.'

'I'll trade you.' Butler takes a moment to look at the window. Blue is perched on the edge of a large, olive tree planter, taking bites out of an apple and staring into space. Butler wipes his lips. Looks back at Pinko.

'You don't have to,' says Pinko, leaning forward, grabbing the neck of the Lagavulin bottle stood by the leg of the desk.

'You're nearly out,' says Butler to the bottle.

Pinko stands and walks to the glass cabinet for a tumbler.

'When I was twenty-one,' says Butler, 'I ran over a young woman.'

Pinko turns to Butler. 'What?'

'Paralysed her.'

He puts the bottle down, holds his mouth open, silent.

'Yeah. Exactly.'

'Jesus,' says Pinko, returning to the chair.

'Yes.'

'You must have felt awful?'

'I still do.'

'Shit… I mean… Did you talk to her? Afterwards?'

Butler leans back in his chair, crosses one leg over the other. 'I went to see her, yes. I still go.'

'Really?'

'I believe that's the right thing to do,' he says. 'It's not ideal but it helps us both, I think. It helps us both to alleviate the…you know,' he shrugs, 'the hurt.'

'Is that why you don't drive?'

Another shrug.

'Butler, I'm really, very sorry.'

'So now,' Butler holds up a hand, 'your thing can't be as bad as that.'

Pinko hangs his clasped hands between his legs, looks at them.

'Shall we work out how you can make peace with that thing? That bad thing?'

Pinko nods, lifts his eyes. 'Alright,' he says. 'We might need a drop more single malt.'

Butler gets up, opens the window. 'Blue!' he yells.

Blue turns his head so that he is staring over his shoulder, his jaws still mashing away at the apple.

'Get us a bottle from the store, will you?'

Blue lets his stare fall over Pinko. 'Aye. Give me a minute,' he yells back.

CHAPTER FIFTY-NINE | August 2032
Pinko

It is morning and Pinko is in bed but awake. The fumes from his mouth are sour in his nose, but the sun is out, at least.

The helicopter is coming today. He'd almost forgotten about that.

He wafts his gaze about the room, then sits up. So it wasn't a dream. 'Make peace with this,' Butler said. Yes, exactly. It is a terrible situation, but it's no different to yesterday. Only that he *knows* more. There is nothing, he says to himself, that will change the past except your perspective.

Butler told him to focus on being a better person from this day forward; to use this experience to be humble and good. To help people. To positively impact lives so that what happened becomes an essential part of creating a better world. He shudders a little as he thinks this to himself but no, *onwards*.

To start with, that child will want for nothing. Pinko will give it the best education. Pinko will ensure it has the best opportunities. It will know its heritage and its birth right. It will be beneficiary of the estate, his offspring. His heir. And Ashleigh will receive a sizeable chunk. That will help make everything better. Not right, but better. He swings his legs out of bed, rests his feet on his Mahabis and sits for a moment. The room is empty now, apart from his round bed, his slippers, and a few clothes in the wardrobe. He'll leave them behind for Gavin, he thinks, as the two men are about the same size. And Gavin seems to like the way he dresses. 'Make peace with this,' he repeats to himself, out loud. At that moment, Jane's ringtone draws him out of his head. He pushes himself off the bed, picks up his phone and hesitates before pressing the green icon.

Then he closes his eyes and waits for her voice, smile-shaped and chiming.

When he opens them, Butler's head is at the door. He is already combed and shaved and moisturized.

'Pinko?' he says.

'I'm on the phone,' Pinko mouths, pointing to the phone.

'Pinko, there's a problem,' says Butler.

'Hello?' says Jane.

'Who are you on the phone to?' Butler whispers. 'Is that Jane?' Pinko nods.

Butler makes slicing motions at his throat, mouths for Pinko to hang up.

'Hold on one second, Jane...' Then to Butler, 'What's going on?'

Butler shakes his head and smiles downwards, his teeth shining wet.

'Jane, I'm going to have to call you back.'

'This is the second time you've said that in two days.'

'I'll call you back.'

'Okay.'

'I will. I'll call you back in just a minute.'

Pinko follows Butler to a small room on the second floor to the far right of the house. 'They must have arrived before I was up,' says Butler. The corridor blurs and pitches like the inside of a ship. Now. Today. The day the helicopter is coming and... They enter the room. It is the size of an en-suite bathroom and is panelled from floor to ceiling in red-stained cedarwood. Pinko can't remember the last time he was in here.

'What's in here?' he asks.

'This screen is linked to the security cameras,' says Butler, and he smirks, and Pinko smirks; it must be all alright if they are both smirking. 'Didn't you know that about your own house?' he adds, sitting at a desk in front of a large TV. 'Look,' says Butler, adjusting the screen so that the focus is on the front porch.

Pinko covers his mouth with his hand.

There they are. About twenty of them. With their smartphones and cameras and microphones and even notepads; crawling over the driveway and flocked around the door.

'It's because I'm leaving,' says Pinko. 'Surely. It must be.'

Butler puffs his breath through closed lips and says, 'I don't know.'

'What are they all still doing in the country?'

'News is news.'

'But...' Pinko shakes his head, glances over to the window, thinks about looking out, then stops himself. 'Where is Blue? Surely *he's* spoken to them. Surely *he* knows what they want.'

'I haven't seen him all morning.'

'It's because I'm leaving, isn't it?' he repeats. 'Butler, why else would they be here?'

'I don't know. I really don't,' says Butler, leaning back in the chair and swinging it slightly. 'Don't worry. I'll go down to them.'

CHAPTER SIXTY | August 2032
Jane

Jane holds her phone to her chest, paces about the hallway, tells herself that he probably has a lot to organise today. 'It's fine,' she says aloud. 'It's all fine.'

She packs the last of her unwanted clothes into a bin bag and tapes an A4 sign to it, reading, 'disaster relief'. She stands back and blinks at it, removes one of her coats from the hallway and folds it into the bag.

Then she checks her phone.

Nothing.

She puts the bag outside, returns to the hall and checks her phone.

She tours the living room, scanning ornaments, books and coasters, in case there is anything she might need. She does the same in the kitchen, opening cupboards and drawers. She has left some crockery, four sets of cutlery, her few remaining tins of beans. If some little wanderer, she thinks, should try her front door, it will be unlocked.

She checks her phone.

Again, nothing. Maybe he's had a change of heart? The thought makes her feel sick.

Jane sits on the stairs and tries to identify the reason for this. Because you don't trust men, says her brain. Her mother comes back to her, bends towards her face – exactly as she used to – hands on hips, elbows well back. *A smart woman*, she says, *reads between the lines.*

The photos in the hallway are deframed, filed one behind the other in a box inside a box inside a bigger box that will go into the helicopter. Likewise for her only vase, her birthday cards from Ashleigh, Ashleigh's folder from primary school, her first tooth box and her baby book.

Pinko freaked out when Jane told him Ashleigh's age. Jane zooms into that detail from the phone call, analyses it from all angles. Beside her, on the stair, is a tiny photobooth picture of

Ashleigh's first passport photo. Her eyes are wide and her wet little mouth hangs open; Jane never did take her abroad.

How did he get her number?

Jane holds her hand to her sternum. Her chest is acidy and full.

Stealing Ashleigh's phone would be like trying to wrench a bone from a Pitbull. Of course, she could always *confront* her…

Jane shakes her head. Gets to her feet. What use is this information, two days before they are due to leave for safety? Together, thinks Jane. Focus on the plan.

The stairwell swells and blurs as Jane treads the stairs. 'You okay?' she calls, when she gets to the top.

Ashleigh is on her back, on her bed. Her hand is rested on the lower lip of her stomach. It's daytime, but the wet in both eyes holds the light from her bedside lamp.

Jane sits on the edge of the bed.

Ashleigh's hipbones jut like two budding horns.

Jane leans forward and whispers: 'You won't feel him kicking yet.'

Ashleigh frowns, opens her mouth…

'The first time you kicked me,' says Jane, 'made me cry.'

'I don't know what you're on about.'

'Your baby, Ashleigh. In your pregnant tummy.'

Ashleigh looks away. 'You're mental.'

Jane takes a deep breath, reaches for Ashleigh's hands, clasped together over her belly.

'His feet are too itsy bitsy to kick with. Isn't that sweet?'

Ashleigh bites her cheek, looks up to the ceiling.

'Itsy bitsy feet made from lemon and lime sorbet.'

Ashleigh laughs, then starts to cry. She sits up and curves herself against her mother.

Jane folds her arms across her back, tells her that her spine is too bumpy, her shoulder blades too sharp. Tells her they must focus on keeeping her healthy, when they get to Finland.

Ashleigh sobs for a while, then wipes her eyes and says, 'I've only just stopped puking.'

'That's normal,' says Jane.

Ashleigh cries again, then asks her mum how she knows that it's a he. Is that something she can tell because she's a veterinary assistant or, like, a mother?

Jane shrugs. 'I don't want to call him "it".'

'Oh,' says Ashleigh. 'I prefer "she".'

'Okay,' Jane nods into the back of her head. 'Whatever you want.'

Ashleigh turns to look at her. 'Are you angry?'

'No.' Jane pushes Ashleigh's hair behind her ears, smiles.

'Do we have to go right now?'

'No.'

'When?'

'They're coming to get us at five.'

'Right.'

They sit quietly for a moment, before Jane asks, 'Do you want to talk about it?'

'What?'

'Your baby.'

Ashleigh shakes her head into Jane's chest. 'Is the telly still working?'

'Only BBC 1.'

'Can we watch it together? Before we leave...'

They sit and watch a rerun of the Antiques Road Show, pretend to giggle at the lady with the peacock fascinator, but are both watching the stately home behind, its reaching Tudor chimneys, the edges of the topiary poking into the frame, the reedy bank of a lake.

'Do you think...' starts Ashleigh.

'What's that?'

'Do you think there'll be, you know, doctors where we're going?'

Jane squeezes her hand. 'Of course there will.'

'Really?'

'We're very lucky, you know.'

'I thought you'd shout at me.'

Jane pulls Ashleigh to her. She would like to ask about the night of the party, at least reassure herself that Ashleigh wasn't hurt or frightened or threatened. She almost asks if the father is still in the picture; but what good would that do, one hour before they are due to escape the most terrifying threat of all? There'll be time enough to unpick the details, thinks Jane. Instead, she asks, 'Did the doctor tell you? That day at Pinko's.'

Ashleigh looks down, pinches the fabric together on the knees of her leggings.

'It's alright,' says Jane. 'I'm just relieved it's only pregnancy. At one point, I thought you had some nasty illness or eating disorder...'

'Do you think I hurt it when I didn't eat?' she blurts.

Jane thinks for a moment, inhales. 'How far along are you?'

'Four months.'

Jane swallows, shakes her head. 'We'll take you to see a doctor when we get to Finland.'

'Do you think it could be blind or something? Because of me?'

'No,' says Jane, pulling her in for a hug. 'She'll be fine.'

Ashleigh nods, blinks at the TV from inside the hug. 'It'll all be underwater soon. All of it.'

Jane looks back at the TV. 'The scientists might have got it wrong.'

'Can we come back if they have?' she says. 'Got it wrong.'

Jane twitches. 'I guess we'll have to see what happens.'

The credits roll upwards and the tinkling piano and horns see out the stately home and the topiary.

'Are we living near him?'

'Pinko?'

'Mm.'

'On his estate, I think. Well no, I don't think. I know.'

'So, right on his estate then?'

'Yes.' She frowns at Ashleigh. 'How do you feel about that?'

Ashleigh shrugs.

Jane reaches for the remote as the one o'clock news drums in, squeezes the volume down.

'We'll have our own cabin.' Jane gets up and looks about the room, shaking the blood back into one foot.

'I saw it in the hall,' says Ashleigh, eyes lolling over the TV. 'Your phone.'

Jane disappears into the hall, locates her phone, tuts at the screen. She wonders if this is the moment to ask Ashleigh about the 'surprise' Pinko's planning for her. She formulates the question in her head, comes back in to find Ashleigh standing up.

'No, Mum,' she says waving for her to get out, then she turns in a circle, looking for the remote.

Pinko's face fades from the TV screen.

'What's going on?' Jane frowns, striding into the room.

'Mum, it's not true,' says Ashleigh. 'It can't be true, can it? They mean you, not me. They must mean you. Look how sick they are. They've got it wrong.'

Jane watches, eyes hard, unblinking, her phone dropping from her hand to the floor.

CHAPTER SIXTY-ONE | August 2032
Ashleigh

It is the next day. When things are about to change and the world becomes very small, like a tunnel, and there is no way of seeing to the end of it, under the duvet feels like the safest bit of the entire earth, because at least there, every part of it is known. When things are about to change, and they don't, even if it's because of a very, very bad thing, knowing that the duvet is waiting in the same place, with the same smells, is actually quite nice. Ashleigh puts her nose well into the fabric and breathes.

Yesterday they – the police – told her to make a statement. Ashleigh said she would, but didn't want to go any further than that.

'What do you mean?' they asked.

She explained that she didn't want anyone to get into trouble.

Her mum sat beside her, kind of separate from it all, as if watching through a window or a TV screen. Every so often, she'd come to the glass, knock on it and say something. At that moment, Jane scoffed, said they would *absolutely* be pressing charges.

'Your mum's right,' said the police officer, raising her eyebrows and tilting her head. 'You're under sixteen, so we have to take this further.'

'Exactly,' said Jane, pulling the same face.

Ashleigh side-eyed Jane. She hadn't slept; her hair slumped in a fuzzy top knot and her bottom lip was scabby from biting at it. For the last couple of weeks, she'd been wandering around in her loose summer dresses, sighing at things that they would probably never see again. But she smiled the whole time, telling Ashleigh how lucky they were. Now, in one wide-eyed, grey-faced look, Ashleigh saw they were back at square one. There would be no Finland, no cabin, no together. Ashleigh nodded slowly to herself as she decided what to say next. It was easier than she thought. Usually, it's not that easy to tell the truth.

'I won't make a statement,' she said. 'It never happened,' she said, then pressed her lips together.

'You just told me it did?'

'I lied.'

At lunchtime, Ashleigh could hear Jane crying in the kitchen, while heating up the last tin of soup. Ashleigh stood in the doorway, leaned against the frame.

'Don't cry.'

Jane jolted, turned, pretended to smile. 'I'm not crying,' she said, coming towards her and drawing her into a hug.

'Are you angry?' asked Ashleigh into her shoulder.

'No. Well, yes. But not at you.'

'Don't be.'

Jane sighed. 'I understand why you said what you said, today. But...'

'So you *are* angry at me.'

'No. I just think he should be punished.'

Ashleigh stared at the bobbles on the shoulder of Jane's old cardigan, then said, 'It wasn't his fault, I swear.'

Jane nodded. 'He never said a word to me, you know.'

'Why would he?'

'Well...' she stood back, pushed her hair from her face. 'Even if we weren't related, you and me, he knew we lived together. That alone seems a bit twisted.'

Ashleigh looked at her stomach, passed her hands over it.

'Every time I think of him doing that. With you. It's...' Jane wrung her hands for a moment, turned in a little circle.

'Mum, don't. It's not what you think.'

'It's horrendous, Ashleigh.'

Ashleigh stared at her mother, tried to imagine what it must be like to believe that your boyfriend has got your daughter pregnant. It was messed up, yes, and bad, but the worst thing about all of this was that they weren't going to Finland. The helicopter had left already – taken most of their stuff. Ashleigh imagined Big Ted squashed inside a box that she would never open. She pulled back a chair, sat down.

'We can still go,' she said. 'Can't we, Mum?'

Jane widened her eyes, 'Are you kidding me?'

'Why not?'

'Ashleigh...'

'Please, Mum...'

'Look what he did to you!' said Jane, gesturing towards her belly. 'You have a baby now. *His* baby.'

Now, under the duvet, she replays her response to this in her mind, while she listens to Jane's long, breathy sobs through the wall. Jane is trying to cry quietly, but the walls are really, really thin. It's all ruined, thinks Ashleigh, as she puts her hands over her ears. Sometimes, if you set your mind to something, it is hard to reset it afterwards. Especially something big. Her mind had been trying reset since yesterday, pretty much, and it felt all wrong. The helicopter had gone. Jane hated Pinko. They would have to go to France. Or she would simply bag up her shame and leave, leave Jane, leave Kent, leave the baby to be looked after by someone who didn't tell lies and destroy futures. Ashleigh's fingers rub together in a silent click. When she comes out from under the duvet, maybe time will have reversed and Jane will be nagging at her, with a smiling mouth, to get her things packed and ready. She jams her eyes shut. What have you done, Ashleigh? The truth wouldn't change their situation. But if she pushed ahead, made the statement, then at least they would get something out of it, she and Jane. He'd have to look after them, give them some money, surely? She tries to make the duvet tighter around her, imagining herself a caterpillar in its cottony cocoon. The world is too big; too grown up. The big lie had been easier to manage when she'd told Pinko. But now everybody knew.

In the kitchen, Ashleigh looked at Jane, took a deep breath. 'That's why I told them it was all a lie.' She spread her hands over her little belly. 'Because I wouldn't want to grow up thinking my dad had done something bad to my mum.'

Jane nodded, put her fists on her hips, nodded some more.

That was the right thing to say, thought Ashleigh. Her mum could make sense of it and it meant that her future wasn't in ruins because of her stupid daughter. 'Will you hate it?'

'The baby?'

'Yeah.'

Jane held her reply between her teeth, then said, 'No. Of course not.'

Ashleigh slit her eyes.

'I won't hate it, honestly.'

'Will you love it, then?'

Jane folded her lips. The soup began to splutter. She turned to it, started to stir.

Ashleigh wiped her eyes on her sleeve and wondered who would love it if *she* didn't deserve to and Jane didn't want to. Who? 'Will you love it, Mum?'

'Of course I will love it,' Jane said into the soup.

CHAPTER SIXTY-TWO | August 2032
Pinko

At the police station, Pinko sits at a rectangular table. He thumbs the corner of it, traces out a rounded edge instead. Someone is talking to him, asking him about the party way back when. He feels his lips parting, his eyes rolling upwards.

'She's a minor; you can't allow her to be interrogated by the press,' he says.

The other person tilts their head, clasps their hands. 'So, you *are* in there?' they say.

The military have largely replaced the police. They are rougher, less patient, it seems, than the jovial local bobby. They have been asking about that night for the last twenty minutes, *what exactly happened? Are there any witnesses? The guy she came to your party with – Gavin – is he still in the country? Did it never cross your mind that she might be underage? Did full sex occur? More than once? Did she consent?* Pinko lets it all slide around him like a bubble of oil. He sits inside and decides he cannot get out, so simply allows it to protect him. He nods, shakes his head, traces that curved edge that isn't there. He can't remember, he honestly can't remember. But there are stills of flashback, and he usually knows when he's had sex; his body feels... well...different, *emptier*, but the hangover that followed that day – the anxiety – engulfed any connection between brain and body. It was as if he existed outside of himself, like now.

'Didn't you realise when you started dating her mother?'

He looks up. What kind of question was that?

'What did you do when you found out she was pregnant?'

That one he can't answer, because it requires more than a yes or a no. Now he is thinking of his niece, Lily, and her sister, Jasmine. What must they think of him, he wonders, as he pictures them realising that Uncle Pinko has done adult things with someone who could very well be their school friend. They will no longer throw their arms around him. They will look at him differently; they might even be scared. Their parents will hesitate before letting him take them to Broadstairs or Bluewater, making up some excuse or wanting to come along too. He imagines himself relinquishing it all; a folder full of deeds handed over to them – Lily, Jasmine, Ashleigh and the baby. *Have it*, he would tell them, *because I don't deserve it*. Love is hot, he thinks, but shame is searing. They can ask him whatever they want, the shame will shroud him, mute him, bow his head. He can't yet see through it.

'When you realised that Miss Ashleigh Pearce was pregnant, what did you do?' They rephrase and repeat this a few more times, before realising he is not being obstinate, he is simply unable to speak.

It had taken them a while to arrive at his house. He thought about Jane. His man was supposed to collect her at five. Five came and went. The man called him from outside her house. 'She's not answering the door.'

'Ah,' Pinko replied. Then, 'This isn't good,' he added to himself, as he tuned into the national news, saw his own face, saw Ashleigh's school photo, saw the front of his house. He called Jane five times, waited three minutes, and called another five times. The press sat on his doorstep until the evening, until the driveway flashed with silent blue and he knew he couldn't stay in that little room any longer. 'Why on earth are you all still in the country?' he asked the waiting group, as the police stepped over the threshold. The flashing intensified, the cameras surged forwards. That question would then be taken out of context, he remembered thinking, broadcast over and over again; they'd been waiting all day for it, after all.

'Is this the first time you've had sex with a minor?' one of them replied as he snapped Pinko at close range. 'Do you consider yourself to be in a relationship with Miss Pearce?' Snap. Pinko closed his eyes, pinched his temples, realised, as beads of rain hung heavy from the twin bay trees, that he was the subject of a scandal. That these cameras would not leave. *I can still win them*, he thought.

'It's raining,' he said. 'I have to speak to the police before I can speak to you. Would you like to wait inside?' Then, 'I really have nothing to hide.'

They lowered their cameras for just a moment, smiled through the openings of their draw-string hoods. Said, *Yeah, great*; said, *thank you*; said, *you wouldn't have some hot water, would you?*

'Of course,' he replied. He invited them in, told them they could photograph whatever they wanted.

Inactivity drove them away. Even journalists have homes to go to, mouths to feed, and they'd certainly put in some mileage today. A few loitered outside in their vans. The police had kept him too long.

Then they gave him ten minutes to freshen up.

Pinko tried to call Jane again, five times. He waited three minutes, then tried five more times.

The world spun in rings about him. He heard whistling and squinted. Through the rings, through the patio doors, Blue trod up the garden, wheeling a barrowful of twigs, shears hanging from his utility belt and over one buttock.

'The police are gearing up to leave,' said Butler. 'You ready?'

A shrug.

Through the patio doors, Blue turned to the side, as if he were being called. A soldier approached him, glanced back at the house, then nodded in the direction of the gazebo. They both walked off towards it and out of sight.

'I'm coming with you,' said Butler.

'Thanks,' Pinko replied. 'Let's see what else they can possibly want.'

Ashleigh. That's what they wanted. They wanted to know her version of events. Pinko nodded at them some more. Shook his head. Traced the curve on the table corner.

Now, they say, 'We need you to stick around for a while.'

At this, he looks up. 'I'm supposed to go to Finland.'

'You'll have to put that off, I'm afraid.'

'But what about the water?'

The soldier scrunches up his face, tilts his head to the side. 'We don't currently have a clear plan for people wanting to leave because of...the water...but we do know that the situation keeps updating itself. We're likely to have some news soon.'

Pinko inhales, feels his knee jigging up and down, his thumbnail picking at the edge of the table. 'I take it I can go home?'

'I'm just going to check that.'

'Thank you,' he says, then holds out his hand.

The police officer nods at the hand, stands up and leaves.

CHAPTER SIXTY-THREE | August 2032
Ashleigh

Ashleigh is in the garden when her cardigan vibrates. She rolls her eyes, wipes the crumbs from her fingers on her thigh, then probes about for the seam of her pocket. Inside is dark and weird, today. It feels like a dull shell. Yesterday it seemed to contain a wriggling, violent creature, but that's gone now, and the house is shattered. Outside is brighter; there are birds in next door's apple tree. If Ashleigh concentrates on all those ordinary things, she can almost pretend everything is normal. Now, she brings the phone to the end of her nose.

I haven't abandoned you. You're still going to Finland.

She frowns, tuts, whispers, 'I knew it', and puts the phone back into her pocket.

As she bites another cinnamon biscuit in half, she wonders how to convince Jane to go. Perhaps she'd have to backtrack again. Insist on the truth: that she's been playing a game, spouting whatever story is needed to make sure they get to safety. It would be awkward, although it's not like they'd be living with him.

It's all so complicated. But at least, she thinks, yesterday is done.

The birds are having some kind of fight now; they sound like a couple of dogs going mental with squeaky toys. Pinko's message grows in her mind, intensifies the sun on her shoulders and the heaviness of her eyelids. She knew he'd come good. When the next text comes through, she jumps to open it.

Wait for my envelope.

CHAPTER SIXTY-FOUR | August 2032
Jane

They sit on Ashleigh's bed in silence, but they both know what the other is thinking. What was the plan now?

Jane has said, several times, that Ashleigh must go to France before the baby comes.

Ashleigh stares at the ceiling, strokes her stomach, lifts cinnamon biscuits from an empty sorbet container that she keeps next to her bed. The dark shadow that ridged her face from her ear to the corner of her mouth is now a little, grey dent in her cheek. She often sits against her headboard with her hair over one shoulder and across one large boob, feeding biscuit after biscuit into her mouth, stroking her belly.

'You'll give yourself diabetes,' says Jane. 'I'm not kidding.'

'The thing is,' says Ashleigh, 'you can't come with me.'

'I know,' says Jane. 'I just feel...stuck.'

'Not really stuck,' she says, through a mouthful of biscuit, 'are you?'

'Well, what am I supposed to do?' says Jane, weaving her fingers through the holes in Ashleigh's quilt. 'You know the rules.'

Ashleigh swallows, pauses, holds her mother in a large, cold gaze. 'Let's stick to the original plan,' she says. 'Think about it, Mum, we can still go to Finland together.'

Jane looks up. 'No way. Forget it.'

Ashleigh blinks. 'Yes, there is a way. The only reason we didn't go is because you refused to answer the door.'

'Are you kidding me?' The thought repulses Jane like an unwanted touch. She'd like to take a shower, get rid of his handprint in her hand, his gaze on her body. All of it makes her itch. And Ashleigh, sitting there like a chubby, lazy cat, has no idea what it would do to Jane to see them breathing the same air. She imagines him now, holed up in his father's office, guzzling scotch. He peers at her over the rim of his glass, winks. The image makes her heave. 'You're too young,' says Jane, composing herself, 'to understand just how traumatic that scenario would be for both of us.'

Ashleigh lifts one eyebrow, drops the other. 'Traumatic?' she says. 'To stay together? To live in a brand new cabin? To be part of the luckiest people on earth right now?' Ashleigh picks up her phone and thumbs through it. 'It's all set up,' she says. 'Mum, we could be on a helicopter by next week.' She turns the phone to show Jane a message. Jane focusses, glances through it, sees who it's from. Nausea spreads into her limbs, pushes her up from the bed. Him, Pinko Stephens, still texting her daughter while all this is going on.

'How long has he been texting you?'

Ashleigh shrinks back a little, her face afraid. 'Mum, calm down—'

'How long, Ashleigh?'

'I don't know...'

Jane grabs the phone, throws it on the floor and stamps on it. Then she heads into the bathroom and vomits into the bath.

CHAPTER SIXTY-FIVE | August 2032
Pinko

I haven't abandoned you. You're still going to Finland. He stops texting, looks up, trails the rings of the ceiling rose with his ambling gaze.

Don't worry.

He hunts around his memory for the last time he saw Jane, his mind's eye plucking out and holding up stills; *and this one?* it says. *And what about this one?* Next to the golden, flaring curlicues of a speckled mirror, holding a rose to her lips, *Are you sure we're allowed in here?* she'd said. Now she cups a ball of hedgehog, in that plastic apron over her green uniform; he smiles, but, no, it wasn't that one. The one he is looking for is downstairs, sat on the round bench in the hall, coat folded over her arm and pulled to her stomach; hearing his own cork slippers whispering away, while her daughter sat in his office with the doctor; pause, rewind, again. It plays. 'Thank you for doing this,' she'd said, and she'd hitched her mouth to the side so she could bite her cheek, fix her eyes on him, hold his good deed to the light. 'I haven't done anything,' he had replied. Then he kissed her cheek, like he would an older, female relative. The memory makes him sneer. Perhaps he even patted the back of her hand then, while his thoughts trod the path back to his father's office and listened at the door.

None of that matters, anymore.

He addresses the envelope to Jane.

Everything will go to Ashleigh and the child. But they are both too young to figure that out now.

He dabs the ink dry, turns the envelope and hovers his fingers above the pen. He would like to write something on the seal. Something cheesy. Something she would laugh at.

He retracts his hand, sits back, looks at the wall.

The dimple below his father's right ear is gone, as is the circle of light in his eye. Paintings do that. Paintings of people you know, thinks Pinko, lifting a crystal tumbler. You pop moods over them like veils. He swallows. So this must be his real mood. Pinko swivels in his captain's chair, once to the left, then to the right.

Back to the left. He stands, picks up his phone, flashes his eyes over the screen and hurls it against the wall.

'I didn't know,' he yells at the painting.

The tapered end of his shoes bunch his toes into hoof-like clumps. He scrapes them off against the leg of the chair.

What if, he thinks, what if you're a man who...

He lifts the stopper on his whiskey decanter.

If you're a man who...

He pours another shot.

A man who...

It doesn't matter.

He lifts the tumbler again. Downs its contents.

And you, says the painting.

His eyes dart to the lips.

And you let my grandson disappear into the mist, it says.

'Grand*son*?' Pinko replies.

The painting says nothing.

'What do *you* know?' He tops up his glass again. 'What mist?'

He looks back to the table, to his phone. But it's gone of course. His gaze falls away to the floor, where it lies, cracked and black.

The note on the desk says, 'Look in the drawer'. He should make it into a label, hang it around he decanter. 'The way that Alice,' he thinks, 'liked to find her notes.' But no, he picks up his pen and draws a line through the writing. The envelopes aren't in the drawer, they are upstairs tucked one behind the other on the top shelf of his wardrobe, between a shoe box and a Fabergé carousel. He moved those two objects up there, so that he could write that exact sentence on the note. He takes another piece of paper, writes again, 'Look in the drawer.' He leans it against the decanter, then takes yet another piece of paper. 'Look in the wardrobe. Between the shoebox and the carousel.' He opens his desk drawer, smirks at its insides and drops the paper inside.

Pinko stands, bows to his father, turns away.

The door clicks shut as he exits the room.

PART FIVE
THE BIRTH

CHAPTER SIXTY-SIX | December 2032
Gavin

Gavin sits at the front of the bus. He did the same on the last bus, just behind the driver. Everyone on that last bus looked at his shoes as they got on. Their pupils fell down to them, tipping like eight-balls rolling to a stop. Then again, he has pushed out his crossed ankles into the aisle, but not so far that people can't get around him. He wears deep, sea-green, spike-studded Louboutin high-tops. Pinko said a long time ago that he didn't like them, that Gavin was welcome to them. He tried them on and they fit perfectly. While he waited for the bus back to London, he sat with his sketchpad and drew them; pulled his foot up to the sink unit in the public loos so he could see them in the mirror, one and then the other; kept running his finger over them to be sure the spike-studs hadn't fallen off. He'd like to do that now, but it is difficult to bend forward, what with the turkey on his lap – cost him thirty quid – and the flowers on top of that. Can only get fresh flowers in London. All blue, they are. He asked the florist to put lavender and thistle in coz his mum likes simple flowers, but the thistle keeps scratching at him no matter which way he turns it, and the lavender has so far attracted two fat bees that sent one passenger shrieking to the back of the bus. Nonetheless, he strains to check his sea-green studs, tries to look out of the window at bits of the town, at all them closed signs, letters looping through the white-washed windows. Only one window, so far, has been smashed down in East Kent. But as the bus came through Lewisham, he saw that the Pets Direct and Carpet Right had been smashed up, innards spewing out of the window like a beaten man's tongue. Also, he swore he'd seen a budgie in an ash tree by the massive car park. That must have been from Pets Direct – weird how that one had gone out of business. Hopefully all the pets had been sent away somewhere safe. His neighbour has arranged for her cat to be put down, Mum said. Fourteen years old, it is; no point in dragging it to France or watching it get caught and eaten if they move inland.

Nuneaton is inland, he remembers thinking.

He straightens his shoulders, blows at the sprig of lavender that lands on his lip as the bus jolts. He would like to put it on the seat next to him, but it is taken. He knew it would be but, if he'd thought about it, he wouldn't have sat *right* next to her. Although, all the other seats are taken anyway, and he didn't want someone else to sit with her.

He tries not to look at the passenger now sat next to him.

She was there, queuing for the bus, just as Padre said she would be, but he didn't know if he was supposed to speak to her. He looked at her while she was in the queue, felt his stomach wobble. She eyeballed him. So he just sat down on one of the benches at Victoria Coach Station, putting all the words in order in his head. He felt a bit whirly about talking to her; especially with all these men harassing women at the moment. Big Carla always comes back from the shops with a different story. One bloke even put his hand in her back pocket. Ryan won't let her go on her own anymore. And if she does, she wears a long, baggy fleece.

If she knew he was coming, perhaps *she* should have spoken to *him*.

The last time they spoke was that night. Way back when. Gavin winces when he thinks about it. Still, she let him sit next to her. Sort of half-smiled at him.

So much has happened.

He looks through the wall in front towards the driver; can't see him but wonders how much he's getting paid. The passenger next to him eyes his turkey, the flowers, his shoes, straightens her back to look some more at his shoes, then stares at his eyes, saying nothing, just staring.

He takes a big breath. 'It's for my mum, the turkey...'

She stares on.

'I told her I'd bring her something from London.'

More staring.

'It's raw... I dunno what you'd do with a raw turkey even if I did give it to you.'

'What makes you think I want it?'

'Coz you're staring. I don't know if you've eaten. Perhaps you thought we'd eat on the way or something.'

'What?'

He closes his mouth and snaps his gaze to the top of the turkey, the thistles.

She deadens her eyes and looks at the wall in front, its Wi-Fi code crossed out, and beyond that, the driver's head.

She looks different with her hair scraped back and no make-up. She's all jumpy, but at the same time her eyes are half-open like she's tired. He swallows, nudges a forget-me-not out of the way so there is nothing between his mouth and her ear, then goes to say something.

She pulls her hood up around her chin. 'Have you seen yourself,' she says, without looking at him, 'compared to everyone on the bus?' She twangs a band on her wrist, takes a long breath. 'You stick out.'

Gavin opens his mouth again. It quivers a bit so he shuts it.

Her nostrils flare and she turns back to the window. He looks at her hoodie, St Christopher hanging over the zipper, ponytail just visible by her throat, cheek unblushed, eyebrow unplucked, rucksack on her lap, (Fila, vintage). She lifts it and stands her feet up on their toes to raise her knees. It is then that he gets a proper look at the hoody, blown and rounded at her stomach, zipper creeping up it like a staircase around the moon.

Padre had told him, but he is still a bit surprised. He stares. She sees him staring and pulls her rucksack closer to her. He thinks of something to say.

'Your baby okay in there? I guess it has everything it needs.'

She rolls her face towards him, then back to the window.

'How old is it?'

'Look, Gavin, I don't really wanna talk,' she says, hugging her rucksack to her.

Gavin bristles. It's the first time she's said his name and he's not sure how he feels about that. He was sort of hoping she'd forgotten him.

The passenger behind shuffles about, then a voice comes from somewhere beside Gavin's shoulder. 'You got a baby?' it says. 'Have you?' Gavin shoots his gaze to the gap in the chairs to see a nose and a fat pair of lips.

'I'm meeting my husband at Dover so forget it,' Ashleigh replies.

'No, you ain't.'

'I am. He's there now.'

'You ain't. That don't make sense.'

'Why?'

'Coz if my wife was pregnant, I wouldn't just leave her. Not here. Not like this.'

'Well, he did.'

'And you're what, eighteen years old? Don't tell me you're married at eighteen.'

'I'm older. I'm not eighteen.'

'You can't just get passage over because of that,' says the face, tilting its chin at her stomach, 'and not take someone along with you.'

'I already told you...' She takes a single-wrapped cinnamon biscuit from her hoodie pocket and crackles off the cellophane.

'It ain't right. It just ain't right,' says the voice.

The world rumbles by for a moment, as her teeth champ through the biscuit.

'If you take me, I'll tell them I'm impotent. I can do that. You wouldn't have to do the immigration wotsit, you know, in front of the jury.'

'I usually carry around pink wafers,' says Gavin, nodding at the wrapper in her hand.

She stares at him, as if he's said something really stupid.

'What the fuck's this got to do with you?' says the face between the seats.

Gavin moves his head towards her, covers the gap in the chairs, and the face. She smirks, swallows her mouthful. 'Ow!' Gavin springs back again. 'You fucking bit me! You fucking bit my hair!'

'This has nothing to do with you, man, with your crap shoes and...flowers.'

'You can't go around biting people!' says Gavin.

'Stay out of it!'

'She's with me!' yells Gavin. 'You can fuck off because she's with me.'

Ashleigh looks at him, head set well back on her neck, inside her hood.

'This is fucking ridiculous,' mumbles the face. A hand wanders through the gap in the chair, grabs Ashleigh by the shoulder. She slaps it away.

'Get off of her!' says Gavin, as he tries to reach around the flowers and smack the hand away.

'She ain't with you! She ain't with no one!'

'I'm taking her to Dover.'

'Oh yeah, of course,' says the face. 'With a turkey and a bunch of flowers. Right-o.'

Gavin opens his mouth, closes it again, readjusts his turkey, then turns to the girl. 'Shall we get off at Canterbury?'

'What?' she says, creasing her eyes. 'Why?'

'You really want to be alone in Dover?'

She shuffles. 'I don't know, I mean, why wouldn't I?' she says. 'I'll be fine.'

'Coz Ryan can drive you. My brother.'

'You don't have to do that,' she says.

'See,' says the face. 'You ain't nothing to do with her!'

'I'm used to dicks like him,' she says.

'What did you call me?' says the face.

Gavin twitches his eyes all over her, manoeuvres to get something from his inside pocket, until his shoulder blocks out the face between the seats. 'If you bite me again, I'll shout for the driver.' He pulls a wad of twenties from his wallet, gives them to Ashleigh, says he'll call Big Carla coz Big Carla's got a mate, a *female* one, a top mate, she works on the ferries. She'll meet her at the port and take the boat with her to France. He won't go to France. He can't do that. There's no way. But she does it all the time. There, back, there, back. Sometimes she gets duty free fags for Ryan...

Ashleigh glares at him, then at the money, then him. 'I don't need anything from you. I don't know why you're doing this.'

'I dunno, I just dunno how much you're going to need,' he says. Padre didn't tell him how much she was going to need.

Her eyes get really narrow, now. 'Gavin, what do you mean?'

He freezes when she says his name again, blinks at her. 'So you haven't forgotten me, then, from Dreamland?'

'Course not.' She smirks. 'Like I said, you stick out.'

He looks towards the front of the bus as it swings into Canterbury bus station, says that usually it would be his stop, says he would have to change in Canterbury; he was considering getting off here and letting her do the extra twenty minutes to Dover alone, but what with that prick behind them... He leans to slide his finger around his spiked studs as the bus slows.

The voice says, 'I can fuckin' hear you, you dick. Why don't you just get off here? Just get off here.'

Gavin shakes his head. 'No way,' he says, and tells him that he'd better fuck off because she's not interested. She sits, mouth open, staring at Gavin's fistful of twenties. The bus driver shouts for him to pipe down. Gavin says there's a young, pregnant girl on the bus who's being harassed. The driver frowns, slows the bus into the bay. The doors open, people outside crowd against it, clutching tenners in their hands, yelping up at the driver like puppies in a pen. Gavin hugs his turkey tightly, looks around at the white buildings, the statue of a little black lamb.

'Let's go,' she says.

'What?'

She is already standing up. 'I want to get off.'

He stands, wobbles his turkey towards the door and they exit the bus, pushing past the driver and through the squabble of people. They stand in the bus shelter as she fiddles with her rucksack. Through the bus window he sees two people sit in the seats they have just left. The doors close, the engine rumbles, the bus draws away. The other poor bastards will have to wait for the next one, or the next one. She checks her stuff.

He re-adjusts the turkey and says, 'What was that all about?'

'Changed my mind,' she says.

At the bus station, they scan the timetable, taking in the red lines running through the cancelled services; the next bus to Dover is in two hours – two hours! She adjusts her hood, buries her hands in her pockets, kicks at the curb-edge. He looks down at her belly, then asks her if she might need something for it, apart from cinnamon biscuits, as pregnant people usually need something for their babies quite regularly, don't they? He fishes about in his pocket and produces two wafers wrapped in kitchen paper (no Clingfilm anymore as Pinko told him it was bad for the environment) and smiles. 'Told you.' Then he explains that they are pink and asks her if it's a girl coz that would match up nicely.

'I don't know,' she says. 'Haven't had a scan.'

He blinks at her. She ignores the wafers and asks him if he knows Canterbury, because she really needs the loo, she's been needing the loo since Bromley. He takes her to the public loos near the bus station, gives her 20p for the door.

He suggests they go to Casper's for ice-cream, thinking that it would be nice and cold for his turkey to sit for a while. When they get there, the windows have been misted over with snow-spray and there's a man in army seconds sleeping in the doorway. Same for Café Rouge, same for the County Hotel. Dammit, the one time he has a pocket full of dosh and all the places worth going to are shut. She tells him that she noticed McDonald's was still open. He shrugs. 'Sounds good.'

Inside, people are laughing, lobbing chips at each other, sat at opened laptops, wearing headphones – or not – making sucky noises on straws, gaping their eyes at the middle distance as they pull bites from lettuce-shedding baps. Gavin and Ashleigh sit at a high table and stare about, falling backwards into England, the way it was before. This is where he tells her. This is where he tells her that he was asked to sit next to her on the bus, have someone meet her at Dover, give her a wad of money. This is where he tells her that he knows she's only young, that too many idiots are about, and so he's been told to look out for her.

She eats a chip and says to him with half-closed eyelids, 'I know, Gavin.'

He sits up, startled. 'How?'

'Padre.'

'You know Padre?'

She flicks her stare around the restaurant. 'He got my attention.'

Gavin nods, 'Yeah, he's good at that.'

She says, 'Do you know my real age?'

'Yes.'

She frowns. 'And you're not weird about that.'

He shrugs. 'No. Why?'

She stares at him for a moment, then says, 'No, nothing.'

Gavin screws up his face as he remembers Padre's words. *The road to Finland has no end. She'll go, by any means, to France.* Gavin remembers thinking that you can't get to Finland by road, anyway. Then Padre looked right into Gavin's eyes and said, *But Little Gavin will come to Liverpool.* Not that he wouldn't mind a daytrip up there, but it would be quite a bus journey, and now wasn't the best time for daytrips. 'You know those ferries go all the time, don't you?' he says, now.

'Yes.'

'You can rock up to that ferry terminal whenever you want…'

'I know.'

'So, like, just out of curiosity…why aren't we going there?'

'You suggested it.'

'Yeah, but *you* decided.'

She sighs, skates about her milkshake-cup on the table.

'Do you miss your mum? Is that it?'

She shrugs her head over to one shoulder.

'I would miss my mum,' he says. 'That's why I'm not going.'

'Really?'

'Mostly, yeah,' he says, leaning over his straw and sucking.

'Where *are* you going, then?'

He swallows and says, 'Nuneaton.'

'Is that in England?'

'Yep.'

'Is it safe there?'

'Dunno.'

She screws up her face and laughs a bit. 'Why go then?'

'Dunno… Smack bang in the middle of the country. Furthest point from any coast. Hopefully won't get flooded.'

'Hopefully?'

'Yeah,' he says, sipping, thinking. 'England is what we know,

I suppose. Ryan's not married. I'm not married. Big Carla's not married. Don't fancy going through all of that...you know.'

'Is that, like, your family?"

'Yeah.'

'So, will you just take a tent or what?'

He shakes his head. 'We're buying a house there.'

'No one's buying a house anywhere in England.'

'I know. It was proper cheap.'

She wrinkles her eyes and giggles.

'Ah, you're laughing, see? That's good.'

They sit. Him slurping, her running her finger around the top of her cup, and he thinks to himself that he's quite relaxed around her, which is weird. Everything that Padre told him made him panic, like properly panic, and this morning before he left, his mum made him bend over his knees and breathe into a paper bag. But then he had to rush around getting to London and lug the turkey about and then he passed the flower shop and before he knew it, he had too much to carry and was almost late for the bus home. But he got there. Would have been nice if she'd said something to him, but this isn't so bad, he thinks. Almost normal.

Now she says, 'I'm scared.'

He looks into her face, then at her belly. 'Oh yeah?'

'Of giving birth on my own.'

'Oh.' He swallows, puts his lips around his milkshake straw and lets his eyes wander over the table. He'd like to say something to her, but he can't get past the word 'birth' and he's got no idea how he's swallowing so much milkshake, when he'd actually quite like to throw up.

'Did you hear me?' she says.

'Mm-hm.' He puts his cup down and says, 'You won't be on your own though. It doesn't usually happen like that...'

'You're sweating,' she says.

'My drink's too cold,' he says, nodding towards the milkshake.

She narrows her eyes, then says, 'I can't even speak French.'

'Oh right... Yeah, me neither. Don't think many people can.'

'I just don't know what it would be like over there. What if I end up giving birth in my room on my own?'

'Is that why you got off the bus?'

Her lips press together and she nods.

'I must admit...' he says, rubbing his chin, 'it is quite scary.'

'I know,' she says, casting her eyes down.

'Why don't you go back to your mum's? Just until you have it?'

Now she looks at her belly and strokes it. 'Mum's gone strange.'

'Why?'

'I don't think she'll like it. The baby.'

Gavin looks at her bump, imagines the little creature inside. Suddenly, he feels sad for it, like it shouldn't have a single person in the world that doesn't love it. It's so tiny, he thinks. It needs love more than anything. 'Everyone loves babies,' he says. 'Especially mums.'

'I've really messed things up and I don't think we can make it work.' She looks up to the side, shakes her head.

'Oh... Well, that's a bit tricky then.'

They finish their milkshakes. Watch entire families with travelling rucksacks, sleeping bags attached to the bottoms, pots and pans clanging behind, mums sighing, kids twirling, pushing each other or sometimes mute, still. He makes getting-up-to-leave noises, pats his pockets, looks around for a bin. She watches, chin in her hand.

'Shall we wander back?' he asks.

'You got kids already?' she replies.

'Um...' he says, flicking a glance at her belly. 'Well, not really. Only Little Carla but she's not mine, like, not *my* daughter but my brother's daughter.'

'Your niece?'

'Yeah. Exactly,' he says, standing up.

She swirls her cup with her straw and lowers her eyelids. 'Do you *want* kids?'

'Well,' he says, looking over at the bin, sitting back down. 'I haven't really thought about it. Bit scary for me, probably.'

She nods deeply, pupils climbing up the wall behind him, along the ceiling...

'Yeah,' he says. 'Bit scary.'

More deep nods.

He feels like he should add something to make him look a bit keener like, 'I'd always take care of it if I had one,' or 'I'd love it if it was actually *here*,' but his words are all sticky and wrong. He looks from her to the bin, from the bin to his watch, gets up, pats his back pockets, picks up the turkey.

'Where are you taking me, then?'

'Dover?' he says, frowning.

'I don't think I want to go to Dover now.'

'Oh,' he says, and thinks about this for a minute. Then he remembers something else that Padre told him. 'Do you wanna get the bus to Margate?'

'Yeah?'

He grins. 'Yeah. You can meet my mum. Ryan will drive you to Dover later.'

She pulls her sleeves over her hands. 'Or I could just get a bus from here. Like we planned.'

'Oh.' His grin shrinks. 'Is that what you want to do?'

She shakes her head, looking at the table. 'Flowers have withered,' she says. 'Let's go.'

CHAPTER SIXTY-SEVEN | December 2032
Ashleigh

By the time Ashleigh arrived at Gavin's house, the whole family were in the kitchen, getting stuff out to lay the table for dinner. A little girl came halfway down the stairs, eyes fixed on Ashleigh's belly. 'Carla, it's past your bedtime,' said Gavin, to which the little girl giggled and scrambled back up to the landing. Ashleigh had only been to Margate once, when she was a baby. Her mum always said it was dodgy, then it got all trendy, then it went back to dodgy again. The beach was nice enough, though. Proper sand and really deep, not that she saw it from the bus, but Gavin told her about it as they rattled through Kent.

Now, Ashleigh takes her shoes off and walks through the lounge to the kitchen, staying close behind Gavin. Normally, she'd be nervous, but at the moment she is just relieved not to be on a ferry in the middle of the Channel. The house smells of something frying – sausages, perhaps? – and makes her want to sit down and stuff her face. She had a McDonald's in Canterbury, but that barely touched the sides. This baby was making up for lost time. She puts a hand on her belly as she thinks about those first few weeks, poor thing must have been starving. She retracts her hand, can't get too attached, she reminds herself.

When she gets to the kitchen, Gavin says, 'Everyone, this is Ashleigh.'

At that moment, she realises she's been holding his sleeve the whole time. She lets go and feels herself get a bit hot in the face.

Gavin's older brother – Ryan? – pulls out a chair and gestures for her to sit down.

An older woman with glasses hanging from her neck, obviously Gavin's mum, turns around and says, 'You're just in time, Ashleigh. I hope you're not vegetarian.'

Ashleigh smiles, shakes her head. 'No.'

Another woman is tweezing crisps into her mouth with her acrylic nails. She is younger, with fierce eyebrows and big earrings. 'I'm Carla,' she says, 'Gavin's older sister.'

Ryan leans over and pinches a crisp from her.

'Oi,' says Carla.

'You'll ruin your dinner,' says Gavin's mum, flicking a tea towel towards the crips bag. 'Oh Gavin, how lovely, are they for me?'

Gavin beams as his mum takes the flowers, puts her glasses on her nose and inspects them.

'And...' says Gavin, handing her the turkey.

Everyone cheers, as if they've only just noticed it, but honestly, it's huge, thinks Ashleigh, how can they have only just seen it?

'Sunday roast,' says Ryan.

Carla turns to Ashleigh. 'You've gotta stay for Mum's Sunday roast.'

Ashleigh hides her mouth in the neck of her hoodie and grins.

'How far gone are you, love?' asks Gavin's mum, as she puts a jug of gravy on the table.

Ashleigh opens her mouth to answer, jolts back into her chair, hand flying to her belly. Ryan and Gavin leap to their feet. Big Carla laughs. 'He proper kicked you there, didn't he?' she says.

Ashleigh exhales, nods, laughs.

'Is she alright then?' Gavin asks around the table, backside hovering over his chair.

'Yeah,' says Ryan, sitting down. 'Just a kick.'

Ashleigh sneezes and Gavin stands again. They laugh at this, especially Ashleigh, who giggles for ages, legs crossed, well after the others have stopped.

'Thirty-seven weeks, I think,' she says to Gavin's mum.

Gavin's mum gapes her eyes. 'You could drop at any minute!'

Ashleigh's smile shrinks into a stiff line. 'I know.'

'Ryan'll take you to Dover later, won't you Ryan?'

Ryan scoffs. 'I can try.'

'What do you mean?' asks Gavin.

'Roads are gridlocked. Probably take us two hours to get there. At least.'

Gavin lets his mouth fall open. 'You're kidding?'

Mum leans over, puts a bowl of mashed potato into the middle of the table. 'Quicker to walk!' she says, laughing. 'Do you like mashed potato, Ashleigh? Done a few sausages as well.'

'Sounds lovely, I'm starving,' she replies, shuffling in her chair, eyeing the food.

'But that means we won't get there until,' Gavin looks at the clock, 'well after eight.'

'Ten, I'd say. Gotta eat first,' says Ryan.

'Where's your suitcase, love?' Mum slides a fried egg onto Ryan's plate.

'There,' says Ashleigh, pointing at her rucksack tucked under the stairs.

'Is that all you've got?'

She nods.

'It's fine, the ferries run all night,' says Ryan. 'You said she can get on any one of them?'

'Yeah,' Gavin replies, looking at Ashleigh. She nods. 'But we gotta make sure she gets on safely.'

'What about stuff for your baby?' asks Mum.

Ashleigh shrugs.

'What ferry would you like to get on?' asks Ryan.

'Dunno.'

'If we drop you there at ten, you won't be over there before midnight.' Ryan looks around the table. 'Then what will she do when she gets to France?' He pulls the bowl of potato towards him.

'And they're an hour ahead,' adds Big Carla.

'*And* they're an hour ahead,' affirms Ryan.

'Will there be someone waiting for you over there?' asks Carla.

'Dunno.'

'We can't just leave her to fend for herself,' says Gavin.

'Watch your elbow, love.' Gavin's mum slides an egg onto Ashleigh's plate. 'Course there is, there must be someone waiting for you in Calais?'

'Dunno,' says Ashleigh, lip quivering. She bends forward, holds her head with her hand.

Gavin's mum puts the frying pan down, lays an arm around her shoulders.

'It's alright, Ashleigh,' says Carla. 'We ain't gonna leave you.'

'No way,' says Gavin's mum. 'We need to get some stuff together for her. We've got Little Carla's baby stuff up in the loft, haven't we, Ryan?'

A tear spirals Ashleigh's wrist.

'No,' says Ryan, putting his cutlery down. 'She's not going over there with a load of stuff and no one to meet her,' he says, looking at Ashleigh, placing a hand on the back of her head. 'We're not leaving you at Dover, tonight or tomorrow or whenever. We're not dropping you off on your own like that.'

Gavin's Mum squeezes Ashleigh into her side. 'I don't think we should worry about this tonight, eh?'

Carla drags her chair over to Ashleigh. 'You can have my room; I'll go in with Little Carla.'

Ashleigh rubs her eyes. Sniffs. Breathes her shoulders upwards. 'Thanks,' she says.

CHAPTER SIXTY-EIGHT | December 2032
Gavin

There's something that's been bugging Gavin for a while now, although he hasn't really had a chance to sit and think about it since the exhibition. He sits in front of a canvas that he's been trying to paint since last week, but the magic has gone from his fingers; he can't feel the movement of the trees like he used to. So much has happened, he thinks again, shaking out his hands.

Ashleigh's been there two weeks – ha! To think she wanted to get on that boat and go to France where she had no one, when she'd got a ready-made family right here. 'It's mum's pancakes, isn't it?' he asked her a couple of days ago. She grinned slowly, the way she does, bumped his shoulder with her own. He didn't mind that. It was nice, actually, to get to a place where they were alright around each other. He would like them to keep her in Margate with them, he thinks, then take her to Nuneaton. There'd be plenty of room for another sister and a baby in Nuneaton. Although, her becoming his sister seemed a bit complicated; there were a few details that needed to be worked out. And she'd already said that she didn't want to stay...

Anyway, the thing that's bugging him.

Gillian.

She asked him the big favour at Pinko's exhibition and he never replied, like he said he would. That's two things he's done wrong by her. The thought of it – the test and the Jury – makes him cringe, like, properly cringe, but he doesn't feel dizzy anymore. In fact, since he's been all matey-matey with Ashleigh, girls don't freak him out quite as much. Not that he'd want to...do that...with Ashleigh. He shudders as his brain shows him a gyrating pelvis and naked buttocks and nipples and...

He scrunches his eyes shut. If only his brain wouldn't do that.

Gillian said they could practise beforehand, as she twisted her fingers and drew her shoulders up to her ears. No-one wants to do it, obviously, but perhaps neither of them were particularly good at it, even under normal circumstances. Perhaps they'd spend a week together, become mates, and then it wouldn't matter if they weren't good at it. Coz they'd laugh about it afterwards. This all seems quite doable, he thinks. But there is a big difference between having a recipe and making a cake.

'Mum,' he says a few days later, bum pressed into the edge of the worktop, hands in pockets.

'Yes, love.'

Gavin's mum sits at the table doing the sudoku, glasses ending halfway down her nose, their gold hangy-chain looping behind her neck.

'Do you remember that lady with the golden eyes?'

She flicks her gaze over her glasses. 'What lady?'

'The one at Pinko's exhibition. *My* exhibition. Do you remember?'

She squints at him.

'Sparkly flip-flops. She wanted to talk to me for a minute. In private.'

His mum puts her pen down, dances her eyes back and forth across her memories. 'Oh yes...I know the one.'

'Well,' says Gavin, 'I think I'd like to take her to France.'

His mum takes her glasses off and squints at him. 'What do you mean?'

'She asked me to.' He curls his big toes upwards and looks at them. His face starts to warm up. 'She doesn't know any other men.'

'But,' says his mum, 'what about—'

'I'd like to do something nice for her to make up for...the car boot sale near the beach...that day.'

'Oh,' she says again, and she makes her eyes really wide. 'Do you feel like you owe her something?'

'I think I owe her everything.'

Gavin's mum sits right back in her chair. 'You know what that will involve, don't you?'

He nods.

They look at each other for a while, then she puts her glasses back on, picks up her pen.

'You're your own man, Gavin,' she says. 'Only you can figure it out.'

Gavin watches while she traces her pen over the empty boxes, trying out the numbers before writing them down properly. His mum was good at doing that, letting him decide for himself. By telling her about it, he'd made it a bit more real. He tunes in to his stomach, his knees, his armpits. Weirdly, they're all alright.

Maybe he can really do this.

CHAPTER SIXTY-NINE | December 2032
Ashleigh

'Do you think we should tell your mother that you're here, sweetheart?' Gavin's mum asks three days later, while folding tea towels and stacking them in a blue, plastic basket.

'No,' says Ashleigh.

They continue folding. In half, then in half again.

'Pass me the peg bag love, just behind you. Ta.' Then, 'You know, I get the feeling that you and your mum don't like each other.'

Ashleigh clutches the tea towel she's folding. 'That's not true,' she says, eyes wide. 'We are, like, best mates.'

'Right…'

'She's always given her all for me.'

'And your dad?'

Ashleigh shrugs.

'So it's just you two, is it?'

'Yes.'

'I'm a mum,' says Gavin's mum.

Ashleigh pouts. 'I know.'

'Ryan had Little Carla when he was seventeen.'

'Did he?'

'Yes. It was all very sudden and we were all a bit shocked.'

'Were you angry?'

'A little bit. His girlfriend was only sixteen. But do you think I'd be without Little Carla?'

'This is more complicated than that,' says Ashleigh, refolding her tea towel.

'Why is it, love?'

Ashleigh powers up a breath, opens her mouth, then shuts it again.

Gavin's mum stops folding, looks straight into Ashleigh's face. 'Your mum will just want to know you're well.'

'Mm. Maybe.'

They carry on folding for a moment. Ashleigh places each folded cloth on her belly until she has a little stack. The baby really is big now, she thinks; it's probably going to come out soon. *She.* Her stomach flutters as she thinks this; she didn't need her science GCSE to know that the birth would be painful. Just one or two of mum's friends was enough, rolling their eyes and making comments about stitches or tearing or… She shudders. But they always had big slanted smiles on their faces, as if they'd done something hard, but worth it. Perhaps it's true that women forget about the pain once they've laid eyes on their baby.

Perhaps it's the best thing in the world.

Ashleigh swallows and finishes her pile. This can't happen to her. It will be removed from her body like a bad tooth. She'll keep it safe while she waits for the tooth fairy, she thinks, and try not to love it. She takes two pegs from the bag, clips one to her sleeve and fiddles with the other one.

Anyway, Padre had promised that she'd see it again. The baby. Although, he had said 'he' not 'it'. *It's 'she',* Ashleigh said. Even though she keeps saying 'it'.

'Silly old man,' she says, squeezing the peg in time to the words.

'What's that, love?'

'I never wanted to keep it,' she says. 'Anyway.'

Gavin's mum stops folding, puts her hands flat on the table, looks at her. 'I'm not surprised.'

Ashleigh tiptoes her irises upwards, meets Gavin's mum's stare. 'I still don't,' she says. 'I don't want my baby. Is that bad?'

Gavin's mum frowns, reaches out a hand and holds Ashleigh's cheek. 'No love. That's very normal.'

CHAPTER SEVENTY | January 2033
Gavin

'Wow, were you hungry, Ash?' says Ryan, at dinner the next evening.

They're all there, including Little Carla, in fact Gavin's mum has only just sat down at the table. The rest of them have started already – that wasn't really polite but ever since they were little, Mum urged them to start before her in case it got cold. Gavin is quite a fast eater, probably the fastest in the family, but he's only about halfway through his veg – he always left the meat 'til last. Ashleigh eats like a gannet. At Christmas, she could have won world records. He looks over at her plate now. It's so clean that he can see the reflection of her pink, onesie cuff, as she picks her teeth with her thumbnail. Big Carla gave her that onesie and she hardly wears anything else. It's big enough for her and her bump and there's plenty of room for the bump to grow.

Ashleigh puts her hand down, licks her front teeth. 'Sorry.'

'Don't be,' says Ryan. 'You're eating for two.'

'Yeah,' she says, holding her belly. 'I'm not actually that hungry, but I think the baby is.'

Ryan says, 'My missus used that excuse with Little Carla all the time. Then four stone later, I was like: you've got to tell that baby that this ain't normal.'

Big Carla rolls her eyes at him, tells him not to be a dick.

'Don't say the 'd' word in front of Little Carla,' says Ryan.

Gavin covers his mouth with the back of his hand. Laughs.

'Every half an hour, it keeps kicking me,' says Ashleigh. 'But not a proper kick.'

Gavin's mum waves her hand at the others to hush them down. 'What do you mean, love?'

'Like, it rocks me from the inside. Like there's a rumbling, right down where I usually get...' she flicks her eyes about the table, tunnels her hands around her mouth '...ladies' pains. It proper shakes me for about twenty seconds, then it's gone.'

Ryan widens his eyes.

'Does it hurt?' asks Gavin's mum.

'Yeah. It does.'

Gavin's mum blinks at her, puts her knife and fork down, opens her mouth to ask another question. Ashleigh interrupts.

'It's just getting too big and too greedy, I think.' She cups a hand over her mouth, 'And d'you know what, I even...' she stops herself when she sees Ryan listening. 'Ryan, don't listen.'

'You even what, love?' says Mum.

'I even peed myself.'

'When?' asks Ryan.

Ashleigh looks as if she's going to tell him to bugger off with his personal questions, then says, 'About four o'clock, when this all started.'

'Are they getting closer together, the rumblings in your tummy?' says Mum.

'Not really. I dunno,' says Ashleigh, spooning more potatoes onto her plate. 'I don't like talking about this in front of you two, it's embarrassing.' She scoops a forkful into her mouth and doesn't lift her eyes to indicate which two she means.

'Ryan, Gavin, take your plates into the living room.'

'No... That's a bit harsh,' says Ashleigh through her mouthful. 'I don't really mind. Don't go.'

'You're in labour, Ash,' says Ryan.

Big Carla gets up, hugs Ashleigh's shoulders. 'We'll help you, don't worry.'

'What do you mean?' says Ashleigh, through a mouthful of potatoes.

'Your baby's coming,' says Ryan,

'But it's too early,' says Ashleigh.

'Mum, should we take her to a hospital?' asks Ryan.

'But it's too early. She's not ready yet...' says Gavin, eyes fixed on Ashleigh's belly. 'The baby's not ready enough to come out.'

'Trust me, it knows when it's time,' says Gavin's mum. 'I reckon she'll be a while yet, but I've got no idea what the traffic will be like...'

'If it comes to it, we'll walk,' says Carla.

'I'll get the car ready,' says Ryan.

Gavin sits upright in his chair, palms flat against his temples.

'I'll pack you a little bag,' says Big Carla.

'I'm not in labour,' says Ashleigh. 'I can pack my own bag.'

'I don't know what to do,' says Gavin, standing up and turning in a circle. 'What shall I do?'

Rough hands clasp his elbows, bringing him to a halt. 'You need to stay here with Little Carla. We can't take her with us, you can look after her,' says his mum, nodding into his eyes.

'Yes,' he says, nodding back, 'alright.'

They thud up and down the stairs for a while, calling to each other about nappies and towels and ladies' whatnots and tea bags and shower gel. Then Ryan is outside the door, honking his horn, and they are rustling back down the stairs. 'Bye Gav,' yells Big Carla. The door shuts behind them and they are gone.

Gavin sits and draws. He outlines a large pregnant belly, then attaches it to the trunk of a chestnut tree, making the branches armlike, the leaves like hair.

Three hours later, they're back, carrying Ashleigh in; she's huffing and puffing and squealing and wanting to sit down, then stand up again, then walk around the coffee table, faster and faster until she has to stop and cling to a chair and bend all the way over, a hand on her hip. His mum tells Ryan to get the neighbour. Not two minutes later, Ryan returns to say she's already gone. 'Right, well, what about Carol's Tanya, isn't she a pharmacist's assistant?' And Ryan sets off again, comes back with Carol's Tanya, who sits and strokes Ashleigh's hand, cowers every time Ashleigh screams and then has to leave the room to be sick.

'Just hold her hand, love,' says Gavin's mum, while she dips to looks between Ashleigh's legs, then pops up to glance at the clock. Then she's asking, 'Can I put my fingers inside?' because it should be like a bagel by now, does she want to push? Does she feel the need to push? And Gavin goes upstairs and sits on the floor in Little Carla's room, in the position he's been told to use if he feels stressed, and Little Carla's headphones are on the rug from where she's been watching *Encanto* on her tablet and so Gavin puts them on and watches the rest.

He wakes up on the floor with one headphone squashed into his cheek. 'Uncle Gavin, there's a baby.' Little Carla shakes his shoulder. 'And you were using *my* headphones!' she adds.

Gavin opens his eyes. 'Is it here?' he asks. 'What is it? Is it big enough?'

'He's tiny coz he's a baby,' says Little Carla, eyes wide. 'But Ashleigh keeps saying he's got a massive head.'

'Is he bigger than a bagel?'

Little Carla giggles, then bends to clutch her knees and laughs some more.

'Is he a boy, then?' says Gavin.

'Yes, Uncle Gavin.' She strides towards him and tugs on his arm. 'Come and see him.'

How nice, Gavin thinks later that evening, to have a onesie that covers everything up so cosily. He looks like he's got paws, not hands and feet. Gavin asks Ashleigh if she's alright, tells her he's sorry for wimping out.

'It's alright. Yeah, I'm okay, yeah.'

'Do you want to see if he'll take your milk?' says Gavin's Mum.

'Nah,' she replies. 'There's the powdered stuff.'

'We've got semi-skimmed in the fridge,' adds Gavin. 'Might want to smell it first…'

'Alright, Ashleigh,' says his mum, ignoring him. 'We'll use the powder.'

The baby gets bigger quickly. Soon they cut holes in the feet of the onesies to free his little toes. Carol's Tanya has still got her keys to the abandoned pharmacy, so they stock up on powdered milk and take it in turns to wind him.

A couple of weeks later, Gavin brings the keys home for the house in Nuneaton. His mum throws her arms around him, starts wrapping lamps and picture frames and her little crystal animals in newspaper, puts them into boxes. Little Carla packs all her Barbies in a suitcase. In the evenings, they let the radio play the news while the baby naps and they eat dinner. Ashleigh would hear the theme tune, then get up and go to the toilet. They notice this and laugh at the fact that the news makes her want to go for a wee.

Then one day, during dinner, she asks, 'I have to go over soon, don't I?'

They all look up at her.

Gavin's mouth is dry. He puts down his fork and says, 'You're coming with us, Ash. To Nuneaton.'

'But it's getting closer, isn't it? The disaster. We're the only ones left on this street.'

They stare around the table at each other. Big Carla snatches a square of kitchen paper from the roll, dabs at the corner of her eye.

'We can't expect her to stay,' says Ryan. 'Most people think we're pretty mental.'

'What do you want to do, Ashleigh?' says Gavin's mum.

A shrug. 'Dunno, really,' she says. 'He's so tiny but...I'm scared of the water coming.'

'Are the rules the same?' asks Ryan. 'Now you've got a baby, can you get over so easily, like, before?'

Ashleigh looks at Gavin.

'I don't know,' says Gavin. 'Don't see why not. He was always there, wasn't he?' pointing at Ashleigh's belly. 'It's just that now he's out.'

'I looked into it,' says Big Carla. 'She can't do *that* for up to six weeks after labour.' She points at her own crotch when she says 'that'.

The table falls quiet. Gavin swirls his spaghetti with his fork. 'Can't we...' he starts, 'can't we keep you with us?'

'Gavin,' says his mum, 'we can't be responsible for that, can we? She wants to go and she's got a small baby. We can't be responsible for that.'

Gavin squints at her. There was something about the way she said 'that' that was a bit weird. She pressed her voice on it, said it more slowly than the other words. 'What do you mean?'

His mum chews, swallows, waves her fork in the air. 'You know...dying here.'

'That's definitely not going to happen,' he replies.

They raise their eyes to him, heads bowed over their plates.

'Course not, Gav,' says Ryan. 'Here, Ash, we've got to register the babe tomorrow, any thoughts on a name?'

'No,' she says, pursing her lips.

'You know, I was thinking that Ryan is a pretty sexy name.'

She laughs at this. 'Alright,' she says. 'Whatever.'

The next morning, they drive to the town hall. They have a video appointment at ten with a clerk in the Falklands, of all places. Why they can't take the call from home is anyone's guess but, whatever; Ryan syphons some petrol from next door's abandoned Toyota and they're on the road by seven-fifteen. Ashleigh takes her rucksack with her, with *all her stuff for the baby*, she tells them. 'If the traffic's anything like it was for the hospital,' she says, 'I'll need it all.'

'Will he definitely be "Ryan", then?'

'Dunno...Yeah, why not?'

Ryan smiles as he drives, slaps Gavin on the knee. 'Did you hear that?'

Gavin says, 'I think she doesn't care what she calls him. If she really wants a nice name, she'll go for Gavin.'

'Righto. Whatever, Gav.'

'She would, wouldn't you?' Gavin catches her eye in the rear-view mirror. She smiles, nods, goes back to watching the city wall, the brown-dry flower beds.

As it happens, there's no traffic, but they get stuck behind the odd army vehicle patrolling the ring road and have to dodge the rubbish that's been dropped or dumped. They slug around the city, trying to avoid it all, then Ashleigh asks them to stop so she can go to the loo.

'Can't really stop and wait for you here, Ash.'

'Just let me out at the lay-by and I'll meet you at the council offices.'

'Are you that desperate?'

'McDonalds is only there. I can nip in quickly,' she says.

Gavin says, 'I'll come with you.'

'No, Gavin. Stay with the baby,' she says, jigging her knees. 'I'm busting, Ryan. My bladder is all weird since I had him.'

'Fine.' Ryan indicates, flicks the hazard lights on. 'Leave your rucksack, we'll bring it with us,' he says.

'It's alright,' she replies, as she opens the door and climbs out. 'Got my ladies' things inside.'

'Oh right, I won't ask,' Ryan says, waving, indicating out again and resuming their crawl around the city wall.

It's dark when they return home. Ryan walks ahead with the baby in his arms. Gavin follows, hands deep inside his pockets.

Gavin's mum is ironing in front of the telly. There are two open suitcases on the sofa next to her, where she seems to be putting the ironed clothes. Gavin notices a large, faded rectangle on the wall, where a picture of Little Carla used to be.

Their mum looks up from a hiss of steam and says, 'Where on earth have you been?'

Gavin sits at the kitchen table, stares at the folded pillowcases. 'She ran off, Mum.'

'Who?' she says, putting her iron down.

'Ashleigh's gone,' says Gavin.

Their mum covers her mouth, shakes her head.

Ryan says, 'Gavin waited at the council offices, while I drove around. We were, what, four hours looking for her?'

Gavin nods deep, slow nods.

'But she might have been taken! Didn't you call the police?' says his mum.

'We found this.' Ryan delves in his pocket and pulls out a folded piece of paper. 'It was in the baby's car seat.'

Gavin's mum takes it, unfolds it and reads the note. 'Gone to France,' she says. 'I know you'll take care of him; I'm too scared to take him with me and too scared to stay.' Gavin's mum folds the note, puts it on the ironing board. 'She reckons she's too young,' she says, as she starts to cry. 'She's not even properly healed yet,' she says. 'She'll get an infection... There are no hospitals.'

Ryan puts his arms around his mother, leans his head against her head and wipes an eye.

Gavin picks up the note, unfolds it, and again reads the PS at the end.

I'd like you to call him Little Gavin.

They spend the evening in the living room, feet curled underneath them on the sofa or armchair, mugs of tea growing cold in their hands. The baby — Little Gavin — is quiet, creaking occasionally as he strains to look at his own hands or to fill his nappy. They lift their eyes to him, pick him up, change him, smile small smiles at him, try not to cry. 'Maybe she'll be back,' says Gavin.

No one replies.

CHAPTER SEVENTY-ONE | February 2033
Gavin

A week later, Gavin finds his mum bawling in the kitchen, surrounded by boxes. He ducks through the door and catches her with her face in her hands. He turns to tiptoe out again – thinking she might like to be on her own – but she draws her hands away, widens her shiny gaze at him and goes about opening the fridge.

'Um...' says Gavin, staring at the fridge door and then back at his mum. 'I just saw you crying, didn't I?'

'I'm alright love,' she says, sniffing.

'Oh right. That's alright then.' He pulls Grandad's chair from the table and sits down. After a minute or two, he notices her shoulders are shaking. He stares at the shoulders, then shuffles to sit on his hands.

'That baby,' says his mum, 'cannot come to Nuneaton.'

'He's got a name now,' says Gavin.

She takes a damp cloth and pushes it over the worktop. 'He needs to get to safety.'

Gavin frowns. Ryan drove them up, the week before, so they could have a look around. It was a bit different to the boarded-up streets of Margate. Inland, he's always believed, is a bit like a flat without a balcony. A good town needs a good beach to sit on, with fresh air and a view all the way to nothing. The massive campsite on the outskirts of Nuneaton didn't help. Mostly vans and caravans – even a few tents – covered acres and acres of farmland. One family had propped up their boat and sat in a row, legs dangling through the railings. Wardens in luminous orange vests stood around a shed by, what Gavin assumed to be, the entrance to the campsite. As Ryan crept along with the traffic, Gavin admired the fairy lights on the shed, the bunting covered A-frame beside it: Welcome To The Centre Of The World, it read. But what struck Gavin most was the smoke from the bonfires. They could see it a mile off, crouching around the town like a dirty spell.

Now he says, 'Little Gavin will be safe with us.'

'No, love,' says his mum, straightening to look at him. 'Because we have chosen to stay.'

'You saw all those people on that campsite,' he says. 'I think we made the right decision. I think we'll be alright.'

'And what if we're not?'

He blinks at her.

She gazes back, eyebrows rearing up to each other. 'Look,' she says, 'he's too little to decide if he wants to stay here – where hardly *anyone* is staying – or go and be guaranteed a chance at life.'

Gavin blinks again.

'We have to make that choice for him. And *I* think,' she says, 'he should be guaranteed a life.'

Gavin rubs his chin with his shoulder, stares at the table. *The road to Finland has no end. She'll go, by any means, to France*, Padre had told him during that awful day that he doesn't like to think about. *But Little Gavin will come to Liverpool*. The France bit is definitely true; she'd be somewhere in the mountains by now, all being well. If the baby was destined for Liverpool, Gavin would strap him into his car seat and drive him there, rather than have some stranger kidnap him. (Well, Ryan would have to drive, of course.) He pictures that tiny person with his little fat lips and curling hands. Little Gavin lives at the edge of them, in his basket at the edge of the sitting room, at mealtimes at the edge of the table. He is hardly there at all, really, because he's so small. Yet, at the same time, he's become the centre of their everything. He is the thing that turns their heads whenever they enter the room. He always gets the first hellos and the last goodbyes. He is the reason for most of their questions. *Is he in bed? Has he eaten? What time did he wake up?* Their lives hinge on all of his little achievements. *He burped today! He smiled at me this morning.* To think of the house without him is as bad as living in it without Ashleigh. They are both my family now, thinks Gavin, and families shouldn't separate. Padre had a habit of getting things spot on, but if the baby goes to Liverpool, how will he be better off than he is here? The water will definitely submerge the coasts, and Liverpool is somewhere by the sea. Miles away from Nuneaton.

His mum is squeezing the drips from a jay cloth. Now she says, 'Is there any way you can…you know…get in touch with his grandmother, love?'

He frowns. 'Grandmother?'

'Yes,' she says. 'Ashleigh's mum.'

'Oh,' he says, squinting into his memory. 'Jane?'

'That's his rightful place, really. If I was his grandmother, I'd want him with me. She must be going out of her mind.' She dries the surface with a tea towel, mouth taut, elbow pistoning. 'Someone should have her number, surely? Someone from Pinko's lot?'

'You're right,' he says. 'I'll call Butler. Butler might know.'

Butler doesn't answer. The call goes straight to the beep. Gavin sighs, taps the edge of his phone against his chin, rocks Little Gavin's crib. He walks around the living room a couple of times, stares at the empty walls for help. Normally, he liked looking at the photos of everyone, especially the one of Ryan and Big Carla having a water fight. He'd taken it right at the moment when Big Carla had squeezed her eyes shut in laughter, while Ryan shot her at close range. All the water droplets catch the light in a shining, glittery way. It's a brilliant photo. There were lots of Little Carla, even one of Ashleigh. Little Gavin would go up in the new house, although he was sort of there already, inside Ashleigh's tummy. Didn't really matter anymore. Now, the photos are nothing but a cluster of bright, magnolia rectangles. All different sizes. His mum has taken every single one down, wrapped them and packed them in a box. Gavin stops pacing and decides to phone the big house – Pinko's house – just to see if anyone is there. That is, after all, the last place he saw Jane. Probably someone would be knocking about.

Blue answers, his voice deep and scratchy. Gavin almost hangs up, but instead says, 'Oh…hello Blue.'

'Hi Gavin.'

'Um…' says Gavin. 'Still there, are you?'

'Aye. Well.'

Blue tells him that he intends to stay until the helicopter leaves at the end of the month. The two security guards would be on it too, with their wives and kids. He says it as if he is smiling, as if he is talking about going for a day trip to the beach. Most people would be this happy, thinks Gavin, about going to Finland.

Sometimes Blue can be alright; he remembers that day on the bus with Martin the Chinchilla, and how Blue had come back the following week to the craft fair to buy Gavin's drawing. Once he gave Gavin a pear when they bumped into each other in Pinko's garden. Then there were other times he had a face like thunder, and wouldn't even look at Gavin whenever he passed him, painting the mural in the main house. And then, sometimes, he was just plain weird. A bit like Padre. Although Padre let you see into him, then explained to you what you were seeing. Blue would do something weird and scurry away; like tidy away Gavin's kit in a locked cupboard without telling him. He and Butler watched him on the CCTV afterwards, scratching their heads disbelievingly.

Gavin asks Blue about Padre. Surely, he'd be gone by now, wouldn't he? As one of Pinko's closest friends, surely he would have boarded a helicopter and disappeared to safety?

'Padre?' Blue laughs. 'No, not Padre. He's still in Liverpool, ready to die the most dramatic of deaths, apparently. His very words.'

'Oh,' says Gavin, and for a moment he is shocked about that, but then he remembers Padre's prophecy about Little Gavin and his heart falls into his knees. A long bright moan bubbles out of the crib. 'Well, I don't know what to do, then. Perhaps I should go to Liverpool.'

Blue sucks in a whisper of air. 'Is that *your* baby, I can hear?' he says, his voice a little higher, a little louder.

Gavin stutters. 'We're looking after him.'

Blue asks, 'Where did he come from, then?'

Gavin feels uneasy about Blue's questions, although he can't work out why. Still, it's not in his nature to tell fibs or avoid the truth. He's nicked a few things in his life, but he could never lie about it when he got caught (he always got caught). 'It's the girl's baby, you know, the scandal…with Pinko…'

'I thought it might be,' says Blue. 'So...you've got Pinko's bairn?'

'He should've been Pinko's baby,' says Gavin, and this thought makes him teary.

'I'd certainly take the boy,' says Blue, before Gavin can finish his sentence.

Gavin takes a slow breath, turns in a circle, looks up at the magnolia, photo squares, then back down to the baby. 'What about Pinko's ex-girlfriend. Jane. Has she left yet?'

'No idea,' says Blue. 'Hasn't she been guaranteed safe passage to Finland?'

'We don't know where she is,' says Gavin. 'Perhaps she's gone over there already to avoid doing that awful test thing in front of the Jury.'

'I'd know if she had,' says Blue.

'How?' says Gavin.

'I just would. And she's got enough money to sink a battleship. She won't be doing the test, you mark my words.'

'Oh.' Gavin's gaze climbs the front room blinds, then slides down the curtains. The test, the pointless test, with its skin and hair and smells... Gillian expands in his mind, sitting on the ring-shaped bench in the centre of Pinko's gallery, one leg crossed over the other. The heel of her sparkly flip-flop flapping.

'Look,' says Blue. 'If Jane's going to Finland anyway, you may as well leave the baby with me...I'll see that they're reunited.'

'Um,' says Gavin, 'I'm gonna call you back if that's alright, Blue?' Then he hangs up.

In the kitchen, Gavin eats three pink wafers, one after the other, while a new plan forms in his mind. This would make everything right, he thinks. He returns to the doorway and rises onto the balls of his feet, so that he can see into Little Gavin's Moses basket. Arms tentacle from the edges and stir the air; bubbles click on his little lips. He's really good, being so small an' all but not getting upset when he's on his own. Perhaps, thinks Gavin, sinking back to his heels, he wouldn't miss us.

It takes him at least an hour to work up the nerve to call her. She slipped him her number at the exhibition, and a few times he'd checked his contact list to make sure it was still there, especially those anxious moments where he knew, he just *knew*, there was no way he could do what she wanted him to do. He plods to the fridge, makes himself a cheese sandwich, then reaches into a bag of Tesco doughnuts – mm, custard today – and fresh too, not the discount ones. The dough hardly resists his teeth as he bites into it and he takes a moment to appreciate how much his life has changed. He makes a cup of tea while having a word with himself about procras... procras... about putting stuff off. There was nothing for it but to ignore the giant, hairy lady-parts that thrust in and out of his mind and press the call button. She probably wouldn't answer anyway...

Gillian picks up after three rings.

'Hello?' she says. Her hello is one, round note with breath-soft edges.

He waits for a moment, licking his lips and willing himself on. Yes, he would do it, he would finally do right by everyone, and this felt so much better than handing the baby over to Blue. 'It's Gavin,' he says, the air disappearing from his throat. 'Do you remember Gavin? I mean me... Do you remember me?'

'Hi, Gavin,' she says. 'How are you?'

He frowns into the phone. 'Are you still here?' he says. 'In England.'

'Yes?' she says, as if it were a question.

'Oh...' he says, then chokes in a breath.

'Are you? Still in England?'

'Yes.'

'Oh right,' she says. 'That's right, you were always going to stay, weren't you?'

'Yes. We're moving to Nuneaton next week.'

'Yes, Nuneaton. That's right. As soon as that?'

'I mean...It's not really soon. It's taken ages.'

'I guess that was to be expected.'

'Yeah...'

Gavin nods through a long pause, holds the back of his head, elbow out.

'I can go with you,' he says, finally.

'Really?'

'If you still want me to.'

'Yes! I mean, I do, I do.'

'You do?'

'Yes.'

'Okay.' Again, he smiles, but realises that he should have thought about this a bit more before calling her. He's really promised it now, and it doesn't feel like doing the right thing, at all. It just feels scary.

'But...' she starts. He can tell just from that 'but' that her fingers are twisting together. 'When? And...how? You're moving next week and we need documents and, well, you know...'

'They can move without me. Ryan's borrowing a van.'

'Oh...Your brother?'

'Yes, my brother.' Then, 'We can get the documents from someone I know,' he says.

'Right.' She sounds like she doesn't believe him.

'No, no, he's legit. He's an ex priest.'

'Well... Um...'

'He can forge the marriage stuff, you know...whatever that is...I don't know what that is...'

'A certificate?'

'Yeah. Maybe.' Gavin scratches his head, tries to think of the word. Perhaps it *is* a certificate...

'Fine,' she says. 'Where do we meet?'

'Well,' he replies, and the words waiting in his mouth are about Little Gavin and Padre and that Gavin will do this to help her, but only because Padre saw it in the future and, in return, she must look after a tiny baby until it's at least sixteen or something. But all those words might seem a bit confusing to someone who doesn't know the full story. I'll get to Liverpool, he thinks, then I'll explain the truth. Just like he did in McDonald's that day with Ashleigh in Canterbury. His heart shrinks a bit when he thinks of Ashleigh. 'Can you get to Liverpool?' he says. 'Soon?'

*

'Why?' says Big Carla at dinner. 'Why does he have to go?'

Gavin sits back. Pulls at the collar of his Matalan polo shirt. It's toad in the hole tonight and he would quite like to enjoy it without Big Carla going off on one, especially about this of all subjects. Mum has always made a decent toad in the hole; the family joke was that it never had a soggy bottom. Ryan was the one to say it tonight and Little Carla laughed and laughed.

'There's no way he's gonna get to France. He gets lost on the way to Londis,' says Big Carla.

'What *are* you on about?' says Ryan. 'Gavin knows the bus system by heart.'

Gavin tries to close his ears, to think about his latest drawing or the new pigeon in the garden or the tiny Coventry City kit that they have ordered for Little Gavin.

His mum holds up a hand, indicating that she would like to speak, but is still finishing her mouthful. Then she swallows and says, 'It's better for the baby, love. It's giving him the best chance he can have.'

'And what about Little Carla?' says Ryan. 'Should we send her off too?'

'Don't be daft,' says his mum. 'Where would we send her?'

'Where will we send *him*?' says Ryan. 'Ash left him with us.'

'Hang on, hang on, shut up a minute,' says Big Carla.

The news jingles in from the living room. The presenter announces the Vatnajökull meltwater has caused the further shifting in the magma chambers and a large rumble has been recorded from Hrafnablótsjökul. The Faroe Islands have been evacuated completely. 'It is most certainly a case of when, not if,' he says.

The tsunami siren wails on Ryan's phone. They shoot their eyes to it, put down their cutlery. Ryan fumbles to shut it off.

'...coming to you live from Krakow,' says the news presenter.

'Where's that?' says Big Carla.

'Poland,' says Gavin, remembering that one of Pinko's mates had moved there.

Ryan picks up his fork and starts eating again. 'London's empty,' he says, through a mouthful of potato.

Upstairs, the baby starts to bleat, then wail. 'I'll go,' says Big Carla, pushing her chair away from the table.

When she's gone, Gavin's mum covers Gavin's hand with her own. 'You're doing the right thing,' she says. 'I'm proud of you.'

Gavin smiles weakly at his mum. 'It would be much easier if Ashleigh was here,' he says.

She makes her eyes all kind. 'I hope she's safe,' she says. 'Let's hope she's gone to find her mum.'

That evening, Gavin asks his mum to stitch a small pouch in the back of Little Gavin's outdoor onesie, right where his nappy would be so that he won't feel it. Gavin takes the birth certificate from his back pocket, reads it again, feeling all proud that he'd managed to acquire it. The name, Little Gavin Pearce, is written in stumpy letters. It was only right that he should have Ashleigh's surname, after all. That's what everyone would have wanted. He folds the paper into the pouch and takes the onesie back to his mum so that she can stitch it in properly. She looks at him and smiles as she cuts the cotton. 'That was a good idea, Gavin.'

Gavin smiles back, then rushes off to tell Little Gavin what he's done. 'You'll wear it on the trip to Europe, Little Gavin,' he says. 'Just in case you get lost. So you'll always know who you are.'

CHAPTER SEVENTY-TWO | February 2033
Gavin

There are no trains up to Liverpool. Gavin checks the bus timetables online, but finds that most of the services are either full or cancelled. Then, of course, what if the volcano erupts and he's halfway up the country on a train or, even worse, on a ferry? Gavin huffs. Puts his phone face down on the kitchen worktop.

'Why are you checking trains?' Ryan looks up. He's painting a tiny, armoured monster at the kitchen table. 'I'll drive you.'

Gavin paces about the kitchen, kneading the front of his jumper. Ryan puts down his paintbrush and frowns. Gavin would like him to say something reassuring; it would be nice to take a bit of this pressure off with a few, kind words.

'You don't have to do this. You don't even know her,' says Ryan.

Gavin nods along, considering this as if it makes complete sense, then he says, 'But it'll make things right. For everyone.'

Ryan tips his head and winces, the way he does when he agrees with something that's right, but it will most likely be rough going. 'And the baby,' he says.

'And the baby,' repeats Gavin.

'But,' says Ryan.

'Go on.'

'Well,' he says, rolling the end of the paint brush, this way, then that. 'Have you ever done this before, bro?'

'What?'

'You know...' and he darts his eyes up to the left and back again.

Gavin squeezes his shoulders right up to his ears. Puts his hands in his pockets.

'Right,' nods Ryan. 'Alright. Don't worry.'

Gavin shuts his eyes and shudders slightly.

'It's not hard,' says Ryan.

'What makes you think I haven't done it before?' says Gavin, eyes still closed.

Ryan is quiet, probably looking Gavin up and down while he thinks about this. 'Course you have, bro,' he says in a gentle voice. 'I never said you hadn't.'

The next day, they set off. The roads are clear from south to north, but Gavin sees in the opposite lane queues of traffic backed up to forever. He says to Ryan, 'I'm sorry, I'm really sorry. Your return journey is going to be shit.' And Ryan shrugs and says, 'It's alright, we're doing the right thing aren't we?' And Gavin thinks about his mum handing them a Tupperware box of sandwiches, then wringing her hands.

'But why Liverpool?' she kept saying.

'I dunno,' said Gavin. 'This Padre bloke can sort out the paperwork, I think. What with him being in that business, an' all.'

'This Padre bloke... Who on earth does he think he is, telling you what you should and shouldn't do?'

'He brought Ashleigh to us.'

Mum said a funny thing then. A really funny thing. She said, 'I know exactly what he's like, Gavin, and just you remember this: he's never shown any interest in you before.'

Gavin frowned. 'Why would he?'

His mum stuttered a bit, then blinked about the room as if her answer were lying around somewhere. 'Just you keep your wits about you...'

Gavin said, 'You know I stole her camera, don't you Mum? She fell over and cut her head open and instead of helping her, I nicked her camera.'

His mum looked away, then; pressing her lips together like she was eating a sour sweet.

'And I'm doing this for the baby as much as for me, remember.'

She nodded and leaned forward to brush down the front of his jacket and straighten his collar. 'You'll come straight back?' she said. 'From France.'

'Yes, Mum.'

Before they left, his mum held little Gavin for a long time, then pushed him into Ryan's arms and dashed off into the kitchen. As they drove away, she didn't wave from the window.

Now, in the car, all these questions roll around in his head about how much he knows this girl and what if the water comes and he can't get back and what if – even worse! – she wants to practise what they have to do before they have to do it. Oh my days, he thinks, holding his cheeks and letting his mouth loll. Oh. My. Days.

'What? What is it?' says Ryan, moving his head back and forth to look at Gavin and the road.

'Nothing.'

'You worried?'

Gavin shrugs.

'We can go back, you know.'

Then the baby starts crying and Gavin turns to coo at him and dance his little bear-toy across the edge of the car seat. He thinks how much he likes the baby and how Ashleigh had trusted them with him and, actually, would she have wanted the baby to go to the continent? If she had, she would have probably taken him herself.

And then his mind winds back to Gillian and she starts to take off some of her clothes and he thinks about what is underneath and what he should touch and what he shouldn't touch and what he should steer well clear of...

He winds down the window, lets the cold air blast through her, as she undoes the top button on her jeans.

The baby is calm now, but he isn't watching the little dancing bear. He is looking outside at the light that bounces from buildings and binbags instead of trees. Or maybe he's just looking at the buildings and the binbags; although Gavin's mum says that he probably can't see very far at the moment, being so little.

'You got the address?' says Ryan.

'Are we there already?'

'We're on the outskirts of Liverpool.'

Gavin swallows back a lump of heart that's heaved its way up to his neck. 'Hang on,' he says. 'It's in my phone.' But as he's giving the address, his voice starts to jump about and Ryan says, 'Calm down. Look at me. Look at me, Gav.'

Gavin looks.

'We can always go back.'

'No,' says Gavin.

'Alright then,' says Ryan, slowing and indicating into a Toby Carvery carpark.

'What are you doing?' says Gavin.

'I'm taking you for a tequila. It'll chill you right out.'

Gavin has only ever tried tequila once and it filled him up so fully with warmth that he tried another. And another. And then he crashed Grandad's Fiat into a telephone box and Ryan told him he could only drink coke from then on.

'Is it even open?' says Gavin, unclicking his seatbelt.

'It's not boarded up,' says Ryan, squinting at the building. 'Let's go check. The baby probably needs changing anyway.'

The pub is full of men sat in rows as if they are at school. But instead of pens, they hold pints, and instead of a blackboard they watch a large TV that hangs from the far wall, spilling out the news.

'Get them in,' says Ryan. 'I'll sort the baby out.'

'Two tequilas, yeah?' says Gavin.

'Don't be daft, I'm driving.'

'Oh yeah.'

Ryan takes the baby to the changing area and Gavin goes to the bar, feeling about in his pocket for a tenner. He comes across the pink wafers – four instead of two – that Mum has wrapped up for him. His stomach pinches.

'He needn't worry. Police aren't breathalysing.'

Gavin turns to the owner of the voice. 'What's that?'

A grey man in a lumberjack shirt sits on a bar stool, pint to his lips.

'They've got a child,' says another man. Younger. Bomber jacket, beard, Converse. 'They won't drink and drive with a child in the back, will they?' He reaches over to the bar and picks up a mug of purple liquid, stringed label hanging over the side.

'I didn't see the child,' says the first man. 'Two men and a child, eh?' Then he scrunches up his face and says, 'Good luck to you,' holding out his pint. He takes a sip, edges off his barstool and waddles off into the depths of the pub.

Gavin stares after him

'It's because he thinks you're gay,' says the other man.

The barman says, 'What can I get you?'

'Why would he think we're gay?' says Gavin.

'You look like a couple with a baby.'

'Yeah, I suppose,' says Gavin. 'But that's my brother.'

'Oh,' says the man, sitting on the empty barstool. 'Cool.'

'Can I get you anything?' says the barman.

'Two tequilas please. Actually, one tequila and a coke.'

'We ran out of coke. We've got lemonade?'

'That'll do,' says Gavin, putting his hands on the bar, then in his pockets, then on the bar, then laughs at himself and says, 'I'm nervous.'

'God, aren't we all,' says the man.

The barman serves the drinks and takes Gavin's tenner from the bar mat. Gavin looks around for Ryan, then downs his tequila, wincing as he does. The warmth floods through his stomach and up to his brain. 'I have to get over to France with a lady and I don't want to go,' he says.

The man turns to face Gavin, tilting his head to one side. 'You don't want to go?'

'Mm-mm,' he says, shaking his head. 'I've just bought a house in Nuneaton.'

The man laughs, a short explosion right at the front of his mouth, then he makes his face serious again. 'Oh, well, it would be a shame to leave that behind.'

'Exactly.'

'And are you here to meet this lady?'

'Yeah.' Gavin lets this thought sink in, then huffs through his nose and shakes his head. Like a horse, he thinks.

'You alright, Gav?'

Ryan's back with Little Gavin in the chest sling.

The man holds out his hand to Ryan and says, 'Hi, I'm Tom.'

Ryan tips his chin, eyes the mug. 'Alright?'

'Nice baby.'

'Thanks.'

'I've got a three-year-old.'

'Have ya?' says Ryan, raising his eyebrows. 'I've got a six-year-old daughter.'

'Lovely. Mine's a girl too. I need to get over to her.'

'Over?'

'Can I have another tequila?' says Gavin to the barman.

'Her mum took her to France,' says Tom, waving a hand past his head. 'Like, months ago. It's been awful.'

'Oh right,' says Ryan.

Gavin downs his next shot and says, 'You're going to France, are ya? Me too.'

The man watches Gavin, licks his bottom lip. 'Well, I'm going via Ireland. Apparently, it's easier that way.'

'Is it?' says Gavin.

'Yeah, um, I'm sorry, what's your name?'

'Gavin.'

'Yeah, Gavin, I mean were you thinking of going back down via the South Coast? From here?'

'No. We're going to Ireland too,' says Gavin, and saying these words, out loud, to a stranger, feels a bit surreal. He feels around for a barstool.

'Steady there,' says Tom, jumping up and helping Gavin onto his stool.

'Why is it better to go through Ireland?' asks Ryan.

Tom pulls his mouth corners down, shakes his head. 'The south coast is a meat market. The ferries are overflowing. Customs officials are violent.' He takes a sip from the mug. 'The chances of being deported are higher.' He shakes his head. 'If you're caught swimming in the Channel, you get thrown into a holding centre in Dover and that's it.'

'What about at Calais?' says Ryan.

'I'd rather take my chances at Cherbourg,' says Tom. 'Who'd have thought we'd be here, eh? Full sex in front of a Jury? What kind of unimaginable BS is that?'

Tom has one hand in his pocket like he is all relaxed, but he is facing them dead on, his eyes all wide and alert, as if Gavin and Ryan are the most interesting people in the world. Gavin frowns at him, wondering what he's after. 'Sounds like you've got it all sussed,' he says. 'Can I have another tequila?'

Tom reaches up and scratches the back of his head. 'Well. Not exactly.'

'Oh yeah?' says Ryan.

'I need a woman,' he says, rolling his eyes. 'I'm ready to go, but I can't find a companion, shall we say.'

Little Gavin starts to fuss and Ryan sways himself this way and that. They all look at the baby for a moment, then Ryan says, 'Gavin, why don't you let Tom go instead of you?'

Gavin has his third tequila to his lips. He lowers it and says, 'How would that work?'

Tom has made his eyes really big and blinky. He says, 'I mean, if you really don't want to go…that would work.'

'Why would you do that?' says Gavin.

Tom stares at him for a minute, then says in a kind voice, 'I need to get my daughter from France, but I can't go because my partner has left me – she took my daughter – and so I am single. As soon as I find a woman who wants to go with me, I can go.'

'So you need a lady. You're looking for a lady.'

Tom nods. 'That's right.'

Gavin squints about him as if he's still trying to get this straight in his head.

'I'm all ready,' says Tom. 'I've got papers and everything.'

'Hang on,' says Gavin, holding his hands to his face. 'This has done my head in. We had a plan,' he says, turning to Ryan. 'Are we changing the plan?'

'You don't want to go, Gav,' says Ryan.

'But what about Little—'

'We could let Tom go over with Gillian and you can come home to Margate and we'll all move to Nuneaton this week. You know, like the *original* plan.'

'But what about Little—'

'Just think, Gavin, you could be home tonight. You would have made things right with Gillian. And Mum'll be so happy.'

'Yes, Ryan, but what about—'

'You'd be up for that Tom, wouldn't you? You don't know the lady…' Ryan tails off, presses his lips together. 'I mean, Gillian would have to agree to this.'

Tom nods. 'Look, I've got a man in Ireland with passports all ready. There's a freezer van driver waiting for me to give him the all clear. We could be there tonight. You wouldn't have to go, Gavin. You could go back to Nuneaton.'

Gavin clutches a tuft of hair in each hand, as the idea dances in his brain. His name sounds weird in the mouth of this stranger.

'Gavin?' says Ryan, 'What do you reckon?'

'We've not moved there yet. We're still in Margate.'

Tom holds his hands out in front of him as if he's ready to catch something. 'Margate, then,' he says. 'Look mate, respectfully, you don't even want to go. I *need* to go.' Tom throws an arm out towards the large telly at the front of the room. 'Have you heard the latest updates? I need to go *soon*.'

The baby fusses and Gavin fixes his eyes on him. Ryan sways from side-to-side, says 'sshh, sshh' and Gavin takes Tom in, from his Converse to his side parting and decides that he doesn't seem dodgy, but this wasn't the plan, and anyway, how much money did he have? He didn't look loaded...Gavin could always give him money, but then, what if he just did a runner and left Gillian stranded? He thinks back to that day on the beach when she lay unmoving on the smooth, fat pebbles and he had scooped up her camera rather than help her. Tom's stare is jumping all over him and Ryan is flicking him pleading looks and Gavin parts his lips and says, 'No. No, thank you.'

Tom sinks a bit. Lowers his hands. 'Hey, it was worth a shot.'

'You seem like a nice bloke, but I had an agreement with Gillian and...well...we planned it all out...'

Ryan is staring widely and shaking his head, agreeing and disagreeing at the same time.

'Tell you what,' says Tom, 'would you take my number? Then if you change your mind at the eleventh hour, I'll step in.'

'You mean like a back-up plan?'

Tom rummages for his phone, 'No harm in having a back-up plan.'

'That seems fair,' says Gavin. 'Alright.'

They get back in the car and Ryan says, 'You are daft, Gavin. That man was put in our way for a reason, you know.'

'Oh yeah?' says Gavin. 'And what would have happened to Little Gavin? You didn't seem to want to answer that question.'

Ryan sighs. 'He would have taken him.'

'Why didn't you tell him that there was a baby involved?'

'Because he wouldn't have agreed. It's one thing finding a partner, but taking a random baby along is a whole other issue.'

Gavin screws up his eyes, 'He wouldn't have taken him, then, would he? You're not making much sense...'

Ryan sighs his head back into the headrest. 'He's a dad. I could see that he wouldn't have abandoned him. He would have figured something out.'

Gavin shakes his head, looks out the window, thinks about what Ryan has just said, shakes his head again. 'You don't know that.'

'Trust me, he wouldn't have left him behind. I'd bet money on it.'

Half an hour later, Ryan stops the car outside the bay window of an old-style barber shop and says, 'If you have any problems, call me.'

Gavin sits stone still in the passenger seat and stares at the red and white striped pole mounted on the house's brick façade. This can't be it, he thinks. It looks like a shop front on Arlington Square: chipped paint and rusting shutters. Padre was way too posh to live here.

'I'm not going home,' says Ryan. 'I'll stay local for the night.'

Gavin frowns. 'Where will you stay?'

Ryan shrugs. 'Travelodge.'

'They're all closed, aren't they?'

'Nah,' says Ryan. 'They'll probably be heaving with couples...' he tapers off.

Gavin shakes his head. 'You can go. Seriously. You can.'

'I'm staying, Gavin,' says Ryan. Then, 'You've got that bloke's number. If it goes wrong, call him, then call me.'

'Alright.'

'And leave the baby.'

Gavin stares, mouth open.

'Look, Gavin, if they don't take the baby with them, we'll just come and get him again. But we have to give him a chance.'

'Okay.'

Ryan leans towards Gavin, looks him straight in the eye. 'We have to.'

'Okay, Ryan.'

Padre opens the door and Gavin is surprised at how tall he is; the last time they saw each other, the old man was sitting down.

Padre lifts his steamy mask and says, 'Hello, Gavin.' His gaze tips down to the car seat and his eyes start to shine. Then he steps aside so that Gavin can walk in, carrying his Umbro sports bag, that he's had since school, and Little Gavin. She is already there – Gillian – sitting at Padre's little pull-out dining table with her ankles crossed and her arms folded, but she looks at him with a big, friendly grin and says, 'Hi, Gavin.'

He relaxes a bit after that. Even her scar looks much better. Almost invisible, now.

But her grin drops as soon as she sees the baby.

The evening passes in blotches, all wobbly and blurred and Gavin can't eat the fish pie that Padre has prepared for them and Gillian's voice is a bit echoey and Padre keeps looking over at Gavin, as if he can see into his insides and Gavin shifts about under his gaze and tries to think of something to say and Gillian is shocked at the baby – *Why did you bring a baby?* – and Gavin says they will have to pretend they're a family, but Gillian is Anglo-Indian and she keeps saying, 'There's no way anyone is going to believe that the blonde, alabaster-skinned baby is mine,' and he has to ask her what 'alabaster' means and she puts her hand to her head and laughs, then looks like she's about to cry, and she doesn't eat her fish pie either.

When Padre is out in the kitchen, she leans forward and says, 'I've never done this before.'

It takes him a moment to realise what she means, and he's not sure if this is a good or a bad thing. 'I've only done it once,' he replies.

She widens her eyes, purses her lips, then explains that she's watched a few YouTube videos and, actually, it might work in their favour, because they will be so engrossed in the act itself that they'll forget they are on display, and Gavin hears her but is distracted by the flesh around her elbows and how he can't see further up her arms because of her sleeves and he doesn't *want* to see further up her arms and along her collar bone and down her chest to her belly and his back has become prickly with sweat and he has to excuse himself and run to the toilet so he can splash his face and cool down. Oh my God, oh my God, he thinks. Oh my God. But Padre stops him on his way back from the toilet and asks him to help with the coffee – Padre can't carry three cups into the living room – and then he says that Gavin shouldn't feel guilty, whatever happens.

'You are the way you are, Gavin,' he says. 'But *I* must protect this bloodline.' Padre nods at the baby, and it doesn't occur to Gavin to wonder why Padre should be so concerned about things like that; he's already thinking ahead, to his new plan. In a few hours, Gavin will give himself a good telling off for letting Gillian down *again*, but not before he gets up in the middle of the night and leaves a big bag of money and a note and gathers up the baby (fucking no way was he going to abandon him) and tries to feel alright about doing a runner. But, just as he is about to leave, the light comes on and Gavin knows that it's Padre come to see what he's up to. He can hear his hissy breathing. Without looking at him, he says, 'I can't do it. I just can't do it.'

And Padre says, 'I know you can't, Gavin, but you must not take that baby.'

Gavin frowns and says, 'I can't leave him.'

Padre says, 'That's my grandson, Gavin.'

And Gavin looks at him, long and hard, trying to figure out how that could be true. Little Gavin lets up sleepy breaths in his arms.

'If he dies,' he says, taking a breath from his mask, 'the magic is gone.'

Gavin would like to get a bit closer, just to reach out and lift Padre's mask, to see more of his face, as if that would help make sense of the situation. Instead, he backs away. 'My brain,' he says, 'can't handle *any* of this.'

Padre wheezes on, but makes his eyes really kind. 'Tom seems like a nice chap.'

The bloke from the pub has been loitering in Gavin's mind since Ryan drove away. He widens his eyes. 'How did you...'

Padre shrugs.

Gavin tightens his fingers around the handle of the car seat. 'But Little Gavin will survive in Nuneaton,' says Gavin. 'With us.'

'The water's coming,' says Padre. 'Give him a chance.'

'Is he really magic?' says Gavin, and he's a bit weepy, so his voice is all trembly.

Padre nods. 'Like me,' he says. 'And you.'

Gavin stares at the baby, while he is sleeping and totally unaware of the conversation happening around him, then sets him down on Padre's rug with the bag and the note, shuts himself out into the world where his mind explodes into a mess of TOO MANY THOUGHTS before he can hold his breath and focus on the one thing he must do. He must stay until the bloke – Tom – picks up the phone. He calls the bloke – Tom – and tells him to turn up the following evening at the old barber's shop on Grafton Street and he almost gives him a heads up about Little Gavin, but his voice gets all wobbly again as it approaches those words and anyway, he shouldn't mention him. He doesn't want to ruin Gillian's chances.

Or Little Gavin's.

Gavin sits with his foot up on the dashboard and his knee right up against the passenger window. He has been rubbing his earlobe throughout the journey, a habit that he gave up when he was a kid. It makes him think of his mum, weirdly, and so he knows he'll probably stop doing it when he's back at home. He wonders how he'll tell her, about what Padre said. He is going over the conversation in his mind when Ryan speaks up.

'You did the right thing, bro.'

'Mm.'

'He'll be alright you know.'

Gavin looks at his phone, at the list of missed calls he's received and ignored. He checks for Gillian's number – she called that morning. There is another number that he doesn't recognise. He bites his lip and presses the green call icon before he can think about it too much. The line beeps like it's in distress and he holds it away from his ear.

'Have you got signal?' he asks Ryan. 'I haven't got signal.'

Ryan shakes his head. 'Network outage. It was on the radio.'

'Yeah?'

'Yeah. It's all getting a bit real now, isn't it?' he says. 'Can you imagine if you'd been stuck in France?'

Gavin is quiet for a while, then says, 'What would our dad have said about all this?'

Ryan flicks him a hard, smiling glance, then looks back at the road. 'Have you gone soft, Gav? Why would you bring him up now?'

Gavin shrugs and is silent for the rest of the journey.

When they get home, their mum answers the door and her face isn't as pleased to see them as he thought it might be. There is a stack of boxes behind her and it's only when he hears the kitchen chair scraping that he asks if Big Carla is home.

'Yes,' says his mum, and she's being all weird like she doesn't want to let them in. 'She's home.'

'You gonna let us in, Mum?'

A lady slides up beside his mum, her hands in her back pockets. Gavin squints for a moment, then his eyelids pop back. 'You're Pinko's girlfriend,' he says. 'Jane.'

CHAPTER SEVENTY-THREE | January 2033
Jane

Some weeks before, the front door slammed. It was like a great thumb and forefinger had hovered level with Jane's sternum and flicked her there. Thwack. Jane jolted, revived, as the dull drum of her heart sharpened. 'Ashleigh?' she called, standing up. She wobbled, sat back down again, reached for the glass of water from the bedside table, then slipped back into hibernation.

That's all she remembers now as she sits on the edge of her bed and wonders what time it is, what *day* it is, even.

Now, the envelope leans against the base of her nightlight. She puts the water down and takes it in her hands.

Jane's Envelope

This is what is written on the front of it. He'd probably formatted each envelope the same way and that disappoints her slightly. She turns it over, then back again, her stomach twisting until she thinks she might gag.

She opens her bedside drawer, slides the envelope inside, closes it.

Ashleigh has an envelope too. It has *Ashleigh's Envelope* written on the front. Butler kept it aside for her. Probably in case it found its way into the wrong hands... Ashleigh went to Pinko's house to collect it in person. Jane slept through all of that, but opened one eye when Ashleigh returned and waved the envelope in front of her.

Jane had groaned and turned her head away.

Now, Jane tries to stand again, smooths her hair, and heads to the landing.

'Ashleigh?'

No answer.

Cinnamon biscuits, Jane thinks, maybe she has gone out to find some more. Although that corner Spar has been fully looted now...

Jane heads to the kitchen to prepare a bowl of baked beans and some crackers. Ashleigh will eat them when she gets home. She needs to up her calorie intake now she's in her third trimester. Jane looks in the cupboard, locates the teabags – only two left – and puts on some water to boil.

The gas is out. Damn.

Jane holds her face in her hands and surveys the kitchen. She walks to the garden door and looks out. The grass is thick and unruly. There are spiky leaves clogging about the base of the little oak tree. She turns away and remembers two full nights of switching off the nightlight, two days of waking up to the envelope. After that, she stopped switching off the light and would often wake in the early hours and stare at her name trapped inside Pinko's handwriting.

She can't have been under for that long, surely?

She tries the gas again. Nothing.

Two hours later, she decides it's time to break out the emergency camping stove. She heats the water and the beans, then stares at the window for so long that the beans get cold again and the air outside greys and darkens.

Finland fills her mind, the cabin with the light-coloured kitchen.

She reheats the water and makes tea for herself, saving the squeezed teabag in a dessert spoon.

It's dark now and Jane is pacing. She gazes up into the stairwell and heads upstairs. Ashleigh's room is empty, but then it has been since the shipment left… She lets her mind imagine their boxed-up things sprawled abandoned on the Finnish coast, then checks for Ashleigh's rucksack. Gone. Perhaps she had lots of shopping to carry? She checks for her purse – also gone. She checks for her toothbrush, her favourite lip-gloss and her clean underwear. Gone, gone, gone. The Saint Christopher that hung from the corner of her mirror is gone. Then she checks the bedside drawer, where she knows Ashleigh stashed the envelope. Gone. But…there is a note.

'Gone to France,' it says. 'Sort yourself out and come over.'

That's when Jane decides to open her envelope.

PART SIX
THE BEGINNING

CHAPTER SEVENTY-FOUR | February 2033
Jane

Matt watches Jane from the passenger seat of the RV. She takes a deep breath and chases it with a swig of coke.

'That's quite a story,' he says, tickling Paris's ears.

She laughs out loud as she realises that he's right; such a complicated chain of events surely can't befall that many people. And all against an apocalyptic backdrop. She has spent the last hour telling her story while he listened along, pulling all the right faces. Now he makes a fist and holds it to his yawning mouth.

'But yours is a fascinating story too,' she says. 'Finding true love like that, I mean, how many people get so lucky?'

'I know,' he says. 'I just cannot believe that she chose me. Without her, I'd be all alone.'

They gaze at their own reflections in the windscreen. The words 'all alone' ring in Jane's ears. *Some people are destined to be alone*, Padre had said not four hours before.

'Do you know,' he says, interrupting her thoughts, 'that every night I fall asleep on her lap in front of the TV? And she just lets me. I know her lap goes numb, but she never wants to wake me.'

'That's nice,' says Jane.

'I always try not to nod off, but I guess her lap makes me feel sleepy.'

'Or safe,' says Jane.

'Yes, safe.' Matt smiles, and he looks as if he wants to say something else. Jane watches, waits for him to straighten out his next sentence.

'You know,' he says, 'I'm glad I met you. I needed to make a decision and, actually, it's not scary at all. We'll be together. Me and her. With a load of money.' He grins at Jane and blushes. 'How can that be scary?'

Jane listens and remembers that it's *his* story too that they are living. That this is a milestone moment in their life's pathway. He inspects Paris' fur with gentle fingers, probably lost in thoughts of her, and Jane thinks at least one good thing will have come out of all of this.

As Matt and Paris doze off in the passenger seat, Jane is left to ponder her usual questions about Ashleigh and the birth and her teeny-tiny baby, and how did this all happen? How did it all happen to her? Stop it, Jane, she thinks. Then she leans her head against the leather headrest and closes her eyes.

By the time the ferry shudders into Dublin, they are both fast asleep in their seats. Jane wakes and looks at the clock. It is 4:30am on Friday 25th February 2033. She has four days to get up to Inverness. Jane turns to Matt. His head is lolling dead-like over his chest and Paris is snoring on his lap.

'Matt,' she whispers.

The head snaps up and the eyes open. Paris registers the movement and directs his eyes upwards without moving his head.

'We're here.'

'Right,' says Matt. 'You okay?'

'Yes, you?'

'Mm-hm,' he says, then the smile appears again as he remembers. 'Never better.' He notices Paris and tickles behind his ears. 'Good morning, buddy.'

Jane asks, 'Do you know what to do?'

He fixes his gaze on the windscreen and nods once. 'When we drive off, she'll come and inspect the motorhome,' he says. 'I mean, she won't *inspect* it, but she'll make as if she will so that her colleagues don't try to. Then she'll wave us through and we'll park a little way up by Starbucks. She'll meet us there in an hour.'

'What if she doesn't show up?'

Matt looks at Jane. 'Don't be daft,' he says. 'We've had this planned for weeks, but we keep backing out because we don't have the money.' His gaze swirls over the parking deck as a few drivers return to their cars. 'Money's not an issue now. We are ready for this, trust me.'

'Okay,' says Jane. 'Fine.'

Matt frowns at her. 'Why wouldn't she show up?'

'I don't know. What if she gets detained?'

He blinks for a moment while he considers this. 'That won't

happen.'

Moonlight cracks through the opening ramp, then widens to a wedge. Jane says, 'Can you give Paris some water please? There's a bottle and a bowl in the back.'

'Yeah, sure,' he replies. 'Come on, buddy.' He turns his seat towards the back of the van and strains Paris off his lap.

By the time he returns to his seat, the cars ahead have started to shift. Matt begins to click his thumbnails together.

'Relax,' says Jane.

But he's not listening. He is looking out the passenger window towards a blonde woman in an orange high-viz waistcoat and blue overalls. Jane notices as she looks up from her clipboard and follows the direction of the motorhome with her eyes. A port hand guides the cars into three lanes and directs each lane towards its own kiosk. Jane follows, then slows to a stop behind the queue of cars to wait her turn at the kiosk. She is about two cars from the front when the blonde woman bangs on Jane's window. Jane opens it.

'I'm going to inspect this vehicle,' she says.

Jane turns to Matt. 'That's fine, isn't it?'

Matt nods at Jane, then smiles at the woman.

She nods back, then boards through the little oblong door on the side and pretends to look around the vehicle.

'You alright, babe?' says Matt, without looking at her.

'Are you sure it's time?' says the woman.

'Oh yeah,' says Matt. 'I've never been so sure.'

The woman appears to think about this, then says: 'How much?'

'One fifty,' says Matt.

'Show me.'

Matt opens the glove compartment to reveal the bundles of fifties.

'Okay,' she says. 'Fine. That's fine.' She hands Jane a sign with a hook cut into it to hang from the driver's mirror. 'Hang this up and they won't stop you at the kiosk.'

Jane nods, noticing that the woman's hand is shaking. 'Thanks,' she says.

'You did well, babe,' says the woman, turning to leave.

'One hour,' says Matt.

'One hour,' says the woman. 'Starbucks.' She climbs out of the oblong door and shuts it.

Matt exhales slowly, then says. 'Right. Good. Let's drive on.'

As they pass the kiosk and head away from the port towards Starbucks, Matt laughs to himself, then clicks his tongue and calls Paris over.

Jane is thinking about the woman, frantic to see the cash. She didn't say hello to Matt, didn't even look at him. Perhaps that's what happens when you don't have family or anyone to be close to, you become mistrustful, no – that's too judgmental. You become a survivor. That would be a better way of putting it.

'Come on, buddy,' says Matt.

'I've noticed that he's stopped barking since you've been in the van.'

Matt says, 'Is his barking that much of a problem?'

'Not really,' says Jane. 'He just doesn't like to be on his own.'

'I get that,' says Matt, scooping Paris up onto his knee again. 'You know, I'll have to go in the back when we park. There might be some colleagues in Starbucks.'

'Fine,' says Jane.

'If they see me, they'll know something's up.'

'Fine,' repeats Jane. 'Get in the back. It might be best if you sit on the floor.'

They pull up into a bay. Matt sits on the floor, cross-legged, grooming Paris with a dog brush. He asks Jane if she can see anyone. Jane squints at the building in front. Starbucks is empty except for a rusty glow from the large window – it's still really early. She's surprised it's even open. Matt tells her that it's open twenty-four hours, in fact, coffee shops are still booming here in Ireland, apparently. Who knows why. They often come here – he and his girlfriend – when he travels over to see her on his days off. They haven't been cleaning the coffee machines lately and an Americano often tastes like cigarette water, but if you go for the creamy ones with the syrups – like a salted caramel or something, you know? – then it just tastes sweet. His girlfriend likes the syrups – she likes anything sweet but, WOW, Jane doesn't need to know all this. He's wittering on about all kinds of crap, he says. It must be nerves. Then Matt is quiet apart from the sshh-sshh of the grooming brush.

Jane says, 'Not at all. I like hearing about normal things, it makes a change.' In fact, all this talk about Matt's relationship lifts her soul a little – something that she didn't think would happen given her recent past. He seems so happy and uncomplicated. 'You just dropped everything and left,' says Jane. 'It's like you were so sure of your togetherness and your plan. What about a suitcase or something? You haven't brought anything with you. Not even a change of clothes.'

He tells her he doesn't need anything. He doesn't have anything of sentimental value because he doesn't have a family. Everything he has is just ahead of him now, within reaching distance. 'I love her,' he says. 'I can't tell you how much.'

Jane smiles through the driver's mirror at Matt, Matt smiles back and, before they can register what is going on the door clicks open and the blonde woman is standing there with a shotgun.

'Give me the money,' she says.

Matt says nothing, but his face flattens right out and his mouth drops open.

Jane turns in her chair. 'Are you kidding me?' she says.

Then a man's voice says, 'Give us the fucking money.'

'This isn't funny,' says Matt. 'What's going on?'

'I knew it,' says Jane, as she leans across to the glove compartment and clicks it open. 'I just knew there was something up with her.'

'Shut up,' says the man, now with his bearded face right in the doorway.

'They're not serious,' says Matt. 'You're not serious, are you baby?'

The 'baby' dents Jane's heart and slows her rummaging hands. She pulls out several piles of cash, then turns her chair.

'I'm sorry,' says the woman to Matt.

Matt hugs Paris to him and drops his gaze to the pile of money in Jane's lap.

Jane says, 'Have you got a bag, or something?'

'What?' says the woman. 'Just give it here.'

The man says, 'We might as well take the van,' as if he is saying that he might as well order a vanilla latte, while he's here.

Jane takes this in and imagines the road down to Rosslare and the helicopter waiting at Inverness and all the little cans and packets stacked up neatly in the RV; the water supply and the commode; the four-tog duvet and the memory-foam mattress. This journey would be much less comfortable without a van, she thinks. And she'll never get to Inverness on time. She narrows her eyes at the woman, takes in the way she holds the shot gun and the way she keeps glancing at Matt as if she really is sorry. 'It's okay,' says Jane. 'I've got a bag. Hang on.' And she turns in her chair back to the wheel.

'I said, we'll take the van,' repeats the man, and he lifts one booted foot into the doorway.

'Fine,' says Jane. 'Just a sec while I...' Then she turns the engine on and slams the motorhome into reverse, curving back onto the road before taking off towards the city. She looks in her wing-mirror to see the man sprawled out on the tarmac, pushing himself to his feet. The woman is still holding on to the doorway, trying to climb inside.

'Has she got the gun?' Jane calls back to Matt.

'No.'

After a minute, Jane slows the motorhome to a stop and shouts, 'Okay, get the fuck out of this van. Go on. Get the fuck out right now.'

The woman ignores Jane, climbs inside and collapses next to Matt. 'I'm sorry, I'm really sorry. He made me do it. I never wanted to.'

Matt looks away from her and says nothing.

'You know,' she says, grasping his neck and pulling herself closer to him. 'You *know* I didn't want to do that.'

Matt shrugs her off, then stands up and takes Paris to the passenger seat.

'Matt, please. You don't know what he's like,' says the woman. 'When you're not here, he bullies me. He overheard you on the walkie-talkie. He wants to get over to the continent.'

Matt sits in the passenger seat, his face solid and his eyes shining. Jane takes in his expression and remembers how closed and sour he was when she was trying to persuade him to come. She turns to the woman and says, 'Leave. Get out.'

'No,' says the woman. 'I'm not going anywhere. Don't leave me with him. Do you know what he'll do to me?'

Jane says, 'You were the one with the gun. Why didn't you just turn it on him?'

The woman breathes heavily and stares at Jane.

'Get out,' says Jane, standing and approaching the woman. 'Get out.'

She is crying now, but she crawls to the door and starts to pull herself up on the handrail.

'Go on,' says Jane, so close now that she can smell the coffee on the woman's breath. 'Fuck off. Quickly.'

The woman is now fully upright at the edge of the door. She turns her head, her face shining and scrunched up, and is about to yell another plea at Matt when Jane pushes her, right in her stomach. She falls from the van and cries out again, a strand of hair sticks to the trickle of snot from her nose and there is a bloody graze on her forearm. She stands and lurches, zombie-like, back towards the doorway. Jane feels her heart pinch a little. Maybe the guy was abusive. Maybe he did force her into this. Before she can say any of this to Matt, the van judders forwards. Jane turns to see that Matt has taken the wheel. She leans out to grab the door and pulls it to a close, and they speed off inland.

CHAPTER SEVENTY-FIVE | February 2033
Jane

They drive for fifteen minutes before Matt says, 'I don't know where I'm going. I need a map or something.'

Matt's eyes have been shining wet since he took the wheel and the rumbling hush of the air conditioning is getting louder with each, wordless minute. Still, he is gentle with his movements, sliding through the gears as if cutting into butter and waving thanks to other drivers for giving way to him. Jane thinks he must be dead inside right now, his body nothing but a robotic shell. She is about to reply, but purses her lips and considers saying what she really wants to say. After a moment, she asks, 'Are you alright?'

'Um,' he says, lifting his hand to scratch the back of his head. 'I'm a bit hungry.'

She looks at the side of his face and laughs. Then apologises for laughing.

'It's fine, but seriously,' he says, 'do you mind if I stop at the next services?'

'We have plenty of food.'

'Do you have Doritos?' he replies.

She tries not to smile again. 'No. No Doritos. You'll have to stop for them.'

They pull into the services and he jumps out saying, 'Back in a tick.' The 'tick' is lost in the air speeding over his body as he rushes away. He looks like someone who is parked on double yellows or desperate to vomit. Jane follows his route with her gaze, not missing his shoulders hunching, his hand wiping one eye. Then the other.

Paris starts barking. Jane hooks him to his lead and takes him for a walk on the green area that frames the car park. When she returns, Matt is still not back.

She tries to call the woman again – Gillian. The phone rings and rings but no one picks up. Not even an answerphone. She tries again and is told that international calls are not possible to this mobile at this time. Fuck, she thinks. But it rang the first time, it'll work again later, it has to. Gavin might have some news, but no, she reasons, she'll try Ashleigh first, even though her phone has been dead for weeks. She clicks call and right away hears, *The person you are calling is not available.* Gavin's number is just under her thumb when Matt opens the passenger door. She jumps and drops her phone.

'Shit,' she says.

'Sorry,' he replies.

'No, don't be...' She tails off as she takes in his face. The skin is thick red and clammy. 'Oh, Matt,' she says.

He looks away. 'I'll be alright.'

'Get in,' she says. 'Before the dog does a runner.'

He climbs up into the passenger seat and shuts the door. Jane notes the lack of Doritos and lets him click his thumb nails together for a minute, before leaning over and clasping one of his hands.

He looks down at her fingers and says, 'If you could have heard all the things she said to me when it was just me and her.'

'I'm so sorry.'

Matt blinks one, large tear onto Jane's hand.

'She probably meant them, Matt. These are weird times and people aren't themselves.'

'Should I go back for her?' he says, looking straight into Jane's eyes.

Jane shrugs. 'What would that achieve?'

'I don't know. She'd come with me though. I'm sure she would.'

'But would you trust her?' asks Jane, wincing at her bluntness.

'You're right,' Matt nods. 'I don't think she really loves me.'

Jane sighs. 'Everyone is desperate at the moment. There's not enough room for love...'

Matt shakes his head. 'I had room,' he says. 'But I'm just destined to be alone.'

Jane's sympathy turns on her in that moment, seeping back through her skin and into her chest. 'Don't say that. Why would you say that?'

Matt frowns. 'It's always been that way, pretty much.'

'But you have your whole life ahead of you. You're, what? Twenty-five?'

'Thirty-seven.'

Jane gapes her eyes. 'Well, I mean, that's still young.'

Matt lets out a long breath. 'Let's not talk about it.'

'This is not your fault, Matt. You're not destined to be alone. No one is.'

Matt nods a few deep nods, then says, 'I'm a bit sore at the moment.'

'Yeah, I'm sorry. Of course you are.' Jane looks through the windscreen at the queue to the petrol station. She realises that the queuers are mostly young men. They stare, as a woman in Lycra gym gear and fluorescent trainers walks past them to put something in the bin. Jane watches the men's faces. They are not leering. They are twitchy, conflicted.

She turns back to Matt. 'Look, you found out the truth about your girlfriend and you got one hundred and fifty grand in the process. When you look back on this, it will feel like a pretty positive moment in your life.'

'I'm not keeping the money,' he says.

'Er,' says Jane. 'Yes, you are.'

'I'm not,' he says. 'I won't pay for someone to love me. And that's my only way out, isn't it? With someone who loves me.' He curls his fingers into speech marks when he says 'love'.

'You can do whatever you want with the money. You don't have to *buy* anyone.'

'Just drop me back to the port,' he says.

Jane scoffs. 'What, Dublin?'

'Yes.'

'Why?' says Jane. Then, 'Doesn't matter. No way.'

'Why not? If I clock on tonight, they won't even realise I've gone.'

'And you seriously want to go back to working there?'

Matt closes his eyes, rubs his forehead. 'I don't know.'

Jane presses her lips together before she says anything else. He's just had a bad shock, she tells herself. Of course he's going to be really fatalist. And anyway, would she risk going back to

Dublin port and bumping into those two loons again? Whatever, she thinks, starting up the van. 'Well,' she says, 'I'll just be driving down to Rosslare while you think about it, okay?'

At that moment, Jane's phone rings.

CHAPTER SEVENTY-SIX | February 2033
Jane

'Hello?' says the woman. Gillian.

'Gillian.' Jane exhales so hard that a small circle of condensation forms on the windscreen. It is Gillian, isn't it? You have no idea how relieved...'

'Who is this?'

'It's Jane. I'm the baby's grandmother. The baby that you're carrying with you – are you at Rosslare? I'm up near Dublin. I'm coming to get him. Have you still got him? Are you—'

'Hello? Who is this? Gavin?'

'Oh no... It's Jane. CAN YOU HEAR ME?'

'Hello?'

'Hello? Hello? I can hear you; can you hear me?'

We need to leave, Gillian.

'I think it might be Gavin.'

Just leave it.

'No! Gillian, I can hear you. Don't hang up...'

In the background, a baby starts to cry.

'Gavin, please stop calling,' says Gillian. Then there's a click. Then silence.

CHAPTER SEVENTY-SEVEN | February 2033
Gavin

Gavin hangs up the phone for the third time in half-an-hour and walks to the fridge. He opens it, slips his phone inside the salad drawer, then presses the door closed with his shoulder. There is hardly any light from the garden today and the kitchen is drowning in shadows. Still, it's the only room that's not in boxes.

The promise he made to himself, to never bother Gillian again, has changed quite a bit since the morning. Since Liverpool, he's lived with a hole in his body, between his breastbone and his belly-button, as if someone has scooped out his core. This morning, his mum held his face and looked at him with that not-quite smile. If an expression could be a sigh, that would be it.

Funny how your mum can know you better than you know yourself. Funny how your mind can drag you one way and your feelings, another. Gavin had never even been to Dover, let alone France; even getting a taxi to Pinko's house in Tunbridge Wells gave him a wobbly tummy. On top of travelling to France was the 'act' itself, or whatever everyone was calling it these days. Gavin shudders just thinking about it.

He moves to sit in his grandad's chair and puts his cheek against the table. It's rough, and a bit sticky, but the cold wood calms him. 'Stop calling,' she kept saying. 'Leave me alone, Gavin.'

Maybe it wasn't such a nice thing to do, swap out one bloke for another. After all, she knew Gavin. She had prepared herself for... him. And then, to bundle her off with someone else – and a baby – can't have been the best turn of events for poor Gillian.

Gavin winces, presses at the hole in his body with one, closed fist. Then he stretches across the table and rubs a finger over Big Carla's etched-in name. The table will go with them to Nuneaton. And Grandad's chair, of course. And Ryan and Little Carla and Big Carla and his mum. But the underbed box with the soft yellow blanket and the rubber giraffe would be a storage box, again. Big Carla was already using Little Gavin's baby wipes to take off her make-up. And last night they slept through, without any tiny, spluttery sneezes and long, gasping wails dragging them barefoot to the kitchen.

Padre messaged him to say they made it to Ireland, the three of them. So that was something. That was a step towards everything being as it should.

Wasn't it?

Gavin thinks of the little onesie, the birth certificate stitched inside, and realises that the patch of table beneath his cheek is now damp with tears. 'We'll be waiting for you in Nuneaton, Little Gavin,' he says into the still, kitchen air, 'when all of this is over.'

CHAPTER SEVENTY-EIGHT | February 2033
Jane

Jane speeds along the M11 to Rosslare. *Sorry, sorry, sorry* loops in her mind when she misses a Stop sign or drives over a mini-roundabout. Matt has surfaced from his misery just enough to step into the role of co-pilot. He tells her where to go, warns her of speed cameras and debris in the road, but also tells her it's okay, it's okay; Gillian and the baby will be stuck at Rosslare for hours. There'll be so many people at the port, he says. It's as busy as the ports in the South of England at the moment, but Rosslare is much smaller, he says. They'll be hours yet.

Jane doesn't respond or nod or acknowledge his presence. When she replays this journey later, she will wish that she had shown him a little more warmth, even as her mind fixated on the image of her daughter's baby, and her eyes swallowed up the road ahead.

They join the queue of traffic miles before they reach the port.

Matt says, 'If we're stuck in it, the chances are they are too.'

'You don't know that,' says Jane. 'They might have had two hours on us.'

'Try calling again.'

She does. The phone rings but there is no answer.

'Try texting,' says Matt.

She does. And for the next three hours she waits for a reply, while she creeps the motorhome forward. What would his name be? What colour hair would he have? How big would he be? She remembers how Ashleigh's tiny fingers curled around anything they could touch and hold. She remembers her chin, slidey with drool. Her closed, creaseless eyes and dumpy shoulders. The rise and fall of her belly.

A question dashes through all of this, the way it always does. That long tunnel of partial awareness she'd lived through not even a month before involved reviewing and re-asking that question until she lost interest in it. There were more important things at stake, she had realised, the day she sat bolt upright in bed and noticed that her Ashleigh, her little soft-bellied baby girl, was no longer there, and that she had no idea when she'd left, where she was, or if she'd come back again.

But that question never got properly answered. Just engulfed by the action of driving, searching, returning, checking and rechecking and calling and driving and searching some more. Now she is closer to getting one of them back than she's ever, ever been. She focusses on what it will feel like to hold the writhing, sleep-suited bundle. All warm and dribbly.

But the question comes back to her again... She acknowledges it and pushes it away.

Instead, she asks Matt, 'What will *you* do when we get there?'

He looks up, startled from their long communal, silence. 'I was just thinking about that.'

'Really?'

'Mm.'

'Have you got a plan?'

'I'm trying to pull one together,' he says. 'But everything seems topsy-turvy, now.' He closes his mouth and looks out of the passenger window.

'Will you see if you can meet someone at Rosslare?' she prompts. 'With the money?'

'I don't want the money.'

Jane frowns. 'Well, what will you do?'

He stares out the window and scratches the stubble on his chin. 'That depends on you.'

'What do you mean?'

'If you have to fetch the baby from France, you'll need someone to...you know...go over with.'

'Oh,' she says.

'You won't be able to pay off the French guards like you did me.'

'It's not that,' she says. 'I just never thought I'd have to go over to France. That hadn't occurred to me.'

She tries not to think about the examination room, the chrome-bright bed, the one-way glass. Her mind produces the images anyway, then it imagines Matt, approaching her. His ginger-root fingers undoing his belt buckle.

Matt turns back to her. 'You haven't eaten,' he says. 'You should eat.'

She twitches her gaze over the cars around them. 'I'm not hungry.'

They enter a lane that siphons off short-stay vehicles and begin to speed past the rows of traffic waiting to park in the designated long-stay. 'You'd think they wouldn't care where they dump their vehicles,' says Jane.

'They must be sticklers for the rules,' Matt replies.

Jane smirks and parks the van. Later, she will remember that bit as probably the last light-hearted moment of her life. 'Is his barking likely to bother anyone?' she asks, jerking her head back to where Paris is sleeping somewhere in the dinette area.

Matt replies, 'He'll be safer in the van.'

He's right, yes, they can't take Paris down through the crowds, where he'd most likely get squashed or lost. Jane will come back for the van, that's for sure. She turns in her chair to watch the rise and fall of his hard, beige tummy. Hopefully some do-gooder won't think he's been abandoned and try to break in and free him. He lifts his head as they prepare to exit the RV, cocking his smoky face at them, until Jane climbs out and shuts him inside.

Together, they follow the signs for the holding area, then descend towards the ferry – small from this distance – and to the noise of car engines and people. On the way, they pass two couples in steamed-up parked cars and hear others panting and scuffling their bodies together in hidden grassy areas. Jane pretends she hasn't seen, her eyes are on the crowd already as she nears the holding area. She uses her vantage point to try and single out a couple and a baby – perhaps a pushchair or a car seat. 'There are more down there,' says Matt. 'Couples, I mean.' And there are. Jane sees a large, swaying blanket a few metres from the edge of the crowd. 'Why here?' she asks Matt.

'They've probably never met before,' he replies. 'They need to practise.'

Jane tries not to think of Ashleigh, but the image comes to her of some man rocking away on top of her daughter, while she gazes off into the distance. The man's face morphs into Pinko's. Jane grits her teeth and presses on along the path to the edge of the group.

What happens next, happens quickly.

'This way,' says Matt, leading her around the edge towards the boarding ramp. 'We'll check the front of the queue first.'

'Okay,' she replies, quickening her feet to keep up.

They walk beside the barrier, scanning the line until they are at the foot of the ramp and cannot go any further.

'They must be somewhere in there,' says Matt, tilting his head towards the holding area.

'That's if they're here at all,' replies Jane. 'What if they're already on the boat?'

As she says this, Jane travels her gaze up along the covered ramp to the boat's entrance. They aren't there, she thinks. Or are they? Would she even see them if they'd hidden the baby? 'Hang on,' she says, as she picks up her phone and tries to call again. 'If it rings, I'll hear it.' But it goes straight to answerphone. Jane drops her hand to her side and sighs at the queue.

'Look,' says Matt. 'Something's happening over there.'

'Where?' Jane follows his finger to a couple just at the entrance to the ramp. The man has been let through, but the woman is standing to the side with a customs official. Jane squints at the woman, the hunch of her shoulders, her sturdy legs, and can't work out why she recognises her. The man is asking something, Jane can almost read his lips and predict the very British response to this kind of thing, *Is there a problem, here?* Jane sees that the man's coat is zipped up to the tip of a little bald head. Shit, a baby. He has a baby-sling underneath his coat. Now he comes back through the barrier towards the woman, who unzips his coat, exposing the baby, pointing from her papers back to the baby – is she saying, 'He's mine'? Or perhaps, 'I'm his mother'? Another guard appears. The woman – Jane has already decided that it's Gillian – and the man, whoever he is, are protesting; their foreheads are frowned into deep ridges and their mouth-movements are quick and large. The guard is not quite as stressed. He holds his arm out towards the other direction like an overly harassed teacher ushering school children. 'They're sending them away.' Jane stops thinking and rushes over to the barrier, 'Hey!' she yells. 'Excuse me! Excuse me! That's my grandson!' she yells. 'They have my grandson!' she yells again, banging on the barrier. 'Please! That's my—'

Matt grabs her arm. 'Jane, you need to get the van.'

'What?' says Jane. 'No.'

'You don't know it's him.'

'It must be!'

'Well, do you think they'll just hand him over to you?'

Jane has fixed her stare on the couple, now disappearing through a door to a portacabin. 'But...' she says, 'I can't just leave.'

'Buy a ticket for the next ferry to Fishguard and then fetch the van. If I'm not on the ferry, wait for me at the other end.'

She darts her gaze over his face, then frowns. 'No,' she says. 'Why would I?'

'Go back,' says Matt. He has made his eyes very large and over pronounces the words right into her face. She takes a step back. 'They'll be split up and sent back to Wales, Jane. It happens all the time. Your only hope is to catch them at the other end.'

'Where are you going?' she asks.

'Just wait for me on the other side,' he says.

Jane nods and pretends to retrace her steps back towards the motorhome. She turns to check if he is still watching her, and only when she sees him disappear into the distance, does she trot back towards the dock and hide herself in the crowd. From there, she observes the portacabin. Every now and then, she scans the dock for Matt. After about twenty minutes, Gillian and the baby exit the back of the cabin and are escorted through a covered walkway to a large concrete building. Jane considers her options. Either she runs down to the building now and tries to get the baby, or she goes back to the RV as Matt has instructed.

Matt. The guy she's known for less than twelve hours.

Sod it, she thinks and runs down to the concrete building, where she locates the entrance. A customs official stops her, asks her what she wants. The woman is short and serious; she moves her whole body to stop Jane.

'Madame, where are you going?'

Jane tries to catch her breath. 'A woman has just been taken in here with my grandson.'

The official looks her up and down, narrows her eyes. 'Grandson?'

'Yes,' says Jane.

'What is she doing with him?'

'She was trying to take him over to the continent.'

'Right,' says the official. 'And do you have evidence of this?'

'Evidence?'

'Yes. That he's your grandson.'

Jane looks hard at the woman, then covers her face with her hands and groans.

The woman sighs. 'If he came in from the UK, he'll be sent straight back. You'll have to take it up with the UK authorities. But you'll need to prove he's your relative.'

'What if he's not sent back?'

'In this kind of situation,' says the woman, 'they all are.'

Jane frowns. 'How long will that take?'

She shrugs one shoulder. 'Hard to say.'

'Will it be today?'

'Um...' says the woman. 'It'll most likely be this week, let's put it that way.'

'This week?'

'Yes.'

'But...'

'Go and buy a ticket.'

'I need him back now...'

'Go and buy a ticket.'

'Can I at least see him?'

'No,' says the woman. 'And I'm afraid you need to leave now.'

CHAPTER SEVENTY-NINE | February 2033
Jane

Jane has her head against the swirly purple and red moquette of the ferry lounge chair. She is the only person in the lounge apart from an old man with a carrier bag. He has not looked at her once and she finds herself staring at him often to make sure of this, or maybe because her eyes have nothing else to look at.

After she was told to leave, she sat at the port for an hour and a half, gazing at the concrete building and willing a closer look at the baby that might not be her grandson, but also might be. In under four days, the helicopter would leave from Inverness. It would take her a day to get there, so she still had plenty of time. If only she could have reached through the wall, lifted the baby out and been on her way. Matt had gone, and at the time she didn't think to ask for his number, not that phones were any good right now. Paris was probably wreaking havoc in the van, yapping his little throat raw. Padre had told her she was doomed to a life of solitude, anyway, so... *Stop making him run,* he'd said. *He's only a baby.* How cruel fate was to dangle him in front of her. If she was really meant to be alone, surely he'd be gone already. They wouldn't be allowed to cross paths like this.

It can't be him, she thought to herself. It's probably not him.

After a while, she bought a ticket and collected the van, rolled it into the green hull of the ferry with only a yellow Mini and a motorbike to share the deck with. She wonders now if either vehicle belongs to the man with the carrier bag. As she thinks this, he looks over at her and stares as if he can't quite figure out how he knows her. His top lip chews low over his bottom one and his eyes are wide. She looks the other way, at a shuddering, fogged-up porthole and clutches an empty polystyrene cup. Perhaps it doesn't matter if it isn't him – the baby. How would she really know? And why would she care? That must be it, she thinks, it's the feeling of them that makes you crave them.

They are an hour into the journey when Jane hears, 'Excuse me,' spoken right into her ear.

She swivels her head. A uniformed woman is standing over her holding a printout of some sort. The ship pitches and the woman steps out her leg to steady herself, then grins at the wobble. Jane lifts one corner of her mouth. The woman seems nice, but why would she stand so close?

'Are you Jane...' she looks at the paper for Jane's last name. 'Just Jane. Are you just Jane?' she tries, smiling again.

'Yes,' says Jane. 'I mean, how do you know?'

'You look very young.'

Jane scowls. 'Excuse me?'

The woman's cheekbones pinken. 'I mean, my colleague would like a word.'

'Why?'

'Nothing to worry about. Would you come with me?'

'She can come out and see me, surely?'

'He,' says the woman, distracted by the printout again. 'Pearce,' she says. 'Are you Jane Pearce?'

Jane stands up. 'You know my surname.'

The woman screws up her face. 'Well, yes...I mean...don't you know why you're here?'

Jane cocks an ear and squints. 'I'm sorry?'

'Matt said you were waiting here with your passport. You know, to collect the infant?'

The words become muffled by dizziness. Jane staggers backwards one step, then rights herself and surges forwards towards the lounge exit. 'Where is he?' she says. 'Where is he?'

'Woah,' says the woman, jogging to keep up. 'Why don't you follow me?'

They leave the lounge area and descend two flights of stairs. The woman strides along the side passageway, passes the empty arcades, the racks of Toblerone and leprechaun figurines, to the stern of the ship. They descend another flight and stop before a keypad. The woman covers it with one hand and types in the code with the other. The door unclicks and they pass through, then turn left into a narrow corridor. They walk for less than ten metres before making a sharp left through another door and there is Matt, sat at a desk, uniform on. He stands, takes Jane's hand, shakes it.

'Ms Pearce,' he says, before she can tell him how pleased she is to see him. 'We forgot to take a copy of your passport.'

'My passport?' says Jane.

Matt loads his stare with meaning, nods slowly at her. 'Your passport. Proof of ID.'

'Oh,' she says. 'Of course.'

She roots around in her bag, pulls out the small, blue booklet and hands it to Matt. He opens it to the photo page, then presses it face down onto a printer. Jane watches the light flash underneath, breathes deeply.

The woman who escorted Jane stands, hands clasped behind her. 'You must have been so worried.'

Jane glances at Matt, he looks up from her passport, nods again. She tries to arrange her face so that she doesn't look confused. 'You have no idea,' she says.

The woman exhales. 'As it happens, lots of babies get stolen from the port. It's terrifying.'

Jane nods. 'I've heard.'

'But to go into your van and steal him...' she shakes her head. 'They must have been following you for a while.'

Matt snaps Jane's passport shut. 'People are desperate,' he says. 'If it will get them where they want, they'll do anything.'

Jane lingers her gaze on him. She knows he means it.

'Good job you stitched his birth certificate into his sleepsuit.'

'Yes...' Again, Jane pulls her mouth into a smile. 'Good thing I did.'

Matt slides a folded piece of yellowed paper into Jane's passport and hands it back to her. 'You might want to stitch that back in,' he says, nodding at the paper.

'Oh,' she says, glancing down at it. 'His birth certificate. Yes, you're right.'

Matt claps his hands. 'Right,' he says. 'Let's get you two reunited.'

Jane puts a hand to her chest, drops her jaw like a fish flipped onto a deck.

'Are you okay?' says the woman.

It is then that Jane's voice fails her. She nods and wheezes, 'Take me to him now. Please.'

CHAPTER EIGHTY | February 2033
Jane

Matt leaves the room and Jane steps forward to follow. As he passes, he winks at her. She pretends not to notice. The woman tells her to take a seat, to wait for him to come back with the baby.

Jane steadies herself. *With the baby.* The seconds can't pass quickly enough, she thinks, as she tries to reconcile all her images of what he looks like, what he smells like, how his little fists ball up as he yawns. In less than a minute, she'll know all of this. In less than thirty seconds, in fact. Her gaze swoops about the room and her fingers tap the edge of the desk. A thought occurs to her.

'What will happen to Gillian?'

'Who's Gillian?' says the guard.

'I mean, the woman who stole him.'

She narrows her eyes. 'She'll be brought back to the UK.'

'Oh,' says Jane.

'How do you know her name?'

Jane opens her mouth without knowing what to say, but then the door clicks open and Matt edges through, making shhh noises and jigging slightly. She dashes over, peers around Matt's body and there he is. The soft, small bundle, eyes closed. The skin is flaky around his eyelids and his lips are wet and fat. Jane swoons, puts her arms out to take him and her passport falls to the floor. She doesn't care. He is in her arms, warm against her, his knees rising lightly, lips suckling once, twice, on nothing, and then he is still again. He has the same large cheeks as Ashleigh, the same widow's peak. She would like to touch his skin but cannot bring herself to disturb him. Her grandson, she thinks, and she squeezes him slightly, all the memories of baby Ashleigh rolling back to her. The night after Ashleigh's birth, Jane stayed awake and stared at her sleeping baby. I can't look away, she thinks to herself now. I just can't.

'We're docking shortly.'

Matt's voice echoes distantly like piped music.

'Okay,' says Jane, without looking up.

'Don't forget your documents,' says the woman, and Jane is aware of something being held out to her. She takes it, her passport with the certificate folded on top – it must have slipped from between the pages when she dropped it – and then she catches something that seizes her. She turns the yellow document to read the writing horizontally, takes in the words once, then twice. By the third read, Matt has taken the baby from her and the woman is helping her into a chair.

'What is it?' says Matt. 'What happened?'

Jane leans forward, her head between her legs, just like she was taught at school. Between deep breaths, she says, 'It can't be true.'

PART SEVEN
THE AFTERMATH

CHAPTER EIGHTY-ONE | September 2032
Gavin

'Take this,' says Butler, as Gavin curves shaky fingers around a tall cup of milk.

'Thanks, Butler,' he says, and starts to cry.

Butler puts a hand on Gavin's upper arm. 'And this is from Pinko. Everyone got one,' says Butler. 'He made sure of that. The name on mine is almost illegible, see?' He holds up his envelope. The 'B' is more like a backwards 'C'.

Gavin stares at his own envelope and pushes it away. Drinks his milk.

Three hours earlier, he is crossing the round lobby. Three at a time he takes the lip-like steps, up past the tree mural and along to the left. He doesn't stop to look at his work as he usually does, but slows to a careful tread inside the corridor, stepping his feet into the parquet squares, searching for Pinko's door. Where is it; which one is it... Then he slides to a halt. Butler is there, wiping his hands on a white towel, which comes away patched with orange and brown. He looks up from his hands, to Gavin, eyes large windows of glare. Gavin feels his fingers splayed at his side, his heels rising from the floor. He looks at him sidelong.

'Alright, Butler?' he manages, slowly with a crack.

'Don't go in there,' Butler replies, in one tone.

Gavin flicks his eyes from Butler to the door. When they flick back again, Butler is shaking his head. The glare grows heavy, droops and splashes onto his cheeks. Gavin unfreezes, sweeps past him, veers towards the curved door, reaches for the round handle, retracts his hand when he sees the crust of vomit, pushes at the door with his shoulder.

He enters the room and immediately makes sense of what he sees. He frowns, gurns, puts his hands to his eyes, then lowers them. He pulls at his shirt, the pockets of his trousers and a cry twists from his throat. His vision blurs as he strides towards Pinko Stephens and slaps him on the shoulder, on the face, on the back, on the face again. Then he bends low to Pinko's scaly lips, his crusted chin and shouts into his eyes. They stare surprised at the extended hand. Something pulls at Gavin's elbow, and he is walking backwards, one foot behind the other. Pinko's face gets smaller and smaller, until it is just a stain amongst the mess of bed.

CHAPTER EIGHTY-TWO | September 2032
Jane

Jane is making instant mashed potato when she receives a phone call.

Tunbridge Wells. Again.

She doesn't answer. She knows very well who's calling her and she has nothing to say to him.

Instead, a minute later, she listens to the answerphone message. Then replays it.

Jane's knees pull her to the ground. The plastic bowlful of off-white slop thuds beside her.

She hears her daughter humming, while brushing her teeth in the bathroom upstairs.

Jane listens to Butler's words. 'The coroner is on his way if you would like to come now. And see him before...'

She mouths the word 'coroner'.

Replays the words 'and see him'.

In the hallway, her eyes watch her front door. Surely he'll knock, any minute now, and laugh, telling her it was all some elaborate joke. But he doesn't. So she crawls into her own heart and holds the phone against it. From her heart, she can slip inside the phone and travel down the line to Pinko's house. Once there, she climbs the stairs, passes Gavin's mural, and walks to Pinko's room. She must only imagine what it looks like, as she has never been inside.

She closes her eyes now, Ashleigh hums on.

In Pinko's room, she approaches his bed, where he lies, bends to his head and holds it in a circle of her arms. Its blond fur smells clean against her face. Its eyes roll upwards to meet hers. 'Come with me,' he says, 'for a moment'. Then they are in his treehouse. She has never been there before, but she can smell the wood creaking, see the weaves in the patchwork blanket. He reaches down a scrabble set from one of the rafters, holds it against his stomach. 'Let's sit here for a while,' he says, 'and play cards, or something.'

'Okay,' she says.

And they do.

'What are you doing on the floor?'

Jane opens her eyes to see Ashleigh standing over her. Or is it Ashleigh? Her red hair hangs jaggedly around her chin and her sweater is so big that Jane can't see the shape of her.

Jane tries to comment on Ashleigh's hair and is sick all over the hall carpet.

'Mum, are you okay?' says Ashleigh. 'What's happened?'

CHAPTER EIGHTY-THREE | October 2032
Ashleigh

Jane is sitting on the edge of her bed. She has been sitting there since she woke up at seven.

It is now eleven.

Ashleigh brings her tea. Jane says nothing, follows Ashleigh's bump with a limping gaze.

Ashleigh folds her arms over her belly. 'What?' she says.

Jane starts to cry.

Twenty minutes later, Ashleigh pops her head around the door, reminds Jane to drink her tea. She ignores the heaving shoulders, the snivels.

Ashleigh disappears again and returns with crackers, takes away the cold tea.

This time, Jane doesn't look at her. She is lying on her side, facing the window. Her breathing is quick and juddery – she is still awake – and her hair is blasted against her head, exposing her dark roots. Ashleigh rounds the bed, looks down at her mother. She takes Jane's phone from the bedside table and types in the pin.

'The funeral has been postponed, pending a coroner's report and a police investigation,' she reads aloud from the internet, catching little bits of Jane's expression in between sentences. She lowers the phone and says, 'You have to get up, Mum.'

Jane says nothing, snaps her stare around Ashleigh's middle like a bite.

Days elapse like this.

The evenings grow dark, as do the plans for Finland. Ashleigh clutches Jane's phone, gazes out the window and wishes she'd kept her fat mouth shut. It would be so easy, thinks Ashleigh, staring at the spindly, baby oak, as nighttime creeps around it, to run away. There is still one bus per week to London. Surely she can get anywhere from London. She looks again at the little picture of the French mountains on Jane's phone, the girls snapped mid-jump-mid-grin. Jane set the image as her background to encourage positive thoughts about Ashleigh's journey. Her own phone is still dead and shattered from where Jane stamped on it. That's really the only thing stopping her from going, leaving without a phone. She doesn't have the guts to loot another and, if she stole her mum's, then *she* wouldn't have a phone. As she thinks this, she waddles back to her own room, to where her own phone has been on charge for the last several weeks. She picks it up, tries to turn it on. Nothing.

She sighs. Puts it back down again. Turns to leave.

She is almost at the door when she hears it, vibrating against the carpet. She strides back over, picks it up and sees an unknown number displayed on the cracked screen. She closes her bedroom door and answers in a whispery voice. 'Hello?'

'Ashleigh?' The voice is wheezy and low.

'Who is this?'

'A friend,' says the voice, before taking in another breath. 'Of Pinko's.'

'What?' says Ashleigh. 'How did you get my number?'

'I know lots of numbers,' he says, all in one breath.

Ashleigh scowls. 'That's a weird thing to say.'

'You must be pleased that your phone's working again.'

She freezes, darts her eyes about her room. 'How do you know it wasn't?'

'I watch people,' says the voice.

'Who is this?'

He ignores her. 'Look, don't feel bad.'

'What?'

'It's not,' he says, 'your fault. Even…if…you think that it is.'

The voice sounds like it's struggling for breath. She runs her tongue over her lips. 'Hang on,' she says. Her left hand is on the door handle and in a few seconds she's across the landing with the phone hidden behind her back. She checks on Jane, still curled over her own knees, this time with her back to the window. Again, that stare, pouncing at her belly. Ashleigh leaves the room and pads down the stairs to the back corner of the kitchen, as far as possible from Jane's room. When she is there, she squats on the floor and says, 'What are you on about?'

'You'll need documents for France.'

'Sorry?'

'They're in London. Everything you need for unhindered passage.'

'London?'

The voice wheezes again. 'The bus leaves tomorrow. But you know this.'

Ashleigh *did* know this. There were stories of scammers, gathering information on their victims, taking over devices. Maybe they hoped to lure her to London, where she'd be sold off to some lonely weirdo so he could claim free passage. 'I'm gonna hang up now.'

'You should think of lies,' he says, in a clearer voice, 'as truths sent to you by destiny.'

Her heart pumps in her ears and the room narrows. 'What's that supposed to mean?'

'Pinko,' he says, 'was *meant* to go. He did all he could in this world.'

They've seen her on telly, they must have done. Her Year 8 school photo; they didn't even pick a recent one. 'I know you're scamming me,' says Ashleigh. 'I know—'

'Gavin,' says the voice, louder now, 'will never leave England.'

'Gavin? What's this got to do with him?'

'He will,' says the voice, 'never leave, but...'

'It's got nothing to do with him.'

'Oh, but it has,' says the voice.

Ashleigh is breathing quickly now; she wraps her free arm over her stomach and glances at the door to the hallway. 'How do you know that?'

'He'll meet you at the station,' says the voice. 'And then, your little boy...will...have...to...go...away from...here.' The 'go' is lost in a prickly intake of breath. 'He'll make sure of that.'

'It's not a boy,' Ashleigh says, tightening her arm around her belly. 'Who is this?' she asks, as the voice tries to regain its control. It wheezes through a few breaths and Ashleigh asks again, 'Is this a joke?'

'It *is* a boy,' it replies finally. 'And I'm Padre.'

At six in the morning, Ashleigh checks on Jane, who is curled into the shape of a foetus. Or maybe a prawn; Ashleigh notes Jane's skinny outline under the blanket. A beam of streetlight lasers through a gap in the curtains and cuts through Jane's ankles. Ashleigh woke at two o'clock. Her feet swung down to the rug and she was up and rummaging through her drawers. By half-two, her rucksack was packed and at the foot of the stairs. Packing was the first stage. Leaving was the second. Ashleigh went back to bed, knowing that if she didn't go through with stage two, it was no biggie, no harm done.

'So, if you're legit, tell me my secret,' she'd said to Padre, on the phone.

'I will tell you your *truth*,' said Padre. 'Your departure will wake your mother. Jane. And your absence will make her love you more. How could it not?'

Ashleigh replays these words now, as she eases the front door shut and glances up at Jane's window.

'I, too, have had to extract myself from people to make them love me,' said Padre. 'It is a strange thing to feel so loved and yet so lonely.'

Ashleigh takes her phone from her pocket, tries to switch it on. The shatter-lines sparkle like spider webs in the streetlight, but the phone is still dead. She'll keep it in case he calls again. Perhaps, one day, he'll tell her she can go home.

'Hardly anyone gets the chance to save their mother,' he'd said. 'And she will thank you for it.'

'I'll save you, Mum,' she says, then puts the phone away and creeps along the pavement into the moonlight.

CHAPTER EIGHTY-FOUR | September 2032
Gavin

A wall. Fancy being buried in a wall. At least in the earth, things will wiggle their way into your coffin and nibble. Afterwards, they'll poop you out into the soil and you'll be sucked up through flower roots. Then you get to sit at the top, in the middle of the flower, and stare at the sun again.

But how can you do that through bricks? You can't.

All these people – and there should be many more – have decorated themselves with round things. Spots, and circles and spirals and hoops and words with lots of 'o's. Gavin looks down at his green Boss suit. No circles here. But it was Pinko's. And it's green. He did like a bit of leafy green. Gavin feels his cheeks pulling downwards. He straightens his tie, looks inside one of his jacket pockets, then the other one, then at the heel of his shoe. No. No good. He'll have to turn to the wall so he can cry a little bit. Just as he pivots his leg around and plants it next to the other one, a sheen catches his eye. He looks up. A man sits in Pinko's desk chair, a hospital mask over his face. Gavin wipes his eyes to see better. The man stares back, removes the mask and stares at Gavin like he's seen something he recognises. Gavin looks away, turns his back to the man and the chair. Then he wipes his nose on his sleeve and decides that he's being a bit rude. So he turns back and walks over.

'Sorry,' he says.

'You're crying,' says the man.

'Yeah,' says Gavin. 'Sorry.'

'Don't suppose you've got any weed?'

'No,' he says. 'But I get asked that sometimes.'

The man shrugs. 'You look like the type.'

Gavin draws in an open-mouthed breath, then mutters, 'I know.'

'I'm sad too, you know,' says the man.

'Is that why you want the weed?'

A nod.

'You shouldn't really be smoking, should you?'

The man waves him away, takes another breath from his mask.

Gavin sways on the spot, but the silence makes him feel funny, so he says, 'Were you like, good mates then?'

The man stares, until Gavin thinks he's not going to answer. Perhaps he can't hear him properly...

'Pinko Stephens has shown me more kindness than any other human being,' he says. 'Throughout his whole life, that man held his heart in the air so that everyone around him might bask in its warmth.'

'Did he?' says Gavin.

'I have watched many people in my time. I *watch* many people still. I am never disappointed by them, because I know how they're going to react, what they'll do, what they won't do...'

Gavin shuffles from foot to foot, holds his elbows behind his back.

'But him...' The man points towards the window to where the wall is. 'He is a mystery. How one man can impart so much good...'

Gavin nods, swallows. That wall, that awful wall. He squeezes his eyes shut, covers his mouth. Why would you work so hard at life just to end up in a wall?

The man says, 'He's not really in there, you know...'

Gavin's eyes snap up.

'Only his body. Not him.'

'How did you know what I was thinking?'

'You know,' he says, taking another drag from his mask, 'I watch a lot of people.'

Gavin nods. 'You said that a minute ago. But I'd already forgotten. Sorry.'

The man smiles through his mask.

'I'm Gavin, by the way.'

'The artist. I know.'

'Really?'

'Yes.'

Gavin grins, looks at his shoes.

'And you are still here,' says the man.

'I am.'

'Where are his other lot, eh? They got their envelopes and went...'

'Well, not exactly...'

The man raises his eyebrows and says, 'Where's Butler?'

'Ah now, that's different. Butler had to go to Germany before the helicopter went.'

'He didn't *have* to, Gavin.'

'You can't blame him.'

'But he had unfinished business here...'

'Oh yeah?'

'Pinko asked him to do something.'

'Really?' frowning. 'What?'

'And now I'm going to ask you to do that thing...'

'Oh, well, um... I'm actually moving to...'

'Nuneaton.'

Gavin stops shuffling. 'How did you know that?'

The man stares, waits.

'You watch people, that's right. I remember now.' Gavin looks to the side, scrunches up his face as if he's doing a really hard sum. 'But how can you see that?'

The man sighs. 'You were saying...'

'Yes. I'm moving soon. I don't know what it is you're gonna ask me, but I've already had some ladies ask me to take them abroad and I can't.' Gavin blushes. 'I'm staying here.'

'One lady,' corrects the man, with a finger in the air. 'Only one lady has asked you and you told her you would think about it.'

Gavin gapes at the man.

'This also involves going abroad. Although whether or not you'll go is yet to be seen.'

'Oh?'

'And *I'm* not asking you, Pinko is.'

Gavin's face starts to twitch. He pulls it back into neutral. Nods.

'You see, there's a girl heading to London... She needs someone to chaperone her.'

'What?'

The man exhales and says in a softer voice. 'To accompany her. To collect her.'

'I don't drive.'

'Take the bus.'

'Oh, I do take the bus quite often actually. Yes, I could take the bus.'

'It's settled then.'

Gavin frowns. 'What is? When do I have to do this?'

'I'll tell you later...' he says, putting the mask back over his face.

'I could get the National Express, but there aren't many of them kicking about these days.'

The man lifts the mask. 'And you owe that lady a favour.'

'What lady?'

'The one who asked you to take her abroad.'

'I know I do. But I'm not sure if I can do it.' Gavin winces, pulls his elbows right in. 'I've never really had a girlfriend.'

The man laughs. Then coughs. Then stops coughing and nods slowly. 'Just that one time, wasn't it?'

Gavin freezes, stares at the man and thinks he's misheard – he must have misheard – but he doesn't want to check in case he hasn't, so he says, 'I'm going to get some chicken satay, do you want some?'

'No, thanks.'

'Alright then.' Gavin puts his hands in his pockets, swings his hips. 'Um, sorry – what's your name?'

The man lifts his mask again. 'Padre.'

'What?'

'PADRE.'

Later, Padre sits in his chair and watches the mourners leave, nodding at them, removing his mask to say 'ba-bye'. They smile back, but their eyes wrinkle a little bit, as if they are confused by him. Some look at the twinkly vase on the desk behind, the round portrait of some old man above it. When they have gone, Padre turns his chair to gaze at the tree on the wall upstairs. He rocks himself to wheel the chair a few centimetres to the right, then has to close his eyes and breathe.

Gavin watches him, his hands clasped around the two pink wafers in his pocket.

How does he know about Nuneaton? he thinks. *And* that thing; the 'once' thing, that makes Gavin shiver just thinking about it. He rubs the wafers more urgently, tries to concentrate on their tiny network of squares, then he has an idea. But the thing about the wafers is that they are most likely too powdery, what with his breathing and everything. He decides to take Pardy something else to eat. Something less powdery than wafers.

His eyes land on a cup of trifle. Trifle is nice and custardy. And some tea to go with it. That would be perfect. He picks up one in each hand and heads over.

'Um, Pardy?' says Gavin.

'Yes?' Padre replies, looking up.

'I drew that, you know. That tree.'

Padre removes his mask. 'I can see the magic in it,' he says. 'I bet your mother loves it.'

'She does.' Gavin grins. 'Um, I brought you some tea.' Padre looks at the cup and saucer in Gavin's left hand. 'And a mini trifle.' Padre looks at the trifle in his right hand. 'Because it occurred to me that no one had brought you anything. And you've been here a while.' Padre looks up into Gavin's eyes and starts to cry. 'Oh shit, no...don't cry,' he says, putting down the tea. Long, trailing tears fall into the red indentations from Padre's mask. Gavin finds the pouch of tissues that his mum put in his breast pocket, offers him one. 'I've got pink wafers instead – would you like one of them?'

Padre shakes his head. 'They...' he clears his throat. 'They are too powdery.'

'That's what I thought,' he says, squatting in front of him.

Then Padre says, 'You watch people, don't you? Like me.'

Gavin squints. Scratches his head.

'You know, Gavin, perhaps you should really, really think about Nuneaton.'

'I have,' he says, making his eyes wide.

A sigh. 'I know.'

'How do you know? I just don't get it, Pardy. It's not that I don't believe you, I'd just like to know how you do it.'

'And how do you make your pictures move?'

Gavin shrugs. 'I don't think they move. I just think they make people's eyes go funny.'

Padre laughs, then twitches his eyes over Gavin, before saying, 'You look like her, you know. Your mother.'

Gavin swallows. 'You know my mum?'

'Be a good lad,' says Padre, 'and fetch me a spoon.'

Gavin goes to collect a teaspoon from the buffet table and wonders how on earth someone like that would know his mum. He brings it back and pushes it into the trifle.

'Thank you,' says Padre, taking the little glass ramekin from him. 'Now before I go, we need to talk about the girl in London. And the baby.'

'About that,' says Gavin, scratching the back of his head. 'You know, Pardy, I'm not too sure about France...'

'Don't you worry,' says Padre. 'She won't go to France. Not before she's had the baby. And that's why she needs you and your family.'

Gavin frowns. 'You want me to take her to Margate?'

Padre digs about in his trifle, finds a strawberry and spoons it up to just in front of his mouth. 'She'll decide that all on her own, don't worry.'

'Mum would love that,' says Gavin, grinning. 'Especially if she has a baby.'

'Good.' Padre swallows the strawberry, then says, wheezily, 'Ashleigh will trust you, Gavin. And she'll love your mum.'

Gavin's ears prick up. He looks straight at Padre and says, 'I know Ashleigh.'

'I know you do.'

Gavin looks left and right; there are still a few people about, so he crouches well down and whispers, 'Did you know it's Pinko's baby she's carrying?'

Padre's mask steams and clears, as he stares at Gavin, unblinking, like he's said something daft.

Gavin stands up straight again. 'Of course you know. You watch people. Sorry.'

Padre lifts his mask. 'That's not Pinko's baby, is it Gavin?' he says. 'It's yours.'

PART EIGHT
THE FINALE

CHAPTER EIGHTY-FIVE | February 2033
Jane

From Fishguard, Jane heads up the coast towards Aberystwyth. The baby sleeps beside her in a makeshift car-seat consisting of two pillows, a cardboard box and some gaffer tape. It is the morning of the 26th. Three days to get all the way up to Inverness. That should be plenty. She could do it in a day if she didn't have a baby to feed and a dog to walk; two days would be fine. Plus, it isn't like she's driving some rust-bucket. The RV is almost new; she's sure of it. She hopes against hope that Ashleigh will be there. Every now and then, she looks over at him, Little Gavin, just long enough to see a lip curl or a finger twitch.

God, that name.

But no, she can't think about that now.

It took her a while to come around after that queasy moment on the ferry. Matt gave her a mug of sweet tea; she'd had enough fat coke to fill an aquarium by that point, but the tea was warm and reviving all the same. As the ferry creaked into dock, he told her she had to get a move on, get down to her vehicle. She scowled at him, unused to his harsh tone, but she wobbled onto her feet. He was, after all, right; he was probably trying to tell her that the helicopter wouldn't wait, without letting the other woman know that they knew each other.

All the same, he asked if he should carry the baby down to the parking decks, and it was then that they could finally talk in private.

'Were you alright up there?' he said, in his normal, nice-ish voice.

'Yeah...just had a bit of a shock.'

'Something to do with the birth certificate?'

She felt herself stumble again, pressed a hand to her stomach and breathed deeply. 'I'll tell you on the way,' she said. 'Not now.'

He stopped just in front of the van, jigging the baby against his shoulder, like he'd done it a thousand times before. 'I'm not coming.'

She blinked. 'What do you mean?'

He shook his head, pressed his lips together. 'You'll go to Finland,' he said, after a moment. 'What do I do then?'

'But...' she said. And she couldn't think of what to say afterwards. There might be space on the helicopter, but what if there wasn't? She could drag him all the way up there, only to leave him waving at her as she took off from the Scottish coast.

'I've got my uniform.' He shrugged. 'No one's asking questions; I guess there's so much movement within staff.'

'What will you do?'

He shrugged again, shifted the baby to the other shoulder. 'I'll sneak on a ferry to France, just as I snuck on the ferry today.'

She scowled. 'And then?'

'I don't know,' he said. 'But what other options do I have?'

She couldn't answer that, instead her lip quivered and whether it was finding the baby, or losing Matt, or realising that Pinko might not be the baby's father, she started to cry. And she hated herself for bawling in front of Matt for what seemed like the third time that day, but when she looked up at him, he was crying too, and he strode towards her, hugged her with his baby-free arm. They stood like that for a moment, a sandwich of strangers.

Jane pushed herself away. 'You're taking the money.'

'No,' said Matt. 'I—'

'Yes,' she said. 'I don't want to hear it. I'm not leaving this boat until you do—'

He sighed, wiped his eyes on his tie. She took the baby from him, told him to go to the glove compartment. He did, and while she danced the baby against her, she heard him say goodbye to Paris.

As she drove away, she tried not to glance in her rear-view mirror, but her eyes disobeyed her. He stood at the edge of the gangway, watching, until she veered slowly to the left and he disappeared from view.

Now, Paris is whining. The baby stares at him with surprised eyes and a round mouth.

'What do you want, Paris?'

Jane stops the motorhome for the third time in an hour. Each time she pulls over, she clicks on his detachable lead and allows herself to be pulled outside, only to watch while Paris snuffles about for ten minutes. She stays close to the door of the motorhome, hanging onto it with the tips of her fingers and glancing through every few seconds to make sure the baby is alright. Little Gavin Pearce.

She shudders.

The second time he whined to go outside, she said, 'I don't have time for this'. The third time, she was concerned. 'What's wrong, wrinkles?' she said. 'Have you got a wee-wee infection?' He closed his panting mouth and moaned high and long from the back of his throat. She checked him over, but it would be hard to tell without monitoring him for a day or so. God, that was the last thing she needed. It wasn't as if they had all the time in the world.

Now she tracks Paris as he sniffs about a tuft of grass; squints to see if anything comes out when he cocks his leg. Then she checks the baby. Thinks about Ashleigh. Tracks Paris again. Baby. Ashleigh. Paris.

Hopefully, Ashleigh will be waiting at Inverness. Even if she is a rebellious little cow, her survival instinct will draw her up to the helipad, surely. Who would choose real danger when they had the option of curling up in the lap of luxury? No sixteen-year-old she knows. That's for sure.

The baby's hand twitches open, then curls over again like an undulant sea creature.

But then there was the problem of getting from Kent to Inverness. Not a simple journey – that's why Pinko had left them the RV, after all. Jane sighs, imagines her daughter roaming the country, baggy and sore. Please be there, Ashleigh. Please. She wipes one eye, then the other, and it is then that she realises the lead is slack. Her gaze snaps upwards, then double takes.

Paris is gone.

CHAPTER EIGHTY-SIX | February 2033
Gavin

Gavin is reading a text from Gillian, when Little Carla takes him by the hand and leads him up the stairs. She is the first one over the threshold of the new house, but she knows exactly where she is going. She ignores the empty picture frames that have been left along the wall of the stairway, and she doesn't notice the notches on her bedroom doorframe. Gavin stops for a moment to touch them, to read the children's names written next to them. The dates. Their heights. 'Come on, Uncle Gavin,' says Little Carla. Gavin enters her room, where she is already sitting on the floor, hugging a large, pink monkey that isn't hers. There is a felt-tip name on the small, white label that protrudes from its bum. Gavin suspects it is one of the names that he has just seen on the doorframe, but he doesn't want to get close enough to read. In one, quick movement, he pinches the tears out of his eyes. Of all the things he thought he'd be feeling today...

Gavin heads over to the window and looks out. Beyond the garden, the hedgerows web through the dull, brown fields. In the far distance, the smoke from the massive campsite smudges through the sky. Even on the clearest days in Margate, the most interesting thing he can see from his bedroom window is next door's neon Santa. It had been on their roof for over a year, now; guarding the empty house. Here, Gavin notices, both neighbours are in their gardens. One moves shadowlike inside their greenhouse, the other scrapes buckets of earth from the ground with a small yellow digger. Bunker, thinks Gavin. Pinko had one.

Gavin's mum is in the back garden, taking a video with her new phone. She didn't expect half an acre of land surrounded by chestnut trees. Gavin should be happy about this too – obviously – but there is a large broom leaning against the garden shed, together with a bucketful of the last of the fallen leaves. They must have done it before they left, he thinks, taking in the trimmed shrubs and the neat flowerbed edges, the window box on the yellow, weatherboard shed. This garden was loved.

'Have you seen my wallpaper?' says Little Carla, tracing a rearing unicorn with her finger.

'Lovely, isn't it?' says Gavin, watching her. But his gaze travels past her, to an open door on the other side of the landing. It has blue walls and a pastel rainbow, only just visible. He leaves Little Carla's room and heads over to it. Inside, he sees the whole of the rainbow painted across the back wall and just to the right, next to the big bay window, is a Moses basket. Gavin smiles and walks up to it, imagining little arms stirring the air, tiny kicking feet. He crouches down, closes his eyes. Little Carla's cousin, he thinks. A real, blood cousin. Gavin reaches into the basket and pretends that he can feel the warmth of a small, firm belly. But his hand presses against the bottom of the basket, damp in the February air. He stands, takes a pill box from his inside pocket and opens it. Inside is a photocopy, folded into a tight rectangle. He unfolds it and reads his name against the word FATHER. Then ARTIST against the word PROFESSION. Then he holds it to his chest and tries not to cry.

'Gavin?' his mum calls from the foot of the stairs. 'There's a frog pond at the end of the garden. Come and see.'

Gavin takes a deep breath, gets himself together. 'Coming, Mum.' He folds the paper, puts it back in the pillbox, then hurries out of the room.

His phone lies face up on the floor, Gillian's text still visible.
I've lost him, Gavin. I've lost the baby.

CHAPTER EIGHTY-SEVEN | February 2033
Jane

Jane spent the best part of an hour wandering the fields beside the A487, calling Paris's name. Then she decided to drive around for a while; he would have covered some ground, probably headed towards a nice, food-smelling house. Paris wasn't the kind of dog to take his chances in a field. He liked his posh grub too much. She crawled the RV through the back lanes, until the baby started crying and the little voice in her head yelled at her that Paris was a lost cause. He might have been picked up by someone, could well be on his way to France by now. And anyway, wouldn't it be daft to miss the flight because she'd wasted all her petrol or blown a tyre? Or she'd run into a sudden, never-ending, traffic jam and had to repeat over and over to herself, *if only I'd left earlier.* Instinct pulls her away from her search. She needs to get going.

As she swings the RV around, she can't help thinking that Padre is watching and has used his omnipotence to make a deal with her. That can be the only explanation, surely: Paris in exchange for the baby. Weirdly, the thought comforts her. He must have seen her strength and realised that, in fact, she will *never* be alone. She is too determined.

Jane sniffs deeply and puts the RV into drive. *I hope he'll be alright, that little pug.* He didn't like the RV, anyway. It made him bark and whine. She glances at the sleeping baby and smiles. He is too young to stay awake for very long. 'It's you and me now,' she says. 'And Mummy. We'll see her soon.'

They head out of Wales and up to Manchester. The hours ahead allow enough space for Jane to indulge happier thoughts. It will all be fine. Padre is making things happen for her, Paris has found a new owner, Ashleigh will be at the heliport. Why wouldn't she? She must have had the same envelope, the same timings. She's had a couple of weeks to think, be scared, be upset and then straighten out her mind and get herself to Scotland. Now the margin of escape is getting narrower, she will *have to* act.

Beyond Manchester, there are fewer abandoned cars on the hard shoulder. With no major port up this far, there's no reason to come here. Still, Jane expected to see a line of traffic in the opposite direction. At Lancaster, she slows down for a mobile speed camera, gawping as she passes it. The last time she saw a real policeman was... She can't even remember. They push on up through the Lake District, where a high-viz official stops Jane at a barrier and asks the purpose of her visit. She explains she is on her way to Scotland and needs somewhere to stop and feed the baby. Jane squints at his lanyard. Space Allocation Officer For Displaced People. If there is a border force in place at the Lake District, that makes Jane a refugee in her own country. Great. A thought strikes her: 'Do you think I'll struggle to get into Scotland?'

The official smirks. 'Once you get to Carlisle, it's business as usual.' He pushes his hands in his pockets and rocks back on his heels. 'It should be like that everywhere, to be fair.'

Jane shrugs. 'I guess people need to act while they can.'

'I'm not so sure, myself,' he says, looking straight at her. Then he asks her to open the door so he can see Little Gavin. Jane rolls her eyes, but obliges.

The official glances at the baby, then returns to his booth, where he retrieves a large-ish box with 0 − 3 MONTHS on the side. 'There's powdered milk, nappies, wipes and a couple of vests in there,' he says, reaching it up to her. 'We've got space on a campsite over by Eskdale if you need to stay here, love.'

Jane feels her chin wobbling. 'No,' she manages, then holds up the box. 'But, thank you for this.'

From Penrith, she makes the short drive to Ullswater to feed the baby and to gaze at the fuzzy green hills. It is her first time here, and the thought that she will never return makes her linger well after the baby is fed. So this is England, she thinks, as she walks up and down beside the RV, patting Little Gavin on the back. The water won't cover these fells, surely? She thinks back to some nineties' disaster movie with a giant tidal wave that engulfed San Francisco. But that was just a film. In real life, tidal waves hit the coast, not entire cities. These hills will still be here, she thinks. The sea won't come that far.

As she pushes on up to the Scottish border, there is a break in the list of thirty-or-so songs that have been looping on the radio since Aberystwyth. The news comes in from Krakow. Urgent rumbles have been recorded in Iceland. Jane finds herself laughing at the word 'urgent', then wiping tears from her eyes. But she is not sad. She feels oddly relieved that it is finally here, that they don't have to wait for the water that *might* come. It will come. And it might engulf the UK, Western Europe, the American coastline and all the poor little islands that sit in its path. But she just can't quite imagine it.

It certainly won't get as far as Nuneaton, she hopes.

Only once it has come will they know what they are dealing with. They can start to rebuild. She might even return to her two-up-two-down in Sittingbourne and pretend that none of this ever happened.

She passes Carlisle, Gretna Green, Lockerbie and Moffat. She notes the way the cars drive about unhurried up here, and the people walking their dogs. The tension that seizes the air south of the border is now undetectable. Funny, she thinks, that Scotland should be directly in range of the mega-tsunami and so theoretically, one of the worst-affected places. Soon, beneath each road sign, and on each motorway bridge, the message HOME IS FREEDOM is graffitied in dark green. The traffic thickens on the outskirts of Glasgow. Cars pass her with posters taped to their back windows. WAKE UP TO THE TRUTH and IT WOULD HAVE HAPPENED BY NOW and A BETTER LIFE IN EUROPE DOESN'T EXIST. At Stirling, she stops for petrol. There is no queue for the shop and, through its window, Jane can just about make out the rows of stocked shelves. The vendor comes out of his kiosk to fill up her tank. He smiles at her, as she watches him in her wingmirror, comments on the weather – it is *surprisingly* sunny – and wishes her a good journey. As he walks away, she notes the words printed on the back of his hoodie: LEAVE MY HOME? FOR LIES?

Jane stares after him, thinks of the last year, the desperation for a survival plan, the shit-show that ensued, and rests her head on the steering wheel. 'Please don't let this all be lies,' she whispers.

Little Gavin rumbles wetly. Jane pulls the van to the side and nips into the back to change his nappy and realises that she hasn't slept since the ferry from Liverpool to Ireland. She yawns and feels as slow and bulky as the RV. Her Satnav says that she has just under three hours to go, but the van will surely take longer – probably nearer to four. And she'd have to stop at least once to feed and change Little Gavin. She yawns again and listens for a moment to the baby's soft breathing. Perhaps now would be a good time for a sleep.

No, she thinks. Not when she is so close…

But her body ignores her, settles itself back into the driver's chair and, right there on the petrol forecourt, she closes her eyes and falls asleep.

She wakes with a start. Little Gavin is crying in the passenger seat, and someone is tapping on the door. Jane plucks the baby out of his car seat, then winds down the window and looks down.

'We heard the bairn and were wondering if you were still alive,' says the assistant, blinking up at her.

'How long was he crying for?'

'Not long. A few minutes. But it's unusual not to wake up when they cry. Are you unwell?'

'No,' says Jane. 'Just very tired.'

'Aye, I can see that.' The man smiles, hands her up a thermos. 'Coffee,' he says. 'You've probably got your own in the back, but it's always nice when someone brings it to you.' He nods at the flask. 'You can keep it.'

He is the second kind stranger to make her well up, today. 'Thank you,' she says.

'No bother,' he replies, turning to leave. 'And you best get on the road before the storm comes.'

Jane turns her gaze to the sky, now too dark to reveal what the weather is doing.

'You've got time to get to Inverness,' he calls over his shoulder. 'But you best leave now.'

Okay, thinks Jane. She tends to the baby, then roars off the forecourt, waving at the kiosk as she goes. She sips at the coffee while she drives. It is earthy and sweet and has been made with oat cream, her absolute favourite. She makes herself sip it slowly and as she joins the motorway, wonders how he knew she liked her coffee like this. *And*, she realises, she never even told him she was going to Inverness.

Padre, she thinks, and the thought warms her. He *is* watching her, and his weird, inexplicable, crazy powers have sent her another ally, just like Matt. The man knocked on her window with *coffee*, for goodness sake. Padre wants them to get to Inverness. Jane smiles at this, presses on the accelerator. Padre is on her side.

They pass through Stirling, Perth and the Cairngorms. It is, by now, the early hours of the 27th of February 2033. The caffeine continues to zing through Jane's blood stream, as she plans what she will say to Ashleigh, how she will hug her. They will spend the next two nights in the RV, then they'll be away, the three of them. But she has to steady her thoughts, bring them back to neutral; she's never been to Inverness before and it is entirely possible that she won't find Ashleigh straight away.

Just get there, she thinks to herself.

During the last stretch of the journey, reason begins to take hold. What if Ashleigh isn't there? Jane wonders. Padre's awful sentence plumes in her mind. She shakes it away, stares hard at the road ahead.

When she arrives at the heliport, she can barely shift the gearstick into park. Her hands are pulsing and her fingertips are shaky. The carpark is almost full, but there are still a few spaces. She glances into the floodlit areas and notes two Porsches, a Bentley, a couple of Land Rovers and a long, thick Hummer. The cars are empty, of course; probably their owners are already in Finland. She had expected to see faces pressed up against the chicken wire that surrounds the heliport, shouting at the procession of high-end cars as they passed through a heavily manned barrier. But there is no-one, not even a guard at the barrier. Not even, Jane realises, a barrier.

It is 2:30am. Jane parks the RV, unstraps the baby and steps out into the carpark. The sky cracks and rumbles; she must have arrived in the nick of time. As she heads for what looks like the terminal, she notices a figure – a woman – walking in the opposite direction.

'You're the last one on the list,' the woman calls.

Jane squints, notes the high-viz, the clipboard and the Kentish accent.

'It means we can leave early,' says the woman, now just a few feet away.

'What do you mean?' says Jane.

The woman stops just in front of Jane and consults her clipboard. 'I checked your number plate on the way in. Jane Pearce, is that right?'

Jane frowns, then nods.

'Great. Everyone else is here.'

Everyone. Jane lurches, giddy. The woman said everyone. Her voice trembles as she repeats the word. 'Everyone?'

'Yes. We'll leave as soon as the storm passes tomorrow.'

'Where is my daughter? Is she here?' Jane says, as the first drops of rain land in her hair. She covers the baby's head with her hand.

The woman pulls up her hood with one hand, checks her clipboard with the other. 'What's her name?' she says.

'Ashleigh Pearce.'

'*Ashleigh* Pearce?'

'Yes.'

The woman studies the list for a moment. 'She's not here.'

Jane freezes.

She scans the list again. 'Nope, she's definitely not here.' She looks up at Jane. 'I'm so sorry.'

'But,' says Jane, 'We can't leave without her.'

The sky cracks again as the rain thickens.

'We *cannot* leave without her,' she repeats.

The woman looks confused. 'She's not on the list,' she says. 'She hasn't got a spot.'

'What?' says Jane.

'She hasn't got a place on the helicopter,' she says.

'I don't understand…'

'I'm sorry,' says the woman, and she drops her eyebrows as if she really is. She reaches out and squeezes Jane's upper arm. 'I'm truly sorry.'

Jane's mouth hangs open as she takes this in, then she's aware of the woman guiding her back to the RV.

'You need to get that baby out of the rain,' says the woman.

'There has to be a mistake,' says Jane, as she lets herself be pushed up into the RV. The woman sits her down, then opens her high-viz jacket and produces a mobile phone. She dials a number and puts it to her ear while Jane blinks at her. It was absolutely obvious that Ashleigh would come to Inverness. Pinko would have given her passage – plus a load of money – it didn't make any sense at all.

The woman calls back to her office, asks after 'an Ashleigh Pearce'. Jane flicks her eyes up when she hears Ashleigh's name, but the rain beating on the roof prevents her from understanding the voice at the other end. 'Right,' says the woman into her phone. 'Right. Yes. Okay.'

'What?' says Jane.

'Yes,' says the woman. 'Right. Okay.' Then she hangs up.

'What is it?'

'She was taken off the manifest,' says the woman. 'Apparently, she's in France.'

Jane doesn't sleep that day, but keeps one eye on the baby and one eye on the window. As soon as the storm clears, she expects to see Ashleigh striding through the wire gate and towards the RV, her headphones around her neck and her smile hitched up to one side. What went wrong? Jane asks herself. Why would an intelligent young girl choose to take her chances out in the wild like that? She had a way out. And all those people, thinks Jane, clambering for the ferry at Rosslare, what would they have given for Ashleigh's ticket to Finland?

Then Jane wonders if Ashleigh really *is* in France.

She might have been kidnapped.

And if she was, what if she's hurt?

But, worst of all, what if she's...

No, thinks Jane. These dark thoughts cannot take root. There is, after all, nothing she can do. Ashleigh ran away from home, gave birth, abandoned her baby... Life has made her independent. A survivor. And anyway, she had no way of getting to Inverness. It was Jane who *really believed* she'd made it true, simply by willing it.

The truth is, Ashleigh was never going to come to Scotland.

The baby starts to fuss. Jane picks him up and jigs him in her arms. Soon they will be in Finland. 'When all of this is over,' she says to Little Gavin, 'when the water *goes* – which it will – you and I will find your mummy.' Little Gavin opens his mouth into his first, wide smile and Jane nods at him, sadly. 'You see? You agree with that, don't you?'

At least, she thinks, Padre's awful premonition was wrong.

Jane arrives at the helipad promptly. She has a rucksack on her back, a sports bag full of cash over her shoulder, and Little Gavin in her arms. Before leaving the RV, she rested her hand on it, thanked it. It had, after all, done its job. Now she watches the large, white helicopter, its blades flopped around it like wilting petals, and tries not to think about Ashleigh. She'll be stuck on a mountain, with any luck, squashed into a room full of fellow asylum seekers. God knows what she had to do to get there...

No.

Don't think about it.

The woman from the day before bustles out from behind her desk. She widens her eyes when she sees Jane. 'Good morning,' she says, voice shaky, before touching her hair, then her cheek, then her ear. 'So you've decided to go, then.'

Jane half smiles, puts down her sports bag, notices the woman's eyes following it down. 'Why wouldn't I?'

The woman shrugs. 'I don't know. What with your daughter... you know.'

Jane nods, her eyes catching the slow rotation of the blades. 'I'm going.'

'Good,' says the woman. 'The others are on board. You need to go through security.'

Jane nods. The woman nods her head towards an airport security belt and tells her to place her bags on it. Jane does as she is told, and is then directed towards a large, metal door. The woman asks Jane if she can hold the baby while she passes through.

Jane scowls. 'Can't I take him?'

The woman smiles and holds out her arms. 'No need,' she says. 'And I take it there's no pug?'

Jane nods sadly. Paris. She'd completely forgotten about him. 'No,' she says, passing Little Gavin over. 'He ran away.'

The woman drops her eyebrows. 'Oh dear. I'm sorry.'

The blades have sped up now. Jane can no longer make out the individual spokes.

'We should get a move on,' says the woman. 'Go through there and hold your arms out. Once you see the green flash, open the opposite door and you'll come out on the other side.'

'Okay,' says Jane.

The woman smiles, bounces Little Gavin lightly. 'Any metals? Jewellery?'

'No,' says Jane.

'Okay then.'

Jane opens the door and enters the room. She holds her arms out and parts her legs slightly. She stands for a few seconds, but there is no flash. She changes position. Waits. Still nothing. She goes back to the door to call out to the woman, but there is no handle on this side. Shit. She goes over to the opposite door and sees it is marked EXIT. This door has a handle. She tries it, but the door won't open. She tries again, shaking the handle. Still, nothing. She starts to call out, then leans right onto the handle. It clicks and the door pops open. Jane stares for a moment into an empty waiting room. She goes back through the door and can see the end of the conveyor belt. As she approaches, she notices the helicopter and freezes.

It hovers in the sky, slowly turning towards the sea.

'Hello?' she yells, looking around. 'Is anyone here?'

Her voice echoes through the empty building.

Jane jumps onto the conveyor belt and crawls to the other side.

'Hello?' she yells again. 'HELLO?'

The woman, the baby and her bags are gone.

CHAPTER EIGHTY-EIGHT | Summer 2033
Ashleigh

The water still hasn't come. Perhaps it was all a lie.

Ashleigh sits at the seventh-floor window of a blocky, concrete building in Arâches-la-Frasse. Usually, it is a ski hotel for families; now it is a refuge for girls and women. Mostly girls. She gets it though, why people would want to come here on holiday. She hasn't been to many places outside of Sittingbourne, but, with all the trees and hills and stuff, this can't be that different from Finland. Why didn't they just come here? The thought pinches her while she contemplates the flint-top mountains; it's as if she's studying a photo. They're real, but she has no idea how high they are. Or how far away. One of the other girls passed her some binoculars earlier that day and, when she focussed them, she could just about make out a person, clinging on somewhere near the top.

There are three of them sharing the room. They are expecting more – the rooms sleep up to six in two set of bunks and a pull-out sofa. The thought of sharing a sofa with a stranger made her feel a bit weird, so she bagsied a bottom bunk as soon as she arrived. The other two got the top bunks. They are from Orkney, right up by Scotland. Sisters. They hugged Ashleigh as she cried that first night. They seemed nice, but Ashleigh couldn't understand much of what they were saying. She thought they might be German.

'What I don't get,' she kept saying, 'is that it's not bad at all. Mum could have come here.'

'Write to her,' said one, pushing her phone into Ashleigh's hands.

Ashleigh pouted and looked away.

'You need a phone,' said the other. 'We can share until you get your own.'

But she had already realised that her mum couldn't have come here. No. Ashleigh couldn't have explained the fact that she lied to get them to Finland. And all that stuff that happened as a result.

Without thinking, she sends her hand up inside her hair and yanks out a few strands, one after the other. She has a small bald patch just above her ear, and she would like to make it perfectly round. She knows this is weird. One of the girls told her that she needs to keep rethinking the memory that makes her pull out her own hair. She needs to take each detail and make it okay, then the memory won't be so bad.

Like the fact that she had sex with Gavin the night of The Last Match.

She met him at Dreamland with her mates the month before. He seemed so sweet and goofy, with his blue slush puppy and his Nokia 3310. And his Coventry City scarf that belonged to his grandad. Pinko got him tickets to The Last Match, at a pub all the way over in Tunbridge Wells, but Gavin had a taxi booked and so invited Ashleigh along. At the pub, they talked for a while about the Intimacy Law and what the hell you were supposed to do if you'd never done it before. Then they got all deep about never being able to enjoy sex, not even once, when they were forced into a life of oppression. And what with The Last Match tapering into 'Sweet Caroline' and all Pinko's mates in their silly hats, they started to get a bit dreamy.

But there was something more, Ashleigh thinks now, something twinkly and warm that squeezed her heart and they kept staring at each other for way too long and soon enough, she'd taken him by the hand and pulled him upstairs. Found an unlocked room.

'You'll have to be in charge,' he said. 'I have no idea what I'm doing.'

'And you think I do?'

It happened, somehow, but Gavin kept his eyes jammed shut and his teeth rammed together. Afterwards, he threw up bright blue sick into the wash basin. Then it was all a bit awkward. Ashleigh bought him a new slush puppy, spiked it with vodka. He was much happier after a few sips. They sat together on the coach to Pinko's, but all the warmth and twinkles had gone and she didn't really talk to him after that.

It was weird. And a bit sticky. Poor Gavin.

She pulls out another few hairs, then sits on her hand. At this rate, the even circle will cover her whole head. Below, she sees the sisters queuing for food in their matching white jumpers. There seems to be an endless supply of brick-shaped cartons containing foul-tasting milk, powdered chocolate, and little pots of mashed-up apple. When Ashleigh runs out of tokens for soup and hard-boiled eggs, she spreads the apple on a crisp-bread and eats it with chocolate milk. She gave the girls her soup token, so they'll probably bring up a bowlful for her. Not that she feels like eating.

At Pinko's party, she went a bit crazy. Maybe to stamp out the memory of what she'd just done, who knows. But everyone thought she was great, and her confidence was sky high. They had a right laugh together, she and Pinko. She'd seen him loads on telly, and then to actually *hang out* with him...

She winces again. Tugs at her hair with the other hand.

After she kissed him, he called her a taxi (which probably came and went, they were up in his room by that point). He forgot about the taxi and told her she had to go to bed. Of course she said she didn't want to, but everything was starting to get a bit blurry, so she didn't put up much of a fight. All those rooms in his big, cake-like mansion and he decided to take her to his.

She remembers him covering her swayingly with the bedspread. 'There's water on the bedside table,' he said, and then leaned over as if to kiss her, but instead put one unsteady finger in the air. 'Water is good,' he said. 'You sleep well now, young lady. Don't come creeping into my room, will you?'

'This *is* your room,' she said. 'You told me that this is your room.'

Thinking about it now, perhaps it wasn't even his room. She wouldn't know. Never will, probably.

He waved her away, stumbled off to the en-suite. She listened to the sounds of rustling clothes and teeth cleaning, then, after a minute, felt a thump on the bed next to her. She looked over, but he was asleep already, his mouth open, his chest bare. He was wearing his pants and shoes. 'I told you this was your room,' she said to him, but he was slowly sucking air down into his belly, his top lip trembling as he exhaled seconds later.

The next time she saw him, he was standing at the door, fully dressed, holding a cappuccino, and Ashleigh soon realised that he couldn't remember a thing.

Ashleigh gazes at the mountains, making sense of it all. *You've been through **a lot**,* the girls keep telling her. *You have nothing to be ashamed of. You behaved like a survivor,* they said. And she liked that.

Still, it's too much to smooth over and make nice right now.

And then there's the worst thing. The most horrible thing of all. And it has nothing to do with making Pinko commit suicide or telling such a huge lie or leaving her mum. All those things wake her up in the night, but *this* thing makes her cry out into the dark.

Ashleigh stands from the window ledge and walks over to her FILA rucksack, all zipped up and stood to attention beside her bunk. She takes an envelope from the front pocket, removes the folded paper, shakes out the little photo and holds it up to the light.

It's the eyes, she thinks, that look right into her. They seem to be moving and, if she doesn't look at it directly, his tongue appears between his lips, the way it used to. As if he had three fat little lips. He must be bigger now; probably doesn't look anything like this anymore. She turns the paper over.

Padre told me where you are, it reads. *I thought you might like this.*

Ashleigh wipes a tear from her cheek. No, Gavin, she didn't like it. It was a knife to her stomach. Jane always used to say, when Ashleigh was hurling abuse at her for being 'unfair' or 'worrying too much', that she would understand when she had her own children.

'I'll find you again,' she says to the photograph, the absent child of the absent child. 'Padre said so.'

If Gavin knows where she is, her mum will find her soon for sure.

She holds the little face to her heart, then takes the phone from her pocket and begins to text.

JANUARY 2034
Hrafnablótsjökul Volcano

Hrafnablótsjökul opens both eyes. Her belly, a swollen, writhing thing, keeps her awake. Her skin is hotter, now. Only the night-cold air calms her as it moves around her back and shoulders. Since that first prickle in her bowels, she has travelled nearly three times around the sun. This is but a speck upon the timeline of the earth, yet never has her magma moved through its chambers this way. Something is different.

She watches the sea and wishes she could fall into it.

Part of her will.

But not yet. Not quite yet.

Author Biography

Born and raised in the South East of England, Lilwall spent several years teaching English in France before returning to the UK to complete her PhD in Creative Writing at the University of Kent. Now a teacher in Creative Writing at the University of Lincoln, she has a passion for imagining odd scenarios and alternative realities, often exploring themes of power imbalance and injustice in her work. Lilwall's debut novel, 'The Biggerers' (Point Blank, One World) established her as a voice to watch in speculative fiction. She co-produces the 'On Silence' literary podcast and serves as a guest editor for 'The Lit' literary journal.

Book Club Questions

1. How does the novel explore class-based disparities in response to disaster, immigration, and asylum-seeking?

2. What do you think was the true purpose of the 'Intimacy Laws'? Do you believe a government could realistically implement such policies in a future crisis?

3. Football is a quintessential part of British identity. How does 'The Last Match' reflect the importance of tradition and cultural rituals during times of crisis?

4. How did your opinion of Pinko, Jane, and Ashleigh—and their relationships with each other—shift over the course of the novel?

5. Pinko and his father are obsessed with wood and rounded objects—wooden buses, watches, and more. What do you think this symbolism suggests, especially in contrast with the novel's modern setting? How does this tension between past and present affect the narrative?

6. Which character had the greatest impact on the plot? Was there a turning point that changed the course of events?

7. Did the ending revelations shift your view of the characters or events? Were you surprised? Why or why not?

8. Do you think Padre's "magic" was real? Was Jane's fate inevitable, or shaped by free will? What does the novel suggest about destiny?

9. What was your first impression of Gavin, and how did this change as the story progressed?

Acknowledgements

With special thanks to everyone who has supported the writing of this novel, including my editor, Isabelle Kenyon, for her insightful guidance and unwavering support throughout this project. I am deeply grateful to my colleagues and students, whose daily interactions continually challenge and inspire me. Many thanks to Matthew Smith and Dan Mandel. Thanks also to Alison Rider, who is my number one fan, and to Imrich Krákorník, who is my number two fan, and whose patience and encouragement is the lifeblood of this story.

10. What role does Gavin's art play in the novel? Do you think his abilities influence the story's direction or outcome?

11. What do you imagine happened to Jane after she was left behind—and what does her ending say about isolation, survival, or loss?

12. Gavin's family is forced inland, unable to escape. How does the novel portray ideas of home, refuge, and moral choice in the face of political and class inequalities?

About Fly on the Wall Press

A publisher with a conscience.
Political, Sustainable, Ethical.
Publishing politically-engaged, international fiction, poetry and cross-genre anthologies on pressing issues. Founded in 2018 by founding editor, Isabelle Kenyon.

Some other publications:

The Devil's Draper by Donna Moore

GRQ by Steven Bernstein

Witchborne by Rachel Grosvenor

New Gillion Street by Elliot J Harper

The Dark Within Them by Isabelle Kenyon

Your Sons and Your Daughters are Beyond by Rosie Garland

Demos Rising edited by Isabelle Kenyon

The Subtle Art of Short Fiction edited by Isabelle Kenyon

The Wager and the Bear by John Ironmonger

The State of Us by Charlie Hill

The Unpicking by Donna Moore

The Sleepless by Liam Bell

Lying Perfectly Still by Laura Fish

Social Media:

@fly_press (X) @flyonthewallpress (Instagram)

@flyonthewallpress (Facebook, Bluesky and TikTok)

www.flyonthewallpress.co.uk